# WAYNE STINNETT

# FALLEN MANGROVE

## A JESSE MCDERMITT NOVEL

*Caribbean Adventure Series*
*Volume 5*

2014

Published by DOWN ISLAND PRESS, 2014
Travelers Rest, SC

Library of Congress cataloging-in-publication Data
Stinnett, Wayne
Fallen Mangrove/Wayne Stinnett
p. cm. - (A Jesse McDermitt novel)
ISBN-13: 978-0692303528 (Down Island Press)
ISBN-10: 0692303529

Graphics by Tim Ebaugh Photography and Design
Edited by Clio Editing Services
Proofreading by Donna Rich
Interior Design by Write.Dream.Repeat. Book Design

This is a work of fiction. Names, characters, and incidents are either the product of the author's imagination or are used fictitiously. Any resemblance to actual persons, living or dead, businesses, companies, events, or locales is entirely coincidental. Most of the locations herein are also fictional, or are used fictitiously. However, I took great pains to depict the location and description of the many well-known islands, locales, beaches, reefs, bars, and restaurants in the Keys, to the best of my ability. The Rusty Anchor is not a real place, but if I were to open a bar in the Florida Keys, it would probably be a lot like depicted here. I've tried my best to convey the island attitude in this work.

# FOREWORD

I'd like to take a minute to thank the people who helped me to write my fifth novel. Through her love, words of encouragement, and support for our dreams, my wife Greta, is by far my biggest fan.

My youngest daughter, Jordy, will be a teenager by the time this book comes out. God help us. She's been the source of a lot of laughs while I'm writing. I wouldn't trade the interruptions for the world.

I drew on my relationship with my older daughter, Laura, in writing parts of this book. She's a strong-willed, independent woman, who is a fantastic mommy to three of my grandkids. My wife's two older kids are always encouraging me also.

Tim Ebaugh, of Tim Ebaugh Photography and Design created yet another great cover, playing with different lighting during a beautiful Florida sunset. You can see more of his work at www.timebaughdesigns.com.

Lastly, where would a writer be without a great editor and proofreader? While I can come up with a decent story line and characters, it's Clio Editing Services who makes it make sense. Donna Rich has final eyes on each of my books, before they get to you. Thanks also to beta readers Sergeant Major Thomas Crisp, USMC (retired), Marcus Lowe, Timothy Artus, Joe Lipshetz, Nicole Godsey, Mike Ramsey, TSgt Alan Fader,

USAF (Retired), and Bill Cooksey. Thanks also to Tripp Wacker of Ryan Aviation Seaplanes Inc. in Palm Coast, FL, for his knowledgeable assistance with the deHavilland Beaver DHC-2 amphibian. Lastly, thanks to my high school classmate, Debbie Kocol, owner of Crystal Waters and Crystal Villas on Elbow Cay, Bahamas, for her valuable assistance with much of the books location.

# DEDICATION

"Certainly there is no hunting like the hunting of man and those who have hunted armed men long enough and liked it, never really care for anything else thereafter."
**Ernest Hemingway**, "On the Blue Water," 1936

If you'd like to receive my monthly newsletter for specials, book recommendations, and updates on coming books, please sign up on my website:

www.waynestinnett.com

**Jesse McDermitt Series**
*Fallen Out*
*Fallen Palm*
*Fallen Hunter*
*Fallen Pride*
*Fallen Mangrove*
*Fallen King*
*Fallen Honor*
*Fallen Tide (November, 2015)*

**Charity Styles Series**
*Merciless Charity*
*Ruthless Charity (Winter, 2016)*
*Heartless Charity (Fall, 2016)*

The Gaspar's Revenge Ship's Store is now open. There you can purchase all kinds of swag related to my books.
WWW.GASPARS-REVENGE.COM

# FALLEN
## MANGROVE

# MAPS

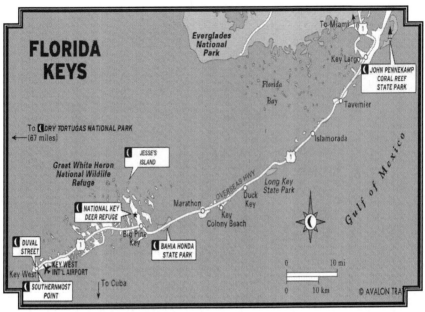

*The Florida Keys*

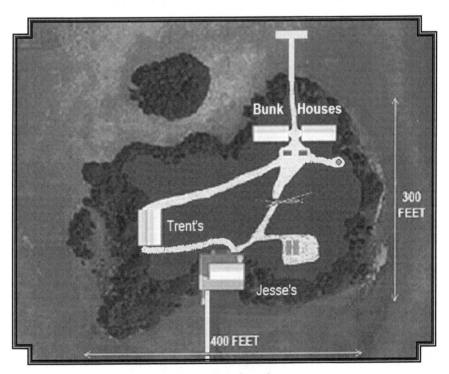

*Jesse's Island*

# PROLOGUE

September, 1566

Try as they might, the crew was unable to stay close to the fleet through the thick fog that enveloped them at dusk. Previous nights hadn't been a problem. The lanterns on the other ships had been visible on the inky blackness of the ocean for nearly a league. Those, however, had been clear nights. On this night, the ship drifted more than sailed, with almost no wind to speak of, shrouded by a dense, heavy fog.

The previous evening, as the fog began to set in, the Captain had suggested to the ship's Master that they might steer slightly more easterly for a time to keep from colliding with one of the other vessels of the fleet in the fog. Eduardo Santiago de Camara was a man of some means in Seville who had served in the Spanish Army and been appointed to his current position as the ship's Captain by the King himself.

The ship's Master thought it unwise, even with the fog bank approaching. He was a younger man, but one who had sailed for many years in the Spanish flotas and worked his way up to his current rank as Master of the carrack *Nuestra Señora de Magdalena y las Angustias*. In deference to His Majesty King Philip II's appointee, he turned to the pilot. Knowing that the Captain had almost no sailing experience at all, Master Miguel Vasquez de Benito gave the order.

"Come easterly one point."

Having overheard the Captain, the pilot, also a seasoned sailor, nodded his understanding to the Master. A course change of one point would only separate them from the rest of the fleet by half a league over half a day. They could easily rejoin the convoy when the sun rose and burned off the fog. The pilot theatrically spun the helm more than half a turn, stopped it and spun it back after a short second's pause. Checking the compass and noting the single degree of course change in the nearly still air, he nodded again to the Master, who smiled.

"I'll be in my quarters if needed," the Captain said and left the poop deck, descending the stairs to his quarters directly below.

The *Magdalena* was a fifteen-year-old square-rigged carrack, built and launched in Seville in 1551. Though much larger and a few years older than most in the fleet, she was still fast enough to keep up with the smaller, newer galleons. This was due in part to her added topsails, bowsprit sails, and lateen-rigged mizzen. It was also due in larger part to her Master and crew.

With a beam of nine meters and a deck length of forty meters, she displaced six-hundred tons when loaded with cargo, passengers, and crew. She was fully loaded on this voyage, having a crew of seventy-five men and an additional twenty-two passengers. Her cargo consisted of silver, gold, rare gems, and pearls bound for the government in Spain, along with trade goods of rum, sugar, spices, tobacco, and silk from the Far East.

The fleet had left Havana Harbor nine days before. Miguel was not very concerned about weather this time of year; it was September, and hurricanes were unlikely. His greatest concerns were the heavy gold and silver in the bottom of the hold and, of course, his passengers. The big ship rode low in the water and was very steady in the strong southwesterly breeze out of Havana.

Before loading in Havana, his Quartermaster had advised removing all of the ballast stones they always added to the hold before leaving the docks in the mouth of Rio Guadalquivir outside of Seville. That was how heavy the treasure currently in the hold was.

They'd sighted Cayo Hueso the evening of the second day and turned east-northeast, following close to the chain of islands known as Los Cayos de Florida. But not too close. The reefs just to the south of those wretched, dry rocks were treacherous and had laid claim to many a ship and man. Although Cayo Hueso had fresh water, it was the only island in the long chain that did, and it produced very little. Save for that one grace and the diminutive deer that could be found on one of the larger islands, none were considered habitable.

For another day and a half, they had the wind astern, sailing at a good speed. The ships made it to the eastern end of the keys and sighted the mainland for the first time. The skies were favorable and the seas nearly calm as they made the turn to the northeast, following the coastline, sometimes less than half a league off shore.

The shallow reefs were fewer here and much closer to shore.

For three more days, they held course, until finally the coastline began to curve away to the northwest and they started to encounter the long, slow-moving rollers of the open ocean. The *Magdalena* trailed the convoy of five caravels and four galleons, the latter bristling with cannons from both sides, on the gently rolling sea.

Two days later, just past midday, they sighted puffy white clouds building to the southeast, indicating the larger islands of the northern Bahamas. Spaniards had killed or enslaved all of the Lucayos, the primitive inhabitants of these northern islands. Since the Spaniards found the islands unsuitable for anything, they had remained uninhabited for more than a generation now.

It was on the evening of their ninth day at sea, of the planned eight-week crossing back to Spain, that they encountered the fog bank. It was unusual this far to the east, but Miguel had seen many unusual things in his twenty years before the mast. He'd started at the age of eight as a page, doing the most menial of tasks aboard ship, then worked his way up to apprentice, which was none the better. He'd then been promoted to able sailor, second mate, first mate, and now Master of his own ship. With the Captain abed, the ship was his. Not that it wasn't when the fool was on deck. He was a mere figurehead, a pompous Lord that had tired of waging war on land and wanted to see the West Indies.

An hour after the sun had gone down, the fog had enveloped them so completely he could see nothing beyond the rails. Having roused himself from his bunk in the officers' quarters, the second mate joined Miguel on the poop deck. Giving the man his heading, Miguel turned command of the ship over to him, then went to his own cabin to sleep.

Miguel hadn't been asleep long when a change in the ship's attitude roused him. He lay in his bunk listening. *Probably just a wharf rat scurrying around*, he thought. Then he felt an almost imperceptible nudge, as if some giant denizen of the deep had gently pushed against the hull of the ship.

He came out of his bunk quickly and made his way to the main deck, where he was dazzled by the number of stars in the sky. The fog had apparently lifted.

He climbed the stairs to the poop deck and spoke to the second mate. "What was it that I felt a moment ago? Did you change course?"

"No, sir," replied the mate, a short, stout, well-seasoned sailor of twelve years with dark curly hair. "We hold the course yet that we've been on for two hours."

Miguel went to the port rail and looked ahead and to the left of the ship. The rest of the fleet was not to be seen, just the eerie darkness of the sea and the stars above it. *Far above*, he thought. *As clear as this night's sky is, I should be able to see stars all the way to the horizon.* The realization hit him—the fog bank. *The rest of the fleet must yet be blanketed in the cursed fog.*

He returned to the helm and called down to the pilot, who was sleeping on a mat on the quarterdeck by the stairs. "Señor Martinez, rouse yourself and give me a knot speed."

Martinez rose from his mat and gathered his knotted line, which was hanging on the bulkhead of the Captain's cabin. It had a triangle of wood attached to the end and knots tied at regular intervals along its length. He descended to the main deck and dropped a third of the coil into the water. A moment later, the wooden triangle caught the water and the line became taut in the pilot's hand.

Miguel turned a sandglass on a bezel and said, "Read it."

The pilot loosened his grip and let the line slide through his hands, counting the knots precisely spaced.

When the thirty-second sandglass ran out, Miguel said, "Time," and looked down over to where the pilot stood, two decks below.

The pilot looked up and said, "Three and a half knots, Master de Benito."

"Three and a half knots? Are you sure?"

"Yes, sir," came the reply.

"Very well, go back to sleep." As he returned to the helm, he muttered, "Three and a half knots." Then he turned to the second mate and asked, "How long ago did the fog lift?"

"Mere minutes after you took to bed, sir," the mate replied.

"I assume the wind picked up slightly about that time?"

"Slowly, sir. Almost imperceptibly. And more southerly."

He looked at the mate in alarm for a moment. *A southerly wind?* He thought. "Three and a half knots for two hours," he muttered again as he looked out toward the fog bank. He calculated the distance in his head. With the rest of the fleet in irons in the fog and the *Magdalena* angling slightly away, the fleet would be nearly two full leagues astern and falling back.

He went to the stern rail but saw no lights save the stars. He knew that this late in the hurricane season, most storms formed in the far eastern ocean, just off the coast of Africa, and remained at low latitudes before turning toward the mainland of Florida or the great cape to its north. Such a storm would produce northerly winds as it approached. While storms that formed early in the season usually rose up south of Cuba in the vast North Sea, or even the large gulf to the west of Florida, some had been known to cross the whole of the peninsula into the Atlantic. These were the storms that brought southerly winds. He'd never heard of a storm late in the season doing this, but it was exactly what he was thinking.

He shouted to the pilot over the rail, "Belay that, Antonio. Roust the navigator, if you would."

A few minutes later, while Miguel considered what they should do, the ship's navigator climbed to the poop deck carrying his charts and logbooks.

"You wished to see me, Master de Benito."

"My apologies for interrupting your slumber, Señor Castellano. What can you tell me of these northern islands? Is there a harbor where a ship can anchor to be safe from a storm?"

"A storm?"

"Supposing there were a storm. Where might we find refuge?"

Juan Castellano was a learned man, tall and slight of build. He'd studied at Universidad de Sevilla, but he had an adventurous spirit that drove him to use his knowledge of astronomy, mathematics, and cartography to secure a position with the Flota de Indias, the Spanish West Indies Fleet.

"Yes, there is such a place," Juan replied. "However, it is many leagues to the south. Between Curateo and San Salvador Island there is a vast sound called Xuma."

"Please show me where it is, Juan."

Choosing one of his charts from his chest, he laid the others aside and rolled it out on the desk behind the helm. "We are northwest of here," he said pointing to a spot on the chart. "This is Isla Barionegne and there are reefs and cays all along the east side."

Moving his finger along the chart marked by many X's, he came to a large island. "This is Lucaioneque, with many small islands to the east, the Abaco Keys."

Pointing to another spot on the chart, he said, "Here is the entrance to Xuma Sound." Looking up at the canvas and then to the stars, he quickly calculated their heading in his head and added, "I fear it is a good two-day sail with favorable winds."

"What about this harbor?" Miguel asked, pointing at a spot nearer their location between Lucaioneque and Barionegne.

"Those waters are controlled by the French, only recently."

Miguel considered what the navigator had shown him. If a hurricane were approaching from the west, it would be wise to sail south toward the sheltered waters of the Sound. *But, what of the rest of the fleet?* He wondered. Again, his thoughts turned toward his primary responsibility—his ship, his cargo, and his passengers.

Miguel had sailed through three hurricanes, the ships he'd crewed sustaining heavy damage and losing many of his fellow crewmen. He seemed to reach a decision and glanced up at his navigator and friend. "It will be a difficult two-day sail, Juan. With many course changes in this unfavorable wind. I fear a late season hurricane is upon us, coming across the peninsula of Florida. Can you get us to this Xuma Sound?"

The navigator again looked up at the stars for a moment and said, "Yes, Miguel. I can get us there. As you said, with this southerly wind, it will be difficult."

Looking around at the horizon, Juan asked, "What of the other ships of the convoy?"

"I know not where they are," Miguel replied. "The Captain ordered a course change to separate us in the fog. It may very well be our saving grace, if indeed this is an east-moving hurricane I feel approaching."

"I will plot a course with appropriate turns to arrive safely as quickly as possible," Juan said.

"If it is a hurricane," said Miguel thoughtfully, "the present wind direction tells me that it will pass to the north of us. Sailing south, even against unfavorable winds, seems most prudent."

A few minutes later, the navigator handed the second mate a scroll on which he'd written the courses to be steered and for how long, throughout the night, barring any change in wind direction. He then went back to his bunk to be rested for the next day. His instructions, as always, were based on a speed of three knots. Though he lacked the intellect of the navigator, the second mate knew the sea and would make adjustments to the timing of the turns if their speed increased or decreased.

After the second mate changed to a southeasterly heading and the sails had been adjusted, Miguel left the poop deck. He went directly to his own cabin two decks below on the quarterdeck to get some rest. The second mate would wake him if conditions changed. The long, gentle rollers soon coaxed him to a deep slumber.

Dawn came and with it the first squall. It didn't last long and failed to produce significant winds or rough seas. Just a late summer rain to the passengers, who were as yet unaware of their course change.

Miguel was at the helm when the Captain came up the stairs to the poop deck. Not being a man of the sea, it took him a moment before realizing they'd altered course.

"Why have we changed course, Señor de Benito?"

"If it please the Captain, sir," Miguel replied. "A sudden change in the wind and the threat of a coming storm at six bells during the first watch, prompted me to alter our course. I fear a hurricane approaches from the west, causing these southerly winds."

"A hurricane? There was a light rain earlier. What gives you cause to think a hurricane approaches?"

"The trade winds have always blown from the west, sir. Late last night, it shifted to a south by southwest wind. My estimation is that the storm will pass to the north of us sometime two days hence. I hope to remove us from its path by then." That seemed to satisfy the Captain and as he turned to leave, he looked ahead of the forecastle, then stopped and turned around.

"Where is the rest of the fleet?"

"By your orders, sir," Miguel replied. "We turned east in the eve. Shortly after nightfall we sailed out of the fog, which seems to have bound the rest of the fleet."

The Captain puffed up slightly. "Very good," he said. "I'm sure they'll be safe. Our first concern is our own cargo and passengers."

"Yes, sir."

Throughout the day, two more short-lived squalls passed, rising quickly out of the southwest, moving northeast. After the second one, Miguel was even more certain that they were running ahead of a slow-moving hurricane coming off the coast of Florida. As nightfall approached he gathered the officers on the quarter deck to inform all of them of his suspicions.

As the sun fell toward the horizon, it illuminated from behind the high clouds that stretched unbroken from north to south, seeming to punctuate his words. "Señores, it is my opinion, and the Captain concurs, that we are running ahead of a slow-moving hurricane which is crossing the Florida peninsula. We have changed course and are making our way to a safe harbor called Xuma Sound, yet another day's sail from here. I fear this storm, which is already within our sight, will be upon us by morn."

"Is there no safe harbor closer, Master de Benito?" asked one of the junior officers.

"Only one," Miguel replied. "A shallow and narrow harbor controlled by the French."

A murmur went around the men gathered before him. He continued, "We will attempt to make it to Xuma Sound. Failing that, we may have to fight a quartering wind and high seas to make the French harbor."

"Any port in a storm," muttered the first mate. "But a French harbor, sir? I'd rather go over the rail."

Whispers of acknowledgement went from man to man, along with nodding heads. "Let's hope it doesn't come to that, Señor Nieves."

Pablo Nieves was a big man, over six feet in height and almost two hundred pounds. He was well liked and respected among the crew, as was Miguel. He'd been first mate aboard the *Magdalena* under Miguel's command for nearly two years.

"Let the crew know, gentlemen. Have them prepare for a storm before night falls. Have the pages go among the sleeping crewmen and tell them. The Captain is informing the passengers now."

By nightfall, the crew had cleared the decks of anything not secured and made ready for the approaching storm. They didn't have long to wait. By the time seven bells rang on the first watch, shortly before midnight, the wind began to increase.

Dawn broke gray and raining, with building seas and near gale force winds. The passengers stayed below deck, save for a single individual, Enzo Navarro. He was a small, fair-haired man in his early twenties. Born in Havana, he was going to Spain for the first time, representing his father's sugar plantation. No stranger to tropical weather and rough seas, he'd spent his youth piloting a small sloop up and down the coast of Cuba, exploring. Enzo stood at the rail, watching the tumultuous sea.

The morning watch crew performed admirably in the building storm, constantly adjusting the sails to the shifting wind conditions at Miguel's orders. The Captain had long since taken leave of the roiling deck, but not before depositing his breakfast over the rail.

"May I come up, Master?" Enzo shouted from the bottom of the stairs. Miguel looked down at the man standing confidently on the main deck, shifting his body weight with the roll of the ship. Though soaked, with his hair pushed back over his scalp, he didn't seem to be bothered by the weather at all.

"Yes, and welcome," Miguel shouted back over the wind.

The young man went up the steps to the poop deck without the aid of the handrail and came to stand next to Miguel, the corners of his mouth turned up slightly as if he were enjoying a bright, sunny day at sea.

"The Captain said on the eve that a hurricane might find us today," Enzo said, taking a quick glance at the compass in its bezel. "From the looks, it's passing to the north. Quite odd."

"You know the sea," Miguel said while studying the passenger. It was more statement than question. He had, of course, met the man before they put to sea in Havana, but he regarded him now in a new light.

"Yes," Enzo replied simply.

The ship was sailing before the wind, which was now nearly straight out of the west. They'd tacked east only hours before as they'd neared the reef north of the island of Lucaioneque. With the island and its reefs now many leagues astern, the crew was preparing to tack again; this turn would put them on a southerly course, directly toward the narrow and quite shallow gap between Curateo and San Salvador. The deeper passage into Xuma Sound to the south of San Salvador could only be approached from the east, and with the wind out of the west, that was impossible. The navigator had assured Miguel that the northern entry to the sound, although shallow, would allow the *Magdalena* passage if he were to stay to the center of the gap between the southern tip of Curateo and Little Island to the east. The gap was only slightly more than two leagues in width and it meant sailing a broad reach along the whole coastline of Curateo.

"Señor Nieves!" Miguel shouted to his first mate on the main deck. The man turned and looked up. "Prepare to come about! Send a page to inform the passengers!"

Pablo quickly grabbed the nearest page and shouted instructions in the boy's ear. As he scurried off, Miguel turned to his guest. "Perhaps you'd find more comfort in your cabin, Señor Navarro."

Enzo grinned. "With your permission, Master de Benito, I am much more comfortable on the deck of a sturdy ship, than restricted to a stifling box of a cabin."

Having seen the page return to the deck, Miguel said, "Very well, Señor." Then shouting to the first mate, he said, "Coming about, Señor Nieves!"

As the crew began to haul on the rigging, Miguel spun the helm to the right, the *Magdalena* responding immediately. The great ship heeled over precariously as it turned, then righted itself slightly as Miguel brought the wheel back to center and the wind filled the sails from abeam, keeping the heavy ship heeled a few degrees. The crew quickly ran up the lateen-rigged mizzen sails on the quarterdeck to aid in steerage, hoisted the bowsprit sails, and brought down the topsails.

"Your crew is exceptional, Master de Benito," Enzo said.

Miguel liked the younger man. "Thank you, señor. And please call me Miguel."

"Then you must call me Enzo, Miguel." He extended his hand and Miguel took it momentarily before bringing it back to the straining wheel.

For the next three hours, the two men talked while Miguel wrestled with the wheel against the quartering wind. The ship was constantly battered by wind and wave as it fought its way forward against the white-capped rollers taking them broadside. At last came the shout from the forecastle, "Land ho!"

"Where away?" shouted Miguel above the rising wind.

"Ten points off the starboard bow! Two leagues!" came the reply from the sharp-eyed lookout.

"Tis much too early," the navigator said, having joined Miguel and Enzo on the poop deck for this last leg toward safe anchorage. "Curateo should be at least another seven hours." Juan Castellano grabbed his own compass and quickly went down the stairs, crossed the main deck and climbed up the stairs to where the lookout stood on the forecastle.

Minutes later he crossed the main deck again, rejoining Miguel and Enzo. "I fear I've made a mistake in calculating our position yesterday," he said. "The land before us is not Curateo, but Lucaioneque. We must sail southeast for twenty leagues to be aligned with a northern approach to the Sound and it will be an additional twenty leagues before we arrive there."

Miguel gave the orders and the crew responded instantly, taking the ship away from the rocky shores of the uninhabited Lucaioneque. After an hour, the wind began to lessen and turned, coming directly astern. This pleased Miguel, as it meant the worst of the storm had passed and was moving north.

Enzo had stayed with Miguel and Juan at the helm throughout the storm, offering observations from time to time on the stalwart crew's abilities. He noted the compass and, perceiving the slight wind change, said, "It seems the worst of the storm has passed well to the north of us. Perhaps we need not the safety of Xuma Sound?"

"Yes, Enzo, it appears we've been blessed," Miguel replied. "However, I think we will continue yet to the Sound. It would be prudent to check for damage in sheltered waters."

The day wore on and soon it was night. They held the southeasterly course well into the night, the seas still battering the starboard bow and occasionally breaking over the deck. Two sailors were swept overboard by one unusually large wave. There was nothing Miguel or the crew could do for them. They were in the hands of God and His mercy.

The pilot kept a continuous reading of the ship's speed at the sound of each bell. When the crew changed watches at eight bells, the freshened crew stood ready to make the turn south. The wind was still astern and they were making almost eight knots. With luck, they'd make Xuma Sound by mid-morning.

Once the turn south was made, Miguel turned the helm over to the second mate and retired to his bunk to try to get some rest. Enzo had left the poop deck only an hour before. The two men had learned they both had a deep, abiding love for the sea, and during the evening and night, they became friends.

Miguel's rest was fitful, but he finally succumbed. He was jarred awake just a few hours later when he was knocked from his bunk. He quickly donned his boots and made his way to the poop deck above the Captain's cabin. The Captain had not been seen since breakfast. The wind had changed once again. It was now coming from the northeast. *Impossible*, thought Miguel, *the wind should still be out of the northwest.*

"It's been coming around steady for three hours," the second mate announced as Miguel crossed the deck toward him. "I was about to send a page to wake you." The deck pitched and heaved in seas much rougher than when Miguel had retired.

Checking the compass, yet knowing the second mate would still have the southeast course, he said, "How can this be? The wind should have gone around to the north, but not continued around to northeast, unless...."

"Unless the storm has changed direction," Juan said as he came up the steps, "circling around us."

The storm had changed direction. Unknown to them, they'd avoided the hurricane when it was at its weakest, after having crossed the Florida peninsula. Once in the open ocean, it had passed north of them, completely destroying the entirety of the treasure fleet before gaining in strength and circling around to the southeast, then to the south. Now it was finally heading west, straight for the safe harbor at which they planned to put in. Miguel realized this, but far too late. By sailing south, they were on an intercept course with the hurricane. He made the decision. There was no other choice and little time to waste.

"We are coming about," he said. "We will make haste for the French harbor."

Again, the big ship heeled sharply in the pitching seas as she turned to the west. Just two days prior, the long, slow rollers had been coming out of the east, lulling him to sleep. Then overnight, the wind-whipped waves had come out of the west, being driven by the storm, colliding with those from the east. Now it was like being in a giant tub as it was sloshed back and forth, then side to side. Towering waves came crashing together from all points of the compass.

An hour into their run for the relative safety of the French harbor, the full fury of the storm was on them. The ship was tossed so much that Miguel was unable to accurately read the compass. The sails were beginning to rip at the seams and the yards were straining severely. With each dive into the trough of a giant wave, the whole of the ocean rose up over the forecastle and the ship dove beneath it, sweeping any hapless sailor who wasn't holding on to something overboard.

The yardarm on the mizzen mast snapped and the upper half of the yard crashed through the poop deck, killing the Captain instantly in his bunk. The loose sheets whipped across the poop deck, their pulleys trying desperately to crush the skull of anyone in the way.

Miguel clung to the wheel while the wind and spray whipped at his clothes, snapping his sleeves. *If we can only make the harbor*, he thought. In the darkness he could only pray that his course was true, and he did. He fought the wheel like a madman as wave after wave came crashing over both the forecastle and main deck.

Above the roar of the wind ripping through the shrouds and stays, Miguel heard an ominous sound. Surf crashing on rock. He'd miscalculated and the wind was driving the ship directly onto the reef. He had to make a choice. *Was the harbor entrance north or south?* He had but seconds to decide, and then he turned the great wheel to starboard. If he was wrong, perhaps they'd miss the reef, or find a hole though it and become beached on the island.

The next sound he heard broke his heart. The sound of the hull being torn open on the submerged reef. The ship shuddered, then spun broadside to the wind. Within seconds she began to roll onto her side. There was no time to give the order to abandon ship. Many of the crew had already been swept from the deck into the sea, the jagged edges of rock and reef putting a quick end to their lives.

Still Miguel clung to the wheel, as if by sheer will he could pull the ship off the reef. Suddenly, everything went black as one of the pulleys on the mizzen sheet connected with the back of his head.

It took only minutes for the ship to break apart in the crashing waves, spilling treasure, cargo, and bodies into the sea. Of the seventy-five crew and twenty-two passengers, only a handful survived the wreck and many of those died struggling in the water.

Miguel found himself in the water, clinging desperately to a length of wood. He had no idea what part of the ship it was from. Fifteen minutes later, he was thrown up onto the beach. For a moment he lay there, thinking he was dead. When he tried to turn his head, the pain in the back of his neck and shoulder told him he was not.

He struggled to his feet and staggered across the sand in the gathering light of dawn. Once he made it to the top of a dune he stopped and looked back through the driving wind and rain. There was no ship to be seen. *Was I thrown overboard and the ship sailed on?*

Then he began to see the flotsam being pushed ahead of the foamy water. Wood, canvas, rope, and everything imaginable. And bodies. He staggered down to the water's edge, forcing himself forward against the wind and spray. The first body he came to was obviously dead, the man's head caved in by a powerful blow.

He nearly retched at the sight but moved on. After finding five people dead, he found the first survivor, Juan Castellano, his left arm bent grotesquely above the elbow. Helping Juan to a sitting position, the man moaned in great pain.

"Juan," Miguel said, "can you hear me?" Juan nodded, his face ashen, blood flowing from an open wound in his scalp.

Miguel pulled his sheathed dagger from his belt. He ripped both sleeves from his shirt and, using the sheath as a splint, he bent Juan's arm back into place, tying the makeshift splint with one sleeve and binding the head wound with the other. He then ripped Juan's right sleeve off and tore it longwise into two pieces. Tying the pieces together he made a sling to hold his friend's arm.

"I must go," he said. "To see if there are others. Can you make it up to the dune?"

"I think so," Juan replied, struggling to his feet.

Miguel left him on his own and went further down the beach. Within ten minutes, he'd made it to a large rock jutting out into the sea and could go no further. Among the dozens of bodies, he'd found two others who were still alive and had tended to them. Going back the way he came, he found one more man who'd just been washed up on the beach. It was Enzo Navarro, struggling to his feet in the heavy surf.

"Enzo!" Miguel shouted. "You're alive!"

"Am I?" the younger man asked, besieged by the pounding waves.

Together the three men made their way back to where Juan waited. The two injured men sat on the lee side of the dune with Juan as Enzo and Miguel went south, looking for others. They found no one else. Out of ninety-seven souls on board, only five had survived.

"Enzo," Miguel said, "I have no idea what island this is, nor if there is food or water here. There are many barrels strewn across the beach. Let us empty the contents and partially bury several of them, open to the rain, for drinking water."

One of the others, Pablo Nieves, was only slightly hurt. "Captain," Pablo said, conveying to the others that Miguel was now the leader. "While you two set about doing that, I will go among the debris in search of any food supplies not ruined by the water. I will also drag the dead higher on the beach. We can bury them after the storm passes."

The three men split up, leaving Juan and the other injured man, the pilot Antonio Martinez, to look after one another's wounds. After two hours of struggling in the heavy surf, wind, and rain, Miguel and Enzo managed to retrieve four sugar barrels, which they emptied and set deep in the sand to gather rain water. Pablo found only a few pounds of salt-dried pork and had dragged twenty-one bodies up to the top of the dune. The others had been claimed by the turbulent sea.

The five men huddled beside a downed coconut palm on the lee side of the high dune for six hours as the storm increased in intensity. Soon it became dark and the storm began to lessen. They tried to sleep, keeping one man on watch at all times, but none slept well through the night.

As dawn broke, the storm had passed, moving off to the northwest with only scattered clouds left behind to show its passage. That and the debris on the beach.

The three men that were able, turned to the grizzly task of burying the dead. Three more bodies had floated up on the beach during the night, making twenty-four graves that would need to be dug. Out of necessity, they were shallow graves. None of the three men digging even considered more than one body per grave; it just wouldn't be proper. The burying took all morning.

Juan left the other injured man and went inland to try to determine where they were. It didn't take long before he reached the western shore and realized they were on one of the many smaller islands, not the main island of Lucaioneque as he'd hoped.

He went north along the western shore, which was mostly tidal swamp and uprooted trees. Soon he came to the tip of the small island, before returning along the eastern shore. He came to a large rock that he had to wade into the water to get around. Miguel saw him approaching and at first thought it was another survivor, until he got closer and could recognize his friend.

"Juan, where did you come from?" he asked as the man approached.

"I crossed the island and came around the northern tip," Juan replied. "This is not Lucaioneque, but one of many smaller keys off its coast. None of which is known to have water or food, save for coconuts. I saw a few trees that bear fruit resembling guava, only smaller. I know not if they are edible." As they walked back to the others

Miguel asked what more Juan knew about these islands and the early inhabitants.

"The Lucayos people were a backward, barbarous people," Juan said. "Much like the Arawaks of Española. They wore little or no clothes and were without inhibition or greed. Some adorned their faces and bodies with paint and jewelry made from shell or bone. There are no native people left on any of these islands. On Española, the Arawak once numbered in the hundreds of scores. Today, there are but a handful."

Miguel considered this. "If they lived here, they ate and drank water."

"Much the way you and Juan have done, they collected vast stores of fresh water from the rain. There has not been any discovered source of fresh water on most of these islands. Their diet was mostly fish, crab, and occasional reptiles that inhabit the interior."

When they arrived back at the makeshift camp they began to devise a plan to survive. The water kegs were half full and if they were careful it would last several weeks. They piled dry wood on the beach to light for a signal fire should they see a ship. Enzo disappeared into the interior and after four hours returned with three large iguanas.

By the end of the second day, they had enough food to last them for several days, certain the rest of the fleet would eventually find them. They turned to the business of trying to recover any of the treasure that they could reach. After three days of diving below the surface they managed to recover quite a bit of the silver, nearly all of the gold and five intact chests of emeralds. They placed the gold and silver in three large chests, and buried them, along with the emeralds, on the lee side of the large rock.

Over the next few days, things worsened on the tiny island. It didn't take long to confirm that they were indeed alone, nor did it take long to confirm there was little food and no water to be found. The temperature was unbearable during the day as the sun never ceased. What trees there might have been at one time had been razed by the hurricane, and little shade was to be found. The crewman, Lugo Esparza, died on the seventh day and was buried on the dune with the others.

"I fear his might be the fate of us all," Juan said after burying the man.

"Nonsense," Miguel replied. "Someone aboard one of the other ships had to have noticed we turned easterly before the fog set in. The rest of the fleet will find us."

"And if they didn't survive?" Pablo asked. "Or sailed on?"

"Then we may be here a while," replied Enzo. "We should find a way to gather fish to eat."

"We will do just that," Miguel said. "And to secure the treasure, we should mark its location somehow."

Enzo bent and picked up a newly fallen green coconut. Tossing it to Miguel he said, "Put use your dagger and inscribe the location with a riddle."

The two men laughed, having shared many riddles over the course of the voyage and to lighten their spirit after arriving on the island.

"I will do just that," Miguel said.

The days turned into weeks and soon the small guava-like fruit was gone. It wasn't long after that before Enzo's foray into the interior resulted in not a single iguana. Nor did he find any the next day. What coconuts they were able to gather soon diminished to the single one carved with the riddle. Miguel had placed the coconut in Juan's chart chest, which had spilled its content of charts into the sea. He placed the chest high in the crook of the only tree that hadn't fallen, a young mangrove.

Rain fell sporadically and the four men used palm leaves to gather more rain into the barrels, but they soon dried up to nothing. With no food or water, their mouths dry and bellies rumbling, it wasn't long before delirium set in. Pablo ran to the sea and drank his fill of the salty brine. Later on that night, he fell ill and died in his sleep.

One by one, the other men met similar fates, until only Miguel was left to bury his new friend, Enzo. The effort of digging the grave, dragging his friend's corpse to it, and covering it, proved to be too much. Captain Miguel de Benito died of exhaustion and thirst while sitting next to the graves of his friends. It was there, after two months on the island, that his body turned to dust and bone and was soon covered by sand.

# CHAPTER ONE

September, 2006

**W**hat's this?" Bob asked, lifting an old chest from the attic floor. Bob Talbot and his new wife, Nikki, had come to Hunters Creek, a suburb south of Orlando, two days earlier on Bob's Indian Chief motorcycle. It was a four-hundred-mile ride from their home on Stock Island in the Keys. They were visiting Nikki's parents to help them move out of their house and into a condo.

"Looks old," Nikki said. "I don't remember ever seeing it before. Anything in it?"

"Like everything else around here." Bob gave the chest a quick shake and something large rattled inside. "Should we open it?"

"The house is a hundred years old—of course everything in it's old. Better set it aside and let Dad open it. It might be personal."

He placed it by the ladder leading down to the second floor. They were nearly finished with the attic and after moving a few other items to the ladder, Nikki went down so her husband could hand the things down to her.

It seemed a shame that her parents were moving out of the old house. It was where she'd grown up and where her father had grown up before her. The home had been in the family for several generations. Her father had offered it to her, but neither she nor Bob wanted to leave the Keys. So for the first time in nearly a hundred years, the old house would be owned by someone unrelated.

They carried the things from the attic down to the kitchen, where her mother was sorting what was to be kept. The upper floor had already been cleared out and everything given away or sold off. Only her parents' bedroom furniture and the furniture in her father's study remained. That would go to the new condo in Satellite Beach, some fifty miles away on the east coast.

Bob gently placed the old chest on the table. Abbey Godsey, Nikki's mom, looked at it with disdain. "Carry that into the study, please, Bob. Frank will have to decide what to do with it."

Bob picked up the chest and carried it through the kitchen and across the hall to his father-in-law's study. Frank Godsey was a retired Orange County Judge and although he liked the man, Bob sensed the Judge was skeptical about Bob's chosen profession. Bob was the First Mate of a combination fishing and diving charter boat out of Marathon.

"Hey, Judge," Bob said from the doorway to the man's inner sanctum, addressing him by his former title out of respect. "Your wife said to bring this to you." Placing the small chest on a table in front of the older man, Bob thought he saw a glimmer in the man's eye.

"Ah, the chest," Frank said and looked up at Bob with a grin. "I've tried to solve the mystery of that thing since I was a kid. My dad gave it to me when Abbey and I married, and his father gave it to him on his wedding day. Story is, that chest has been handed down from father to first son for over two centuries and not a one of us has ever figured out the mystery."

His face changed, a look of melancholy replacing the glimmer of fun that had been there. "Have a seat, Bob, and I'll tell you the story." When Bob sat down across from the older man, he noticed another facial change, to an expression of resolve.

"I have no son to give this chest to," he finally said. "Nikki's my only child, so this thing's yours now."

He proceeded to tell Bob about his early family history. The Judge's fifth great-grandfather, Quincy Godsey, had been a sea-faring man. He'd been born in Charleston, South Carolina, during the American Revolution and went to sea at an early age. At twenty-five, two years after the birth of his first son in 1802, his ship ran aground off the island of Elbow Cay in the northern Bahamas. At the time, it had only recently been settled by colonial Loyalists who had left Charleston after the war. The situation with the British on the islands and the former colonists was tenuous at best. As it turned out, one of the first settlers on the island knew Quincy's mother, Elizabeth. Quincy was by that time the First Mate of the merchant ship *Gloria* and was able to negotiate a price with the local wreckers to help pull the ship off of a sandbar, with the help of Winston Malone, the son of his mother's friend.

While waiting for the tide to rise the following day, young Quincy went exploring on the northern shore of the island. A recent hurricane had submerged that part of the island and most of the trees had been swept away. Quincy's sharp eyes noticed something unusual in the high boughs of an ancient mangrove that had been toppled by the wind and waves. The branches had grown around and encased an ancient chest that was now exposed after the branches had broken apart.

With some difficulty, Quincy was able to remove the chest and open it. The chest was watertight and when he opened it he found nothing more than a coconut inside. It was at this part of the story that Nikki came into the study and the Judge opened the chest, revealing the coconut.

"A coconut?" she asked. "Your ancestors handed down a coconut through how many generations?"

Bob was enthralled with the story and said, "Eight, beginning with your sixth great-grandfather, Captain Quincy Godfrey."

The Judge smiled. "Nine now," he said as he closed the chest and pushed it toward Bob. "If you can't figure out the mystery, give it to my grandson."

"You're giving this to us?" Nikki asked.

"It needs a new home and a new set of eyes on it. Do you know Spanish?"

"I speak a little," Bob replied. "Everyone in south Florida does. Why?"

"There's some sort of riddle carved into the coconut and it's in Spanish. Old Spanish. And parts of it have just faded away with time and can't even be guessed at."

"Thanks, Judge," Bob said. "Means a lot to me. What have eight generations learned so far?"

"Almost nothing," the Judge replied. "A few words translated, but like I said, it's old Spanish. Even people in Spain don't talk like that anymore. I'll tell you exactly what my dad told me forty-two years ago. It's better if you just start from scratch."

Bob studied the chest a moment. It was longer than normal, nearly two feet, but only about a foot tall and less than that in width. The top was rounded and it had two ornate iron straps that became the hinges on one side and the clasps on the other.

"Did any of your ancestors learn anything about the chest itself?" Bob asked.

"The box?" asked the Judge. "No, not that I know of."

"Is it the original box the coconut was found in?"

The Judge sat forward, glancing curiously from the chest to Bob and back again. "So far as I know," he replied at last. "I don't see why anyone would have put it in a different box. Why?"

"I have a friend that can probably tell us where and when the box was made," Bob said.

"The 'when' was figured out a long time ago," said the Judge. "The coconut has a date carved into it—September twenty-third, 1566. It's partially rubbed off, but still legible."

Nikki sat down next to her father. "1566? That's right after Columbus discovered America."

The Judge snorted and grinned. "A lifetime after, Peanut. And Columbus didn't 'discover' anything, least of all America."

She looked from her father to Bob with a puzzled glance. Bob explained, "The Judge is right. Columbus first landed on the islands of the northern Bahamas, where he was greeted by the people that lived there. Being a staunch Catholic, he named the first island San Salvador, after the Savior, and the second Santa Maria de la Concepción, after the Virgin Mary. It wasn't until his third voyage that he landed on the mainland of South America. Thinking it was an island he named it Isla Santa, now called Venezuela. He was greeted by the people that lived there, also. You can't really 'discover' a land where people already live."

"You know your history, Bob," the Judge quipped.

"It was my favorite subject all through school."

"Back to the box," the Judge said. "If the writing on the coconut is in Spanish and dated 1566, why wouldn't you think the box was the same?"

"No reason to think it's not," Bob replied. "However, the early explorers bought and traded things all over the known world. Whoever put that coconut in the box might have bought it somewhere in their travels. It's at least worth finding out. It's in pretty good shape and could be worth a fortune itself."

"Why would they put it inside a tree?" the Judge asked.

"You said the tree was a huge mangrove," Bob replied. "The chest might have been placed in the branches of a small tree to protect it from the water and the tree grew around it. What year did you say Quincy found it?"

"His son, George, was two years old, so it would have been around 1804."

Bob let out a low whistle. "If the date's right, the chest was in that tree for almost two hundred and forty years.

I know mangroves live over two hundred years sometimes, so it's possible."

"You've already figured out a part of this mystery nobody else has," the Judge said, smiling. "I've no doubt you'll be the one to finally solve it."

A horn sounded from outside the house and Abbey shouted, "The moving van is here."

Within a few hours, the movers had everything loaded on the truck and had left for the coast. Bob and Nikki, along with her parents, stood outside the old house as Frank and Abbey said their goodbyes to the neighbors, some of whom Frank had known all his life.

"You sure you won't reconsider?" Abbey asked Nikki.

"About the house?"

"Yes, it's been in your father's family since they moved down here from Charleston during the War of 1812."

"We like it in the Keys, Mom," Nikki said. "It's where our roots will be planted."

Frank and Abbey took one last look at the old house, with its stately oaks dripping with Spanish moss, before handing the keys to the real estate agent who had just arrived. With that last formality, they each hugged their daughter and son-in-law, got in Frank's big Mercury and drove away.

The day before, Nikki had arranged a small van to pick up the few things she wanted to keep and had them shipped to their home on Stock Island. Bob had strapped the chest to the small luggage rack on the back of the motorcycle after first stuffing it with padding that one of the movers had given him to keep the coconut from bouncing around inside. The ride back home was uneventful and they arrived in Marathon just before sunset.

# CHAPTER TWO

S houldn't they be here already?" Rusty asked. I rolled my eyes at my old friend. He'd asked the same question about every fifteen minutes since I got here. Deuce had called me at zero six hundred to say they were passing Alligator Reef, and I'd come down to the *Rusty Anchor* in my skiff from my island in the Content Keys.

"Dammit, Rusty!" I said a bit too excitedly, causing Pescador to lift his shaggy black head from the floor. "They'll be here when they get here. It's a sailboat, not a Donzi. The wind's light, so they're probably under power." Pescador is my dog. I found him a year ago, stranded on a sandbar after a hurricane, catching fish. He was catching the fish, not me. Turns out that even though I'm a licensed offshore fishing charter boat Captain, my dog was the better fisherman—hence his name, Spanish for fisherman. He's been living with me ever since.

My relationship with the short, three-hundred-pound, bald, bearded man on the other side of the bar went back much further, nearly three decades. We first met on a Greyhound bus headed to Parris Island in the early summer of 1979. We were in the same platoon in Boot Camp and were stationed together a couple of times before he left the Marine Corps. I was his best man when he married his high school sweetheart in 1981 and sat next to him at her funeral, just two years later. She died giving birth to their only child, Julie, named for her mother, Juliet.

We'd stayed in touch over the years since he'd returned home to the Keys to take care of his daughter. I'd visited from time to time, staying at his home in Marathon. Seven years ago last June, I retired from the Corps after twenty years of service and moved down here myself. I'd always loved the Keys, ever since I was a kid growing up in Fort Myers. I'd also stood as best man when Julie married Deuce. They were due back from their honeymoon today. The wedding was almost two months ago and had been marred by an explosion that took the life of a young man I'd grown to trust.

I first met Deuce when he was just a teen. His father was Rusty's and my Platoon Sergeant when we were stationed together in Okinawa, Japan. Sergeant Russ Livingston, Senior, and I became friends, and when we both found ourselves stationed in North Carolina together, we took every opportunity we could to go diving. Many times we came to the Keys, and we'd sat right at this very bar on more than one occasion.

I met Russell "Deuce" Livingston, Junior, for the second time when he came here looking for me. His dad had been murdered and Deuce wanted to spread his ashes on a reef we'd both loved. By then Deuce was a Lieutenant

Commander in the Navy SEALs. Together, we'd found the man that killed his dad. His bleached bones can probably still be found on a tiny island just a few miles from mine.

Deuce and two of his best operatives had left the SEALs and gone to work for Homeland Security. The group of men that his dad's killer belonged to also happened to be responsible for the death of my own wife. It didn't take much for Deuce and his merry band of misfits to rope me into working with them. They now trained and lived part-time on my little island.

"Are you losing your hearing, man?" Rusty shouted, interrupting my thoughts.

"Sorry. What were you saying?"

"I asked what time was it that Deuce called you?"

"Probably about the same time Julie called you, numb-nuts. As soon as they got in range of a cell tower. About zero six hundred."

He looked at the clock on the wall over the bar and said, "Well, that was nine hours ago."

Just then, Jimmy walked in. He used to be my First Mate until about a year ago, and now he worked part-time at the bar.

"Jimmy," I said, "thank God you're here. Take over so me and Rusty can go down to the boat ramp, will ya?"

"Take over what, dude? You two are the only ones in here."

"Just watch the bar," Rusty said as he came from behind the large slab of oak.

Rusty and I left the bar, with Pescador trotting ahead of us, and walked down the crushed-shell drive to the boat ramp at the back of the property. It was more like a pair of overgrown ruts through the backyard than a driveway. This land had been in his family for several generations. An old shack off to the east of the boat ramp was where Rusty's grandfather had once made illegal rum during Prohibition. Now it was where Rufus, Rusty's old Jamaican cook, lived and whiled away his retirement.

We got to the boat ramp and sat down at a small table under the shade of an old gumbo-limbo tree. Beyond was the Atlantic Ocean. More precisely, Hawk Channel and the Straits of Florida, a narrow funnel between the Florida coast and the islands of Cuba to the south and the Bahamas to the east. Through this funnel ran the greatest river on Earth, the Gulf Stream, moving warm water from the Gulf of Mexico through the Straits and up into the North Atlantic. It was this current that Britain owed its climate to.

"What time is it?" Rusty asked again.

"Ten minutes later than last time you asked," I replied. "You're acting like a worried dad whose daughter's out on prom night with Alice Cooper."

"Jesse, she's my only kin. And these last two months has been the longest we've been apart since the day she was born."

"What about when she went through basic?" I asked. Julie had enlisted in the Coast Guard nearly a year ago.

"I flew up every other weekend."

"Really?" I said incredulously. "Bet that went over well with her CO."

He stood up suddenly. "Hey! There they are!"

I looked where he was pointing and sure enough, I saw the distinctive red and white sails on Deuce and Julie's blue Whitby ketch clearing the point at Key Colony

Beach. Although the wind was light, I'd been wrong assuming they were under power. They had every inch of
canvas up. Still, it took twenty minutes before they made
the turn toward Rusty's channel, started the little diesel
engine and dropped the sails, then another ten minutes
before they putted into the canal and were tied up at the
docks.

"It's a great boat, Dad," Julie said after we'd helped
them tie up and were seated at the bar. "She sails really well, whether in light wind or heavy seas. We finally
came up with a name—*James Caird*."

Rusty smiled as he wiped down glasses behind the bar.
He'd never been a fan of wind power, but seeing the boat
under full sail in winds too light for most sailboats, he
was starting to change his mind. A little.

"Shackleton's lifeboat," he said. "I never thought you
paid much attention to those old sea stories I told you."

"She told me about it," Deuce said. "I remembered hearing about it in college, but she made the story come alive
one night while sailing in the Leewards. When we made
port the next day, we looked it up on the Web—," The
sound of a motorcycle outside interrupted the debate
between power and sail. A moment later my First Mate,
Bob Talbot, and his wife, Nikki, walked in. Bob had been
a Navy Corpsman with 1st Battalion, 9th Marines when
they met. Nikki had been a Marine clerk at 9th Marines'
regimental headquarters. In the Corps, we affectionately
called all our Corpsmen 'Doc', even though they weren't
really doctors. Doc was carrying what looked like a treasure chest. Pescador rose from his spot next to my stool
at the end of the bar and trotted over to them to welcome
them by allowing each to give him an ear scratch.

"Hey, Doc," I said as Pescador accepted the ear scratch from both of them. "How'd the move go, Nikki?"

They walked over and Doc placed the chest on the end of the bar as Rusty slid two cold Dos Equis in front of them. Rusty had a terrific memory for what people liked to drink.

"It was pretty emotional, Jesse," Nikki said. "Their house has been in the family for almost a hundred years."

"I can understand that," Rusty said. "My great-grandpa built this place and the house. My grandpa rebuilt them after both were blown down in the Labor Day hurricane of thirty-five."

"Where'd you get the chart chest?" Deuce asked.

"Chart chest?" Doc said.

"That's what it looks like," Deuce said, pointing at the chest on the bar. "A sixteenth-century chart chest. I'm guessing German."

"German?" Doc said with a quizzical expression. "We were thinking it was Spanish."

Deuce walked over to the end of the bar and examined it more closely. "No, not Spanish," he said. "They used mostly brass fittings. These are iron. And in damned good shape, too. Is it real?"

"As far as we know," Doc replied. "Nikki's dad gave it to us."

"Is it full of doubloons?" Rusty whispered with a grin.

"Nope, nothing in it but a coconut," Doc said. Then with a half grin, he added, "And a riddle."

"A coconut?" Julie asked.

Doc unclasped the chest and opened it, taking out an old, dried-out coconut that looked like it'd been baked and placing it on the bar. He turned to Deuce and asked, "So, what's a chart chest?"

Deuce was still examining the chest. "Usually longer than a standard chest, like this. Also, like this one, it has a seal around the inside, making it watertight. They were carried by ship's navigators and used to keep their nautical charts, logbooks, and diaries dry. I'm almost certain that's what you have here. What made you think it was Spanish?"

"This right here," Jimmy said. "The coconut has Spanish writing on it."

"What's it say, Jimmy?" I asked, knowing that he had a pretty good knowledge of the language.

"I can only make out a few words," he replied, studying it. "The date is definitely September twenty-third, 1566, even though part of it is rubbed away. First part says something about mist, then something about a woman." Turning the nut, he pointed to two more words, adding, "This word here, 'suprimio,' means suppressed, and this one means trade. It's not like any Spanish I've ever read, though."

"Dad said it's old Spanish," Nikki said. "From the old country."

"You should let Chyrel take a look at it," Deuce said. "I can call her and ask her to come down."

"No need," I said. "She's up on the island. She bought herself a little skiff and has been exploring for the last month."

Chyrel Koshinski is our resident tech guru. She handles all of the communications and computer wizardry for Deuce's Homeland Security team. Just over a year ago, while serving as a SEAL Team Commander, Deuce was recruited by the Department of Homeland Security to create and head up a team of the best operators from military, civilian, and investigative services. Their mission at the time was to monitor and, if need be, intervene in the ever-growing terrorist threat in the Caribbean and south Florida. I serve as a transporter, occasionally moving field operators and equipment around on my boat, *Gaspar's Revenge*. She's a forty-five-foot Rampage fishing boat, perfect for moving small groups around undetected. Chyrel joined the team out of the CIA and proved extremely valuable this past year in the takedown of some high-level terrorists, drug smugglers and murderers.

"What can she do with it?" Nikki asked.

"For one thing," Deuce replied, "she can enter the writing into her computer's translator. She probably has some forensics tools to bring the words into sharper focus, too. Any idea what it all means?"

Doc grinned and said, "Better open a few more beers for everyone, Rusty. I'll tell you the story that was told to me." In fifteen minutes, Doc had spun a tale of Spanish treasure, shipwrecks and early American history.

"So this chest," Rusty said, "was found *inside* a busted-up mangrove tree?"

"That's the story," Doc replied. "I asked the Judge if he could give me any more information on what his ancestors might have found out about it, but he said it would be better to start from scratch."

"I know a little bit about the early Spaniards in the West Indies, man" Jimmy said. "They were brutal, dude. They believed what they had to offer the natives of the islands was worth all the gold and silver they could carry off. The islanders didn't have much need of what the

Spaniards offered, namely the Roman Catholic religion and civilization. For over two hundred years, anyone that wouldn't accept those gifts were usually put to death in a lot of nasty ways, including Protestants. From when Columbus first landed in 1492 to 1530, less than forty years later, all but a handful of the native people of the Caribbean were murdered or enslaved. By the date on this nut, the Spaniards controlled all of the Caribbean, with forts in Cuba, Florida, and South America, and they'd begun moving cargo and treasure from the Orient across the Pacific to southern Mexico and Panama. From there, they took it overland to El Caribe and eventually to Spain. The age of the Conquistadors, man."

"So, why would someone put the coconut in a chest meant to keep charts dry?" Julie asked.

"That's easy," Rusty said. "To protect the nut."

"Okay, so why hide it inside a tree, instead of burying it?"

"Ever see how a tree can grow around a rope or chain-link fence?" I asked. "If whoever put that nut in the chest, did it over four hundred years ago, he might have simply put the chest in the crook of a tree for safe keeping, and the tree grew around it."

"Exactly what I told the Judge," Doc said with a crooked grin.

"Still begs the question, why did he want to protect the nut?" Julie asked.

"Seems to me," Doc said with that half grin of his, "there's really only one answer to that. He didn't have anything else to draw a treasure map on."

Looking at the others, I thought it over. Many years ago, me and Deuce's dad found a little treasure up in

Fort Pierce. Last year, Deuce's dad was killed looking for another treasure, when he found part of it. Earlier this year, me, Deuce, and Rusty went up there and found the rest. It was enough that Deuce and Julie's kids wouldn't have to worry about college, Rusty could do some renovations on the bar and his house, and I was able to spread a little around the tiny community that had grown up on my island.

Besides myself, I had a caretaker who had his own little house and looked after things for me. We'd started a fledgling business growing vegetables and crawfish in an aquaculture system. The sale of the crawfish was becoming pretty lucrative for him, his wife, and their two small children.

At any given time, there might be a few others living in two small bunkhouses, and the vegetable garden had quickly become a part-time hobby for many of them during their downtime. These were members of Deuce's team and they ranged from a former female Olympic swimmer turned Miami cop to a number of SpecOps-type guys from the SEALs, Marine Recon, Army Rangers, CIA, and the Coast Guard's elite Maritime Enforcement.

"You guys in a hurry to get home?" I asked. "We can head up to the island and see what Chyrel can do right now."

"I have to work in the morning," Nikki said. "You go ahead, Bob. Call me when you get there."

"Let me know what you find out," Deuce said. "We'll come up in the morning. We have a lot of things to do on the boat this evening."

Doc and I walked out to the docks behind the bar, where he kissed his wife goodbye and we shoved off after I promised her I'd have him home before she got off work. Pescador took his usual spot on the casting deck. We'd just cleared the jetty when we heard Doc's motorcycle start up and I brought my little skiff up on plane.

We turned toward the Seven Mile Bridge and skimmed across the skinny water between East Sister Rock and Boot Key. Rounding the tip of Boot Key and turning north, I pushed the throttle a little more. Crossing under the bridge, we heard a horn behind us. We both looked back and saw Nikki waving as she headed up the long span on Doc's motorcycle. We waved back.

I turned more westerly and wound my way through the small islands of Cocoanut, Teakettle, and Sandfly Keys. Looking over at Doc, I could tell he was happy to be back on the water. Being cooped up sixty miles inland doesn't sit well with a waterman.

It was only twenty miles in the skiff, and it took only thirty minutes to get to my island. I'd bought it and the *Revenge* a month after I retired from the Corps in '99, pretty much on a whim. I did some work on it off and on for a couple of years and camped out there when the weather was cool, until I met a woman named Alex. We became friends, but after a little more than a year, she'd had to go back to Oregon to take care of a sick brother. I really went to work on it then. In less than a year, I'd built my little house on stilts, mostly from scrap lumber I'd picked up at the Miami shipping docks and fallen hardwood trees that I'd cut up and had milled in Homestead. The pilings were concrete and went down into the limestone and coral base quite a few feet. All in all, it was a simple, sturdy little house. The first I'd ever owned.

When Alex had returned to the Keys a year ago, we'd both realized our friendship had changed to a lot more than that while she'd been gone. She loved the little house and we'd both realized we wanted to live out our lives there. In a week, we were married. She was murdered the next day.

That was when I fell in with Deuce and his team on a more permanent basis. Together we'd found those responsible and dealt with them in our own way. Not really vigilantism, as Deuce's team had the full backing of the federal government, but none of those guys will ever hurt anyone again.

Since then, I'd added the two bunkhouses, the aquaculture system, a battery shack, a generator system, and a water maker. With the addition of my caretaker Carl Trent's little house, we had five permanent structures. Together, they didn't add up to the square footage of a decent-sized house on the mainland, but it was home for us.

I keep my boats under the house to avoid prying eyes. When I'd first built the house, the channel I'd dug by hand was barely deep enough for the skiff and the underside of the house was open. After Alex died, I redoubled my efforts and dredged the channel eight feet deep and twenty wide, building a pier on top of the spoils and enclosing the area under the house, adding large doors to the south side.

Using the fob on my keychain, I released the latch and the east door slowly began to swing open on its spring-loaded hinges as a light came on inside. The main house was still completely on its own solar and wind system that charged a bank of deep-cycle marine batteries.

All of the electric in the house was twelve volt. The doors had an electric motor that pulled them closed.

When I'd originally built the place, I'd had it in mind to dock the *Revenge* under there, so I'd built it with the floor beams fourteen feet above the high tide. There are two bays, with a narrow dock all the way around three sides and another narrow dock in the center, and large hanging closets for gear at the front of each of the three docks.

The *Revenge* was tied up on the far western side. Over the last year, I'd acquired a few other boats. As a wedding gift, Deuce and Julie had given us Russ's twenty-foot Grady-White. It now belonged to the Trents. I'd given it to them so Carl's wife, Charlie, could get back and forth to go shopping on Big Pine Key and take their kids to school. It was tied off against the far eastern dock, along with my late wife's red Maverick Mirage skiff. Tied up to the center pier on the east side was a thirty-two-foot Winter center console named *El Cazador*, the Hunter. It fell into our possession last winter, having been confiscated during a drug bust. On the opposite side of the center dock was a Cigarette 42x, one of the fastest boats on the water. It came to us from the terrorist smuggler who was ultimately responsible for my wife's death. The previous owner didn't have any more use for it now that he was vacationing in Guantanamo Bay, Cuba, as a guest of the federal government.

I turned the skiff around in front of the house and backed it in between *Cazador* and the Grady, tying off sideways to the rear pier behind *Cazador*. I was surprised there wasn't a welcoming committee. Usually the Trents' two kids were always at the dock when any boat came in.

47

"We weren't up there long," Doc said, "but it's sure great to be back down here."

As we stepped up onto the pier, I said, "I was worried Nikki might con you into accepting the Judge's house."

He handed the chest up to me before climbing out. "I kind of got the impression she was reluctant to give it up, but in the end she loves it down here as much as I do."

Walking around the back of the docks and along the western pier to the door, I clicked the fob again to close the doors and said, "I wonder where everyone is."

The door opened just as I reached it. "Hey, Jesse," Carl said, standing in the doorway. "Welcome back, Doc."

"Thanks, Carl," Doc said. "It's good to be back."

"Where is everyone?" I asked.

"I heard you coming. Tony's down by the fire pit telling a story to the kids, Chyrel, and Charlie."

"The man can spin a tale," Doc said with a chuckle.

Pescador looked up at me, his ears up and tail wagging. "Go ahead," I said, and he bolted up the steps.

Carl grinned and asked, "What's in the treasure chest?"

"We're hoping Chyrel can tell us. It's a coconut with some kind of riddle carved into it."

"A riddle? Don't mention that to Charlie."

"Don't mention what to me?" Trent's wife asked from the top of the steps leading up to the deck surrounding three sides of my little stilt house.

"Oh?" Doc said, glancing at Carl. Then looking up at Charlie he asked, "You good at riddles, are you?"

"Can't resist trying to figure one out," she replied, smiling. "Welcome home, Doc."

We crossed the deck together and I told the others to go ahead while I put away some things. I went inside and switched on the single lamp in the main room. My house really only has two rooms, three if you count the head. The main room is a combination galley and living room, with a small propane stove and sink in one corner. By the door is a small propane-fired refrigerator and across the room is a tiny table and two chairs, next to a small pantry. The living room part has a pair of recliners, with a small table between them. The rest of the room is cluttered with work benches, outboard motor parts and a wood-burning potbellied stove.

Beyond the living room are two doors. The one on the left is the head and the one on the right goes to my bedroom. It's equally Spartan, with nothing more than a queen-sized bed and a chest of drawers. It has two windows, one looking out over the deck to the large clearing in the middle of the island and the other looking east, over the treetops to the multicolored waters of the flats and the Gulf beyond. I usually slept aboard the *Revenge*, as I'd sort of grown fond of air conditioning, and allowed any couples visiting to use the house. Although it'd been a year since my wife was killed and I'd enjoyed the company of a couple of women in the last few months, I wasn't ready to share that bedroom on a permanent basis yet.

I opened the pantry door and put my go bag inside, took my Sig Sauer P-226 and holster from the small of my back and placed it on a shelf above the bag. I never go anywhere unarmed, but here on the island I felt safe. Only one person had ever made it to the shore undetected, but trying to get through the thick tangle of vegetation around the clearing was a different story. Pescador's sharp ears had alerted us, and the intruder ended up with a huge knot on his head from a heavy lignum vitae tree branch, swung by Deuce.

I took a six pack of Red Stripe from the refrigerator and went back down to the docks. I stepped aboard the *Revenge* and went across the wide cockpit and up the steps into the salon, turning on the cockpit light and overhead lights in the salon and galley. Putting the beer in the fridge, I heard the generator start up. It was controlled by a voltage regulator and came on automatically whenever the onboard house batteries, which were separate from the engine's batteries, got too low.

I went back upstairs to the deck and looked out over the north rail as the last rays of the sun painted the few clouds to the west a dark red and purple. I couldn't help but think, *Red sky at night*, as I looked out over the island. Doc, Carl, and Charlie were standing around the fire pit on the northeast side of the clearing, with Tony, Chyrel, and the Trents' two kids.

Directly across from my house stood the two tiny bunkhouses I'd built and Carl had remodeled. Originally, each had had six sets of bunk beds and a small desk at one end. I'd failed to take into account that lodging for women and an office might be needed, so Carl had converted the bunkhouse on the west side. He put up a wall separating two sets of bunks from the others, then turned the two in the smaller part of the bunkhouse so they were against the new wall, leaving more space for all of Chyrel's electronic gizmos.

Just in front of the two bunkhouses were two identical heavy wooden picnic tables, a flagpole at one end and a huge stone fireplace and grill at the other. Originally, that's where most of the cooking was done. When Carl built his house on the west side, overlooking the small beach and sandbar, I'd bought a top-of-the-line-oven for it. A big, commercial type oven and six-burner stove. Charlie cooked for everyone and a few times that had been more than twenty people.

I heard a small splash to my right and glanced over. There was a widening circle in the first tank of the aquaculture system we'd built. Carl was in the process of enlarging it, but for now there were only three tanks, each twenty feet by eight feet. He'd added the third just a few weeks earlier. The first tank was deeper than the other two, which were up on a platform so the tops were slightly higher than the first one. In the first were crawfish, separated into several sections with different-size mesh so the bigger ones couldn't eat the littler ones. The second tank held a system of racks that grew several kinds of vegetables. The third one was to grow even more vegetables, and the one Trent was now building would grow tilapia, a farm-raised freshwater food fish that tastes like snapper.

Water was pumped from the bottom of the crawfish tank up to the first vegetable tank, where it flowed through to the second one before being gravity fed back to the crawfish. The nitrates in the water from the crawfish tank fed the plants, and the oxygenated water from the plants was returned to the crawfish tank. It was all Greek to me, but Trent had a friend in South America doing it and learned all there was to it. Apparently, it was working, because we always had fresh tomatoes, broccoli, and lettuce. He wanted to try to grow corn in the third tank, and the shoots were just starting to come up.

# CHAPTER THREE

I t was two hours later, after the Trents had gone to put the kids to bed, that Chyrel came out of her little office, the coconut in one hand and a file folder in the other.

"I used the laser scanner to capture the markings digitally," she said. "I had to do a few passes and jigsaw them together." She lost me at the word laser. She handed the nut back to Doc, who put it back in the chest. "Then I upped the contrast, fiddled with the levels, and cleaned up the image some." I nodded as Chyrel went into an indepth explanation of pixels, resolution, and a histogram she'd edited to "punch up latent markings." I knew if I asked about whatever that meant we'd lose thirty minutes. She was the guru, so I let her do her job. "My guess is that those worn places were caused by decades of wind blowing the tree it was hidden in and moving the coconut around inside the box."

"So, after all your techno magic, what does it say?" Doc asked.

She opened the file and handed the three of us sheets of paper, then turned so that the light from a gas lantern fell across her shoulder. "It says, '*Después de la niebla, la tempestad recato atravesó el istmo y nos rodearon y ahora la mujer inquieta ahora descansa. Su envío suprimido fuera el pilar prodigioso ochenta contundentes avances ausente del comercio. 23 de septiembre, 1566.*' That's one really old coconut."

"Jimmy said he recognized a few words," I said. "Mist, woman, suppressed, and trade. But, he said it was what he called 'old Spanish,' not like the Cuban that's spoken around here."

"I spent a year in Rota," Tony said. "Gimme some light." Tony Jacobs was one of Deuce's first recruits, along with another member of his SEAL team, Art Newman. Tony's a wiry, very dark-skinned, easy going black guy. His dedication to service was evident by his just being here. Last winter, he was captured by a terrorist cell operating out of Cuba and tortured. They'd cut off the tips of his right forefinger and middle finger, at the first knuckle. His only response, once we got him out, was that he was glad the SEALs had taught him how to shoot with either hand.

"Yeah, this is a riddle, all right," Tony said. "And Jimmy was right—this is Castilian Spanish, but written in sort of a medieval way, maybe. I think it says, 'After the mist, the diffident tempest traversed the isthmus and surrounded us and now the restless woman now sleeps. Her consignment suppressed outside the prodigious mainstay eighty forceful advances absent from trade. September twenty-third, 1566.'"

"No," Chyrel said. "The computer says *descansa* means rests, not sleeps."

"You sure?" Tony asked. "Not really much difference."

"In a riddle," Charlie said as she came across the clearing, "a subtle difference in wording is huge. Rests means to cease being active, but sleep is the suspension of consciousness. Mind if I have a look?"

"I'm lousy at riddles," I said and handed Charlie the translation.

"Hmmm," she muttered. "Did you notice that the two words near the end of the first sentence in the Spanish text start with uppercase letters, while the rest of it is normal?"

"Huh," Tony and Chyrel said in unison.

"Is that important?" Tony asked.

"It is if it's intentional. The writer of a riddle usually does everything intentionally. Makes me think that the M and I might be initials, or Mujer Inquieta is a title, or maybe a name, not just an adjective and noun."

"Chyrel," Doc said. "Do you think you can find—"

Chyrel interrupted him, saying, "A list of possible Spanish shipwreck locations in September, 1566?"

Doc grinned. "You don't think they kept really accurate GPS records back then? No, I was thinking a list of names of ships that never arrived in Spain? Maybe one about this time with the initials M I?"

"No," she replied, smiling. "No GPS back then. But they kept very accurate lists of ship departures and arrivals. Most Spanish ships going up through the Windward Passage, which we now call the Gulf Stream, were treasure ships headed to Spain. Coming from Spain they used the equatorial route following the trade winds and carried commercial goods to their outposts in the Caribbean."

"Trade?" I asked. "Absent from trade?"

"Hah!" Charlie exclaimed. "He used synonyms. Absent could be away from. As in the opposite way of the trade winds."

I gave that a thought. "The trade winds for the northern route to Spain obviously blow toward the east, so he meant west?"

"How long would it take a Spanish treasure galleon to sail from Havana to wherever the coconut was found?" Chyrel asked.

"It was found on Elbow Cay, in the Abacos," Doc said.

"Ships in those days followed landmarks as much as they could, staying close to shore," I said. "They'd stay in deeper water once out of sight of land, and they probably didn't travel more than a hundred miles a day. Chyrel, calculate the distance from Havana to Key West, then along the Keys and east coast up to the northern Bahamas. That could give us a departure date."

She headed back inside to her computer. "Okay," I said. "What's that give us?"

Charlie pondered the translation. "After the mist, the diffident tempest traversed the isthmus and surrounded us." She thought it over then said, "Mist could be fog. A diffident tempest, maybe a backward storm?"

"A backward storm?" I asked. "No storm in the northern hemisphere circulates backward."

"No," Doc said, getting excited. "But sometimes a hurricane will move east instead of west. Usually in September hurricanes form in the eastern Atlantic, but now and then one will form in the Gulf of Mexico and cross Florida into the Atlantic."

"Traversed the isthmus!" Charlie said. "Crossed Florida."

"Okay," I said. "So, after a fog, a hurricane crossed Florida and passed them. Probably to the north, which caused them to sail south to get away from it. That would make sense as to why they wrecked in the Bahamas. If it circled them, it could have caught them in open water and driven them onto Elbow Cay."

"Then the rest," Charlie said, "and now a ship, maybe named after someone with the initials M I, finally rests. Her consignment, meaning cargo, suppressed outside the prodigious mainstay, I'm guessing that's some nautical term, eighty forceful advances to the west."

"On land," Doc said, "distances are sometimes measured in paces. Advances?"

"Okay, eighty forceful paces then," Charlie said. "If it is paces, then forceful paces must mean long paces. But what's a prodigious mainstay? 'Prodigious' means amazing or impressive."

"Eighty long paces?" I thought out loud. "A regular pace is about thirty inches, a long pace could be anywhere from thirty-six to forty-eight inches. That'd be two hundred and forty to three hundred and twenty feet. Probably less, depending on the terrain. What was the word for 'mainstay' in Spanish again?" I asked.

"Pilar," Tony said. "Pillar? Like a big rock or spire?"

"The restless woman finally rests," I thought out loud again. "Her cargo suppressed. Buried?"

"Of course!" Doc shouted. "What else do pirates do with treasure?"

"Outside the giant rock or spire, eighty long paces west?" Tony asked. "Outside would have to mean away from the water, or inland, right?"

"After the fog the hurricane crossed Florida and circled around us and now the restless woman finally rests," Charlie began, really getting excited. "Her cargo buried inland from the giant rock two to three hundred feet west. It would have to be a giant rock. They couldn't mean anything that might not be there in a few years. Maybe they knew they were going to die and wanted to leave a clue for another Spanish ship."

"Now all we need is a ship's name, and to find the giant rock," Doc said.

"Do you know exactly where on Elbow Cay the chest was found?" I asked.

"The Judge said his fifth great-grandfather found it while walking on the northern beaches of the island. He was waiting for the tide to rise to refloat their ship, which was stuck on a sandbar."

"Satellite view!" Tony and I said together. We all jumped up and headed toward the western bunkhouse and Chyrel's little office.

Chyrel was just coming out when we got there. "Not a galleon at all," she said as she turned and went back inside, the rest of us crowding around her desk. "There was a fleet of four galleons, five caravels, and one carrack that left Havana in early September. I didn't even have to calculate the distance. They were the only ships that didn't make it to Spain in the summer and fall of 1566. A carrack is much larger than a caravel or galleon. This particular carrack was the *Nuestra Señora de Magdalena* y las Angustias, or Our Lady of Magdalena and Anxieties. The Restless Woman."

"Can you pull up a satellite view of the northern part of Elbow Cay?" I said.

"Satellite time is expensive," Chyrel replied.

"Doesn't have to be live," I said. "Even an aerial picture might do the trick. We're looking for a large rock on the eastern shore of the northern part of the island."

A moment later, she zoomed in on the beaches of Elbow Cay, north of Hope Town.

"There," I said, pointing at a place that jutted out into the water. "Zoom in on that."

"It's a big rock, all right," Doc said. "But look at the scale. The island's only a little more than a hundred feet from beach to bay."

"Zoom back out," Tony said.

Chyrel zoomed back out and scrolled the screen down, showing the beach further north.

"What's that?" I asked

"Looks like a house," Chyrel said.

"Yeah, but the way that piece of land juts out, it's got to be built on a huge boulder," I said. "Zoom back out,"

"The island's a lot wider there," Tony said. "Almost a quarter mile or so."

"You think that's it?" Doc asked.

"No way to know for sure," I replied. "Hell, the rock we're looking for might even be underwater now."

"It probably is," Chyrel said. "I'll check into it some more tomorrow. Erosion data for most coastal areas has been collected for several decades. I might be able to extrapolate that data and create a computer model that could simulate what the coastline of the island looked like four hundred and forty years ago."

"You can do that?" Doc asked.

Tony laughed and said, "Doc, when it comes to computers, there's not much beyond her capability."

"Thanks, Tony. Now all of you scram. I'm going to bed," Chyrel said. As we left the little office, Charlie said she was also going to bed and headed off to their little house.

"You guys really think there's a treasure?" Tony asked.

"Maybe Chyrel can find out more about the fleet tomorrow," I said. "I know the Spaniards had a full manifest of every ship's cargo and most of the time, there was more aboard than what the manifest said. I just put some beer in the fridge on the boat—you guys wanna join me?"

We sat in the salon and Tony pulled the sheet of paper out of his pocket along with a printout of the satellite view. "Let's suppose for a minute that this ship, *Magdalena*, was the ship that Doc's chest came from. Do you think they all wrecked there?"

"September's still hurricane season," I said. "And the clues point toward their being sunk during a storm. That's what most likely happened, since none of the eight ships made it to Spain. The history books are full of entire fleets being wiped out by hurricanes."

"Okay," Tony said. "So what happened to the other treasure ships? I'm just guessing here, but wouldn't they all have been carrying treasure?"

"Probably," Doc said. "Chyrel said the carrack was much larger than the caravels and galleons, which were very heavily armed. Being larger, you'd assume they were much sturdier and slower. Maybe the other ships broke apart in the storm and never made it to land, or maybe they made it further south, trying to run from the storm."

Tony shuddered. "Nasty way to go."

I grabbed a pencil from a drawer and handed it to Tony. "Let's write down everything we have questions about. The manifest, for one. The size difference between a carrack and a galleon, for another. Also, if they were driven onto the island by a hurricane, the storm didn't stop there. We think it crossed Florida, looped around to the south, then west, and it probably made landfall again on the mainland somewhere else. Maybe she can look through early American archives for hurricanes that made landfall in September of 1566."

"What would that tell us?" Doc asked.

"I'm wondering if it was this one ship, or the whole fleet, that strayed so far out of the shipping lanes," I replied. "They should have been well to the north of the Abacos and if they were caught in a storm, they would have been sunk at sea, or driven onto the mainland. If we knew the storm's track, we might even have a starting point for where the rest of the fleet went down."

"Chyrel said it was bigger than the others," Tony said. "Maybe during the fog, they steered away from the smaller ships to avoid a collision."

"That makes perfect sense," Doc replied. "If we know the location of one ship and the track of the storm, we might be able to predict where the others sank also."

"You want to find the whole fleet?" I asked.

"Finding a deep-water wreck would probably be beyond what we can do," he replied. "But narrowing the location would be something, wouldn't it?"

"That takes us to the next step, Doc. There's two options for if and when we find any treasure and you should decide up front which route you're gonna take."

"What's that?" he asked.

"About twenty years ago," I began, "me and Deuce's dad found some treasure. A bunch of silver coins. We found it in a place we shouldn't have been looking. That said, our only recourse was to sell it to a less-than-reputable collector who probably melted it all down."

"I'm not sure I follow you," Doc said.

"If these clues do lead you to a 1566 Spanish treasure ship, the government of Spain is going to declare ownership and the government of the Bahamas is going to declare sovereignty. You'll be lucky to get a tenth of the actual worth after months in Admiralty Court, but you will have the satisfaction of getting your picture in papers all over the world and you might have a wing to some museum in Spain named after you."

"The alternative would be what you and Deuce's dad did? Sell it on the black market?"

"Didn't sit well with me either, but it was Russ's find and I left it up to him."

"The historical value of finding this one ship could be really significant," Tony said.

"No need on deciding right now," Doc said. "We don't know anything about these ships and for all we know, they all were loaded with rum."

I laughed. "If it had a cargo of four-hundred-year-old rum, that'd be worth keeping secret."

"Then we'll wait until tomorrow and see if Chyrel can find a manifest," Doc said.

I walked up to the deck with the two men and sat down at the table on the rear deck to finish my beer as they headed across the clearing to the bunkhouse. It was clear and cooler than it had been in a while. After a few minutes, my eyes adjusted and the vastness of the night sky revealed itself. Rusty had taught me years ago how to read the timeless and predictable stars to figure my location. Now I didn't even need a clock. Knowing the month, I could tell the time by where the stars were. The Pleiades were rising out of the east. The Seven Sisters are a winter constellation. Fleeing Orion, they were a reminder to early seafarers to leave their ships tied to the docks and tend the land. It was also a reminder to me that it was late, so I turned in.

# CHAPTER FOUR

The phone on the desk was ringing as the slight, balding man walked into his office. He picked it up and spoke into the receiver, "Good morning, Florida Historical Society."

"I think we have something," came a voice over the phone.

"Who is this?" the man said.

"I just listened to the tape," said the voice. "They have a lead on another treasure find."

The man in the office was middle-aged and out of shape. Not that he'd ever been in good shape. He was five feet seven inches tall and a flabby one hundred seventy pounds. His skin was chalky from lack of sunshine and his hairline seemed to be in a race with time to see if it could reach the bald spot in back before the bald spot reached it. He walked over and closed his office door before speaking again.

"You're sure?" he asked.

"Listen for yourself," said the voice on the phone. Then after a couple of clicks, a different voice, tinny and slightly distorted, came over the phone. "*If these clues do lead you to a 1566 Spanish treasure ship, the government of Spain is going to declare ownership and the government of the Bahamas is going to declare sovereignty. You'll be lucky to get a tenth of the actual worth after years in court, but you will have the satisfaction of getting your picture in papers all over the world and you might have a wing to some museum in Spain named after you.*" Then there was another click and the man's voice came back on. "The name of the ship is *Magdalena*. There's more on the tape. See if you can find out anything on the ship. You should come down here. Today."

The man loosened his cheap necktie and thought for a moment while checking his calendar. "I can't get away this morning," he finally said. "But I can be down there this afternoon." Without a word, the call was ended and he placed the receiver in its cradle.

# CHAPTER FIVE

A gentle wind was blowing from the west, my hammock swaying slightly to the beat of the song in my head. I could hear the gentle whoosh of the tiny waves as they washed ashore just a few yards away. The smell of fresh rain, frangipani, and jasmine filled my nostrils with an intoxicating fragrance. A light, warm rain fell on my face, but that didn't bother me. I opened my eyes to the sight of the fronds of a coconut palm being gently pushed by the breeze above my head. The sun was just showing through the trees to my left, silhouetting a woman in a white blouse and tight jeans. Her wet blouse was plastered to her body like a second skin, showing off her ample curves and the flatness of her belly. Her thick blond hair fell across her face and draped her shoulders, rainwater dripping from the ends.

Her voice sounded like an angel. "Red sky in morn, Captain Sleepy Head."

I bolted upright in my bed. "Alex!"

The only answer to my shout was the sound of a light rain on the metal roof of my little stilt house. I rose from our bed, went into the galley where the coffee was already brewing, and poured a cup. I started to sit down at the little table when I heard footsteps coming up the rear steps. I walked over and opened the door as Tony and Carl came across the deck. Both men were dressed in standard island attire, cargo pants and bare feet.

"Thought I heard a shout," Tony said with a worried look.

"Spilled hot coffee on my hand," I lied. "Want some?" It wasn't the first time my late wife had come to me in a dream. It seemed to happen as a warning of something ahead. *Red sky in morn?* I thought.

"Sure," they both replied. I poured two more cups and we sat down.

"Got the tilapia tank done," Carl said. "It's filling now. I'm going up to Homestead this afternoon in Skeeter's flatbed to pick up the fry."

"Already?" I asked.

"Yeah, Tony and I were up early and finished plumbing it just before the rain started. Doesn't look like it'll last long. It's already light to the east."

"Doc was up late," Tony said. "Filling Nikki in on what we'd learned. I think he's leaning toward making the search public."

"I hope he does," I said. "If that rock with the house on it is where the riddle is pointing, it won't be much fun digging up someone's yard in the middle of the night."

Tony laughed and said, "No, it could get downright troublesome, too."

"Let's go check out what you guys got done," I said.

We walked down to the aquaculture setup on the southeast side of the clearing. My island's pretty small and beginning to get crowded. At just over two acres, the clearing in the middle takes up the majority of it and it's barely one hundred feet across at its narrowest. Still, it's more than double the diameter of a helicopter's rotor, and more than one competent chopper jock has landed here. The new fourth tank was filling fast. It and the tank with the crawfish were tucked back under the tree line for shading, but the two growing tanks were out in the sun. I noticed the plumbing was in a loop, from the new fish tank to the crawfish tank and from there to the first farm tank, then the second, before dumping back into the fish tank.

"The intake from the new tank goes all the way to the bottom," Carl said. "The bottom of the tank is covered with a raised screen to allow the fish waste to fall through."

"They'll breed, right?" I asked. "What about the eggs?"

"We'll be raising Nile Tilapia, which are mouth brooders," Carl said. "At the far end are a bunch of foot-long PVC pipes, all strapped together and anchored on the bottom. That's where the males will build their nests and where the eggs are laid. Once the eggs are fertilized, the females will take them in their mouths and leave the nests. They hatch in the female's mouth and she'll release them when they're ready to swim, usually a week to ten days after laying."

"So why is the intake at the bottom?" Tony asked.

"It'll help keep the water clear," Carl explained. "The solid waste from the fish will fall through the mesh and be siphoned up along with the water as the water's pumped out of the crawfish tank up into the farm tanks. The crawfish will feed on anything edible in the fish's waste and break it up, so it can flow more easily through the pumps and bio filters to the plants. The bio filters break the ammonia down into nitrite and then further into nitrate, which the plants thrive on."

"Glad you know what you're doing, Carl," I said. "It's all Greek to me."

I could hear the sound of an outboard approaching from the southeast. I left them there and went back up to the deck. Looking out beyond Harbor Channel, I could see Rusty's familiar skiff approaching. He had Deuce with him.

"Why didn't Julie come with you?" I asked once we'd tied Rusty's skiff off to the south dock.

"She's nesting," Rusty said. "Run us off, so she could get their boat cleaned up."

"She's kind of fussy about that," Deuce said. "Two months of sailing all over the Caribbean has been kind of rough on the interior."

We walked up to the deck, then down the back steps and across the clearing. Doc was sitting with Chyrel at one of the tables outside the bunkhouses. We brought Rusty and Deuce up to speed on what was written on the coconut, the translation, and what we thought it all meant.

"Sounds to me like you guys are goin' on a treasure hunt," Rusty said.

"We have a lot more to find out before we go off looking for anything," Doc said.

"I found dozens of geological survey reports dating back to the late 1920s," Chyrel said. "They contain beach erosion data on Elbow Cay. Using those, along with dozens of early nautical charts, I was able to create a drawing of what the coast line might have looked like four hundred and forty years ago. The island has lost a good three hundred feet of beach. That's why there are so many exposed rocks along the shoreline. The rock with the house on it was well inland back then, and bigger. The rock that's now well offshore was on the beach then."

Tony gave her the list of things we'd thought of last night, and she disappeared into her little office. She'd printed out many nautical charts of the northern Bahamas dating back to the early 1600s and a history of the islands. The Spanish had had little use for the tiny islands, except to enslave the populace that had once lived and flourished there. By the early 1500s, there were no people on any of the Abacos. Ownership passed back and forth between England and Spain until 1783, when England ceded Florida to Spain in exchange for the Bahamas.

Doc pointed at the satellite view. "According to the scale, two to three hundred feet west of that rock is quite a ways offshore today."

"Early nautical charts were very accurate as far as latitude," Rusty said. "That's just a simple matter of shooting the North Star. But determining longitude was still a matter of sailing due east or west and measuring speed to determine distance. Very unreliable"

He pulled out a chart dated 1728 and placed it next to one dated 1898. "See how wide they show Abaco here and again a hundred and seventy years later?" Before anyone could answer, he placed a modern chart over them, and pointing to the narrow isthmus between the southern end of Abaco and the northern end, he said, "The reality is that the island narrows to just a few yards here."

"Okay, what's your point?" I asked.

"Even this early map shows Hole Rok, now called Hole in the Wall, at the southern tip of Abaco. Major landmarks for navigation were usually pretty accurate. Life depended on it. This early one shows a rock offshore of Isla Lucayoneque and the reef beyond."

"I see what you mean," Tony said. "If that rock was offshore almost two hundred and eighty years ago, it was probably offshore a hundred and sixty years before that."

"I'd bet on it," Doc said. "My money's on the big rock with the house on it being the 'prodigious mainstay' clue on the coconut."

"Have you decided, Doc?" I asked. "This is your call, yours and Nikki's."

"We talked about it last night. If we go after the treasure, we agree we should do it right. Announce our findings and everything."

Chyrel came out of the office with a file folder and handed it to Doc. "Maybe you should call Nikki back and go over what I found here. You can use my office."

Doc opened the file and scanned the first document. "Are you sure about this?"

Cheryl nodded, "Like I said, the Spanish kept very good records, but from what I've read, there was usually a lot of contraband in the form of pesos and jewels that weren't on the manifest." Doc walked toward the office, flipping through more pages.

"What'd you find out?" I asked.

She turned to the four of us and said, "The *Magdalena* carried one and a half million pesos, along with about two thousand pounds of gold and three twenty-pound chests of uncut emeralds."

"Holy shit!" Rusty exclaimed. "A peso is just shy of an ounce. At today's price, worth about thirteen bucks. That's almost twenty million dollars, right there."

"Gold's at about eight hundred an ounce," Tony said. "That's what? Another two and a half million?"

"Twenty-five million," Chyrel said with a smile. "You didn't carry one of those zeroes."

Only minutes later Doc came out of the office and walked back toward us. "Just this ship alone carried about fifty million in silver and gold, plus another two million in emeralds. Nikki and I both agree, we still should do what's right."

I smiled, knowing that was a hard decision, but he'd made the right one. *Hell*, I thought, *ten percent of fifty million is still a huge chunk of change.*

"Further," he said, "we thought it right to split anything we find with everyone here that's helped figure out where to look."

"The find's yours," Rusty said. "You get half off the top."

Doc started to say something, but I interrupted him. "And don't argue about it."

"Well, I am going to argue," Doc said.

"Look, old son," Rusty said. "You and your missus are the rightful owners of whatever you find. You got more than just the two of you to think about. You'll have kids someday."

"Trust me, Doc," Deuce said. "You're not gonna win this argument. They did the same with me."

"And from the story you told," I added, "you have quite a few generations to satisfy."

Chyrel stood up and said, "I'll get started right away on the protocol of who needs to be alerted for you and try to get a handle on the salvage laws in the Bahamas."

# CHAPTER SIX

The drive through Miami rush hour traffic had been a nightmare with the air conditioner barely working in his ten-year-old Buick LeSabre. By the time he got on the Florida Turnpike in Orlando, he'd already had to remove his three-year-old, off-the-rack coat and tie. The drive from Orlando to West Palm Beach was three hours of adrenaline rush, dodging demented truckers and wandering tourists. Then it seemed that everything south of Palm Beach was under construction, slowing traffic to a crawl for thirty-five miles.

That delay put him on the Sawgrass Expressway and Homestead Extension during rush hour, another harrowing sixty miles of hell. He debated the wisdom of getting off the interstate and taking the surface streets, but decided against it. He'd heard a lot of bad things about Miami and his directions had his destination just a couple of blocks off the Turnpike. After three hours of stop-and-go traffic, choking on car and truck fumes, he finally took the Southwest 184th Street exit to Cutler Ridge and turned right. Just ahead on the left in a small strip mall was the Presidente Supermarket he'd been told to look for. He turned into the little parking lot and looked at the signs over the few stores that were occupied. Around the grocery store was an eclectic assortment of bail bondsmen, pawn shops, and Cuban restaurants, with heavy bars over the windows and doors.

Finding the right office, he pulled into a parking spot and shut off the engine, which chugged a couple of times in the stifling heat before finally wheezing to a stop. He got out and looked around. The man he was meeting, Chase Conner, had once worked for the Florida Department of Revenue. He'd been fired just a few months earlier for accepting a bribe from an undercover Florida Department of Law Enforcement agent and now ran a small accounting business. It was shortly before he was fired that Conner had approached him about bugging the boat of another man they were both going to meet, concerning the sale of Confederate gold bars to the Florida Historical Society. Conner represented both the state and the IRS. He hadn't wanted to go along, but Conner had been persuasive, suggesting that if the man on the boat got wind of another treasure find, they might be able to get to it first and get rich selling the treasure on the black market. *People all over Florida were getting rich doing a lot less*, Owen Bradbury thought. Looking at the eleven gold bars which the Society had purchased from the man on the boat every day didn't make it any easier to resist.

Bradbury, Assistant Curator of the Florida Historical Society in Orlando, Florida, tried the glass door to the office and found it locked. There was a button on the door frame, so he pushed it and heard a bonging sound from somewhere inside. He waited and could barely see movement through the heavily-tinted glass of the door. The lock clicked and the door opened, releasing a blast of cold air and revealing a tall, sandy-haired man of average weight in a blue three-piece suit.

"Mister Bradbury," Chase Conner said as he pushed the door wider. "So nice to see you again. Hope the drive down wasn't too bad. Come in, there's some people who have already arrived that I'd like you to meet."

The inside of the office was darker. As Bradbury's eyes adjusted from the white hot sunlight of south Florida, he made out the four people sitting in the office. A woman sat in a comfortable-looking chair in front of a desk, along with a man in a suit. A third chair to the woman's left was empty, as was the chair behind the desk.

There were two other men sitting on a sofa against the wall. These men caught Bradbury's attention immediately. Both were large men; he could tell they were tall even sitting down. Their light sports jackets didn't conceal the fact that both men were heavily muscled, with broad shoulders, thick, corded necks, and barrel chests. The men had serious-looking faces and wore nearly identical crew cuts. *Heavy brass bookends*, Bradbury thought. The man sitting with the woman stood up and came across the room, extending his hand.

"Mister Bradbury, my name is Valentin Madic. I'm pleased to finally meet the brains behind this endeavor."

Bradbury took the man's hand, which nearly crushed his own. Madic was only slightly taller than Bradbury, who stood at five feet eight inches. A first guess would put him in his late thirties, but looking closer, Bradbury could tell he was older, probably in his fifties. He was trim and looked like he took great care in his appearance, though his cheeks were pocked with acne scars. His eyes drew Bradbury instantly. They looked like two vacant ice-blue orbs, never moving, showing no emotion. They fixed Bradbury with a steady, appraising gaze.

What Bradbury now had in his briefcase gave him the confidence his appearance didn't otherwise show. He felt the confidence of knowledge grow inside him. The fact that Madic had called him the 'brains behind this endeavor' confirmed it in his mind. Finding what he'd found earlier in the day on his computer, Bradbury actually felt more confident than he'd ever felt before. And now, here was a man that looked like he could provide the means for him to finally get what he felt he deserved.

"This is my personal assistant, Tena Horvac," Madic said as the woman rose and turned toward him. She was extremely attractive and also impeccably dressed in a black pencil skirt, light blue blouse and black jacket. She looked to be in her mid-thirties, but Bradbury had never been good at judging the age of a beautiful woman. She was fair-skinned, almost pale, but with a light coconut or olive undertone speaking toward mixed ancestry. She matched her boss in height and moved with a precise, athletic measure, flowing like liquid metal. *No, not athletic*, Bradbury thought. *More fluid and graceful, like a jungle cat, a jaguar.* Every movement she made seemed both calculated and graceful at the same time. It was a delight just to watch her cross a room. Her hair was black, piled into a bun on the back of her head, and her eyes were the darkest eyes Bradbury had ever seen, like lucid pools of India ink. "Very nice to meet you both," Bradbury said, turning toward the two men on the couch, expecting them to stand and be introduced also. Both men met him with flat, expressionless stares, which he returned.

"These are two of my men," Madic said dismissively.

"Have a seat, Mister Bradbury," Conner said, walking toward the chair behind the desk.

Madic and the woman sat back down in their chairs, leaving Bradbury with the only other chair in the office, next to the woman. He sat down, placing his briefcase on his knees. "I thought it was just going to be the two of us, Mister Conner."

"The two of us would never be able to do this alone," Conner said. "And please, call me Chase. It's Owen, right?"

"Yes, Owen is fine."

"Owen, Mister Madic here is a local businessman. A very successful and busy local businessman. He has access to many of the things we'll need if we're going to have any chance of pulling this off. More than anything, boats and manpower."

"So far," Madic said with just a trace of accent, "I haven't heard anything that would interest me in participating in anything. Perhaps you have something, Mister Bradbury." Bradbury looked across the cheap desk at Conner, who nodded.

Madic didn't seem the type to use first names. "Mister Madic, would fifty million dollars interest you enough?"

"Did you say fifty million?" Madic asked, his vacant, shark-like eyes showing brief surprise. Bradbury noticed the woman seemed not to react at all.

Bradbury opened his briefcase and removed a file. Opening it he said, "This is a manifest. The Spanish were very good at accounting for cargo transported back to Spain. This lists the cargo aboard the Spanish carrack *Nuestra Señora de Magdalena y las Angustias*, which sailed out of Havana on September third, 1566 and was never seen again. Among the hides, sugar, molasses, rum, and other assorted trade goods, she carried one and a half million pesos, two thousand pounds of gold, and three chests of uncut emeralds. The silver and gold alone would be valued today at fifty million dollars, just in commodity value. Intrinsic value and historical value could easily double that amount. And it wasn't the only ship in the fleet, just the largest."

The woman spoke for the first time, her voice as fluid as her movements. Resonant and businesslike, also with just a touch of an accent that he couldn't place. "And you know the whereabouts?"

# CHAPTER SEVEN

W e finalized a loose plan by noon. Chyrel gave Rusty all the information she found that he'd need for salvage rights. Rusty, Deuce, and Doc went home by early afternoon to get started on planning the treasure hunt. Using his license as a salvor, Rusty made inquiries to learn more about salvage laws in the Bahamas. Deuce would decide on two more from his team to come along for security. Carl would use the *Cazador* to bring non-perishable supplies up from Big Pine and stow them aboard the *Revenge,* along with a list of equipment we'd put together over the next week. Chyrel dug through computer files for any reference to storms on the mainland and in the northern Caribbean in September of 1566 and found quite a bit of information.

A journal from a Priest, Father Lopez de Mendoza Grajales, who'd founded the first Catholic mission in Saint Augustine just a year before described a fierce storm that came out of the wilderness to the southwest and moved offshore in early September. A single Lucayan slave washed up on shore three days later. He spoke only his native tongue, but the Priest managed to find out that although the slave didn't know the name of the ship he was on, he was able to convey that it had been one of ten ships in a fleet that left Havana nine days earlier. The Priest further described a second, even more powerful hurricane coming off the ocean from the southeast less than a week later.

"This is important information," I told Chyrel and Tony over coffee in the salon that evening. "It could mean that the slave was on one of the other ships in the fleet and they sank in the storm about the time the *Magdalena* turned south."

"Then the hurricane circled around the northern Bahamas as the *Magdalena* sailed south," she added, "eventually driving the ship onto Elbow Cay, where the crew probably died from dehydration. There's no source of fresh water on the island."

"But not before salvaging the treasure and burying it on the island. I wonder how many people survived the wreck and why didn't they turn north after the hurricane passed the first time."

"The manifest said they had a crew of seventy-five," Tony said. "Plus twenty-two passengers. Maybe they had damage and were looking for someplace to make repairs. The *Mag* was the largest. Ten ships? Maybe five to eight hundred people in all?"

"And only the one slave survived the wreck of the other nine?" Chyrel asked.

"Probably only a small handful survived the wreck on Elbow Cay," I said. "Ever wonder why early sailors wore a gold ring in their ear?"

"I'm guessing it wasn't a fashion statement?" Chyrel asked.

"Back then, few people knew how to swim, even sailors. Among Christian sailors, their greatest fear was drowning at sea and not getting a proper burial. The gold ring was to pay for one, if their body floated up on shore."

"So, not knowing how to swim would mean most of the passengers and crew drowned." Tony added. "With all the native Lucayans gone from the island, there wasn't anyone there to help the survivors. I don't know which would be worse, drowning or dying of thirst."

"I'm taking the *Revenge* to the *Anchor* for a day or so in the morning. Either of you want some shore leave?"

"I'm fine," Chyrel said. "Charlie and I are going fly fishing tomorrow."

"I'm in," Tony replied. "Seafood's great, but I could sure use a steak."

Early the next morning, with Pescador tagging along, we were up on plane, headed northeast up Harbor Channel. It took another forty-five minutes to reach the Seven Mile Bridge and the channel to the *Rusty Anchor* just around the tip of Boot Key.

Deuce and Julie were sitting in the cockpit of their Whitby as we came down the long canal. Deuce came over, helped us tie off the *Revenge*, and then came aboard.

"I was just about to call you," he said. "Charity called this morning. I'd left a message on her cell last night to call me." Charity Styles was one of Deuce's team members. She'd been a martial arts instructor for Miami-Dade Police Department and an Olympic swimmer prior to that, before being recruited by Homeland Security as a member of Deuce's team. Several months earlier she'd gotten close to a young Marine named Jared Williams who we'd all grown to like. He died in the attack at Deuce and Julie's wedding, but he saved many lives that day.

"How's she doing?" I asked.

"She sounded fine. She opened a private dojo up in Key Largo. Said she hoped we'd get an assignment soon, she was getting bored. I told her about what we had planned and asked if she'd like to go along as added security. She jumped at it. I also called Andrew. He's in."

Andrew Bourke came to Deuce's team from the Coast Guard's Maritime Enforcement, where he was a Senior Chief Petty Officer. A quiet and unassuming man in his mid-forties, he was looking at retirement and decided a change of venue might be better. He handled a lot of the cross-training in small boat boarding tactics for the team.

"When did you tell them to come down?" I asked.

"Charity will be here this evening and stay the night aboard our boat. Andrew got a lead on a mini LED infrared spotlight and is fashioning a receptacle for the *Revenge's* bow light."

"The *Revenge* doesn't have bow lights."

"It was a suggestion from the Director after reading our boarding practices report," Deuce said. "It'll be really small, hardly noticeable." Retired Colonel Travis Stockwell was Deuce's boss, the Associate Deputy Director, Caribbean Counterterrorism Command, Department of Homeland Security. He was a former Ranger and we were in Somalia at the same time in 1992, though we'd never met until just a few months ago.

Tony and I sat down at the bar and Deuce went back to his boat. Apparently boats need to be cleaned now and then, and he and Julie had been neglecting it for a few weeks.

"Morning, Jesse," Jimmy said from behind the bar. "Hi, Tony. Breakfast or beer?"

"Both?" Tony asked.

"Coffee for me, Jimmy," I said. "I have to drive up to the mainland today."

Tony looked over at me. "Was I volunteered to do something I wasn't told about?"

I laughed and replied, "Only if you want to. I'm going up to Miami to see someone about supplies I ordered a few weeks ago."

"What kind of supplies?"

"The loud kind."

"I'm in," he said, then to Jimmy he added, "Just coffee for me, too. And whatever Rufus recommends for breakfast."

"Double that," I said as Jimmy poured our mugs. "Where's Rusty?"

"He went down island, to upgrade his salvor's permit."

"Upgrade?" I asked.

"Yeah," Jimmy replied, "to international. And the Bahamas requires a whole different permit to salvage a ship's cargo that's found on land."

We both ate quickly. I told Jimmy to let Rusty know we were going to be gone most of the day, but would be back by evening. Ten minutes later, we were passing under the gumbo-limbo and oak branches that shade and nearly obscure the entrance to the *Anchor*. I turned *The Beast* north onto US-1.

My truck is a 1973 International Travelall, sort of an SUV on steroids. I bought it over seven years earlier, when I first arrived in the Keys after retiring. It just seemed to call out to me at the time. Since then, friends had chipped in and done a complete makeover while I was in the hospital last spring. They left the exterior just the way it was, scratched, dented, and fading to rust in places. They simply cleaned it up, shot it with clear coat to stop the rust from getting worse, and mounted a huge brush guard, winch, and oversized wheels and tires. It looked like a jacked-up junker. But under the hood, the tired old American Motors small block V-8 gas engine had been replaced with a monster Cummins supercharged diesel engine that produces four hundred and fifty horses and over eight hundred pounds of torque. The axles and transfer case were also replaced with heavy-duty Ford units. Inside, my friends had gutted the interior, reupholstered the backseat, and replaced the front bench seat with comfortable air ride seats. A console was added, with a completely new dashboard and gauges, air conditioning, and a nice sound system.

As the tires set up a hum on the highway passing Duck Key, Tony asked, "Where exactly are we going in Miami that's gonna take all day to get there and back?"

"I lied," I replied. "Didn't want anyone in the bar knowing my business. We're headed to a little town on the west coast. LaBelle, near Fort Myers. An old friend lives there who has access to just about anything."

"That would mean something you can't get locally, then?"

"Yeah, I think you'll approve."

The old International drove and handled like a brand new rig, the big engine not even breaking a sweat at highway speed, and we got to my friend's place of business before noon. I'd gone to high school and later served with Billy Rainwater, a Seminole Indian who lived near where I grew up in Fort Myers. He loved four-wheeling and had a collection of off-road vehicles. He ran a business customizing other people's trucks, and he also ran an import/export business on the side, with a very limited clientele. I'd called him several weeks earlier and told him what I was in the market for and he called back a few days ago to tell me my order had been filled.

I eased the big truck under the shade of an ancient cypress tree on the edge of Billy's crushed-shell parking area. His shop was nothing more than an old steel building, with two garage bay doors and a small office. It had once been a gas station, back when we were kids. Billy came out of the shade of one of the garage bays, lazily striding toward us as we got out. He still wore his hair long in a ponytail and dressed like he probably had every day for thirty years—jeans, boots, and a western-style plaid shirt.

"That don't sound like no AMC, Kemosabe," Billy said, extending his hand. I took his extended arm, grabbing his forearm in the Indian way, then pulled him in for a slap on the back. I hadn't seen Billy in over seven years, but it felt like it was only yesterday that we watched as a young woman put eight rounds into a man who had kidnapped her. He and I had been hunting the man, an escaped convict that nobody will ever find or miss.

"Good to see you again, brother," I said, releasing the bear hug. "This is my friend, Tony."

Billy turned and offered his hand to Tony and said, "Any friend of Jesse's is someone I'd take a bullet for." When Tony took his hand, Billy turned it and looked down where Tony was missing the first knuckle of his index and middle fingers. Without a word passing between them, Billy seemed to sense it happened in a violent way and wasn't accidental.

Turning back to me he said, "Am I nuts, or did I hear a 6.7 liter Cummins pull in here?" I popped the hood and let him ogle the truck for a few minutes. Finally closing the hood, he leaned on the brush guard and said, "I have everything you wanted. All boxed up in the rear of the shop. Why don't you back this beast in and we can get her loaded up."

Tony and I got in the truck and backed it into the bay Billy had disappeared into. When we were clear, Billy pulled both rolling doors down and joined us at the back of the truck.

"Now that's rare," Billy said pointing at the back of *The Beast*.

"What's that?" I asked.

"Barn doors on a seventy-three. Most of them had a tailgate."

He walked over to where a heavy tarp covered some boxes and pulled it off. Sliding the crate beneath it over, he unlatched it and opened it. "Exactly like you specified," he said. "I won't even bother asking what it mounts on."

Inside was a titanium mounting bracket that would fit securely into the deck mount where the fighting chair goes in the cockpit of the *Revenge*. It was three feet long but telescoped up to five feet in four inch increments, with large locking pins that slid through holes drilled in it. It had a folding tripod with rubber feet that extended out from the base post thirty-six inches and locked into place twenty-four inches up from the end of the base post. At the top was a swivel yoke. It was perfect. I closed the case and Tony helped me lift it and put it in the back of the truck.

Billy pulled the tarp back further, uncovering a second crate equal in size and shape to the first. "I've only been asked to find one of these five times. The other four, I pretended it was something I couldn't get my hands on."

When he unlatched and opened it, Tony laughed and exclaimed, "A Ma Deuce? Are you fucking kidding me?" Inside was a completely reconditioned Browning M2A1 .50 caliber machine gun, with two brand new lightweight quick change barrels, affectionately called Ma Deuce.

I closed the lid and latched it, and we loaded it into the truck as Billy dragged out three smaller boxes from under the tarp. Inside the first were a dozen hand grenades, and the second one held ten pounds of C4 plastic explosive. The last box, smaller still, held two dozen electronic blasting caps and two handheld transmitters. I carefully carried them to the truck, setting them inside, away from the C4. Billy put another box in, covered everything with the tarp, and said, "The box of ammo is complimentary, old friend."

I closed the doors on the back of the truck, pulled a roll of hundred-dollar bills from my pocket, and handed it to Billy. "Thanks, again. You seriously need to get down to the Keys and do some fishing." He shoved the roll of bills in his pocket and invited us to sit and have a beer. We sat down in three chairs and talked for a while longer, but Tony and I had a five-hour drive back to Marathon and it would be at the speed limit all the way.

When we were back in the truck, heading east out of LaBelle on Highway 80, Tony asked, "What in the world did you buy a fifty for? I'm not knocking it, they can chew things up in a hurry, but what are you gonna do with it?"

I glanced at Tony and said, "I built storage places under the sofa and settee, false bottoms, really. They can only be accessed from the engine room. The inside of each is the exact dimensions of the M2 and stand. I already had the securing mounts made and installed in each one. Just pull down a panel in the overhead and release the catches, and they both come right out. If anyone is chasing us, they're gonna find out the *Revenge* can have a tail stinger in about a minute."

"That's jacked!" Tony said, slapping the dash a bit too enthusiastically. "Ya know what? I never shot one."

"Really? We'll get 'em stowed and mounted tonight and in the morning me and you can take the *Revenge* out, run a couple drills, and see how long it takes to set it up to fire. We can shoot up that box of ammo that Billy included, too."

We stopped in the little town of Belle Glade, at the southern tip of Lake Okeechobee. After refueling we were back on the road for the long sixty-mile stretch across the Everglades to Miami. Once on the interstate, I moved to the far left lane and tried to keep to a sedate speed. The big truck, with its monster tires and brush guard, was more than imposing enough to get slower commuters to move out of the way without having to get too close behind them. But it still took over an hour to travel forty miles to Homestead. Once we got on US-1 out of Homestead, the traffic thinned out quite a bit. It was a weekday in early fall so the next seventy miles went by quickly.

We arrived back at the *Anchor* and I backed the truck up close to the *Revenge*. It only took a few minutes to move our cargo aboard. Both the stand and the machine gun fit the recesses and securing brackets perfectly. *Thanks, Pap*, I said to myself. My grandparents had raised me from the age of eight and my grandfather had been an architect. I never realized how much I'd learned just watching him work at his drafting table. I drew the plans myself for the individual brackets and the recessed compartments. I designed each compartment in two pieces and had separate carpenters build them. The brackets were aluminum, coated with rubber anywhere they came in contact with metal. Once they were secured and the panel closed, you'd have to know they were there to find them.

# CHAPTER EIGHT

**W**hen we finished putting the machine gun and stand away, Charity had arrived and Julie was satisfied enough with the condition of the *James Caird* that she released Deuce to have a beer while the two women caught up.

"Are you serious?" Deuce asked in a hushed whisper. "You bought a fifty caliber machine gun? What the hell are you afraid of, Jesse?"

"Not a damned thing," I said with a lopsided grin, then drained my bottle. Rusty had another one in front of me before I set the empty on the bar. "It's just in case. Somebody who knows these waters really well once told me you can never have enough firepower."

"Actually," Rusty said, wiping down the bar, "I think I said the more the better, not the bigger the better."

"Tony and I are going out in the morning to try it out—you guys wanna go?"

"Yeah," Deuce said. "Julie and Charity are going shopping in the morning."

"Count me out," Rusty said, reaching for the phone that was ringing below the bar. "Gotta stay by the phone. Waiting for a call from Nassau about the onshore salvage permit. They're balking because I won't give them the exact location." Then into the phone he said, *Rusty Anchor Bar and Grill.*" After listening for a minute he said, "Yeah, he's right here in front of me, hang on."

When Rusty extended the phone to me he said, "It's Pam, at the bank. Wants to talk to you."

I took the phone from him and, stretching the cord, walked to the end of the bar. Pam Lamarre is the manager of the State Bank of the Florida Keys, trustee of my estate, and a close friend.

"Hey, Pam, what's up?"

"Hi, Jesse. I have a visitor outside my office that's looking for you. She claims to be your daughter and tracked you to here at the bank. I can't give out customer information, you know that. I didn't even know you had a daughter."

*My daughter,* I thought. *Which one?* I'd been sending cards with checks tucked inside for birthdays and Christmas for the last twenty-three years. Until last July, none had ever been cashed. The one to my youngest daughter, Kim, had been cashed at a bank in North Carolina just after her birthday.

"Jesse, are you there?"

"Yeah, I'm here. Is her name Kim?"

"Yes, she's sitting outside my office right now. Would you like to talk to her?"

"No," I said. "Keep her there, I'll be there in five minutes."

I handed the phone back to Rusty and told him I'd be back soon, then headed out and jumped in *The Beast*. I pulled into the bank parking lot four minutes later. When I walked through the door, I glanced around. Two girls sat in chairs just outside Pam's office. I hadn't seen my youngest daughter since she was five months old, but I recognized her immediately. It was almost like looking in a weird mirror and seeing a reflection of yourself, younger and a different gender.

She had sandy brown hair, past her shoulders, and blue eyes. The girl sitting next to her was half a head shorter. As I started walking across the lobby she saw me and our eyes met. She stood up and met me in the middle of the lobby.

"Daddy?"

"Kim? How'd you find me?"

She flung her arms around my neck. "It is you! I knew Momma was lying."

Pam came out of the office and said, "If you'd like to have some privacy, Jesse, the conference room is available."

She showed us to a small room with blinds on the windows and door. When Pam left and closed the door, Kim introduced me to her friend, Megan, and we sat down.

"First, what did you mean by 'your mother was lying to you'?" I asked.

"Growing up, Momma didn't talk about you very much. Eve told me stories about how big you were and how strong, but when I asked Momma, she'd go on and on about how you were a trained assassin that went all over the world killing women and children. When I was ten, she told us your past had finally caught up to you and you were dead. Just before my last birthday, I found a card from you in the mail and confronted her about it. She tried to take it from me, but I wouldn't let her have it. I put the money you sent in my own account and have been saving all summer to come down here."

"Wait a minute," I said. "It's September. Shouldn't you be in school? Does your mom know you're down here?"

"See, Megan," Kim said to her friend, who looked to be a couple years older. "I was right. If he was as bad as Momma said, he wouldn't be worried about my not being in school."

Then she turned to me. "I skipped a year in middle school and graduated last May. I told Momma I wanted to wait a year before college, so I'd be with my own age group again, and I wanted to go to Miami and see Eve."

"Eve?" I said. "What's she doing in Miami? Wait, back up. So your mom thinks you're in Miami?"

Kim went on to tell me that my other daughter, Eve, had graduated from Duke University last winter. A week later, she'd married a man she'd been dating for two years who was in his last year of law school at Duke, and Eve and Nick now lived in Miami. Then she told me I would be a grandfather in two months. *A grandfather?* I thought. *Me?*

We talked for another ten minutes and she told me how she had driven to Miami and stayed with Eve and Nick the first night. The next morning she told Eve I wasn't dead, but I lived in the Keys and she was going to find me. Her friend, Megan, lived nearby and they came down together.

Apparently my ex had continued to express her increasingly liberal notions about me, the Corps, and the military in general as nothing but knuckle-dragging Neanderthal baby killers. She'd taken the kids and left me in '89, when I was with FAST, the Fleet Antiterrorism Security Team. We were deployed to Panama without even being allowed to make a phone call before departing. That was five days before Kim's first Christmas. I got to see my daughters a few times over the next few months, but was deployed again the following summer for the run-up to Desert Shield.

Sandy's parents in Virginia hired a very good lawyer and she divorced me while I was deployed. Since I didn't show up at the divorce hearing, she got full custody and stayed in Virginia. They'd moved back to North Carolina just three years ago.

Kim went on to describe my ex as having a far-left ideology about nearly everything. She was a member of PETA, Greenpeace, and several other of what Kim called "tree hugger" organizations. She turned vegan and pushed her lifestyle on the girls and continually described me to the girls as having been a very dangerous man. Eve turned out a lot like her, but Kim bucked her at every turn from the way she described the relationship. Both girls did very well in school, Eve graduating college in three and a half years and Kim graduating high school at sixteen.

"I don't think I ever believed what she said about you," Kim admitted. "So I decided to come and find out for myself."

"Where are you staying?" I asked, noting that the lobby was now empty and Pam was standing by the door.

"Actually, Mister McDermitt," Megan said, "I can't stay. I live in Miami and we were planning to drive back tonight. My boyfriend already said he'd come get me if Kim decided to stay."

Before I even knew it I looked at my daughter and said, "That's ridiculous. You can stay with me and drive back to Miami tomorrow, or whenever you want to go."

"You're sure?" Kim said, smiling. Ten minutes later, Megan called her boyfriend and told him where to pick her up as we were pulling into the crushed-shell driveway to the *Anchor*.

"You live in a bar?" Kim asked.

"No, I live on a little island north of here, but for the next couple of days, I'm staying here on my boat." I pointed to the *Revenge*, tied up at the near end of the dock, the blue overhead lights illuminating the bridge and cockpit.

"Oh, cool," she squealed. "The really big one?"

"Come on inside," I said, stepping out of the truck. "You can meet some of my friends."

We stepped through the door and I immediately felt the tension. It hung in the air like ozone after a lightning strike. Deuce and Julie were sitting at the far end of the bar with Charity and Tony. A few local fishermen I recognized were scattered around at tables, but it was the two guys standing at the near end of the bar that caught my attention. They both reminded me of coastal oak trees I'd seen in North Carolina, massive limbs hanging to the ground. They were dressed in nearly identical gray sports coats, bulging at the shoulders, with two square heads sitting on top of them. One stood slightly behind and to the side of the other, who was doing all the talking.

"Then I'll speak with the owner, fat man!"

Although the two men were at least six inches taller than Rusty's five foot six, the man lacked a reverse gear. He'd never backed down from anyone and a whole lot of tougher-looking men had earned a trip to the hospital for underestimating both his speed and his ability. I caught Deuce's eye and with a look held him in place. Whatever was going on, Rusty was up to it.

"I *am* the owner, musclehead," Rusty growled at the taller man. "And I told you, I ain't serving you."

I put a hand on Kim's shoulder, holding her and Megan at the door, as I stepped around the tables to the left, coming into full view of the second man. When he saw me his right hand started to move toward the inside of his jacket, but I was ready for it. Nobody wears a sports coat in the Keys unless they're hiding something under it. My hand was already on the grip of my own Sig P-226, in a holster at my back under my tee shirt.

I had it out, held solidly in both hands and pointed right at the man's sizable chest, before he even got his right hand inside his jacket where I presumed a gun would be.

"We don't allow guns in here, gentlemen," I said.

The leader saw me in his peripheral vision as I stepped further to the left. He started to reach inside his jacket, but Rusty was well ahead of him and leveled his deck sweeper on the man. It's a sawed-off twelve-gauge shotgun with the butt removed. The sudden scraping of chairs as the men at the tables behind the two strangers scrambled to get out of the line of fire covered the sound of Deuce, Julie, Tony, and Charity coming off their stools and leveling more guns at the two intruders. Deuce came up behind the second man. He moved with the silence and speed that only comes from training and was at the second man's shoulder in a second.

"Very slowly," Deuce whispered to the man, who looked around at all the guns suddenly pointed at him and his friend. "With just your thumb and middle finger, pull that gun on out of there and hold it up above your head."

"You heard the man," Rusty snarled menacingly. "And I mean *real* slow. This sweeper has a hair trigger and I'm just a mite jumpy right now. I'd hate to have to clean brain matter from the wall and ceiling."

I saw the fight go out of both men's eyes and they did as they were told. I stepped behind the first man and took his gun as Deuce disarmed the second man. I shoved the man's gun into the large pocket of my cargo pants and quickly patted him down. I found a small revolver in a holster on his left ankle and shoved it in my other pocket. Deuce had done the same thing and then took the second man by the collar and walked him backwards until he fell into a chair.

"There seems to be a lot of guns for a place that does not allow them," the first man said with a slight accent I couldn't place.

"Owner's friends are exempted from all bar rules," Rusty said. As quickly as the sweeper appeared, it disappeared. Rusty kept it in a long custom holster mounted under the end of the bar. Loaded with buckshot. Deuce and I both tucked our own guns away.

"Is this where all the locals gang up and beat shit out of interlopers?" the man asked. *East European, I thought. Not Germany, maybe one of the Baltic countries.*

"No," Rusty said. "This is where you speak civilly to the owner and air your grievance. I said I ain't gonna serve you two and then you hadda go all Billy Badass, two against one. Your partner's sitting this dance out now."

He looked down at Rusty then over at me. "I don't like odds. Your friends will come to rescue."

I laughed lightly. "He doesn't need any help from us. But, if he says the word, I'll gladly gather up what pieces are left over and carry you to the hospital in Miami, where I'll swear on a stack of Bibles you stepped in front of a bus in Coconut Grove."

The man made a sudden move, his left hand streaking out in a quick, sharp uppercut aimed at Rusty's jaw. Rusty stepped forward, lifting his shoulder and arm at the same time, so the punch went under his left arm. Spinning quickly, he took the man by the wrist and jerked back, pulling him off balance. As he came around, Rusty's other hand went up, his big palm slapping the man in the back of the head with a crack, and shoved his face into the massive wooden armrest on the edge of the bar. In a blur, he snatched the man's coat collar and stood him back up, while sweeping his legs out from under him from behind. As he was going down, Rusty's left fist hit him squarely in the center of the chest with a thud. He hit the deck flat on his back and didn't move.

"You!" Rusty roared, pointing at the second man. "Clean this mess up and get out of here. Either of you comes back, I'll shoot you at the door."

The second man rose slowly, warily. He looked at Deuce, standing behind and to his right, then me, then at Rusty. He shrugged and stepped forward. Bending down, he got his buddy under the arms and dragged him toward the door.

I motioned Kim and Megan to come over beside me. Kim seemed to be frozen at the door, one hand in her purse, staring at the man lifting his friend. When they finally moved my way, I drew them behind me as the man struggled to get his unconscious friend outside. As he neared the door, he seemed to notice the girls for the first time, glancing at them for a moment, but settling on Kim for longer than necessary. I knew that look. Hell, I'd given that look more than once. But not toward a child. There was something else in his eyes. A sadistic quality that spoke volumes.

Something clicked in my brain. A feeling I hadn't experienced in a long time. It was akin to when my oldest daughter disappeared once in a grocery store as a toddler. The look he gave my daughter made my skin crawl. When the screen door slammed shut, I went over to it and watched as he hoisted the man's weight easily onto his shoulder. No easy task; the first man probably weighed more than my two hundred and thirty pounds. He carried him to a big brown sedan, where he dumped him unceremoniously into the backseat.

I walked back over to Kim and took her hand. "Are you all right?" She looked me straight in the eye. Though not frightened, she was obviously shaken. I grinned and said, "Your mom wasn't completely wrong. Just about who we're dangerous toward. Come. Meet my friends."

She relaxed a little and I saw the fear melt away from her eyes as I pulled her toward the end of the bar.

"What was that all about?" I asked Rusty.

"Coupla loud mouths, I thought at first. Said they were looking for you and Doc. When I asked 'Jesse who?' they got belligerent."

I went behind him and rang the brass ship's bell to get everyone's attention. Not that I needed to—everyone's eyes were on Kim and Megan anyway, wondering who they were.

"Everyone, this is Kim and Megan." Then I grinned and added, "Kim McDermitt. My youngest daughter."

Julie was first to get up and came around the bar to where we stood. "Hi, Kim," she said, giving her a hug. "Jesse's been like my second dad, so I guess that makes us almost sisters. I'm Julie. These other lunatic gunmen are my father, Rusty, my husband, Russell, and our good friends, Charity and Tony."

Deuce stepped up to take her hand and said, "I remember when you were born. I was about fourteen and our dads were stationed together. It was just before my dad left the Corps."

Rusty leaned on the bar and said, "I remember your mom and sister. You favor your mom some. Me and your dad were stationed together a few times. We stood up for one another when we each got married."

"Really nice to meet you, Kim," Tony said, shaking her hand. "Your dad saved my life not long ago. Deuce's too."

"I'm kind of confused," Kim said. "You've all known each other since before I was born?"

"All but me," Tony said.

"And me," added Jimmy, from behind the far end of the bar.

"Rusty and I met on the bus going up to Parris Island for Boot Camp," I explained. "Being the only two from Florida, we became good friends. When he got married, I was his best man. A couple years later, we were stationed together in Japan and Deuce's dad was our Platoon Sergeant. I met your mom when I came back to Camp Lejeune the following year. When we got married, Rusty was my best man."

I pulled the two guns I'd taken from one of the guys out of my pocket and placed them on the bar. "What'd you get, Deuce?"

He pulled out the gun he'd taken from the second man and placed it next to my two. "Looks like we have a pair," he said.

Rusty picked one up and looked it over. "Looks like a Springfield XD, but it must be some kind of foreign knockoff."

Deuce picked up the second one and said, "No, this is the real deal, Rusty. Springfield bought the rights to the Croatian-made HS2000. Both of these are authentic Croatian military sidearms. What about the revolver?"

I picked it up and examined it. It was a nasty-looking pistol, the barrel no more than two and a half inches, barely longer than the cylinder. "It's Serbian," I said, opening the cylinder and removing one of the rounds. "A Zastava three-fifty-seven magnum. I thought that guy had an accent. Could be a Serb."

"My guess would be Croatian," Tony said. "Former military, from the look of them. Their pilots were issued the Zastava."

"Are you going to see Sherri anytime soon?" I asked Deuce.

Sherri Fallon was one of Deuce's team members. A former armorer with the Miami-Dade Police Department, she was now his weapons expert.

"Later this week," he replied.

Rusty produced a small box from under the bar, placed the HS2000 in it, and slid it across the bar to Deuce. He and I placed the other two guns in the box and Deuce closed the lid and set it aside to give to Sherri when he saw her. She'd run ballistic checks on all three to see if they'd been used in any crimes and if so, she'd file a report with a complete description of the two men.

After an hour of everyone talking at once, Megan's boyfriend arrived and she left with him. I noticed Kim yawn and suggested we go to the boat. I said she could have the master stateroom and I'd bunk with Tony in the guest stateroom.

"There's someone else on board you'll have to make friends with," I said.

When we approached the cockpit of the *Revenge*, Pescador stood and raised his shaggy head above the gunwale. "This is my friend, Pescador. He thinks it's his boat, so you'll have to ask his permission to go aboard."

"What a cute dog," she said. "Why do you call him Fisherman?"

"You know some Spanish?"

"I'm pretty fluent, took Spanish in school every year for seven years."

"When I found him a year ago, he was stranded on a sandbar and I watched him catch a fish in the shallows."

She turned to the dog and asked, "Puedo ir a bordo, Pescador?" To my surprise, he barked once and laid back down in the corner of the cockpit. She turned to me and asked, "You taught him Spanish, too?"

"I never even knew he could speak it," I said as I stepped over the gunwale and unlocked the hatch to the salon.

When we entered the salon, I switched on the recessed lights and disarmed the alarm system. She exclaimed, "Wow! This is amazing."

"I didn't even ask if you'd had anything to eat."

"You cook, Dad?"

*Dad?* I thought. *That's gonna take some getting used to.*

"If need be," I replied with a grin. "Usually, I eat whatever Rufus has on the menu at the bar, or whatever my caretakers on the island whip up. But, in a pinch, I can make a decent meal."

"We ate just before we got to the bank," she replied. "Who's Rufus and who are your caretakers?"

"Rufus is Rusty's Jamaican chef. Have a seat. Want something to drink?"

"Water, or juice, if you have it."

"My caretakers are Carl and Charlie Trent. They take care of everything on my little island."

I got two large mangoes from the fridge, dropped them in the blender with some ice, and switched it on. After a moment, I switched it off and poured two glasses of mango smoothie.

"Permission to board?" came Tony's voice from outside, followed by a quick reply from Pescador.

"I just thought of something," I said as Tony came in through the hatch. "Regardless of whether you believed your mom, you just came onto a boat with two men you don't even know."

"I'm not naive, Dad. I'm just a very good judge of people. That, and I have a thirty-eight in my purse."

Tony laughed as he got a beer from the fridge. "Like father, like daughter."

"You're carrying?" I asked.

"Everywhere I go," she replied. "That's something else you should know about Mom and Eve. They're both totally anti-gun. I go to the range every weekend. The lady at the bank seemed really nice," Kim went on. "She said she'd grown up here and knew everyone. After she called you on the phone and said you were coming over, she told me you were one of the nicest people she's ever done business with. Does this boat have a bathroom?"

I pointed forward and said, "On a boat, it's called a head. Forward is the master stateroom, if you want to put your things away. It has a private head to starboard. That means...."

"The right side," she interrupted. "I don't have much, just a go bag I always carry on day trips."

Tony laughed once more, "Yep, like father, like daughter."

"I'll take you shopping in the morning, if you want to stay longer. Do you have a phone? You should call Eve if she's expecting you back in Miami tonight."

"Yeah, she's a bit of a drama queen, though. If you hear shouting, it's not me."

She went forward to the stateroom and closed the hatch. Tony said, "I guess tomorrow's activity is canceled?"

I looked at him, puzzled for a moment. Then I remembered. "Maybe, maybe not. Depends on how far the apple fell."

"What apple?" Kim asked, coming out of the stateroom. "I got Eve's voicemail and left a message that I'd be staying a few days. Her and Nick were going out with his dad's partners and their wives."

"If you can hold off shopping until afternoon," I explained, "several of us are going shooting in the morning."

"Can I shoot my gun? I have three speedloaders, all loaded."

"Apparently, not too far," Tony said, grinning from ear to ear.

"Do you shoot, too, Tony?" she asked. "I couldn't help notice your trigger finger is missing."

"Oh, that," he replied, holding up his right hand and waggling the stumps of his index and middle fingers. "Luckily, I was trained to shoot with either hand."

"How'd you lose it?" she asked with child-like innocence.

Tony looked at me and I nodded. While I made another batch of mango smoothies, he went on to tell the whole story about how he was part of an anti-terrorist team for DHS and had gone into Cuba to get intel on a suspected arms merchant, but was captured, beaten, and tortured. He overdramatized the part where Deuce and I, along with several other of Deuce's team, went in to get him out.

"So, let me get this straight," Kim said after Tony finished. "You and all the others I met tonight are government agents?"

"No, not all of us," I replied. "I'm just sort of a 'transporter on call' and Jimmy and Rusty aren't affiliated at all."

"But, wouldn't all this be like classified stuff? Like, 'I can tell you, but I'd have to kill you' kind of stuff?"

"Our team is still in the training stage, more or less," Tony replied. "Some things we aren't allowed to talk about outside the team. What we can talk about is pretty limited, only among family. They have a need to know."

"So, can I go shooting too?" she asked enthusiastically.

"Sure," I said. "But you might want to save your ammo for your six-gun. I'll let you use one of mine."

# CHAPTER NINE

Y ou let a little fat man take you down?" Tena Horvac shouted at the two bodyguards. "And you let
him take your guns? Imbeciles!"

"There were eight of them," Borislav Varga retorted,
perhaps a bit too assertively.

"When Ivo carried you in here," the woman hissed, "he
said it was only the short, fat one that took you down."

Tena Horvac was a strikingly beautiful woman on the
outside, but inside, she was colder than ice and her eyes
reflected that now. She was born just south of the small
fishing village of Punat, on the island of Krk, an island in
the Adriatic Sea, off the coast of Croatia. Her father was a
poor fisherman, but he was also a Chavano, a sorcerer, of
the once nomadic Romani people that settled there. He
used his spells and concoctions for good, to help others.
Tena recognized her own powers early in life and knew
instinctually that they were greater than her father's. She
also knew her powers were darker. At the age of twelve,

she sought out a local Borsaki woman, an evil witch of the gypsy people. The woman instantly recognized that Tena was a powerful young girl, but unfocused. Dusanka Tadic agreed to teach the girl all she knew of gadjo magic, and before she turned sixteen and had blossomed into a beautiful woman, Tena had become a Mamuna, or Night Hag, a person capable of inflicting total paralysis or even death with a simple incantation.

Borislav looked down at his feet. He was a brute of a man, powerfully built with a cruel nature. In Croatia, he'd already shot and killed a man before he was thirteen. At sixteen, he was bigger than most men, heavily muscled and quick on his feet. It was then that he first killed a man with his bare hands and found that he enjoyed watching the life go out of a person's eyes, face to face. He'd also killed women barehanded. Prostitutes in Croatia's capital city of Zagreb, where he was raised, were more than plentiful and usually very cheap. They were never missed. He found that he received greater satisfaction when strangling a prostitute during climax, watching her face as the life drained from her eyes. He'd come to the United States just five years earlier and made his way to Miami, where a sizable Croat population existed. That was where he met Valentin Madic.

The fat man had surprised him, that's all. But he dared not contradict Tena Horvac. The woman standing before him scared him more than any man. He knew of her past and her training as a Romani witch. He also knew what had happened to the gang that had defiled her as a young woman.

"Yes, ma'am," he replied, not wishing to anger her further. "It was just the one. It will not happen again."

"This group?" she said. "They seem to be trained somewhat and well-armed?"

"Yes, ma'am."

She turned and walked across the darkened room and stood looking out the window overlooking Biscayne Bay. Her lithe frame was silhouetted by the bright lights of South Beach. The two men couldn't help but notice the light shined through the flimsy material of her blouse and skirt, accentuating the curves of her body. "We will have to try a different approach, then. It was wrong to assume these men would be soft and compliant like Conner and Bradbury. Conner said his latest recording revealed they would be going to Elbow Cay in the Bahamas soon. We'll set up as near there as we can without drawing attention. If we can't find the location of the treasure and get to it before them, we'll take it from them afterward."

She turned and glided across the office to her desk, where she opened her ledger and took out a company credit card. She handed it to Borislav. "Put together a team. The two of you and two women, preferably. That way you won't stand out. Secure four rooms at the best hotel you can find on Elbow Cay. The two of you will go there also, but the two women will work in the field. One room will be for Mister Madic and one will be for me. Also, make arrangements to have a boat at our disposal, a large and fast boat."

"Yes, ma'am," Borislav replied as he took the card and put it in a pocket inside his jacket. He was already wondering how expensive an island prostitute was.

Tena turned to the other man. "Ivo, you will fly me there tomorrow morning. Then come back here to bring the others over, once Borislav has put them together."

Ivo Novosel had served in the Croatian Air Force from 1991 to 1994, during the country's war for independence from Yugoslavia. At only twenty-two, he was considered too young for combat flying and had flown the Canadian-built Bombardier Challenger CL-600 passenger jet, transporting Officers and other dignitaries to and from negotiations in Belgrade and around to the different bases in Croatia. He was removed from the military when his superiors discovered he'd raped a fifteen-year-old girl. But she wasn't the first, nor the last. He came to the United States with Borislav five years earlier and while eating in a Serbian restaurant, the two of them had met Valentin Madic. When Madic had learned Ivo was a pilot, he'd hired both of them on the spot. A month later, Madic bought a two-year-old CL-604, the newer version of the plane Ivo had flown in Croatia.

"I will have the plane ready before sunrise," Ivo replied, and the two men left the office.

Tena sat down at her desk and made a number of phone calls, the first of which was to Madic, who was in his own office just down the hall. She told him about the incident down in the Keys with the two bodyguards and the information Conner had called her with just an hour ago.

"It seems these men aren't the type to be intimidated," Madic told her. "How do you suggest we proceed?"

"I've already ordered Borislav to assemble a team, two men and two women. I will go over to this island tomorrow to look around. If you are able, you should join me there as soon as possible. If we are able to get the location from the Americans, we can try to get to the spot before them. If not, we can take the treasure from them by force."

"I will be tied up here for three days. Handle it for me."

Before she could respond, he ended the call.

# CHAPTER TEN

I woke just before dawn, the smell of coffee from the galley drawing me from my single bunk in the guest stateroom like a moth to a flame. It can sleep three people, with a Pullman-type folding bunk above the two side-by-side bunks. The inboard bunk can slide over to make a cozy double bed for couples.

I was pulling on a tee shirt as I stepped up into the galley. Kim was already there, eating a bowl of corn flakes with a cup of coffee. "Hope you don't mind," she said. I nodded and went for the coffeemaker. After I'd poured a cup and drank about half, Tony came up the steps.

"You can't talk to him until he's had coffee," Tony said.

"Come on, I'm not that grumpy."

"I was hungry," Kim said, "so I just made myself at home."

"Mi casa es tu casa," I said. "Or barco, as the case may be. But you should have waited. Rufus makes the best Jamaican omelet you'll ever eat."

"Oh, I can always eat more," she said. "I'm still growing." I noticed she was wearing a bathing suit top and cut-off jeans.

"I have some shirts that'll fit you," I said. "The sun on the water can burn you fast."

"Are you being a prudish father?" she asked.

"Maybe," I said with a grin. "But it's true about the sun. Look in the hanging closet in your stateroom."

"We're going out on the water?" she asked as she went forward to her stateroom. "I thought we were going to a shooting range."

"We're going shooting," Tony said, "but not at a range, although I did set one up the other day on the island."

"You did?" I asked. "I didn't see it."

"That little mangrove-covered sandbar on the north side, west of the dock," he said. "Nothing much, just some target stands."

"I thought you meant one of your shirts," Kim said, stepping back up to the galley and pulling on a long-sleeved woman's shirt. It had belonged to Alex.

"I figured you were about the same size," I said. "Come on, let's go eat."

We walked up the dock to the bar and went inside, the smell of fresh herbs and spices, along with frying bacon and sausage, filling our nostrils.

An hour later, our appetites sated, we boarded the *Revenge* and took a thermos of coffee up to the bridge as the sun climbed above the horizon across the yard to the east. I showed Kim the controls and where everything was located and asked if she did a lot of boating.

"A little," she replied. "But never on a boat this big."

"It's really calm and where we're going it'll be calmer, but there's some motion sickness pills down in the galley if you think you need them."

She laughed. "The few times I've been out on the ocean, everyone else got seasick, but not me. I'll be fine, Dad."

A moment later Deuce, Julie, and Charity joined us, having had breakfast aboard the *James Caird*. I started the engines while Tony untied the lines, then shoved the bow away from the dock and jumped aboard. Kim sat next to me in the second chair, while Julie and Charity sat on the bench in front of the helm. Tony climbed up and sat next to Deuce on the port-side bench and we idled down the long canal toward the open ocean.

"Push the throttles about halfway forward," I said to Kim when we cleared the breakwater.

She grinned, reached over, and shoved the throttles forward. The response from the twin 1015 horsepower engines was immediate, lifting the bow and dropping the stern as the big boat surged forward and came up on plane. I kept us heading due south until we were a mile offshore, then turned west, passing to the north of East Washerwoman Shoal. A few minutes later, I turned north into Moser Channel and sailed under the Seven Mile Bridge, nudging the throttles a bit more to twenty-five knots.

"Where are we going?" Kim asked.

"We're leaving the state," I replied. Grinning, I added, "We'll go about five miles north, into the Gulf. That's outside state-controlled waters."

"What exactly are we going to shoot at in the middle of nowhere?"

"First, I want to see how you handle a gun. Have you ever shot a semi auto?"

"A few times. I'll buy one when I'm old enough. My Colt was given to me a couple of years ago."

*Who would give a gun to a fifteen-year-old girl?* I wondered, but I let it go. If she wanted to tell me, she would.

"Anyone want more coffee?" I asked, shaking the empty thermos.

"Want me to go down and refill it?" Kim asked.

"No, I'll get it. Take the helm," I said as I stood up.

Kim looked up at me with her eyes wide. "You want me to drive your boat?"

"You drive a car," I replied. "I want you to pilot my boat. Just keep it at a heading of three hundred and twenty degrees. If the water starts to change to green ahead and sort of flattens out, that'll be Horseshoe Bank. Turn due north when you see it."

She moved over to the first chair and I let go of the helm. She looked at the compass directly in front of her and made a small adjustment. "What if I hit something?"

"You'll do fine," I replied. "There's nothing out here to hit except Horseshoe, and you'll know it when you see it. Just pick out a cloud on the horizon and steer toward it. If you concentrate on the compass, you might miss something in the water."

I went below and refilled the thermos, then climbed back up to the bridge. Kim started to get up and I put a hand on her shoulder and took the second seat, noticing that she'd already turned due north. I glanced to port and saw the shallows of Horseshoe Bank about a quarter mile away. She was dead center in the natural channel and we had over ten feet under the keel.

"From here, we're just a few minutes until we're out-side state waters. Want to try her at full speed?"

"It goes faster than this?" Kim asked. "We're already going almost thirty miles per hour."

"Yeah, there's a lot of throttle left. She'll do forty-five knots if the conditions are right."

A second later she smiled and said, "That's just a little over fifty miles per hour. Can I?"

I nodded and she pushed both throttles to the stops, the big boat surging ahead, as Kim grinned broadly over at me.

"As a friend once said to me," I quipped. 'The worm done turned.'"

"Yeah," Tony said. "It surely has."

Five minutes later, we crossed into federal waters. "We better switch places now," I said. "We're going to anchor up in a few more miles."

"Hey, where is your island, anyway?" Kim asked as she got up from the helm and I slid over.

I pointed southwest and said, "About ten miles that way. We can stop by for lunch after we're done shooting out here."

"That's still puzzling me. Why did we come way out here in the ocean, er, I mean Gulf, to shoot?"

Deuce chuckled and said, "Because your dad had some harebrained idea about mounting a machine gun in the cockpit."

"A machine gun?"

"They're not exactly legal," I replied.

"Where is it?"

"Stored in the engine room," I explained. "Tony and I figured we'd run some timed tests to see how long it takes to mount it and get it ready to fire."

A few minutes later, I pulled back on the throttle and slowed to twenty-five knots again. I looked at the GPS and sonar until I found the waypoint I'd marked some years ago. It was a shoal about eight feet deep. I turned and lined up on it, then dropped the throttles further until we came off plane. I'd dived this spot a couple times and knew there was a wide patch of sandy bottom to the south of the shoal, which was mostly a coral-encrusted limestone rock formation.

Tony was on the bow and had unchocked the anchor chain. When we were over the center of the sandy patch, he gave me the signal, and I released the clutch on the windlass and reversed the engines. I paid out about thirty feet, then reengaged the clutch to set the anchor. Once I was satisfied we were stationary, I shut down the engines.

"All right," I said. "Let's go down to the galley, so I can get a few things and you can get your purse. I want to check you out on your wheel gun, if you don't mind."

"No problem, Dad," she replied as she climbed down the ladder to the cockpit.

I spread a large cloth I use for gun cleaning on the settee table and went forward to the stateroom, with Kim following me. Kneeling, I keyed in the code that releases the lock on the bunk and raised it up. Inside were several long fly rod cases, half a dozen small chests, and one large chest. I picked up one of the small chests, then lowered the bunk.

"What's in all the boxes?" Kim asked.

"I'd tell you, but then I'd have to kill you." She slugged me in the shoulder and laughed. She had a nice laugh. "Come on up to the salon," I said. "I want to look at your gun." The others had come into the salon and were sitting on the sofa, Deuce was in the galley making another pot of coffee.

"Take your Colt and set it on the table," I said, opening the chest and removing one of my Sig Sauer handguns. I checked the grip and locked the slide back, then set it on the table. Kim opened her purse and unzipped a side compartment. Reaching in, she pulled out a snub-nosed Colt. Releasing the cylinder, she opened it and pushed the ejector rod, dropping six .38 Special cartridges onto the table, before handing it to me.

"You don't leave the chamber under the hammer empty?" I asked.

"No need to," Kim replied, grinning. "That's a Colt Detective Special. They were mostly used by undercover cops. It has a hammer block that prevents the firing pin from striking the primer unless the trigger is pulled. You can throw it at the ground and it won't go off."

I looked at Deuce and caught his almost imperceptible nod of appreciation as he poured two cups of coffee and handed me one. He and I had grown close this past year, and we seemed to be able to communicate a lot just through a nod or expression. His dad and I had been the same way.

"Really? I'm not real well versed in revolvers," I lied. "How accurate is it?"

"Pretty accurate at close range," she replied, taking the gun back from my hand and reloading it. "I really don't have a lot of experience, though. Yours is a Sig Sauer?"

"Yeah, it's a P229, a smaller version of the P226 I usually carry. Thought you'd like to try it out."

"It's the same gun the Coast Guard issues us," Julie said.

"You were in the Coast Guard?" Kim asked.

"I still am. Temporarily assigned to my husband's team so I can keep an eye on him," she replied, nudging Deuce with her elbow.

The six of us went out into the cockpit. Tony had rigged one of my casting rods with a two-liter plastic bottle tied to the line. He pulled it from the rod holder and, stepping to the transom, cast it about twenty-five feet astern.

"You do have targets," Kim said, smiling.

"A little different than shooting at static targets," I said. "It's bobbing in the water and we're standing on a moving deck. Go ahead."

She had her purse hanging from her left shoulder and reached in and pulled out the Colt. Aiming, she fired three quick shots, hitting the bottle once and coming very close with the other two shots.

Tony stood up from where he'd been lounging on the gunwale, his back against the bulkhead. "Pretty good shooting. All three would be center mass on a target. Where'd you learn to shoot?"

"Mom dated a cop for a while. He took us all to a shooting range one time. Eve and Mom hated it, but I had a blast. He and I went back a few times and he taught me to shoot. That's who gave me the gun."

Tony pointed aft and said, "It's gonna sink—get it."

Kim turned and aimed the Colt again. She took her time and fired three more rounds. The first two hit the water very close to the top of the bottle, the only part sticking up. The third round hit the cap and sent it flying off, just as the bottle sank.

Tony reeled the line in and pulled the bottle out of the water. He cut the line with a pocket knife, removing the bottle, and tied a new one to it before casting it out to about the same spot.

I handed her the Sig and a loaded magazine. "You said you shot an auto a few times. Try it out."

She slid the magazine in, racked the slide, and aimed at the bottle bobbing in the water. I could see her finger slowly taking the slack up from the trigger until it fired. She fired two more in quick succession and the bottle disappeared under the surface.

When Tony reeled it in, it had three holes through the big Pepsi logo. Tony whistled softly. "All three could fit under a quarter," he said. "Very impressive. How often do you shoot?"

"I go to an indoor range every Monday and Thursday," Kim replied. "One of the guys that works there lets me shoot anything in the case. I shoot my own gun every time and something else after that." Turning to me, she said, "Last week, he let me shoot a Desert Eagle."

"That's overkill," I said, laughing as she extended the Sig to me. "No, you keep it. You seem to be a pretty good match."

"Really?" she asked. "You're giving it to me?"

I nodded, and she removed the magazine, ejected the chambered round, and set the gun on the fighting chair, then threw her arms around my neck. "Thanks, Dad."

"Okay, let's get to what we came out here for," I said. "Everyone up to the bridge. Tony, you'll go first, mounting it solo. Then we'll try you and Deuce working together."

Kim looked puzzled, but we all climbed up to the bridge. I turned the bezel on my dive watch to the minute hand, waited for the second hand to reach twelve, and said, "Go!"

Tony climbed quickly down to the cockpit, lifted the fighting chair clear and laid it out of the way on the deck. Then he went down to the engine room and soon came out with the custom-built mount. As he opened the tripod legs and slid it into the chair's receiver, the legs clicked as they locked into place.

"That must have set you back a few bucks," Charity said as Tony disappeared into the engine room again. "Is that milled aluminum?"

"Titanium," I replied.

Tony came out into the cockpit again, carrying the receiver, and inserted the pintle into the yoke, locking it into position. Unlike a standard tripod for the M2, this one didn't have a traversing and elevating mechanism, so the gun was free to swing by hand. Not as accurate, but good enough for our use.

"Two minutes," I called down as Tony disappeared into the engine room again.

A moment later he reappeared with the barrel, screwed it into place, and disappeared once more, as I shouted, "Three minutes."

When he came out of the engine room a third time, he was carrying an ammo box and a bucket. He hung the bucket on a small hook that I'd had Billy add to the bottom of the receiver. He attached the ammo can to the side, opened it, and raised the cover on the receiver. Pulling the belt from the ammo can, he slapped it across the feed slide and slammed the cover down. Racking the bolt handle back twice, he shouted, "Done!"

"Three minutes and fifty-four seconds," I shouted. "Pretty good for a first time."

I went down and helped him disassemble the gun and put everything away. When we got back up to the bridge, Kim asked, "A machine gun? Aren't you going to shoot it?"

"In a few minutes," I replied. "Let's see how fast two can do it first." I looked over at Deuce and said, "Ready?"

"Always," he replied.

I turned the bezel and waited for the second hand again. "Go," I shouted, and both Tony and Deuce went down the ladder.

Tony disappeared into the engine room and Deuce removed the fighting chair, laying it aside once more. Tony appeared at the hatch and handed the mount up to Deuce, who turned and mounted it quickly, locking the legs in place. Tony reappeared at the hatch and Deuce took the receiver from him and mounted it to the yoke. When Tony came out with the barrel, he handed it to Deuce then grabbed the bucket and ammo can from under the steps. While Deuce threaded the barrel in, Tony set the bucket aside and mounted the ammo can. Deuce finished with the barrel and as Tony loaded the weapon, Deuce hung the bucket below it.

Tony slammed the cover shut and yelled, "Done!"

I looked at my watch, which hadn't quite reached one minute. "Fifty-eight seconds!" I shouted.

Deuce looked up from the cockpit and said, "Plenty quick enough if trouble comes. But will this mount hold up?"

"It should," I said. "That titanium can take a heck of a pounding and each part is a solid milled piece. Only one way to find out. Let her rip!"

Tony turned toward the machine gun, raised the handles, and aimed astern. He fired a quick three-round burst, and the vibration could be felt even on the bridge. Half a mile astern, three geysers shot up from the water.

"You want to shoot it?" I asked Kim.

"You bet," she replied and climbed down to stand beside Deuce as Tony let loose with a long ten-round burst, the spent casings dropping neatly out of the bottom into the bucket.

Tony stepped aside and explained how the paddle trigger worked and how to aim, then Kim stepped up and fired a five-round burst, slightly higher than Tony's. Nearly a mile away, five quick geysers reported the location of impact. She fired another five-round burst, which landed about where Tony's had. We spent the rest of the morning disassembling the weapon and trying to better our time at setting it up, then everyone had a turn at firing it.

It occurred to me that if the need for the weapon ever arose, we'd probably be underway when it happened. So we pulled the hook and headed west, with Tony and Deuce practicing both solo and team set ups. It proved to be a bit more difficult, but not by more than half a minute working as a team and about a minute working solo. Tony almost dropped the receiver on one setup and I made a mental note to have some slip proof rubber pads made to fit the entire deck, to be used any time a mission came up.

Finally, we headed for the island to get lunch. On the way, Deuce got a call from Doc. I listened to the one-sided conversation and when he disconnected, he said, "Doc's been trying to reach you, but his calls keep going to voice mail. Where's your phone?"

I had to think for a minute. "Top tackle drawer, I think. Battery's dead."

"So, where's your charger?" he then asked.

"Pretty sure that's down in the engine room."

Deuce and Julie both laughed, knowing my dislike for the device. Kim said, "I couldn't live without my phone."

"I can. If it's important, they'll leave a message. If it's real important, they can find me."

"Well," Deuce said, "when you charge it up, you'll find that Doc left you three messages. I told him we'd be at the island for a little while, but would be back in Marathon before dark. He's going to meet us there."

Thirty minutes later, I slowed as we entered Harbor Channel. At the mouth of my channel, I reversed the engines, used the key fob to open the west door below the house, and started backing the *Revenge* up the channel. Kim stood next to me as I turned and put my back to the wheel, steering the big boat mostly by throttle control.

"Wow," she said. "It's like Robinson Crusoe on steroids. You really built it yourself?"

"The main house and the basic bunkhouses, yeah. But a lot of people chipped in with the rest."

"What rest?"

"You'll see," I replied, grinning.

"Is that a racing boat?" Kim asked, pointing at the Cigarette 42x tied to the center dock under the house.

"It belonged to some bad people," Deuce said. "They no longer have any use for it, so we took it."

Carl and Charlie's kids met us at the dock and Carl Junior helped tie us off. I introduced Kim to them and little Patty said, "Mister Jesse is your daddy?"

The two of them took Kim by the hands and led her toward the door then up to the deck. The rest of us followed. When I got to the deck, Kim was standing by the table at the far corner, looking out over the island.

"It's beautiful," she said, when I walked up next to her. The others went on down the back steps and continued to the two tables by the bunkhouse. "What's that over there?" she asked, pointing to the aquaculture system.

"We grow some of our own food here. Tomatoes, green beans, some peppers and squash, mostly. That's Carl and Charlie's house," I said, pointing. "They keep things running here and pretty much take care of everything."

She turned toward me. "Whose shirt is this I'm wearing?"

"I was married almost a year ago. Her name was Alex and it belonged to her. Come on, you must be starved." We went down to the tables and joined the others. I introduced Kim to Carl, Charlie, and Chyrel.

"Y'all sit down and relax," Charlie said. "I'll slice some fruit before lunch."

While enjoying a lunch of grunts and a summer squash casserole, Carl explained to Kim how the little garden worked. I noticed Pescador raise his head and cock his ears toward the west. A moment later, I heard an airplane approaching. While it's not unusual to hear

private planes out here, the sound of a sixty-year-old radial engine in a plane flying low enough to scare flying
fish into flight meant only one thing. It was my friend
and part-time mechanic, Dave Williams. I listened as the
slight sound grew louder. Looking around, I noticed only
Pescador, Deuce, and Tony seemed to hear it.

Suddenly, Dave's deHavilland Beaver flew over at tree-
top level, rising up over the Trents' house, climbing and
banking to the south. Dave's son was the young man who
was killed in the explosion a couple of months ago, on
the day Deuce and Julie were married.

"What the hell?" Kim said as she involuntarily ducked
and stared after the plane disappearing into the late
morning sun.

"A friend of mine," I said. "Come on, you'll like this," I
added as I rose from my seat and headed down the path
between the two bunkhouses. The others followed along,
Kim catching up and walking beside me. I glanced back
and saw the flag flapping lightly in a westerly breeze
and could hear Dave banking the plane around in a wide
turn to line up for an upwind water landing.

We reached the end of the pier on the north side of the
island and I pointed the plane out to Kim. He was about
a mile out, leveling off and descending. Having chopped
the throttle, we could no longer hear the sound of the big
radial.

"What's he doing?" Kim asked.

"Stopping by for a visit," I said. "His name's Dave and
he does some mechanical work on the boats for me."

"He's going to land on the water? It's a seaplane?"

"A 1953 deHavilland Beaver."

When the plane was a few hundred yards out and just feet off the water, he flared and gently touched the surface with the pontoons. The plane skipped across the light chop, then settled into the water a little. Dave increased the throttle, keeping it up on plane until he was just a hundred feet from the pier. There, he cut the engine to an idle and it settled down in the water and decreased speed to a walk. Ten feet from the pier, he cut power, opened the left door, and stood on the pontoon with a rope coiled in his hand.

Tony caught the tossed coil and we all ducked as the big wing went over the tee-shaped pier. Tony walked the line to the eastern end of the tee before taking the slack and bringing the plane to a stop just a couple of feet away. Dave tied the line off to a cleat on the pontoon aft of the doors while Julie deftly tossed another line over a cleat forward of the doors. They both hauled on the lines, bringing the pontoon up to the rubber bumpers on the pier, and Dave stepped up.

"Hey, Dave," I said, taking his hand. "What brings you up here?" Dave and his wife live on Stock Island, just before Key West. He does some charter fishing in the back country, using kayaks he carries in his plane to get clients to places other guides can't.

"We're moving back to Kentucky," he said as he pulled a box out of the cargo area in back and handed it to Tony. "This is for Charlie," he told him. Turning back to me, he said, "I wanted to give you the first option on buying my plane."

I'd just spent two months getting my private pilot's license and seaplane certificate. Dave knew I was looking to buy a plane, since most of my flying time had been in his Beaver with him and my instructor and we'd discussed the merits of a lot of planes. I'd been planning to wait until I finished my multi-engine certification. I wanted a Beechcraft King Air for its range.

He reached in and grabbed a second box, which he handed to Julie, and said, "This one's for Charlie, too." Turning to Deuce he said, "That last one in there is for Carl, Deuce. Mind getting it? It's pretty heavy."

"Why don't you take it back to Kentucky?" I asked as we walked up the pier. "Oh, Dave, this is my daughter, Kim. Kim, meet Dave Williams."

He stopped and turned to the two of us. "Your daughter?" He took the hand she offered and looked closely at her. "Yeah, I can see the resemblance." He turned and started walking again. "We bought a place up in the hills, no water around. This plane belongs down here."

I looked back at the Beaver and said, "Yeah, she's perfect for this area, that's for sure. I've been waiting until I get my multi cert. I want to get a King Air, but if she's really available, yeah, I'd consider taking her off your hands."

# CHAPTER ELEVEN

How long will you be staying on the island, Miss Bonamy?" asked the desk clerk at Hope Town Harbour Lodge on Elbow Cay.

"Indefinitely," Ettaleigh Bonamy replied. "I would think a week. I apologize for the short notice."

"It's no trouble, ma'am. Your assistant booked two of our ocean view cottages and two of our main lodge rooms for one week. If you will need them longer than that, please see me a day in advance. This is our slow time of year and we should have no trouble extending the reservations."

She leaned over to read his name tag and said, "Thank you, Paul. Can you have a bottle of wine sent to my cottage? A Chanson Chablis, perhaps?"

"Yes, ma'am. Right away." He turned and beckoned a bellman with his finger. "James, please take Miss Bonamy's bags to cottage two."

The young man was quick to gather up the woman's three bags. "Follow me, ma'am."

She left the office and followed the man through a network of ivy and palm-covered walkways, arriving at the middle of three small cottages. They were quaint and rustic-looking on the outside, but appeared to be meticulously maintained, as did the surrounding lawn and vegetation. He unlocked the door and held it open for her, then followed her in.

Placing the key on a small table by the door and the bags at the foot of the king-sized bed, he turned and asked, "Can I bring you anything, ma'am?"

"Thank you," she said, handing him a ten-dollar bill. "That will be all."

"Thank you, ma'am," he said, taking the bill and pocketing it instantly. "If I may?"

She was looking out the open French door at the deck with a custom gas grill and the ocean just beyond. She looked back at him over her shoulder. "Yes?"

"I don't mean to be nosy, but your name? Are you related to the Bonamy family that once lived down on Long Island?"

She smiled, her full lips exposing perfectly straight teeth, turned and said, "Very distantly related, yes. You know island history very well. You're speaking of Bromfield Bonamy, of course?" The young man blushed slightly, something Ettaleigh found enticing. At thirty-six she was in the prime of her life, physically and emotionally. She preferred young men like this one—they usually had an appetite and stamina that at times even matched her own.

"Yes, ma'am," he said. "A very colorful character in our islands' history. Will there be anything else?"

"No, thank you, James." She cocked her head in a seductive manner and asked, "If I do need something, should I call you?"

James tried to control his reaction, but it didn't work, as his cheeks colored once more. He was twenty-three years old and had never met such an exotically beautiful woman as this.

"I'm on duty until five, ma'am," he stammered.

"What if I need something after five?" she asked, gliding toward him. "How can I reach you?"

James couldn't believe what he was hearing. Local island girls flirted with him often and he was considered a good-looking young man. He'd watched the rich, beautiful women that visited the Lodge from all over the world with no small amount of lust, but he had never made an advance. It would cost him his job and they were hard to come by on a small island. Yet, here was an exquisitely beautiful older woman making advances on him.

He'd had his own business cards made up, as he was an accomplished spear fisherman and sold his catch all over Great Abaco, Elbow Cay, and Man-O-War Cay. He pulled one out of his pocket, knowing it wasn't a very good idea. But his libido had another idea.

"I catch fish to sell," he stammered again. "For the grill," he added, pointing out to the deck. "If you want some, call me." He handed her the card, hoping it sounded innocent enough if she wasn't coming on to him and suggestive enough if she was. She slid the card inside the top of her blouse, which caused James to become noticeably excited.

There was a knock at the door. James turned and opened it, then left the cottage as the wine steward entered. The wine steward was an older black man who placed the tray on the table and offered to open the bottle for her. She thanked him and said she was going to change and go for a swim first. She tipped him and he left immediately.

Opening the single French door to the deck, a breeze blew in carrying the fresh, salty scent of the sea and sand with it, gently ruffling her loose-fitting pleated blue skirt. She stepped outside and marveled at the lush tropical foliage that separated the cottages. There was a narrow path through the low vegetation that went over the dune to the beach, which appeared to be completely deserted.

She welcomed times like this. Her job was very demanding and when an opportunity to indulge herself was presented, she took advantage of it. Technically still on the clock, she'd arrived on Elbow Cay a few days ahead of her employer to make sure the accommodations were suitable, make arrangements for the business they would be conducting, and ensure their business would proceed uninterrupted.

Going back inside, she quickly unpacked her suitcases and put her things away, making sure the young man's card wasn't lost. Then she changed into a backless yellow one-piece bathing suit, cut high at the thigh and low at the neck. The suit accentuated her long legs, narrow flat belly, and modest bosom. She released the single pin in her hair that held it in a bun and it cascaded across her shoulders, like a dark wave, reaching the middle of her back.

The history of the Bonamy family in the islands was colorful indeed. Bromfield Bonamy was one of the first settlers on Long Island, just after the American Revolution. As a Loyalist to the Crown, he fled Charleston with many others to settle the deserted islands of the northern Bahamas. He received a land grant of four hundred acres from King George III and settled there to grow Sea Island cotton. After a caterpillar infestation destroyed the crops in 1796, he turned to piracy. Not in the truest sense of the word. He sailed his private warship, *Ballahoo*, throughout the northern Bahamas, preying solely on American cargo ships. Bonamy led an otherwise secluded life on his large plantation. Although he never married, he fathered fourteen children with several native slave women he brought up from Hispaniola. Their descendants were now scattered all over the Bahamas, Florida, even all the way up to Charleston.

Those slaves weren't of African origin, but were from the nearly decimated original inhabitants of the Bahama Islands, the Lucaya. Like Ettaleigh, they were a dark-skinned, handsome people with long, straight black hair and dark eyes. By 1550, they had all been killed or enslaved by the Spanish, leaving the northern islands uninhabited for over two hundred years. The Spaniards considered the low-lying islands unsuitable for growing anything and the waters too treacherous. The ancestry of the Lucaya can be traced back to the people that inhabited North and South America long before the first Europeans arrived.

Ettaleigh walked out onto the deck and leaned against the rail, facing an easterly breeze. The light wind lifted a few strands of hair from her shoulders. She looked up and down the beach, then lifted her face to the warm sun with her eyes closed, as if meditating.

She left the private deck and followed the path down to the beach, not having any particular destination or direction in mind. She was nearly to the water's edge before she saw anyone's footprints in the sand. She turned and went in the direction the footsteps had come from.

James watched her come out of the back of the cottage from his vantage point on the second-floor balcony of the main lodge. He knew he hadn't been dreaming by the way she'd slipped the card into her bra as she touched her lips with her tongue. He watched her walk to the water's edge and turn south toward the cove, her dark skin and hair all the more exotic in the yellow bathing suit she wore.

As Ettaleigh walked, she marveled at the beautiful lush shoreline. Coconut palms leaned out over the beach from the dune, where clumps of sawgrass and sea grape marked the edge of vegetation. The water was crystal clear and she could easily see the scattered rock outcroppings just below the water's surface. Further out, the bottom fell away quickly and the water turned from green to a deep, cobalt blue less than a hundred yards from shore.

She walked for over a mile and never saw another person. *Slow season*, she thought. *That's an understatement.* She came to a rock outcropping that jutted out into the water at high tide and curved away to a sheltered area beyond. The tide was low, so she continued around the rock, marveling at the home built on its bluff. Beyond the protected water was a ten-foot limestone cliff. She waded right into the calmer water until it came to mid-thigh. Seeing no obstacles in the little cove, she jack-knifed her lithe body and dived beneath the surface. Her long black hair streaming behind her, she swam underwater for ten yards before surfacing face first in waist-deep water, which left her hair streaming down the middle of her back.

The mixture of the cool water and warm sun seemed to rejuvenate and excite her after the flight and boat ride to get to the island. She'd have all day tomorrow and possibly the next day alone, before her employer and their business associates arrived. More than enough time to relax and unwind. *Enough time to test that young man's stamina and endurance*, she thought. Again she dove under the water, cooling her body and mind, both of which needed it.

She came up out of the water and brought her hair around her shoulder, wringing the water out of it. Returning to the beach, she walked slowly back toward the cottage, retracing her steps. *I will call him tonight after dinner*, she thought. She looked forward to it, wondering if he could last as long as his youth suggested. If not, she had ways of arousing even the most exhausted lover.

# CHAPTER TWELVE

D ave and I agreed on a price. It didn't take much haggling, but we did anyway, because that's how things are done in the Keys. He would fly back to Boca Chica, clean her up, and do a complete service on her before I picked her up in two days. We would be going to Elbow Cay in a week and I suddenly had a crazy idea to fly over ahead of time to get a bird's eye view of the areas where we thought the treasure was buried.

After Dave left, I brought everyone back down to the *Anchor*. Kim and I were sitting on a table out back by the boat ramp with Pescador, waiting for the sunset. It had become my and his ritual and I wanted to share it with my daughter.

"Hey, Dad?"

"Yeah?"

"You think I could stay with you for a while? A couple days or a week maybe? I'd like to get to know you better."

I gave that some serious thought. I hadn't seen my daughter since she was just five months old and we barely knew each other. We had a trip coming up and might be gone for several days, but I wanted to get to know her as well.

"A couple of days, sure. Several of us are going to the Bahamas on business later this week, though. Might be gone a week."

"Government business?"

This was as good a time as any, so while we watched the sun sink toward the horizon, I told her about her grandfather who was killed in Vietnam and her grandmother who couldn't continue alone and took her own life. I told her about her great-grandparents who raised me and about the time Deuce's dad and I found treasure in Fort Pierce. I told her about the inheritance Pap and Mam left me. I told her about the gold that Deuce, Rusty, and I found last spring. I told her everything we knew about the treasure we were looking for and finally, I told her all about Alex and everything she left me, both material and emotional. Somewhere during all that, the sun set with a spectacular display of light and color.

"You reached out to me, Kim. With all the stories your mom told you, that was a big step. I'm glad you did."

"Somehow, I was certain that none of it was true. I love your little island and your friends. Can I stay? I promise I won't get in the way."

"You'll never be in the way," I said. "Call your sister and tell her you'll be staying down here a little longer. Call your mom, too. You're only seventeen, but you're out of high school and can make a decision like that on your own. Still, you should call her."

She threw her arms around my neck. "Thanks, Dad."

"Let's go get something to eat, then we'll have to go do some shopping."

Thirty minutes later, we pulled out of the parking lot in *The Beast* and headed north on US-1 a couple of blocks to Anthony's Ladies Apparel, where Kim picked out a few dressy tops and shorts, along with a new swimsuit, some shoes, and underwear.

Then we stopped at Keykers Tropical Clothing Store and I bought her some proper working clothes. Living and working on a boat or an island, outside in the hot sun all day, requires a specialized kind of wardrobe. Tough-wearing long-sleeved shirts and long pants, boat shoes, wraparound sunglasses and long-billed fishing hats. Tourists flock to the Keys to worship the sun, but those of us who work under it seek the shade.

When we got back to the *Anchor*, Deuce and Julie were sitting at a table with Doc, his wife, Nikki, Charity, Tony, and Andrew Bourke, who had just arrived an hour earlier. We joined them at the long table. I introduced Kim to Andrew and told everyone that she knew all about the upcoming trip and would be staying with me for a couple of days.

"Deuce just told me you bought Dave's plane," Bourke said. "Congratulations." Bourke is my age, a little shorter, but the same weight, with broad shoulders and a thick chest. He always seemed to be able to maintain an even keel, even in the most hectic situations.

"We were just talking," Deuce said. "And the idea came up that it might help if we could do a flyover and have a look from above before we go over there."

"I'd bet a dollar that was your idea, Deuce."

"Yeah," he replied. "You don't think it's a good idea?"

"Yeah, that's how I knew it was yours. I just thought the same thing an hour ago." Deuce and I always seemed to be on the exact same page.

"I made preliminary reservations at a resort," Doc said. "It's privately owned and only a few miles from where the dig site is. It's called Crystal Waters and Villas and it has a large dock on the lee side, a big main house and five smaller detached villas. I reserved the main house, but someone needs to call the lady. My credit card doesn't have a high enough limit."

I handed Kim my credit card, grinned, and said, "Give Kim the number, she'll call and confirm it." She went over to Doc, who gave her a slip of paper with the name and number on it then started outside to make her calls. "And Kim, get any GPS numbers they have." She gave me a thumbs up and went out the door.

I turned to Rusty. "Do you think I could put some tie-downs over on the corner of the property, between the canal and the ramp? Until I can build something out on the island."

"What? I'm your friggin' airport now?" Then he winked and nodded and the deal was done. "I finally got the information I needed to get my salvage license approved in the islands. They were hesitant, because I wouldn't give them the location we wanted to survey. I finally got them to understand that if someone other than a licensed salvor found it, like say the property owner, then the government might not get anything. At least with me, they know they're dealing with a professional. I just need to go over there and sign some papers, or have them shipped here."

"Let's me, you, and Doc fly over the day after tomorrow," I said. "We can land in Nassau, clear customs, sign for your license and then do a flyover of the location and where we'll be staying."

Rusty got up to get one of the patrons at the bar a fresh beer and brought back refills of everyone's drinks. He sat back down and said, "With only four locations over there to check out, we'll probably only need a few days."

"Four locations?" Doc asked. "I thought we had it narrowed down to one place."

Tony said, "Chyrel's model of the shoreline four hundred and forty years ago shows a large limestone formation that's now a large rock jutting out of the water a hundred yards from the beach. It was once connected to land until about three hundred years ago. Plus she found two more large limestone outcroppings on parts of the island that were wide enough. One's almost to the northern tip of the island and another is further south than the one we were sure of. Back then, she says it was a lot larger and inland from the beach about twenty yards. Now it's the southern edge of a small cove."

We talked for another hour and I could see that Kim was getting tired. It'd been a pretty exciting day for her, I guess. "Where are you staying, Andrew?" I asked.

"I was hoping to hitch a ride up to the island," he replied. "But it looks like you're docked for the night."

"Kim can bunk with me on the *Caird*," Charity said.

Kim had just returned from making her phone calls and said, "On the blue sailboat? That'd be cool!" Handing my card back to me, she added, "Everything's all set at Crystal Waters. The main house and the villas have different names, but one owner. Crystal Waters is close to the dock and Crystal Villas is down the hill to the east, nearer the beach."

I glanced at Charity, who smiled. "All right, Andrew," I said. "You can bunk with Tony and I'll take back my stateroom."

"Let's go get your stuff, Kim," Charity said. "I'm about beat."

As they got up to leave, Deuce asked, "When will Dave have the plane ready?"

"Tomorrow evening," I replied. "He said he'd spend the whole day servicing and cleaning everything. I can pick it up the next morning."

# CHAPTER THIRTEEN

I pay your firm to do things for me," Valentin Madic said.

The older man sitting across the mahogany desk from him removed his reading glasses and placed them next to the documents he'd been given to read. "Yes, Valentin, my firm has done quite a bit of work for you. We know the law and more importantly, we know how to keep from going afoul of that law. I'm not saying what you want done can't be done. It just has to be done delicately, taking the proper steps in the proper order, with the right amount of time between each. This ensures that no red flags go up anywhere. What you ask will take at least two months, probably ten weeks."

Madic sat back in the chair. He thought of the clown he'd once seen at a circus when he was a child. The clown had dozens of plates spinning on sticks and had to move quickly from one to another to keep them from falling. Recently, he'd begun to feel just like that clown. He was in the office of the patriarch and lead partner of the law firm that handled many of his legal dealings and a few that were slightly less legal.

"Very well," he said. "If it takes that long, then it does. I have faith in you and your team, Alfredo."

"We'll get started on it immediately," the older man said. "Now, that other matter. The background investigation of certain people you asked about. Only two of the license plate numbers you provided came back to anyone living at that address. From that, I have the dossiers of three people. The owner of the establishment, his daughter, and her husband. My people asked around discreetly about who the others might be, since you could only provide first names. Island people are very tight-lipped, but we learned one of them. His dossier is here also."

Madic picked up the four files and looked through each, with a bit more than a cursory glance. Finally, he looked up and said, "Two Navy men, a Marine and a woman in the Coast Guard?"

"That's all we've found so far. The owner of the bar served many years ago and his daughter is in the Coast Guard Reserves. Only her husband has recent military service. There's nothing anywhere that we have access to that says anything about him since he left the Navy almost two years ago. The last man left the Navy eight years ago. He was a medical specialist."

Madic closed the files and put them in his briefcase. "Thank you, Alfredo," he said as he rose from the chair.

The older man stood up and walked around the desk, shaking Madic's hand. "I'll keep you abreast of each step along the way and how long we should wait until the next one, but I don't foresee this taking longer than ten weeks."

Madic left the inner office, nodded to the secretary, and continued on through to the hallway, where he took an elevator to the ground floor. As he got into his Mercedes, his phone rang. He glanced at the caller ID and answered the phone.

"Valentin, we've learned more," came Tena Horvac's voice over the phone. "From the listening device that Ivo planted in the bar. They will fly an advance party to the island in two days."

"No mention of the location?"

"Nothing yet. There are now four possible locations. They will use the airplane to look at each from the air. I know three are within a few miles of the northern end of the island and the fourth is offshore. They all reference large rock outcroppings."

"Two days?" Madic said. "Will our people be in place?"

"This is just an advance party that will fly over. Our people will be in place before the rest arrive. We know where they will be staying now, also."

"Very good. I should be over there within three days. Let me know if anything else is learned."

# CHAPTER FOURTEEN

I woke early and after pouring a mug and thermos of coffee, I climbed up to the bridge. It was still dark, but the eastern sky was showing a tinge of purple. I could see light spilling across the dock from the *James Caird*, but so far nobody had emerged.

A light went on in the back of the bar, so I knew Rufus was up and getting breakfast ready. Rusty now had eight liveaboards at his dock. A month earlier, he only had a couple. He raised his dockage rate by ten dollars a week and included a free breakfast buffet every morning from zero six hundred to zero seven hundred for the liveaboards. Nobody grumbled and word spread to other marinas. Now, there were at least twenty people every morning, those not docked there paying ten bucks a head for Rufus's Caribbean breakfast buffet.

Kim and Charity climbed up to the dock from the *Caird* and both started my way. "Grab a coupla mugs from the galley," I said. They did and climbed up to the bridge as Deuce and Julie emerged from their boat also.

"How many people can that plane you bought carry?" Kim asked when she sat down in the second seat and Charity sat on the port-side bench, being her usual quiet self.

I laughed and said, "You want to go to the Bahamas, too?"

"I have a passport," she said by way of a reply.

"Flying over open water in a fifty-three-year-old airplane?"

"Please..."

"Yeah, you can come. And to answer your question, it can carry six people, plus the pilot."

"Got an email from the Director," Deuce said as he and Julie walked up to my dock, hand in hand. The Director is Deuce's usual reference to his boss, Travis Stockwell. His full title is Associate Director, Caribbean Counterterrorism Command, Department of Homeland Security. He was an easygoing man in his early fifties who had taken over when Deuce's former boss, Jason Smith, went rogue and nearly killed both of us, along with the President. Stockwell had worked his way up through the ranks in the Army's famed 82nd Airborne Division, first as Enlisted and later as an Officer. He'd retired after thirty years in the Army and was tapped to take charge of Deuce's team and expand it.

"What's the Colonel up to?" I asked.

"We have a new operator joining us in the next week or so," Deuce replied. "Bender just retired from the Secret Service."

Paul Bender was the head of the Presidential Detail when the President and Secretary of Homeland Security came down to the Keys for a little fishing last summer. He was a professional all the way and even though our first meeting didn't go so well, I liked the guy.

"Bender?" I asked. "He struck me as career Secret Service."

"The political writing is on the wall," Deuce said.

Bourke and Tony emerged from the salon and together we all went over to the bar for breakfast. While eating breakfast in a bar might seem strange to some people, here in the Keys they're the primary social gathering places for locals. The *Anchor* isn't on any tour maps and unlike *Dockside*, which is a popular restaurant and bar just half a mile away, it's been able to retain its local attitude, where nearly everyone that walked in is known to everyone else. Rusty had seen the need for such a place years ago and had been building it up for just that. His dad had run it as a bait shop and bar for years. With Rufus's food now a local attraction in itself, Rusty was already in the process of planning a full kitchen addition to the place.

While we ate, we discussed what would be needed the next morning. With five people already aboard, we wouldn't be able to take much of anything in the way of cargo or gear. Our plan was for me to fly the Beaver from Key West to Marathon and pick up the others. Then we'd fly on to Nassau to clear customs and refuel. We'd be on the ground in Nassau a couple of hours, while Rusty went to the government complex to get his license and permit. From there, we'd do a couple of low-level flyovers of the four sites and where we'd be staying on Elbow Cay. With nearly five hours of flight time, we should have plenty of daylight.

Bourke said he could go to the Home Depot, pick up some bags of concrete, large eyebolts, and other hardware, and set three tie-downs near the boat ramp while we were gone. He'd just need a few minutes to look at the plane and determine where to set them. Charity volunteered to help him any way she could.

"When I get that done, I'll mount that infrared light I got for you," Bourke said. "I think you'll like the look of it once it's installed."

Counting the short hop from Key West to here, we'd be flying almost seven hundred miles, refueling in Nassau and Miami to clear customs both ways and arriving back at the *Anchor* before dark. I called Key West airport and filed a flight plan, departing at 0800 and returning about 1700.

With nothing much to do the rest of the day, I asked to borrow Rusty's skiff so I could show Kim around the nearby islands and do some fishing. We packed some water and food into his little skiff and headed out, going east and then north through Vaca Cut and into the Gulf of Mexico. I pointed out a few of the landmarks, told her the names of the islands we passed, and explained what history of the islands I'd acquired after living here for over seven years. We circled the east end of the Knights Key, passing under the Seven Mile Bridge and back into the Atlantic. I showed her the mansion built on East Sister Rock, before turning into Sister Creek. We toured Boot Key Harbor, stopping to say hi to a couple of liveaboards I knew.

Exiting the harbor on the west side, we went back under the Seven Mile Bridge and anchored on Bethel Bank to fish for snapper. We spent an hour there, talking and getting to know one another better as we fished. After catching a half dozen good-sized snapper and putting them in the fish box, we skirted Pigeon Key, then went west following the Seven Mile Bridge. I explained to my daughter about the early settlers and "Flagler's Folly," as the early railroad was known.

Henry Flagler was a prominent business man that developed a railroad and a number of resorts along Florida's east coast in the 1800s. Not satisfied when the rail reached Miami at the turn of the century, he decided to extend it over a network of more than forty bridges, all the way to Key West. Other businessmen of the time thought him mad calling it the "railroad that went to sea" and dubbed his endeavor "Flagler's Folly". In truth, the man had great insight. Pigeon Key is now a tourist attraction, set up like the early settlers in the area had lived. When we reached Spanish Harbor, I turned north and followed Bogie Channel toward No Name Bridge.

"You feel like a pizza for lunch?" I asked.

"I'd love a pizza. Don't tell me there's a Pizza Hut out here on these islands."

"Not a Pizza Hut, but I know a place that makes the best pizza in all of south Florida. It's more of a restaurant and bar, called No Name Pub."

"Why don't they give it a name?"

I just shrugged and turned into the marina at Old Wooden Bridge Cottages, just before the bridge. I tied up just short of the fuel dock and we got out. From there it was a short walk to No Name Pub.

Kim wasn't exactly prepared for what she found once we went inside. Nearly every bare surface—walls, ceiling, posts, and bar—was covered with dollar bills. We ordered our pizza at the bar and got a couple of cans of Coke, then walked out the back to the terrace area.

"You were right," Kim said, after eating her fourth slice. "This is the best pizza I ever had."

I asked the waitress for a marker and she produced one instantly from her back pocket. I handed it to Kim along with a dollar bill and said, "It's a tradition for first-time visitors. Write your name on it and we'll staple it somewhere on the way out."

She scrawled her name on the left side of the bill and slid it over to me, along with the marker. "You sign it, too, Dad."

I did as she asked and I stapled it on a slightly bare spot on the ceiling, right by the door. Walking back to the boat, she asked where we were going from there and what we were going to do with the fish we'd caught.

"We'll cross the skinny water up to the island and drop the fish off with Charlie. We always need more fish."

We got back in the boat and headed out of the marina, turning north and following the shoreline. I kept close to the west bank, idling along, scanning the shore. Finally, I saw three Key deer feeding in a small grassy area and turned in, killing the motor.

"They're so tiny," Kim whispered, watching the buck and two does eating. "They're no bigger than your dog."

We watched them graze for a moment, then started the engine and threaded between Cutoe Key and the peninsula on the southeast corner of Howe Key. Ten minutes later, we tied up at the south dock and started unloading our catch.

"Rusty said he wanted first dibs on our first batch of crawfish," Carl said while we helped him clean the fish. "I can have two coolers full in just a few minutes, if you're headed back that way."

"Go ahead and box them up," I said. "We'll head straight there from here."

A half hour later, with the snapper in the freezer and two coolers full of crawfish on the skiff, we headed south through Big Spanish Channel to the southern tip of Little Pine Key, then made a beeline for the hump in the Seven Mile Bridge. Idling back up the canal to the *Anchor*, I asked Kim if she'd had a good time.

"It's nothing like I thought it'd be," she said. "Driving down, we only got to see what the islands looked like from the highway. All those little islands up around you are way prettier."

It was midafternoon, but a cool front had moved through and it looked as if the sky would split open any minute, so we hurried with the coolers and made it inside just as the first fat drops of rain started to fall.

"What's in the coolers?" Julie asked from behind the bar.

"Crawfish," I replied. "Rusty said he wanted the first harvest."

"Dot di little lobstah he was talkin' bout?" Rufus asked, as he came in the back door.

"You have a recipe for crawfish, Rufus?" I asked.

"Dunt know," he replied. "Nevah see one. Lemme see dem."

I set one of the coolers on a table and opened it. "Careful, they have pincers."

He reached in and pulled one out, its pincers reaching back for his fingers as it slapped its tail, trying to get free. "Dem er janga," he said, dropping it back into the cooler with a grin on his face. "Di hill peoples got many recipes fer dem, mon." He carried one of the coolers out the back door, then returned and carried the second one away, still grinning.

# CHAPTER FIFTEEN

E ttaleigh finished her dinner in the Great Harbor Room at the lodge. She'd considered going to one of the restaurants in town but had some last minute business to take care of and brought her laptop computer to the restaurant at the lodge. Besides, it had a very good reputation and she'd been looking forward to their fresh seafood.

While she waited for her broiled lobster tail to arrive, she put a tiny earphone in and plugged it into the laptop. She didn't want the other diners to have to listen to what was on the recorded message. After listening, she emailed the audio file to an associate. That business taken care of, she made one quick call to her employer to relay an update concerning their business on the island and then gazed out at the ocean as the sun cast long shadows across the sand. When she got back to her cottage, she made one more call after locating the business card the young man had left.

James was hesitant about answering his phone when it rang. It was an international number. He'd thought about the woman all that afternoon and evening. In the end he decided he had been imagining things, and besides, there was just too much chance of losing his job, anyway. He was sitting in his little fishing boat, about to go out to the reef and spear some fish. He fished at night most of the time, usually alone. Finally, he answered it.

"Hi, James, this is Ettaleigh Bonamy," came a seductive voice over the phone. "We met this afternoon. I'm staying at the lodge."

"Yes, ma'am, I remember."

"I was wondering if I could persuade you to be my escort this evening. I want to go out drinking and dancing before my business associates arrive."

"Dancing?"

"Do you have access to a boat? Perhaps you could give me a tour of some of the clubs over on Great Abaco. My treat."

"Yeah, I could do that," he blurted out. "I'm sitting in my boat right now."

"Where is it? What should I wear?"

He was relieved that she wanted to go somewhere off island, but he was still having trouble believing she had any kind of sexual intent. If anything, she would probably leave him tired and frustrated by the end of the night and he had to be at work at seven o'clock in the morning.

"It's at the post office dock," he replied. "Maybe a three-minute walk north from the lodge on the bay side. Everywhere on the islands is barefoot casual. There's a place called the Jib Room over on Abaco that has a live band."

"I can be at the dock in ten minutes," Ettaleigh said and ended the call. She was wearing a lightweight black sundress with a tropical floral pattern. She took a moment at the mirror, applying just the right amount of gloss to her full lips. Slipping her feet into a pair of beach sandals, she started for the door. As an afterthought, she grabbed her heels and shoved them in her oversized purse.

Ettaleigh made it to the dock in just over ten minutes and found the young man waiting. She got that tingling feeling down low as she approached him. He was tall, several inches taller than her five nine. His hair was loose and wild-looking now, where it had been tied back earlier in the day. He was powerfully built and Ettaleigh looked forward to seeing if his ability matched his physique.

"Am I keeping you from your fishing?" she asked, pouting, while making no attempt at all to hide the fact that she was looking him over from head to toe, lingering at his groin.

"No, ma'am," he replied. "Probably wouldn't be a good night on the reef anyway."

"Okay, first things first, James. I'm Ettaleigh and we're going out drinking and dancing. So, please stop with the ma'am. I'm only a few years older than you," she lied. "Secondly, I have every intention of screwing your brains out later, maybe right there in that boat of yours."

James stood there in disbelief. He'd had sex with a number of girls up on the casting deck of his boat, under the stars, out on the bay. He much preferred it to a bed. He smiled hungrily at this beautiful, sexy woman and said, "Yes, ma'am."

She smiled wickedly and allowed him to help her step down into the little boat. Two minutes later, he was picking his way through the many boats at anchor in the little bay, headed north with her sitting beside him. Once clear of the bay and into the narrow channel to the open water between the islands, he pushed down the throttle and the little boat flew across the glassy water. Although it was dark, the moon was bright and James knew every rock and coral head in the area.

Ettaleigh pulled her hair over her left shoulder and held it in place against the wind with one hand while she clutched James's upper arm with the other for balance. She couldn't see much past the front of the little boat, but he seemed to be very competent at the wheel. Coupled with the darkness all around them and the speed they were going, the flexing muscle of the arm under her fingertips added to her excitement.

Fifteen minutes later, they were tying up to the dock at the Jib Room. James was a pretty good dancer and for an hour, the two rarely left the dance floor. When the music slowed, they embraced and crushed themselves together, making it obvious to one another what their physical needs were.

Finally, they left the club to go to a more out-of-the-way bar on Great Guana Cay to the north. Feeling the effect of the two rum drinks she'd had, she made no effort to disguise her desire. She took a flask from her purse and offered it to James.

"This is my own little concoction," she said, smiling. "It boosts a person's energy level."

Sensing his reluctance, she drank a third of it herself and again offered it to James. He took the flask and gulped down the rest of the sweet liquid.

They only made it halfway across the narrow sound. Her hands were all over him, which caused James to turn and head for a very secluded little beach on Great Abaco, across from Great Guana. The beach was on a tiny island just beyond a spit of land that jutted several hundred feet out into the water. As they approached, James could see that it was obviously deserted, but he decided not to land and cut the engine. He went up to the bow and dropped his anchor thirty feet from shore. This little stretch of sand was well known to young couples in search of a quiet place to be alone and sometimes it was host to a bonfire party with dozens of people.

When he turned around, Ettaleigh was all over him again, urgently pulling his shirt off and tugging down his shorts. It'd been many months since she'd last had a man, and she slowly knelt before him, eager to get started.

Forty strenuous minutes later, they pulled the anchor and headed across to Great Guana and Nipper's Beach Bar. There, they danced, drank more rum, and fed one another fresh barbequed shrimp for over an hour. The combination of the rum drinks and the energy drink loosened Ettaleigh up even more, if that was possible. She wasn't quite satisfied yet and asked James to walk her along the beach. Once outside the pool of light from the bar, she turned into his embrace. Lifting one long leg and wrapping it around him, she drew him in and they made love again while standing and gyrating to the seductive beat of the island band just a few yards away.

On the return to Hope Town Harbour, they stopped once more and anchored in the lee of a tiny sandbar. Stripping off their clothes, they both slipped into the water and swam to the shallows, where they coupled once more in waist-deep water.

Walking back along Queen's Highway to the lodge, she felt fairly satisfied but was already looking forward to tomorrow.

# CHAPTER SIXTEEN

Sitting on the table behind the *Anchor* with Kim, Pescador laying at our feet under the table, we watched the sun slide slowly toward the horizon. "You know," Kim said, "the whole time I've been down here, I haven't checked to see what time it was."

"You adapt pretty quick," I said. "We call it 'island time.' It's measured by the sun, moon, and tides, not by a clock or calendar."

As we talked, the sun moved closer and closer to the far horizon, bathing the scattered clouds left over after the rain with an orange and pink glow as it slowly sank below the tree line. The view from my island is much better, but we enjoyed the time just the same. With the sun behind the trees, we walked back to the bar for supper.

Rufus's janga soup was a huge hit. People from all over the island must have smelled it simmering away in one of his large black pots behind the bar. For nearly six years, he'd been cooking on a small deck using gas-fired burners with nothing more than a tarp for cover. It was amazing what came out of those pots and pans. We retired early, Kim bunking with Charity again.

I woke before sunrise, repacked my go bag for flying, and packed another, smaller bag that I would leave in *The Beast* or, if there was a good stash spot on the plane, I'd take it with me.

I'd arranged to meet Dave at the Key West Airport at zero seven hundred, give him the cashier's check for the amount we agreed on and take possession of my plane. Since I had more than a hundred hours of flight time in her already, both Dave and I agreed we were a good fit for each other.

It was only a fifty-mile drive and normally it could be done in about an hour, but occasionally it might take way longer. Dave and his wife had business in Miami later in the day and he promised to drive *The Beast* to Marathon and drop it off for me and continue in their own car. I'd decided to leave at zero five thirty and grab a breakfast sandwich at some fast food place. So, I filled a thermos, grabbed a mug of coffee, and fired up *The Beast* in the quiet, early morning glow.

Having no delays, I arrived early at the airport. Dave was already there and came around the front of the plane as I pulled up on the starboard side.

"Looks like it's gonna be a great day for flying," he said, walking up to me and extending his hand.

"Hope it stays that way," I replied, shaking hands. "A few of us are going to fly over to Nassau."

I carried my bag over to the plane and Dave said, "I have something to show you."

After I'd stowed and secured my bag in the aft cabin, Dave climbed in and went forward to the flight deck. He sat down in the left seat and said, "Lift the co-pilot's seat."

I knew both seats had storage underneath, accessed by pulling a strap located between the seat cushion and backrest. I pulled it open and found the usual logs, charts, and emergency first aid kit.

"Now pull down on the springs of the seat bottom," he said.

I pulled down on the springs that cushioned the bottom and the whole seat bottom gave way with a click, folding back down normally. I immediately recognized two things. The spring assembly was fake, almost identical to the real spring assembly still attached to the seat cushion. The back side of the fake assembly, now facing up, had the unmistakable outline of a handgun and magazine created with foam padding.

I grinned at my friend. "You know me all too well, Dave."

"Thought you might need a place to stash something inconspicuously."

I raised the false bottom and it clicked back into place on the underside of the seat cushion. Looking closely, I saw there was no way you could tell it was there unless you already knew. I went back out to *The Beast* and grabbed my other bag.

Together, we did a complete and thorough walk-around inspection, checking all the control surfaces and paying close attention to the floats. He gave me the card of a mechanic that worked for Key West Seaplane Adventures and did some work on the side. He'd already given the man my name and suggested I give him a call to arrange a regular servicing schedule.

Once Dave left, I did the preflight, walked the props to clear any oil from the lower cylinders, and started the burly radial engine. It fired, chugged, and belched smoke, then settled into a smooth idle. The smoke was normal and I'd come to enjoy the smell of partially burned avgas. I let the engine warm up at high idle for a few minutes, then contacted ground control and requested taxi instructions.

"Beaver one three eight five, Key West ground. Good morning, Jesse. You're cleared for VFR to fifty-five hundred feet. Taxi via Bravo, hold short runway niner."

I greeted the controller, repeated and acknowledged the instructions, then lowered the idle and released the brakes. The Beaver was produced in two forms: the standard wheeled tail dragger model and as a float plane. An industrious flyer in Saint Paul, Minnesota saw the need for an amphibian and started a company called WipAire, where he designed replacement floats with retractable wheels for a variety of planes, including the Beaver.

I taxied to the end of the runway and did a quick run-up, checking the gauges, then switched the radio to air traffic control and requested takeoff instructions.

"Beaver one three eight five, Key West Tower. Traffic two miles outbound is a Beechcraft King Air. Runway niner, light wind zero niner five at five, clouds are scattered and visibility is ten miles. You are cleared for takeoff. Report clear to the southeast. Have a safe flight."

I repeated his instructions and released the brake, giving the plane a little throttle and turning onto the runway. I knew from experience that I'd use only about half the runway. After putting on my sunglasses, I pulled down the flap lever to thirty-five percent and bumped the throttle up to takeoff speed. In just over two hundred yards, I'd reached eighty-five knots and pulled back slightly on the yoke. The plane responded instantly, lifting off the runway and climbing slowly. I drifted slightly to the right and quickly used the foot pedals and wheel to get back on course, but over corrected and drifted left. At two hundred feet I passed over the end of the runway. Checking the air speed indicator, I raised the flaps and flipped the switch that activated the hydraulic pumps, raising the gear up into the floats. I pulled back a little more on the yoke to increase the rate of climb, while banking southeast out over the sparkling water.

I radioed ATC that I was clear of the field and leveled off at eight hundred feet, turning slightly north of due east to follow the island chain toward Marathon. I reached over and lowered the sunscreen on the passenger side to block the rising sun. I was flying. And in my very own plane. The feeling was exhilarating. I banked a little to the right, flying further out over the water then back to the left, toward the island chain. *What a rush!* I thought.

At that low altitude, I could see people on the decks of their boats as they headed out for a day of fishing and I recognized one or two boats. When someone waved, I banked left and right to wave the wings back in return. *Yep, I'm flying my own plane,* I thought. I got the same feeling that I did seven years earlier, when I took the helm of the *Revenge* for the first time.

In my head, I could hear Jimmy's voice. He went up to Miami with Rusty and me to buy the *Revenge* and on the way back with her, he asked, "What do you think you're gonna call her, man?" Then he went on to tell me about the pirate Jose Gaspar. It occurred to me that this was the second time I'd taken off in something without a name.

As I followed US-1 back toward Marathon, I began to think of appropriate names. I'd always been impressed with the nose art on bombers from World War II and thought it would be a pretty cool idea to paint something on the cowling. I still wanted to get the King Air one day and maybe even one of those old flying boats that were used for passenger service to the islands many years ago, before airports and runways were built. Since this plane would be used primarily for hopping around the hundreds of islands that make up the Keys, I decided on *Island Hopper*.

Flying low over the water gave me a sense of what the islands might have looked like a century earlier, except for the constant ribbon of asphalt that is US-1. These islands have a long and sordid history, dating back long before Europeans ever laid eyes on them. I could almost imagine looking down and seeing the early Spanish ship convoys as they made their way across the Florida Straits from Cuba, then east and north along the Keys and the mainland.

It only took twenty minutes to get back to Marathon. *No tourist traffic jams up here*, I thought. I radioed Marathon Airport to get permission for a water landing in Vaca Key Bight.

"Beaver one three eight five, Marathon Tower. No traffic at this time, wind calm, overfly the bight to check for surface traffic."

The winds were exactly as I'd hoped for. Almost dead calm. I acknowledged his instructions and dropped down to five hundred feet as I crossed over Boot Key Harbor and banked slightly to the south as I reduced power and lowered the flaps twenty degrees. Seeing no boats in the shallow water or coming out of the several channels, I banked further south until I was off Key Colony Beach, then began a tight turn to the north, finally lining up for an approach parallel to US-1 and the airport runway just beyond it. As I came over Key Colony Beach, I checked the four advisory lights again to make sure the gear was up and reduced power even more. I pushed the yoke forward, lining up on the microwave tower on Sombrero Beach Road, which was near the entrance to Rusty's canal.

Dropping down to just thirty feet, I leveled off and pulled the flap lever to thirty-five degrees, reducing power even more. The plane dropped slowly and just a few feet off the water, I pulled back lightly on the yoke and flared her out just a bit too early. The pontoons making soft contact with the glassy surface and bouncing a few feet back up in the air before settling back on the water. I held the yoke back as surface friction brought the speed down and she settled into the water. Before dropping down off plane, I gave her more throttle and used the rudder pedals to turn toward the canal. I could see Rusty and Bourke by the boat ramp and just a hundred feet from shore, I dropped the engine to an idle and she settled down into the water, barely moving forward.

I lowered the landing gear, checking the four blue lights on the dash to ensure they were locked down as I approached the wide boat ramp. Just before making contact, I pushed the throttle forward and the big radial responded with a roar. Once up the ramp and on level ground, I rolled about twenty yards further to get a bit more room for turning toward the ramp later. I hit the right brake and rudder pedal, spinning the big plane ninety degrees before stopping it. I let the engine idle down for a moment, then shut her down.

When I climbed down, Bourke was waiting with a can of spray paint in his hand, which I assumed he was going to use to mark the spots for the tie-downs. "This is a really beautiful bird, Jesse."

"Yeah, she is," I said as Rusty walked up.

"If this is where you intend to tie her down, I'll go ahead and mark the tie-down locations," Bourke said

I glanced at Rusty. "Think this will be out of the way?"

"Can we shove it back a bit? It'll make turning to get back down the ramp easier."

With Rusty in the center pushing on the crossmember and Bourke and me pushing on the floats, we managed to push it back about twenty feet.

Rusty surveyed the parking job and said, "If we poured a level concrete pad here with a curb at the back, it'd be a lot easier to push and you could set the anchors in the pad."

"I can do that," Bourke said.

"I'll have Julie call the Home Depot," Rusty said. "They can have one of them trailer mixers and enough concrete bags to do the job delivered here in an hour. Figure up what you need to make it about three inches thick and let her know."

Bourke pulled a tape measure from his pocket and began making measurements while Rusty and I walked down the crushed-shell path to the bar.

"I didn't intend it to be a permanent thing," I said.

"Then it won't be," he replied. "Up to you. But you could pick up clients here and get them out to more remote fishing spots." Then he grinned and added, "Course, I get twenty percent."

"Always the hustler, huh?"

# CHAPTER SEVENTEEN

W e had the plane loaded in fifteen minutes and everyone climbed aboard. Even though it was early, the sound of the big radial engine coming up the ramp drew a good-sized crowd for our departure. While they boarded, I ran through a preflight check and started the engine. Once everyone was settled and strapped in, I stood on the right rudder pedal and pushed the throttle up just enough to get her rolling. Once the bow wheels were pointing down the ramp, gravity took over and I pulled her down to an idle, using the brakes to steer down the center of the ramp. The nose gear on a Beaver isn't steerable. The nose wheels on the front of each float are on casters like a shopping cart, which makes maneuvering a little difficult. Ten feet from the water, I had her lined up perfectly and just let her roll on down into the water.

Idling across the shallows, I raised the landing gear, checking the lights to make sure the wheels were fully retracted. When we were a good hundred feet from shore I called Marathon airport again for permission to take off.

"Beaver one three eight five, Marathon Tower. Traffic outbound is a Cessna Caravan at three miles. Light wind zero niner zero at five. If surface traffic is clear, you're clear to takeoff."

I repeated the instructions, checked for boats and, seeing none, I turned her into the wind. I had Kim riding shotgun, with Rusty, Deuce, and Doc in back. I lowered the flaps to thirty-five degrees and pushed the throttle to full power, lining up just to the south of the last marker for Vaca Cut channel.

The plane was up on the step in less than two hundred feet and skipped over the glassy water for another six hundred feet when I could feel her pulling toward the sky. Easing back on the yoke, she came up off the water smoothly. A moment later I raised the flaps and landing gear, banking southeast and climbing. Once a few miles out over the Straits, I leveled off at five thousand feet, turned to a heading of eighty-five degrees and reduced power to an efficient cruising speed of one hundred and forty miles per hour.

"It's almost two hours to Nassau," I said over the intercom.

"Will we be over water all the way?" Kim asked.

"In a little over an hour, we'll fly over the northern tip of Andros Island," I replied. "Other than that, there won't be anything to see but water."

"This is all very cool, Dad."

"You want to drive a little bit?" I asked her.

"Me? Fly a plane? I only got my license to drive a car two years ago."

"There's nothing to it," I said. "Pull back a little to go up and push forward a little to go down. Other than that, just keep her aimed at that cloud way up ahead."

"Are you sure it's okay?" she asked, reaching for the yoke.

I raised both hands and said, "Off stick."

Kim took the yoke in her hands, grinning, and asked, "I'm flying?"

"Yeah, you're flying. Now turn the wheel just a little to the right while you pull back slightly and press lightly on the right pedal." She did as I told her and the plane banked to the right. "Now do the same thing to the left and bring us back on course for that cloud."

She banked slowly to the left and lined back up on the cloud. I noticed the altimeter dropped about a hundred feet but didn't say anything.

"Our altitude changed," she said, as if reading my mind.

"Yeah, it'll do that when banking. It's a heavy plane and kind of slides downward whichever way you're banking. With practice you'll get better at maintaining altitude in a turn."

I took the controls back and brought us back up to five thousand feet. Rusty and Doc started talking about the salvage law requirements in the Bahamas and Kim and I enjoyed watching the ocean slip by below us. After about an hour we could see clouds building up ahead, a sure sign of land.

I pointed out the little village of Owen's Town and Stafford Creek as we flew over the island. *One day,* I thought, *I'll have to bring her here to see the blue holes.*

Flying back out over the ocean again, I contacted Lynden Pindling International Airport on Nassau when we were ten miles out and requested approach and landing instructions.

A distinctly island voice came back to me, saying, "Beaver one three eight five, Pindling Tower. I have you ten miles out. Traffic three miles inbound is an L-1011 heavy. Runway fourteen, light wind one fifteen at six, clouds are scattered and visibility is ten miles. Cleared to land."

I acknowledged the instructions and started searching the sky for the airliner. Spotting it, I began an easy turn to fall in behind it. Five miles out from the runway, I reduced power and started to descend. A mile out, I lowered the flaps and landing gear, checking the lights to make sure they locked into position.

We didn't need a third of the runway the airliner used as I came in over the glide path and touched down a hundred yards beyond the west end of the runway. Once on the ground I switched to the ground control frequency and requested taxi instructions to the fixed-base operator Deuce had arranged for fueling and clearing customs. Ground control directed us to Odyssey FBO, where I turned the plane around so it was facing the taxiway.

Doc handed down the two bags we'd packed with extra food, water, and other emergency provisions, and I placed them on the ground, open. We all walked inside with our passports, leaving the doors open also. It's been my experience that it's far easier making everything as accessible as possible when arriving in the islands. It didn't hurt to have a twenty in each pocket either.

We cleared customs with no trouble and a customs officer accompanied me out to the plane while Rusty made arrangements for a van to take us to the government offices. The customs officer wore a name tag that read only Joshua.

"Dat one beautiful plane, mon," Joshua said as we approached the Beaver. "What yeah?"

"It's a fifty-three," I replied, handing him the signed and notarized bill of sale, title, and registration. "Just bought it this morning."

He looked from the plane to me and back to the plane. "I know dis plane." He stopped and turned toward me. "You bought dis from Mistuh Williams?"

"You know Dave?" I asked.

He smiled, his white teeth seeming to glow against the darkness of his skin. "Ya, mon. He been through heah many times. Mind if I go aboard?"

Knowing it wouldn't matter if I minded or not and wondering if Dave had made a good impression here, I said, "Sure, feel free."

He stepped up on the starboard pontoon and opened the door. He went straight for the seat cushion, lifting it and rummaging through the contents before stepping down with the plane's logbook.

"Dese not necessary, but Mistuh Williams like gettin' it stamped. If ya like, I can run dis into di office?"

I took the book from him and thumbed through it. There were stamps from many airports all over the southeastern United States and half the Caribbean.

Thumbing back through the first few pages, I saw airport stamps from several places in Canada and Alaska.

"He never mentioned this," I said, grinning. "But yeah, it's pretty cool. A lot of history in this little book." I handed it back to him and he went back inside.

A moment later, he came back out, followed by the others. A fuel truck pulled up and an Odyssey worker began refueling the tanks.

"Here ya go, Mistuh McDermitt," Joshua said, handing me the planes log book and my passport. "Ever ting is irey. Soon's dat mon finish fuelin' ya and di van get here, yuh can lock her up and go. He wheel her up to doze tie-downs when he done."

I looked and realized that while I'd turned correctly, I'd missed the tie-downs by ten feet. I didn't notice them and hadn't even thought of tying her down. Like the Keys, the weather on these islands could change in half a heartbeat. Not a mistake I'd make again.

I pulled both hands out of my pockets, turned to Joshua and extending my hand, I palmed a twenty into his while handing him a business card with my left hand. "Thanks, Joshua. It's been a pleasure meeting you. If you get over to Marathon and want to dive the Stream or fish the back country, look me up."

He lifted the *Gaspar's Revenge Charters* business card to his eyes while smoothly pocketing the bill in his pants. Sticking the card in his shirt pocket as the van pulled alongside us, he said, "I do dat."

I closed and locked the doors of the plane. Deuce had already taken care of paying for the fuel, so we climbed into the van and headed for the government office.

It took less than twenty minutes there for Rusty to finish his application and get his Bahamian salvor's license and permit. That done, we stopped at a little outdoor restaurant on the way back to the airport and had conch fritters and Caribbean gumbo.

We were back in the air before noon, well ahead of the schedule I'd planned. From Nassau to Elbow Cay took less than an hour. I contacted Marsh Harbour Airport and got clearance to do a few low-level flybys of Elbow Cay and the surrounding islands for photography.

"Beaver one three eight five, Marsh Harbour Tower. Minimum altitude is three hundred feet anywhere within the Bahamian five-mile limit."

I acknowledged him and dropped down to four hundred feet, following the coast of narrow Tilloo Cay to the south of Elbow Cay. At this altitude, the coastline of the two islands seemed almost as one. It was easy to see that many years ago, they had been a single island, now separated by Tilloo Cut.

Approaching the cut, I dropped the speed and lowered the flaps ten degrees. I adjusted the throttle to maintain ninety miles per hour as we passed the cut and followed the shoreline northward.

"There's where we'll be staying," Doc said, having taken over as co-pilot. "The light blue house on the hill with the townhouses below it."

Passing it, I banked left and turned a slow circle around the property. It looked like a great place for a vacation get away. Deuce used a digital camera with a zoom lens and took a couple of dozen pictures of the property from all angles.

Reaching the beach again, we continued north along the coast. Rusty had the printout Chyrel had given him, with the four locations marked on it.

"The first is just ahead," he said over the intercom. "The cove with the low limestone cliff on the south side."

I spotted it and again turned a slow circle while Deuce took another twenty or so pictures. Crossing the beach once more, we continued north. The next one was easy to find. It was a massive rock formation with a house sitting right on top of it. Whoever owned it sure had a great view of both the ocean and the beaches north and south of it.

"The next one is offshore," Rusty said as I began the same lazy turn around the house. "When you come out of the turn, head north-northeast. It's about a half mile north of this rock and a half mile offshore."

Deuce got pictures all the way around the house and I set the heading Rusty had given me. I spotted the rock jutting up out of the sea and banked right to line up for another circle around it.

"When you finish the circle," Deuce said, "head out to sea a ways and fly back due west about a hundred yards north of it."

I knew what he wanted. To photograph the area "eighty great advances" to the west of the rock. As I overflew the area, I banked slightly left and kicked the right rudder pedal, causing the plane to fly a straight line while banked to the left, giving Deuce a much better view. I heard the fast clicking of about a hundred frames, stopping only when we reached the beach.

"The next one's on the northern tip of the island," Rusty said.

Banking left again, I circled a group of small, quaint-looking cottages sitting right behind the dune and then continued north along the beach. Out of the corner of my eye, I saw color and movement. Glancing over, I saw someone standing on the deck of the middle cottage. A dark-haired woman in a yellow bathing suit was looking up at us as we flew over. She had a flowered sarong around her waist, but one very shapely, tanned leg was exposed. She waved and, not wanting to appear suspicious, I waggled the wings in return before looking ahead again to find the last rock outcropping.

"What the heck was all that about?" Rusty asked from the back seat. "Something wrong with the plane?"

"Just saying hi," I replied, seeing a large rock outcropping jutting out into the sea thirty or forty feet.

"Well, quit bein' so danged friendly," he said. "You're bouncing the passengers around."

Approaching the rock, I turned another slow circle around it while Deuce took more pictures. As I circled, I looked off to the south and saw the woman still standing on the deck, watching us. Even at this distance, I could tell she was attractive.

# CHAPTER EIGHTEEN

James managed to get to work on time, but it was an effort. He'd never met a woman as aggressive and tenacious as Ettaleigh. He managed to crawl into bed at two o'clock and when he woke, every muscle in his body was stiff from overexertion.

He'd seen her once already that morning. She'd come down to the restaurant for a late breakfast, dressed in a strapless yellow sundress and flat sandals. Though he was completely exhausted from the night before, the mere sight of her excited him. This he couldn't understand. He'd seen plenty of attractive women, but this woman seemed to have an effect on him that no other woman ever had and that he was powerless to control.

Shortly after breakfast the head desk clerk, Paul, summoned him. "The guest in cottage number two has asked for you," he said. "She needs more towels and asked if she could talk to you for a moment about taking her fishing. I've warned you about soliciting the guests, James."

"She asked if I had a boat," James replied, not really lying. "I just gave her my card. If you like, I can tell her no and refer her to someone else."

Paul thought about it a moment. Employees becoming overly friendly with guests had always been a problem, but James was one of his hardest workers and was well-known all around the islands as being a professional on the water. Besides, the guest had called the desk to ask if it would be acceptable instead of calling James directly.

"No," he replied. "If the lady and her party want you to take them fishing, that will be all right. But, only on your days off, or after work. I can't get someone to fill in on short notice."

James went to the laundry, got a bundle of still-warm towels from the shelf, along with a couple of hand towels, and went to cottage number two.

He knocked on the door and after a moment it opened. She reached out and grabbed his arm, dragging him inside. She wore a yellow bikini, covered with a tight-fitting black mesh dress that extended to her wrists and middle thigh. It had a loop that encircled her middle fingers to hold the sleeves in place and she was wearing black high heels.

She took the towels and tossed them on the bed as she dragged him across the room to the open French door. Without saying a word, she lifted the bottom of the dress above her hips and pulled her bikini bottom off, tossing it on the bed also.

He was already fully aroused before she bent and released him from his shorts, then turned her back. Gripping the insides of the open doorframe, she arched her back, turning her head and smiling seductively at him.

"You have about ten minutes before you'll be missed, James. Don't waste any of it staring."

Temporarily sated, Ettaleigh sent her new boy toy on his way, telling him to return by way of the secluded deck when he took his lunch break. In her business life, she had to maintain a certain aloofness to be effective at her job. These business preparation trips were sometimes the only way she could let loose and satisfy her physical needs. Since they were few and far between, she'd learned to be more aggressive and take what she wanted during the short time she was preparing for upcoming business.

Occasionally, she would have a day off on a weekend and would rent a car and drive to another city, where she could go on the hunt for strong young men at will. She had no problem with using modern chemistry to ensure a willing partner and would add a second dose if a man showed even the slightest sign of faltering. So far, this one had remained more than ready, even twelve hours after the first dose.

Opening her laptop she read a few emails, responding to those that required a response, then listened to the latest audio clip sent to her from one of her associates. She played it back and listened closer, then forwarded the audio file to her employer along with a message explaining what she thought this new development would mean for their business plans.

Her immediate work completed, she decided to get a couple of hours in the sun on the secluded deck before lunch. As she lay on the recliner, enjoying the warmth of the sun and the tingling sensation of the cool ocean breeze on her bare skin, she heard the sound of an airplane. She rose from the recliner and stood at the deck's rail, searching the sky.

She spotted the bright red seaplane circling the house on the rock to the south of her cottage. It then flew a mile offshore and circled a large rock that protruded up from the ocean bottom, undercut all around from the constant wave action. The plane circled the rock and then flew out to sea before turning and coming back toward the beach. It flew over just to the north of her cottage and turned a slow, lazy circle to the south before heading north along the coast once more.

The plane moved so slowly, she wondered how it even stayed in the air. As it flew over the water just offshore, she saw the pilot turn and look down at her. She smiled and waved and the plane dipped its wings in return before moving further up the beach and performing another lazy circle.

She saw James approaching from the beach, carrying one of those large umbrellas people use to ward off the sun. She smiled again. *What friendly people these islanders are*, she thought as she went back inside the cottage, leaving the door open once more.

# CHAPTER NINETEEN

After flying over the last of the rocks Chyrel had marked on the map, I turned due east and followed the southern shoreline of Grand Bahama Island at eight hundred feet. Reaching Freeport, I turned southwest toward Miami and climbed to five thousand feet.

"Is the water here always so clear?" Kim asked. "I can see the bottom."

"Pretty much all the time," Rusty explained. "The Gulf Stream moves north between Florida and these islands, drawing water out of the islands with the rise and fall of the tide. Kind of like a giant filter."

For the next two hours as we flew steadily back toward civilization, conversation centered on the hunt for the treasure and in what order we should search the four areas.

We arrived at Miami International Airport just before sixteen hundred and had no problems clearing customs, refueling, and taking off once more toward Marathon.

Kim would be leaving to drive back up to Miami in the morning and I was already beginning to miss her. I now wanted more than anything to meet my oldest daughter, Eve.

Forty minutes after leaving Miami, I contacted Marathon Airport about a water landing in the Bight. They gave me the go ahead and told me wind speed was up to ten knots, so a downwind landing was out of the question. I flew over Vaca Cut and checked the water in the bight for boats. One was heading out of the cut, but it would be well clear before I touched down. I banked right and circled Sombrero Beach, flying over Boot Key Harbor and reducing speed. A few minutes later, we came in low over the trees and settled into the water at the end of Rusty's channel.

I kept the plane up on the step and turned around, taxiing toward the boat ramp with the wind behind us. Dave had warned me about downwind taxis and I kept the yoke forward so the wind held the tail down. Approaching the ramp, I lowered the landing gear and powered up to climb out of the water.

I could see that Bourke was just finishing up the concrete pad, but it'd be a day or two before the concrete cured enough to park on it. I turned sharply to the right at the top of the ramp, stopped the plane so we could push it back alongside the newly poured pad, and shut down the engine.

Both Bourke and Charity were waiting to lend a hand pushing the plane back once everyone was off. A moment later, we had it where we wanted it and I saw that Bourke had figured on this and put temporary tie-downs under the wings and another under the tail. Once she was tied down, everyone headed to the bar to get something to eat.

With all the details and arrangements hammered out, there was little to do until morning. As we ate Rufus's pork roast and seasoned vegetables, we continued the discussion from the plane about which site to search first.

"The largest rock is the one with the house on it," Rusty argued. "If I was to get marooned on a deserted island, I'd pick a spot like that to make camp."

Kim picked up one of the many photos Deuce had printed out from his little office on the *Caird* and said, "See how this rock's undercut all the way around the bottom? I bet it was a whole lot bigger four hundred years ago."

"You might be right, Kim," Deuce said. "There's been a lot of wave action in the last four hundred years and according to Chyrel sea levels have risen a few feet too."

"I suggest we work south to north," Doc said. "The offshore one and the one on the northern tip will be difficult. The area west of it is vacant land, just tangled mangroves and brush."

As sunset approached, Kim and I made our way out to the boat ramp to watch the sunset. Sitting on the table, with Pescador sniffing his way along the seawall, Kim said, "I want to stay here."

"Stay here?" I asked.

"Here in the Keys. Not permanently, just until I start college next year. I don't have a job to get back to and I've already decided on putting college off until next year."

"What's your mom gonna say about that?"

"It's not for her to decide," she replied forcefully. "I have my own car that I bought with my own money and have been making my own decisions about everything for a long time."

"You remind me a lot of myself when I was younger. Pap raised me to think and do for myself at an early age."

"So, can I stay?"

I thought about what she was asking. Living on an island with basically no electricity, no television, and spotty cell service didn't seem like something most teenagers would aspire to.

"There's not very much to do on the island," I said. "We fish and dive for lobster, work in the little garden, but mostly I just wait for the next part of life to happen. Pretty boring."

"Sounds like just what I need. Will you teach me to dive?" she asked, as if the decision was already made.

In fact, it was. "Yeah, I can teach you to dive."

"And to fly, too?"

I glanced over at the plane, its red aluminum skin glistening in the late evening sun. *Island Hopper*, I thought. *That's just what we'll do.*

"Yeah, I'll teach you to fly, too."

We talked some more as the sun performed its mesmerizing dance of colors, finally deciding that Kim would return to Miami in the morning before we departed for the Bahamas and she'd return in a week. Then we went back to the boat to turn in early.

Dawn broke overcast and cooler, with a fifteen-knot wind out of the northeast. It was going to make the crossing difficult. I considered postponing our departure, but then I thought about those who would be crossing on the boat. Deuce and Tony were both Navy SEALs, Bourke and Julie were Coasties, Doc was a Navy Corpsman, his wife Nikki was a Marine, and Charity was once an Olympic swimmer. While I was sure of the first five, I had no idea how Nikki and Charity would handle a ten-hour crossing of the Gulf Stream and Bahama Banks then around the north end of Andros and across the Tongue of the Ocean, or TOTO, to New Providence Island. I planned to refuel there and spend the night. After that would be another four hours to Elbow Cay in some of the deepest waters of the Atlantic—the northern dogleg of the TOTO.

I got part of my answer when I stepped up into the galley, where I smelled bacon and coffee. Kim and Charity were making breakfast and whispering quietly. I was surprised they'd been able to board without me noticing. I cast a stern look at Pescador and headed to the coffeepot.

Waiting until I'd downed a third of my cup, Charity said, "Looks like it's going to be a fun crossing."

"You're still going to leave in this storm?" Kim asked with a concerned expression on her face.

Tony and Bourke stumbled up into the galley and headed straight to the coffeepot. "It won't be so bad," Tony said. "Ten-foot seas crossing the Stream. Nothing the *Revenge* can't handle."

I leaned against the island cabinet and nodded at Kim. "We'll be fine, it's just a small blow. What time are you headed back to Miami?"

"Right after breakfast," she replied.

"Will you remember—" I started.

"To call you when I get there? Will your cellphone work that far from land?"

"Yeah, I'll forward my cell to a satellite phone. It'll make me feel better knowing you got back okay."

She smiled and said, "I will if you promise to call me from Nassau and Elbow Cay."

"Deal," I said with a grin.

From outside I heard Deuce call out, "Permission to board?" A single bark from Pescador was all the answer he needed. Deuce, Julie, Doc, Nikki, and Rusty came through the hatch a moment later.

"Everyone grab a plate," Charity said. "Nothing fancy, just scrambled eggs, bacon, and toast."

It was cramped inside, so me, Rusty, and Bourke took our plates up to the bridge. I wanted to familiarize Bourke with the details of operating the *Revenge*, since the three of us would be posing as crew, taking three couples to the islands, in case anyone got nosy.

Kim took our plates after we'd finished eating and I started the engines. Doc and Tony set about casting off the mooring lines, while I walked Kim to her car.

"Be careful," I said. "And tell your sister I said hello."

"Don't forget to call me when you get to Nassau tonight," she said. "And I'll call you as soon as I get to Eve's."

I hugged her, kissed her forehead, and watched as she backed out and drove down the crushed-shell driveway. I suddenly experienced a great sense of loss. Though I hadn't seen her for most of her life, watching her leave was like having a part of me taken away.

When I got back to the *Revenge*, Tony and Bourke were at the bow rail and stern, ready to shove off. I stepped aboard and they pushed first the bow, then the stern away from the dock as I climbed up to the bridge. Doc was in the second seat and switched on the bright spotlights mounted on the roof, illuminating the canal and the foredeck, where Pescador sat looking forward. I put the starboard engine into gear first, then the port engine, straightening the boat in the middle of the canal. With Rusty finishing the breakfast dishes in the galley, everyone was able to sit on the bridge, though it was a bit cramped.

We slowly idled down the canal to open water. Once we cleared the jetty, the waves starting slapping the hull and I pushed the throttle up to cruising speed, the engines lifting the big boat up onto plane, where the *Revenge* took the waves with no problem. The real trouble would hit once we reached the Gulf Stream. Seas there would likely be a lot rougher.

I knew Rusty was readying the cabin for rough water, so I kept inside the reef and ran Hawk Channel northeast. I sent Tony and Doc down to help him, knowing that we'd be encountering more direct wind and larger waves as we followed the curve of the Keys more and more northerly.

Originally, we'd planned to get outside the reef and just set a straight course for the north end of Andros. However, just like a battle plan, it was tossed as soon as we engaged the enemy. Today's enemy was Mother Nature. I kept the NOAA Weather Radio turned up, the mechanical voice droning on monotonously as we followed the markers up the Intracoastal Waterway. This plot would keep us in fairly sheltered water, cutting our time in the open water of Florida Strait to only sixty miles while only adding about forty miles to the run. We all agreed it would be worth the time.

Rusty, Tony, and Doc soon joined us on the bridge. Rusty took the second seat while Doc sat with Bourke and Deuce, leaving Tony standing up front with the women. He always seemed to prefer standing.

"Everything's secure," Rusty said.

"Thanks," I replied. "We're gonna run on the inside to Biscayne Bay."

"Probably wise. Which way's the storm headed?"

"Stalled out over Florida Bay," Deuce replied. "We should punch out of it, when we get to Bimini."

"Hugging the flats all the way to Fowey Rocks?" Rusty asked.

"It'll add two hours, but it should keep the pounding to a minimum," I replied.

An hour later it became obvious we had made the right decision. Passing Tavernier the curve of the Keys had us headed straight into the wind and waves. Seas were still fairly calm at only three to four feet and barely noticeable. The chatter on the VHF from fishing boats out on the Strait told us that it was far worse on the outside.

Twenty minutes later, as we were passing north Key Largo, my cellphone chirped from my shirt pocket. Deuce looked at me with a surprised expression. It was Kim calling to tell me she'd made it to Eve's house and asking how things were going. I told her our change in plans and that I'd call her back once we reached Bimini then I ended the call.

"You have your phone on you?" Deuce asked, incredulous. "And it's charged?" Rusty nudged me with his elbow and grinned. While Julie was at Coast Guard basic training and Maritime Enforcement School, he was never more than an arm's length from his phone.

"I keep it close by whenever I'm expecting an important call," I replied.

It took another two hours before we turned toward open water just north of Legare Anchorage. As we made the turn, I called Pescador off the foredeck. He seemed a bit reluctant but picked his way along the starboard side to the cockpit, where he made two turns around his favorite spot by the transom door before lying down. The seas picked up dramatically as we passed from the relatively sheltered water of the Intracoastal just south of Star Reef and out into the wide open Atlantic. The sonar showed the bottom falling away sharply and just a mile out, it was beyond the range of my sonar.

Either the fishing boats earlier were exaggerating or it had calmed some. It would still be a rough two-hour crossing, with wind-driven waves rolling out of the northeast at eight feet, but they were spaced well apart. Nothing the *Revenge* couldn't handle with ease. I even nudged the throttle up to thirty knots, taking the rollers on the port bow, its sweeping Carolina flare knocking them down with only occasional spray over the foredeck and a bit of a nudge sideways. I looked down to the cockpit and saw Pescador curled up sleeping, blissfully unaware of the rough seas.

Halfway across the Strait, I called the dockmaster in Bimini to see what the weather there was like. He reported seas weren't very favorable for small craft and asked if I had a slip arranged at my destination. When I told him where we were headed and said that I did have a slip reserved for the night, he suggested that we continue on to our final destination to clear customs.

Just like that, we went from behind schedule to ahead of schedule. After passing Bimini, we headed out onto the Great Bahama Bank, a huge, sandy, shallow part of the ocean west of Andros and south of Grand Bahama. We broke out of the overcast sky and into sunshine thirty minutes later, the rolling waves falling away to nothing soon after we got out onto the vast submerged plain. The water across the bank is always crystal clear and usually very calm.

Because it was out of the currents, the water was warmer and more prone to evaporation. This caused a higher salinity, restricting growth of sea grasses and corals. We now had the sun slightly off the starboard beam, and our shadow, flying across the sandy bottom twenty feet below, was clearly visible off the port bow. Having gained back the time we'd lost, I suggested we anchor up for lunch. Nikki and Charity went below to get it ready as we dropped anchor in ten feet of water, where there was barely a ripple.

Getting underway a short time later, we soon crossed into the TOTO north of Andros via "The Pocket," the deep-water triangular part of the Northwest Channel. The change here was even more dramatic than leaving the Intracoastal. The flats funnel through a deep chasm at the north end in a very narrow canyon that was once an ancient river. It's always a bit disconcerting when looking at it on a chart. Even though there's plenty of depth on either side, the drop-off from twenty feet to over six thousand feet is one of the steepest anywhere in the world.

In less than a minute, the bottom dropped far beyond the range of my sonar. This huge trench between Andros and New Providence is over a mile deep, its waters changing from the crystal clear of the bank, where minute details of the bottom can easily be seen, to the cobalt blue of the deep in just a matter of minutes as we passed the Northwest Channel light.

Just before sunset we arrived in Nassau Harbor, which is actually a channel between New Providence Island and Paradise Island. I'd reserved a slip for the night several days earlier at Hurricane Hole Marina, a small deep-water marina on the south side of Paradise Island. I called the dockmaster at Hurricane Hole on the VHF while Doc ran up the yellow quarantine flag and informed him of our arrival. He directed me to the fuel dock and told me once I was fueled to go to slip number forty-eight, between the office and Green Parrot, on the west side of the marina. As we idled into the deep little bay, I was glad I'd reserved a slip—they were all full but one. After fueling, I backed into the slip where the dockmaster stood ready and helped tie the *Revenge* off.

After introducing himself and noticing Pescador sitting in the corner of the cockpit, he said, "You are aware that your dog cannot leave di marina."

"He's no problem. He won't even leave the boat, except to pee on that tree," I said, pointing to a tree just across the dock area. Pescador immediately vaulted the gunwale and trotted to the tree, where he hiked his leg before returning to his spot by the transom door and sitting down again.

I went with the dockmaster to the customs office to register the *Revenge* while Rusty and Bourke hosed down the boat. After I'd completed the paperwork and getting my cruising and fishing permits, the customs officer accompanied me back to the boat, where he boarded and performed a cursory inspection before stamping all our passports. Doc lowered the quarantine flag after the customs officer left and we decided to visit the Green Parrot to eat. It was literally just a few steps from the dock.

Our waitress was able to get us two adjoining tables on the deck that were large enough to seat all nine of us and we sat down to watch the sun disappear to the west. I sat where I could see both the *Revenge* and the door from the bar. Our drinks came very quickly and our food wasn't far behind.

I'd already paid for two rooms at the Best Western for Deuce, Julie, Doc, and Nikki, just a few minutes' walk from the marina. I'd give up my stateroom on the boat for Charity and Tony, Rusty, and Bourke could take the crew cabin while I slept in the salon.

When Charity started to object, I said flatly, "I never sleep in the stateroom when I'm in a strange port, anyway. Pescador sleeps by the door and I always sleep on the sofa right next to it."

# CHAPTER TWENTY

Alfredo Maggio met with his son, Nicholas, and the four people his son had chosen to handle a task for him at his favorite Cuban restaurant in south Miami Beach. Although Alfredo's firm was considered one of the most reputable law firms in Miami, occasionally an opportunity presented itself that might run afoul of the law, which involved hiring people from outside the firm. People with questionable ethics and morals. The four people sitting with Alfredo and his son were these kind of people.

They were seated at a large booth in the back of the restaurant. He always insisted on meeting these kind of people in a place like this. How they reacted to dining in a five-star restaurant told him a great deal about whether they would be up to certain tasks.

Their table was the only one occupied in the back part of the restaurant. Alfredo sat at the head of the table and

Nicholas at the other end, the two couples sat across from one another, the men at Alfredo's end.

"You're certain none of the principals has seen any of you?" Alfredo asked both men.

"Not a chance, Mister Maggio," replied Jose Reynolds, a first-generation Marielista whose mother had once been a Havana prostitute and now ran a high-end escort service. She brought her young son to Miami during the Mariel Boatlift in late 1980.

"We talked only to acquaintances of some of the friends of the principals for a week," added the other man, Gary Lopez. "Our probing probably wasn't even noticed by them. We were just two tourist couples looking for a good time."

Alfredo had utilized the services of both men on several occasions. Reynolds looked more like a surfer than a private investigator. Tall and lanky, with fair hair and blue eyes that belied his Cuban ancestry. He had no qualms about doing things outside the law—if the money was right.

Lopez was Reynolds's business partner. He appeared to be just another of the hundreds of successful young Cuban businessmen in the area. The two men's success in their business, both legal and illegal, was due in large part to their ability not to look like investigators or criminals.

The two women, a brunette and redhead, both of Hispanic descent, were strikingly beautiful; each looked perfectly natural on the arm of the two men. They both worked for Reynolds's mother as high-class call girls. They would look and act correctly whether at a ballet, an opera, or a dinner party—or in bed. Such were the requirements of their employer.

Consuelo Reynolds had married an American shortly after arriving in the States, twenty-six years earlier, and her new husband had adopted her two-year-old bastard son. She went back to her old line of work after her elderly husband died suddenly of a heart attack in 1982. No longer a streetwalker, she'd used her late husband's insurance money to become a very successful madam, picking out the most beautiful and talented of Miami's many ladies of the evening. Her clientele demanded a certain level of confidentiality, which Madam Reynolds not only delivered but exceeded. Her business grew, her client list becoming a veritable "who's who" among entertainment, government, and aristocracy.

"I have some limited background information on some of the people I sent you down to investigate," Alfredo said. "What more do you have to add?"

The redhead opened a briefcase and passed two files to both Alfredo and Nicholas. The two men opened them and flipped through the pages. "The owner of the establishment is a lifelong resident of the Keys," she said. "Fourth generation, in fact. As you already know, he served in the Marines for four years, but that was over twenty-five years ago. He's also a licensed salvor and has recovered the contents of a number of vessels over the years. Aside from that, he appears to be a run-of-the-mill bar owner. His only child is currently in the Coast Guard Reserves. Neither of them have anything that stands out, or that could be used as leverage to persuade the others. The daughter's husband has only been around the Keys for about a year and doesn't seem to have a job of any kind. They live on a sailboat behind the restaurant and bar that her father owns. He doesn't seem to be hurting for money; his share from their last find seems to be supporting them."

Reynolds took two more files from the briefcase, handing one to each of the lawyers. "Robert Talbot came to Key West five years ago, took a job as a deckhand and later First Mate on a shrimp boat. He and his wife, Nicole, met when they were stationed together, he in the Navy and she in the Marine Corps. She works as a waitress at a number of places in Key West and he works as a mechanic at a motorcycle dealer in Key West. Her father is a recently retired Judge from up near Orlando. The shrimp boat was put up for sale last winter and he's basically been unemployed, except for working part-time at the motorcycle dealer and an occasional charter with a number of fishing boats. Nothing we learned suggests he's involved in any kind of criminal activity at all."

The brunette spoke for the first time. "Actually, aside from frequenting the bar owned by Thurman, there's no connection between any of them. All of them being former military is coincidental, with the exception of the bar owner and the boat owner. Those people seem to naturally drift together. The black man called Tony and the woman called Chyrel are unknown to anyone in the area. While talking to one man, a long-haired boat bum, I sensed he was being kind of secretive about the owner of the boat, McDermitt. Those islanders don't gossip much about each other."

Reynolds took the final two files from the briefcase and handed them to the father and son. "McDermitt was stationed with the bar owner in the early eighties.

They were close friends and when he retired, he went to the Keys, where his friend lived, to build a charter business. That was over six years ago. Aside from his owning the boat and a small island north of Big Pine Key, we learned very little. People seemed more secretive about him than any of the others. He stays to himself mostly and is thought to be honest, trustworthy, and an exceptional fisherman. In all, these people seem to be exactly as they appear. A group of people struggling to make an honest living in the islands who stumbled on information about a treasure."

"What can you add, Nicholas?" Alfredo finally asked, lifting his gaze to his only son.

Nicholas looked up at his father, then at the two men, when his attention was diverted to the opening of the restaurant. Valentin Madic had just entered with his two bodyguards. On their way to their table, Madic looked through the glass partition. His father, Reynolds, and the woman sitting next to him followed Nick's gaze. Madic looked from one person to another, finally nodding a salute to the elder Maggio at the head of the table.

"Keep your eye out for that man while you're over there," Nicholas said after Madic went on past the partition. "Let me know immediately if you see him."

"Who is he?" Reynolds asked.

"Someone you don't want to cross," Alfredo said.

"You're wrong about McDermitt," the younger Maggio said to both Lopez and Reynolds. "He's anything but an honest fisherman. He's a very dangerous man who has killed a lot of people all over the world. Sometimes just for sport."

"And just how do you know this, Mister Maggio?" asked Reynolds, skeptically.

"I'm married to his daughter," Nick replied.

# CHAPTER TWENTY-ONE

While waiting for our food, I called Kim to let her know we'd arrived in Nassau safely. After a moment of talking, I noticed one of the couples at the next table seemed to be paying a little too much attention to my conversation. I really don't like nosy people, so I cut the call short, promising to call her from Elbow Cay tomorrow about noon.

When we'd finished our meal, we said goodnight and split up, agreeing to a 0700 departure time. I took a mug of coffee up to the bridge and sat watching the comings and goings in the marina. I would have liked a beer, but whenever I was in a place I wasn't real familiar with, I steered clear. I watched as the two couples that had sat at the table next to us came out of the restaurant. As they began walking around the marina to the far side, following the same path Deuce and the others had taken minutes before, it struck me as odd when they seemed intentionally not to look my way. The *Revenge* is a head turner in any marina and people have nearly walked off the docks looking at her graceful lines. Something about these four just didn't sit right with me.

I called Deuce and he answered on the first ring. "How do you make them?" he asked, as if he were sitting right next to me and making the same observations. He was a lot like his dad in that respect. Russ and I could carry on whole conversations with just a glance and a nod.

"The redhead and the guy she's hanging all over were eavesdropping when I called Kim. Neither man looks armed. They're taking the same path out of the marina you did, about fifty meters behind you."

"We've doubled back from the far side of the office. Should pass them any second." Then he started talking to me as though to an employee. "I'll be there in a minute, Captain. I don't know why you can't seem to handle it yourself."

Knowing they were walking past the two couples, I played with him a little. "Swabbing the deck is for squids, I have your swab and bucket ready."

A moment later he said, "They seemed surprised and tried real hard to not look at us."

"They did the same thing leaving the Parrot," I said. "Something's not right with them."

A few minutes later, everyone was back aboard the *Revenge*, gathered in the salon. Comparing mental notes from the restaurant, it seemed the two couples came up on Doc and Tony's radar also. This didn't surprise me: both men had served in Iraq and Afghanistan, where every person on the street is a potential combatant.

"It wasn't so much how they acted or what they did," Tony said, "more like how they didn't act and what they didn't do."

As the two couples approached them, Julie had pretended to take a picture of the marina with her wide-angle digital camera and managed to get all four in the shot.

Deuce was already on the phone, calling Chyrel, as I booted up my laptop. It was a gift from Deuce last year, replacing my old one. Though it looked exactly like the old one, it was packed with high-tech gadgetry. I clicked on the *Soft Jazz* icon on the desktop and a window opened for video conferencing.

"I'm sending you the picture now," Deuce said after putting the data card from Julie's camera into his phone. "Call Jesse's laptop when you find anything."

Chyrel had priority access to the FBI's central computer and its powerful facial recognition software. Even the low-light image would be enough for her to identify the four people if they had any kind of record.

"Where is she?" I asked, meaning Chyrel.

"Her and Charlie just got back from fly fishing. She shouldn't be more than a few minutes." Moments later, the laptop beeped and Deuce sat down, turning it toward him and clicking the incoming call button.

Chyrel's face filled the screen, with a smaller window showing Deuce at the bottom. "That didn't take long," he said.

"I got a hit right away on one person who lives in Miami, so I prompted the software to search the data base starting in Miami and the south Florida area." Chyrel said. "It only had to go as far as Miami-Dade to get the other three." The video screen switched to a display showing four police mug shots. It was the two couples from the restaurant, though the mug shots were far less flattering than they looked in person. The screen changed to a picture of just one of the men, the sandy haired one, with an arrest record below it.

"This is Jose Reynolds," Chyrel said. "American citizen, born in Cuba to a Marielista mother and adopted by her American husband. He's a private investigator, but when he was younger he had a few scrapes with the law. He was a person of interest in a number of disappearances in south Florida, some trafficking charges, but nothing stuck. His mother is Consuelo Reynolds."

"*The* Consuelo Reynolds?" I asked.

"Yeah, more money than God," Chyrel said. "If a judge isn't one of her clients, he's on her payroll. The Teflon Madam, they call her."

The screen switched to the other man's picture and arrest record. "This is Gary Lopez," Chyrel said. "American national, parents both from Cuba. He's Reynolds's business partner, also a private investigator and also with a less-than-stellar record. He did two years upstate for involuntary manslaughter. Pled down from murder two. A few arrests for B and E, drugs, and soliciting."

The screen switched to the two women, side by side. "The redhead is Bianca Garcia. Puerto Rican-born, natural citizen. More than ten arrests in Puerto Rico for prostitution, but only one in the US. Bailed out and fine paid by Consuelo Reynolds. The brunette is Faye Raminez, American national, Cuban parents, both dead under suspicious circumstances. Several arrests for prostitution in Las Vegas. Arrested for killing a john in Miami two months ago. She claimed self-defense at the arraignment through a court-appointed attorney and was held over for trial. Alfredo Maggio, senior partner of the law firm representing Consuelo Reynolds, took the case pro bono the next day, right after she was visited in jail by Consuelo Reynolds. Charges were dropped by the DA a day later."

"I swear I've seen them before," I said. "In the Keys."

"So, we're being followed across the ocean by an escort service?" Tony asked. "I don't get the connection."

"Could just be two rich guys taking a couple hookers to the islands," Charity said.

Deuce and I looked at one another. I could tell he thought them just as hokey as I did. Reading body language when everyone around you is a possible enemy is something that's hard to learn, but necessary in some of the places we'd both been.

Deuce shook his head. "I don't think so."

"Me either," I said. "What do we do?"

"If we leave now, we can be on Elbow Cay before dawn," Bourke offered.

"Run from two hookers and a couple of private dicks?" Doc asked.

"'Live to fight another day,'" Bourke said. "Oliver Goldsmith."

"'But he who is battle slain, can never rise to fight again,'" Doc replied, finishing the quote. "What? You think they want to kill us?"

"It'll be hard to follow us in the dark, whether by boat or plane," Bourke said. "If we see them on Elbow Cay, we'll know they're following us."

I glanced at Deuce, who nodded almost imperceptibly. "Cast off, Rusty. Me and you have first watch."

It only took five minutes for Rusty and Bourke to cast off the lines. While I warmed up the engines, Doc kept an eye all around the approaches to the marina with a night vision monocular. I plotted a course using the GPS coordinates the owner of the resort on Elbow Cay had given Doc, with a waypoint at Tilloo Cut. The GPS plotter automatically plotted a course through the cut and around the shallows of Tahiti Beach to the channel that ended at the resort's dock. *Man, I love technology*, I thought. *If only the damned thing could tell me if and why we were being followed.*

The why was obvious. We'd done our best to keep the treasure a secret, but somehow it got out. That, or I'm just paranoid. I had my doubts about them not being able to follow us by air. We'd be one of a very small number of boats on the water at night and these waters are noted for phytoplankton that glow when disturbed. We'd leave a trail in the water a blind man could follow. I planned to ruin any chance of them following us on the water by making a high-speed crossing of the Northeast Providence Channel.

While Doc kept watch, I went below to my stateroom and punched in the code to raise the bunk. Among the many reel cases, I grabbed one marked "Penn heavy-duty Squall Level reel" and went back through the salon and up to the bridge. Rusty and Bourke stepped into the cockpit and I put the engines in gear, switching on the powerful spotlights.

Leaving the marina, I turned west into Nassau Harbor and brought the big boat up onto plane immediately. After we cleared the two bridges, I pushed the throttle further, increasing our speed to thirty-five knots. Moments later, we left the channel and I turned north-northeast for Elbow Cay. I opened the reel case and took out two pairs of Pulsar Edge night vision goggles and fitted one set over my head while handing the other one to Rusty.

"You remember the last time we took off in a boat wearing these things?" Rusty asked. It'd been just over six years ago, with a hurricane bearing down on us as we were holed up in Tarpon Bay, way up in the Everglades. Kidnappers, plotting to take a woman we were anchored up with and another boater's wife and daughters, had tried to sneak up on our anchorage. They were unsuccessful.

"I remember we came out on top," I replied vaguely.

"Wonder what ever happened to that guy," Rusty wondered.

*He died*, I thought. *And it wasn't pretty.* I'd never told Rusty, or anyone else for that matter, what had happened.

"No idea," I lied. "Some say he got eaten by gators."

"Yeah, right," Rusty said.

I switched on the intercom and grabbed the mic. "Y'all might as well try to get whatever rest you can. It's a hundred miles of deep, open ocean to Tilloo Cut and we'll be there in less than three hours. No guarantee of a smooth ride."

Once clear of the outer channel markers, I keyed the mic again. "Going dark on the bridge," I said as I switched off the spots and all the lights on the bridge. Pulling the electronics down in front of my eyes, I turned it on and the world came into focus in a grayish green light. The red and green markers just below the pulpit cast a bright green semicircle of light on the water for a good fifty yards, and the goggles easily picked up the horizon and stars, along with the lights from other boats far in the distance. Someone smoking a cigarette a mile away would be bathed in a bright green light.

I found the new toggle switch Bourke had installed for the infrared spotlight, which he'd mounted inconspicuously in the leading edge of the pulpit trim, and switched it on. Having looked at the tiny light up close, I really didn't expect much, though Bourke swore it would make a huge difference. He was right. The tiny IR spotlight lit up the water directly ahead for almost half a mile.

I pushed the throttles to their stops and the big boat surged forward. At least the seas were calm, just low wind-driven rollers no more than two feet high and spaced so far apart they had very little effect on the boat.

Minutes later, Deuce, Tony, and Doc joined us on the bridge with mugs and thermoses, filling the mugs by feel and handing them to me and Rusty. "Where's your monocular?" Deuce asked.

I handed it to him and he switched it on while hanging on the rail and looking aft. Tony held what looked like his cell phone in his hand. He waved it around the bridge and as he started passing it over the console I realized what he was doing.

Rusty started to say something, but I interrupted him. "You're not gonna get a signal out here, Tony."

Tony held up one finger then pointed below. A few minutes later he finished and put his phone away. "We found a bug in the salon," he said. "Bridge is all clear."

"What kind of bug?" I asked.

"Not a sophisticated one," Deuce replied as Bourke joined us. "It's a voice-activated recorder. Only records

216

when someone is talking and then shuts off. It's capable of sending a microburst of data twice a day, purging what was previously recorded."

"The rest of the cabin's clear," Bourke said. "Just the one in the salon."

"Sounds pretty damned sophisticated to me," Rusty said. "How'd it get there? You always lock up the salon and set the alarm, right?"

I thought back over the last couple of weeks. "There's no chance anyone planted a bug recently."

Deuce leaned on the rail, still looking through the monocular toward the channel. "Doesn't have to have been recently. Recording only when there's sound, then sending it in a short burst, the battery could last for months, especially if it were quiet most of the time."

I thought back further. The *Revenge* had been docked at the island for most of the last couple months. I hadn't taken out a charter since midsummer. To get back and forth to Big Pine or Marathon, I usually used my skiff. If I needed to haul anything heavy or go offshore, I'd been using the *Cazador* a lot. It's a big, diesel powered, thirty-two-foot center console built by Winter Boats up in Raleigh.

"Remember the first night we figured out what was written on the coconut?" Tony said. "Me, you, and Doc sat in the salon and talked about it."

"That doesn't make sense," Doc said. "They would have had to bug the boat before we even knew about the treasure. That means the bug was for something else altogether. Have you pissed anyone off recently, Jesse?"

I laughed and replied, "You better get a notepad." Then it occurred to me. The only time strangers had been aboard my boat was months before, when the President came down for a little fishing.

"Any chance the Secret Service planted it?" I asked. "That's the last time any strangers were aboard."

I knew that Deuce had a great deal of respect for the other agencies he had to work with sometimes. I could see him mulling it over in the green glow of the optics. "I don't think so," he said. "The Director was in the cabin the whole time."

I'd never met either the President or Secretary Chertoff before that day and only knew them by reputation. Both struck me as honorable and besides, it'd be beneath their respective offices to bug a civilian. I did know Colonel Stockwell and had a great deal of respect for him. I thought about that whole day, who all was on the boat and who might have had unaccompanied access to the salon. Deuce was right, except for one short moment.

"Before they went into the cabin," I said. "The other two agents under Bender went in to clear the cabin ahead of the President."

"You're right," Doc said. "But why would the Secret Service want to bug the boat?"

"I don't think it was them," Bourke said. "They have access to a lot more sophisticated equipment and would have planted more than one."

"Is the bug still active?" I asked.

"No," Bourke replied. "I deactivated it. Once it was shut down, I checked the battery level. It was down to just five percent. Whoever planted it will assume the battery died."

"You know I don't believe in coincidences, Deuce," I said.

"Nor do I," he replied, still looking aft through the monocular. "Can you see that go-fast boat on your radar?"

I'd been busy watching the water ahead of us. The radar was on, but with the backlight turned off. I leaned forward and looked at it through the night vision goggles. There was a boat just coming out of the channel and another boat two miles ahead of us.

"Got him," I said. "You think that's them?"

Deuce worked the zoom function on the monocular, steading himself with the rail. The radar showed the boat was about a mile back and gaining speed.

"Can't really tell for sure," he said. "I count at least two people aboard."

"Why don't we find out?" I said, looking closer at the radar screen. "Keep an eye on him. There's another boat two miles ahead of us, going about half our speed."

I could clearly see the phytoplankton in the boat's wake and slowly steered over into it. "I'm going to overtake the boat ahead. We're in his wake now. We'll be on top of it before the go-fast is within half a mile. At that point, we'll go completely dark and turn hard to the east, then come around behind him. If it works and it is them following us, they'll think the boat ahead is us."

"Good thinking," Deuce said.

"Rusty, range me on both boats," I said while grabbing the mic and switching to boat-wide intercom. "Y'all hang on down there. In a few minutes, I'm going to kill all the lights and make a hard right turn."

Julie's voice came back over the intercom, "We're ready."

"Fifteen hundred meters ahead, closing fast," Rusty said. "Twenty-five hundred meters behind, closing faster."

"He's right in our wake," Deuce said. "Where you joined the wake of the slower boat, his is fainter. The go-fast might not even see it."

"That's what I'm counting on," I said. I could clearly see the boat ahead with the aid of the IR spot. It was an older sports fisherman, looked like about a thirty-five footer. Close enough in size and shape to the *Revenge* that it might fool them.

"Five hundred meters ahead," Rusty said, staring intently at the radar screen. "A thousand meters behind."

It was going to be close. I stood up, straining to see better and put my finger on the master light switch.

"Deuce, you see a radar dome?" I asked.

"No dome," he replied. "Not even an arch. It's them, though."

"Two hundred meters," Rusty shouted. "She's barely making fifteen knots. One hundred meters ahead and five hundred astern. Fifty meters!"

"Going dark!" I shouted and flipped the master switch while spinning the wheel to starboard.

At forty-five knots, the *Revenge* responded immediately. We angled quickly away from the other fishing boat. I could see the two men on its bridge very clearly, backlit by their forward spotlights. Neither man saw or heard us as we turned away to the east, accelerating in a straight line once I spun the wheel back.

"He's slowing," Deuce said.

I continued an easterly course for half a minute, then grabbed the mic again and shouted, "Another hard right!"

"He's gone dark and dropped to the same speed as the other boat," Deuce said. "It worked. Looks like a thirty-eight foot Top Gun."

I dropped the throttles back to cruising speed and began a sweeping turn that would bring us up behind the Cigarette. After a couple of minutes, we were about a half mile behind them and I brought the throttles back to match the speed of the other two boats.

I keyed the mic again and said, "Come on up to the bridge."

There was no moon and high, wispy clouds blocked most of the stars. I reached up and switched on the dim red light mounted to the overhead. There was little chance we would be seen at this distance and our followers were likely all looking straight ahead at the lights of the other boat. A moment later, Julie and Charity had joined us.

"What do you want to do, Deuce?" I said.

"As I see it, we have two options," he began. "We could easily hightail it east or west, put some distance between us and then continue on to Elbow Cay, staying blacked out until we're well ahead of them. If they realize that other boat isn't the *Revenge*, they'll come on fast and might find us. The other option is to ask them why the hell they're following us."

"Yeah," Bourke growled. "I'd kinda like to know that, too."

I looked up at Deuce and he nodded. "Take the helm, Rusty," I said as I got up and went down the ladder. I switched the night vision back on and went quickly through the salon and down into the forward stateroom, where I knelt and punched in the code on the keypad.

Pulling the lever next to it, the bunk slowly raised up on hydraulic pistons. I grabbed two reel cases, both marked "Penn Senator," and set them on the deck. I also grabbed a small tackle box marked "Dry Flies" and lowered the bunk back down. Back out in the cockpit, I handed the three boxes up to Deuce then climbed up to the bridge.

Deuce opened the box of flies first and took out six earwigs, very compact communication devices that are inserted in the ear and pick up sound from the jaw bone. I passed them out to Julie, Bourke, Tony, Rusty, and Deuce, keeping one for myself. I'd had the opportunity to watch Deuce in action a few times and we'd practiced what we were about to do a number of times with the 42x.

"Bourke, you'll board with Tony and Julie," Deuce said. "I'll back you up from the foredeck. Arm yourselves."

Each of the two larger reel cases held two Sig Sauer 9mm semiautos, with a holster and two magazines for each. All were fully loaded with twenty rounds of hollow points. "The pulpit will be three feet above the engine cover on the Cigarette. We've trained to do this exact thing several times from this very boat onto the exact same kind of boat—piece of cake."

He looked ahead through the monocular and said, "They're all facing forward and haven't moved. Odds are they won't even hear us over their own engines. Move fast and shut down their engines quickly."

Deuce looked at me and said, "At the instant Bourke steps off, hit the spots and go to neutral. Watch me for signals."

"Roger that," I said as I nudged the throttle up a hair. The four of them climbed down from the bridge as we slowly crept up on the other boat from behind.

We had trained for this quite a few times before Deuce and Julie's wedding. Bourke and Julie had both been well trained in boarding tactics, along with Ralph Goodman, another member of Deuce's team, through the Coast Guard's Maritime Enforcement School. We'd used the *Revenge* and a Cigarette 42x that we'd confiscated almost a year ago and found using the pulpit to be far better than trying to come alongside. In a beam boarding, the Cigarette could simply turn away and leave us in its wake. The boat ahead of us was also a Cigarette and nearly identical to the one we'd trained on. This technique relied completely on surprise, as there was no way the *Revenge* could chase down the go-fast boat.

Rusty and I put the earwigs in and switched them on, and then we checked com between all six of us. "Going dark," I whispered as I switched on the goggles, and Rusty reached up and turned off the red overhead light. Even if they looked aft it was doubtful they'd see us in the almost complete darkness, especially after they'd been straining to see the lights of the boat they were following.

The problem was, the boarding team couldn't see much better and we only had the two sets of Pulsars, a fact that I promised myself then and there to rectify. Bourke was in the front of the pulpit and had already removed the forward bar. They knew to watch out for the windlass and chain and the three of them all stood in the pulpit, each with a hand on the others' shoulders. All of them were looking down at the water about ten feet in front of the boat, keeping their eyes off the sports fisherman's lights ahead of the Cigarette to preserve their night vision. They were relying on me to bring the target boat into their line of sight and then Deuce would direct me with hand signals, as we'd practiced dozens of times.

Rusty kept watching the radar and quietly counted off the distance until the stern of the Cigarette disappeared from my view under our bow. We knew from experience that we were only fifteen feet behind the other boat now and both Rusty and I kept our eyes on Deuce. The last ten feet were the hardest, as we would also be fighting the backwash from the other boat's propellers and riding up on the bulge of water abaft their transom. I had one hand on the throttles and Rusty had his finger on the spotlight switch.

Deuce had his right hand up, opening and closing his fist and bringing us closer to the slow-moving Cigarette. The two women were behind the men, one standing between the two front seats, the other leaning over the man's shoulder at the helm, talking to him. Behind them was about three feet of open deck and four seats facing forward. The boat had the typically long engine cover, as Cigarettes are narrow boats, with the two engines mounted in a staggered fashion instead of side by side in the narrow engine compartment.

"Go!" Deuce whispered as he dropped his fist out to the right.

Rusty hit the spotlight switch and I dropped the throttles to neutral at the same time that the boarding party surged forward as one, jumping down three feet to the engine cover below and scrambling across it.

Bourke and Tony each grabbed one of the women by the hair, pulling them backward into the seats just as the powerful spotlights lit up the cockpit.

One of the women, the redhead, tried to scramble to her feet, but Julie gave her a shove, forcing both of them to the far left side of the boat while she vaulted to the right side and drew her Sig. Her cap was pulled low to block the light and as she brought her Sig up, she yelled, "Don't move!"

Tony was less subtle. As the guy in the left seat started to turn, Tony caught him in the temple with a right cross, dropping him in a heap on the deck in front of his seat.

Bourke put his Sig in the driver's face and reached in front of him and shut down both engines before the man could even react to his sudden appearance. He then reached across the man and grabbed his shirt at the shoulder. Yanking him out of his seat and spinning him around, he shoved him to the deck, face down.

Bourke's booming voice came over my earwig, "Target is secure."

I turned on the master light switch and checked the radar. Seeing nothing coming our way, I idled over next to the Cigarette. Doc and Rusty tied us off to the go-fast boat as Tony and Bourke put flex cuffs on our followers and sat them all in the rear seats. I turned a spotlight around and shined it down in the cockpit. I saw that the guy Tony clocked was Jose Reynolds, the son of one of the most successful madams in Florida. He was just coming around and looked very confused, having no idea what had hit him.

Deuce stepped up onto the gunwale, then dropped lightly to the deck of the other boat. At six feet tall and a shade over two hundred pounds, he moved like a man much smaller. Julie stuck her Sig into the holster clipped to the waistband of her shorts and went forward to check the boats instrumentation. Tony and Bourke stood behind the front seats, having holstered their weapons to bind the four.

Deuce stood between his two men with his hands on his hips, looking the captives over. They didn't look very happy. "You said you saw them before, Captain?" he called up to me.

Following his lead and not using names, I replied, "That's right. On Big Pine a couple days ago."

"Why are you following us?" he growled at Lopez.

Lopez looked up at him, his eyes dark and menacing. "No hablo inglés."

"Por qué estabas siguiéndonos, idiota?"

The man's eyes flashed with hatred and he tugged at the flex cuffs binding his wrists. It was useless, of course.

Deuce looked over at Reynolds and said, "You two are way out of your league here, Reynolds."

"How the hell do you know my—"

"Shut up, fool!" Lopez hissed.

"If I don't get an answer pretty quick, one of you is going to become shark food," Deuce said.

I kept checking the radar to make sure the other boat continued on. They were now two miles ahead and still moving north-northeast.

Deuce looked up and saw me checking. "How far out of Nassau Harbor are we?"

"Just eight miles," I replied.

"How far away is that other boat? Think they'll hear a gunshot?"

I looked down at the radar again. "Two and a half miles and moving away. Pescador would be quieter. Messier, but quieter."

At the mention of his name, the big, shaggy dog stood up with his front paws on the gunwale, snarling at the four people in the back of the Cigarette.

"Go aboard, Pescador," I said. He leaped over the gunwale, landing softly at Deuce's side, and turned slowly toward the four people. The women were now visibly frightened as the dog snarled, showing his inch-long yellow fangs, saliva dripping from his lower lips and the hair all the way down his neck and back standing on end. A low rumble emanated from deep inside his wide chest. Sometimes, even I couldn't tell if his displays were just for show or if he was about to rip into flesh.

Lopez must have had a bad experience with a dog at some time in his life, because his eyes no longer showed hatred but were now filled with panic.

"Señor Lopez, les presento a Pescador," Deuce said, introducing the private dick. "Pescador, say hi to Señor Lopez."

Pescador moved slowly toward Lopez. Sitting in the low seat, he was at eye level with the huge, shaggy head coming right up to his. The low rumble emanated from Pescador's chest again as he bared his teeth, yellow eyes locked on Lopez's nearly hysterical eyes. Pescador's favorite food is fish and he always has really terrible fish breath.

"Call it off, man!" he shouted. "We'll talk! We'll talk!"

"Pescador!" I shouted, actually afraid he was about to attack. A year ago, a man had stabbed me with a switchblade knife and Pescador went straight for the man's throat, tearing it open and sending blood everywhere. He didn't die quickly. Pescador quickly lunged up and over Lopez's head, landing on the engine cover before jumping back across to the *Revenge*.

Deuce knelt in front of Lopez. "I'm only going to ask one more time. If I don't get what I think is an honest answer, I'll have the Captain's dog eat your nuts right in front of you. Now, who sent you?"

Lopez swallowed hard, glancing across at Pescador then back up at Deuce, all the fire gone from his eyes. "We were told to find out as much about who all of you are and to follow you all the way to Elbow Cay if we had to."

"Still doesn't answer my question," Deuce said. "Shall I get the dog?"

"Alfredo Maggio hired us," Reynolds blurted out.

# CHAPTER TWENTY-TWO

I'm still at a loss to understand why you brought them in, in the first place?" Owen Bradbury asked.

Once again, he was at Chase Conner's office in south Miami. The office was actually located in Cutler Ridge, but to Owen everything south of Palm Beach was Miami and lately, you couldn't really tell when you'd left one city and entered another, beginning well north of Palm Beach and going all the way down to Homestead.

"They have the money and the muscle, Owen. We don't. We've been all around this. The knowledge is key and that's what we have."

"Play it back," Bradbury said.

Conner brought the audio file back up on his laptop and clicked play for the third time. The two men leaned in closer to the laptop's speakers. The first voice was tinny and slightly distorted, as if the recording had picked up someone on the boat talking on a speakerphone with someone else.

"*I got a hit right away on one person who lives in Miami, so I prompted the software to search the data base starting in Miami and the south Florida area. It only had to go as far as Miami-Dade to get the other three.*"

Conner stopped the recording. "I think they're talking to this Chyrel woman over a computer video feed. Listen to this next part—it sounds as though she's showing them a computer file, identifying people that are following McDermitt and his party."

He clicked the play button again and heard clinking noises, as if someone were pouring a drink, then the woman's voice continued, "*This is Jose Reynolds. American citizen, born in Cuba to a Marielista mother and adopted by her American husband. He's a private investigator, but when he was younger he had a few scrapes with the law. He was a person of interest in a number of disappearances in south Florida, some trafficking charges, but nothing stuck. His mother is Consuelo Reynolds.*"

Bradbury stopped the recording this time. "How did Conseulo Reynolds become a part of this?" he asked. Without waiting for a response he stood quickly, turning and lifting both arms out to the side in dismay. He suddenly turned again and put his palms on Conner's desk. "She has Senators and Congressmen as clients, for God's sake. Not to mention a lot of very large men of unsavory character for employees."

Conner leaned back in his chair, surprised at Bradbury's uncharacteristic display. "That does present a problem—it looks like her people have figured out what McDermitt's after, too." Conner clicked play again.

The next voice was familiar to both of them. They'd met the man in person. "*The Consuelo Reynolds?*" McDermitt asked.

"*Yeah, more money than God,*" the tinny-sounding woman's voice replied. "*If a Judge isn't one of her clients, he's on her payroll. The Teflon Madam, they call her.*"

There was a few seconds of silence, then the Chyrel woman said, "*This is Gary Lopez. American national, parents both from Cuba. He's Reynolds's business partner, also a private investigator and also with a less-than-stellar record. He did two years upstate for involuntary manslaughter. Pled down from murder two. A few arrests for B and E, drugs, and soliciting.*"

Bradbury stopped his pacing, leaned over, and clicked the pause button. "Murder? Breaking and entering?"

"Madic's people have a worse reputation, Owen. That's the kind of people we have to have to get this done." He sat back in his chair, clasped his hands behind his head, and continued. "Look, what's the worst that can happen? The two factions collide with McDermitt in the middle? Madic's going to come out on top of that, I promise. And we get our share. The best thing that could happen? They all kill each other and we hire someone else to go get the treasure. Or just do it ourselves."

"What about the two women with this new group? I watch those forensic shows. Bad women are far more dangerous than bad men."

Conner leaned forward and clicked the play button again. Once more the woman was doing all the talking. It puzzled both Conner and Bradbury, but both agreed that she seemed to be the one in charge of things. "*The redhead is Bianca Garcia. Puerto Rican-born, natural citi-*

zen. *More than ten arrests in Puerto Rico for prostitution, but only one in the US. Bailed out and fine paid by Consuelo Reynolds. The brunette is Faye Raminez, American national, Cuban parents, both dead under suspicious circumstances. Several arrests for prostitution in Las Vegas. Arrested for killing a john in Miami two months ago. She claimed self-defense at the arraignment through a court-appointed attorney and was held over for trial. Alfredo Maggio, senior partner of the law firm representing Consuelo Reynolds, took the case pro bono the next day, right after she was visited in jail by Consuelo Reynolds. Charges were dropped by the DA a day later."* Bradbury stopped the recording this time, sitting back down and looking at Conner with his face close to the desk lamp. "A murderer? Maybe she killed her parents, too? That's bad enough. What's worse is that I don't see how McDermitt and his people manage to get this kind of information so fast."

"They probably have a computer hacker working for them," Conner replied, sitting forward with his arms crossed on the edge of the desk. "Remember, they have quite a bit of money now."

Conner clicked play again. McDermitt's voice came over the speakers next, discussing the four people they'd just learned about. The two people he was talking with, Conner and Bradbury both agreed, sounded like the two that were on the boat with him in one of the earlier recordings.

*"I swear I've seen them before. In the Keys."* McDermitt said.

*"So, we're being followed across the ocean by an escort service?"* the unidentified black man responded. *"I don't get the connection."*

"*Could just be two rich guys taking a couple hookers to the islands,*" a new woman's voice said.

"*I don't think so,*" another man's authoritative voice said after a short pause. Both men surmised it sounded like the quiet man with the crew cut they'd met on the boat with McDermitt that day.

"*Me either. What do we do?*" McDermitt asked.

Another man's voice, one that neither Conner nor Bradbury had ever heard, spoke next. His voice was deep and booming. Both men thought that he must be a large man, based solely on the tenor of his voice.

"*If we leave now, we can be on Elbow Cay before dawn,*" he said in a quiet, even tone.

"*Run from two hookers and a couple of private dicks?*"

Conner stopped the recording. "That guy there," Conner said. "I'm certain he's the one they call 'Doc.' Apparently, from the other recordings, he's the one who found the first clue about the treasure and brought in McDermitt and the others."

Conner clicked play again and the big man with the booming voice quoted one of Bradbury's favorite playwrights, Oliver Goldsmith, and the man named Doc finished the prose.

"*'Live to fight another day.'*"

"*'But he who is battle slain, can never rise to fight again.' What? You think they want to kill us?*"

Another Goldsmith verse came to Bradbury's mind just then. Ill fares the land, to hastening ills a prey. Where wealth accumulates and men decay. *They both should have read more Goldsmith,* Bradbury thought. *Maybe I should, too.*

"*It'll be hard to follow us in the dark, whether by boat or plane. If we see them on Elbow Cay, we'll know they're following us,*" the big voice said.

There was a few seconds of silence, then McDermitt said, "*Cast off, Rusty. Me and you have first watch.*"

There were a lot of rustling noises, then what sounded like a door closing. After that, nothing but silence for thirty seconds and the recording ended.

"Do you think we should—"

"Tell Madic there's more of them on the boat than we originally thought?" Conner interrupted, sitting back in his chair again. "No. I think we should just let this play out. In hindsight, we should have planted more than just one listening device. They seem to spend more time outside the cabin than inside."

Bradbury leaned back in his chair, deep in thought. He wasn't a criminal and couldn't think like a criminal. But how this would play out looked obvious. Two different factions, both with deep pockets, plenty of manpower, and connections to the criminal world, seemed to be converging on McDermitt and his people. And it was he and Conner that had pointed them out.

# CHAPTER TWENTY-THREE

Tony and Julie remained on the Cigarette, while the rest of us went into the salon to talk about what to do next. The four captives didn't know anything about the bug—at least they said they didn't.

"I still want to know how this Maggio guy was able to get a bug on my boat," I told Deuce.

"We might never find out," Deuce replied. "The two things have to be connected, though. Those four are just subcontractors. It was most likely another sub that managed to get aboard undetected."

Bourke cleared his throat. "The question we need an answer to right now is, what do we do with those four?"

"You're right," I said. "We're sitting out here in the open, tied off to a boat that for all we know could be stolen, with four captives aboard."

Deuce thought for a moment, then said, "We can't just release them. Their boss will only send more and probably better."

"I don't like the other option," Tony said.

"Don't worry, Tony," Deuce replied, clapping him on the shoulder as he made his way past him to the coffee-maker. "We're not going to kill them, either."

"All that's left is to sit on them," Bourke said. "That could be dangerous. If we were in the Keys, sure. But we're in a different country here."

"There's a tiny sandbar with a few trees, twelve miles southeast of here," I said. "It's a mile off of Rose Island. Completely uninhabited."

"We could be days on Elbow Cay doing the search." Deuce said. "Maybe a week. I get what you mean, but that'd be worse than putting a bullet in their heads and dumping them here. Do you know of a deserted island closer to Elbow Cay, where we can run food and water out to them?"

I turned to Rusty. He'd been running back and forth to these islands since he was a kid. Rusty leaned back on the couch, clutching his hands over his huge girth, with an equally huge grin on his face.

"Yeah," Rusty said, as Julie came in through the hatch. "There's a few, but most are day trips for snorkelers and picnickers. I know the perfect place to stash them, though. It ain't a deserted island. It's on Great Abaco, in fact."

"Hole in the Wall Light?" Julie asked.

Rusty said, "Yep," then stood up and crossed the salon to where Deuce and I stood on the other side of the cab-inet in the galley. "An old guy I know lives at the light-house there. Someone from Marsh Harbour brings him supplies the first of every month. He's basically a squat-ter, but nobody seems to mind. Other than that, hardly anyone ever goes there. It's a hardscrabble three-mile hike to a rock and dirt track that ya gotta have four wheel drive to get over. Then it's another thirteen miles of a bone-rattling two-hour drive to get to the first paved road. Might as well be uninhabited."

"How well do you know this guy?" Deuce asked.

"Well enough. He'll welcome the company. I told you about Charles, didn't I, Jesse?"

"The crazy guy that eats land crabs?"

"He's the one. Spent three weeks stranded on an island as a kid and never been right since. He's somewhere between seventy and a hundred years old. Even he don't know for sure."

"Will they be safe there?" Deuce asked.

"The south end of Abaco is as barren as the moon and north of the light is mile after mile of jungle. Those four don't have to know they're twenty-five miles from a settlement at Sandy Point. Even if they did, they'd turn back before they got five miles. They're city people."

"I didn't even know that light was manned," I said.

Rusty laughed. "I wouldn't exactly call having King Charles living there the same thing as being manned. It's automated, no need for anyone to be there, but he's kinda took to maintaining it some. There's a deep-water sand beach to the east of the hole that's usually protected from wind and wave. We'll have to take 'em overland from there about half mile to the light."

"Will your friend be safe from them?" Deuce asked.

"King Charles?" Rusty asked with a chuckle. "He's crazy but he ain't stupid. Never goes anywhere without his old Navy Colt. He sleeps in the top of the light. Thinks the land crabs' ghosts come after him at night, so he locks himself in there. We can put them in the light keeper's house and leave enough food and water to last a couple of days. Tied or untied, they ain't goin' anywhere."

"Okay, what do we do with the boat?" Bourke asked.

"I can answer that," Julie said. "It's a rental, believe it or not. Rented to the Maggio and Maggio Law Firm, in Miami. I found the rental contract on board. It's not overdue for ten more days and the tanks are nearly full."

"Then we take it with us," Deuce said.

"It's a hundred miles from here to Tilloo Cut," I said. With a stop for maybe an hour along the way, we'd make it there before sunrise.

"Hole in the Wall is halfway there," Rusty said. "And no more'n two miles outta the way."

# CHAPTER TWENTY-FOUR

W ho do we have here?" Madic asked his pilot.

Ivo Novosel rose as his employer boarded the plane. "Mister Madic, I wasn't expecting you for another hour."

Borislav Varga ducked and turned sideways to get his wide shoulders through the door of the plane. He carried two suitcases, which he quickly stowed in a small closet under a counter.

"We're leaving early," Madic said.

"I'll start the preflight, sir," Ivo said, hurrying toward the cockpit. The two women sitting in front of Madic stood and walked over to him.

"Mister Madic," Borislav said, "this is Elana Galic and Sabina Duric. Miss Horvac selected them herself."

"Close the door, Borislav," Madic said as he stared at the two women. Of course, he already knew who the two women were. Tena was very good at selecting the right people for the right job. He was slightly taken aback at their appearance. Both were skilled freelance assassins, Galic from New York and Duric from Chicago. Based on their backgrounds, he'd expected them to look more menacing somehow. The two women standing before him looked more like librarians. Attractive, but not beautiful. Slender, but with a lithesome athletic quality.

Madic stepped forward, extending his hand. "Pleasure to meet you," he said, shaking hands with both women as he appraised each in turn. "Tena told me of your backgrounds, but she didn't say anything about how beautiful you would be."

Neither woman responded to the compliment, just as he expected. The taller of the two, Elana, had long, dark blond hair, streaked by the sun and pulled back in a loose ponytail. Her eyes were a clear, dark blue, giving her more of a California look than that of a woman trained to use a rifle at long range, or to slip stealthily into a private residence and administer a lethal poison to a sleeping target.

Sabina was an inch or two shorter than Elana's five foot four, and both women combined probably didn't equal Borislav's two hundred and forty pounds. Sabina had dark brown hair, emerald-green eyes, and a lighter complexion than Elana. She had a small scar, barely noticeable, just above her right eye and wore her hair short, barely to her collar, with bangs cut straight to hide the scar. Her tiny physique and agile body allowed her to get in close to her unsuspecting target. She preferred quieter weapons, like a knife or garrote.

"Please, sit," Madic said, sweeping his hand to the four seats in back of the main cabin, facing inboard. Beyond that was his private office. Borislav joined Ivo on the flight deck. Though not a flyer, he was very adept with electronics and acted as Ivo's navigator.

The two women sat down in adjacent seats and Madic sat across from them. "Tena tells me that she chose the two of you for both your ability and your adaptability. She has given you both the basic itinerary, yes?"

The two women nodded in unison. "The two of you, along with Ivo and Borislav as backup, will be following a group of people who are looking for something of great value. I plan to have it when it's found. Originally, we'd hoped to locate it and beat them to it, but that would involve more people than I wish. When these people find what they are looking for, we will simply take it from them. If they offer resistance, we will kill them all."

"What do you know about the targets?" Sabina asked without a trace of accent.

"They are four men. Two of them are about my age and single. The other two are about your age and married. All of them were formerly with the U.S. military."

Again, the two women nodded in unison, their expressions neutral. "Borislav and Ivo are known to them," Madic said, "so they will stay in the background until needed. I want the two of you to infiltrate their group. By whatever means necessary."

The two women glanced at one another. Though they'd never met, each knew of the other's ability and background. Both had used sex to get close to their targets in the past. It was just another tool in their belts. One that worked very well.

"You understand what I mean when I say whatever means necessary?"

"Yes," replied Elana, who also had no detectable accent. "We are to seduce two of them. Or all four at once, if need be. It is not a problem."

"No problem at all," echoed Sabina with a seductive smile.

Madic smiled. As an organizer, Tena was far above anyone else he'd ever known. The subtle nuances of their business dealings, fitting the right people to the right task and overseeing everything from a distance, were what made her so valuable to him.

"Mister Madic," came Ivo's voice over the intercom. "We've been cleared for takeoff."

Madic flipped a switch on the bulkhead between the cabin and his private office and asked, "How long before we arrive?"

"Just under an hour, sir."

"You may take off, Ivo," he replied as he switched off the intercom. "Why don't we go into my office for the flight over," he said to the two women with a hungry leer.

# CHAPTER TWENTY-FIVE

The crossing to Great Abaco took less than two hours at twenty-five knots. I ran with the bridge lights doused, relying on the night vision goggles.

Rusty piloted the Cigarette and stayed in my wake a hundred feet back, completely blacked out except his stern light. Wearing the goggles and communicating with the earwigs, he could stay close enough that we only presented a single radar image to anyone watching.

Arriving at Hole in the Wall just before midnight, I dropped down to idle and passed just west of the long, narrow peninsula. Rusty held off until I was anchored in ten feet of water about thirty feet from shore. Anchored fore and aft, Rusty came alongside and tied off. The earlier haze had disappeared and the moon was rising over Hole in the Wall, which has been a landmark for mariners for centuries. This rock ridge, extending several hundred feet south of the eastern shore of Great Abaco, has a hole cut through it by wave action and a natural arch spanning the opening. It's been recorded on maps dating back three hundred years.

With the additional light, the night vision goggles weren't needed. Using just the moonlight and the red overhead light on the bridge, we quickly transferred bottled water and food for four days over to the Cigarette. Rusty, Deuce, and I would take the four captives to the beach while the others waited on the *Revenge*.

Once the supplies were on board, we shoved off and idled over toward the powdery white sand beach. Rusty nudged the Cigarette forward until the bow made contact with the bottom. He revved the engines quickly, lifting the bow and driving us another three feet onto the soft sand. The stern still had five feet to the bottom, the dropoff was so steep.

One by one, we moved our prisoners to the beach. The women were easy. Still bound, Deuce had them sit on the gunwale with their legs hanging overboard. I stood alongside in waist-deep water and carried the redhead over my shoulder first. I set her on her feet in knee-deep water where she could stand up by herself.

The dark-haired woman, Faye Raminez, struggled a little as I lifted her off the gunwale and onto my shoulder. As I trudged toward shore, she twisted her body around and angrily whispered in my other ear, "Who the hell are you people?"

"Shut up and wait here," I said, depositing her on her feet in the water.

The two men were even easier. Deuce just rolled them each off the gunwale, where they struggled to get their feet under them, gasping for air and spitting water. I dragged each by his shirt collar to shore, where Rusty waited.

Though the water was very calm, he insisted on setting an anchor in the soft sand. Pescador jumped down from the bow of the boat and nuzzled my hand for an ear scratch. I looked up to the cliff as the bright beam from the lighthouse now concealed beyond it swept over us, shining its warning out over the water.

I scanned the whole area in the moonlight. Standing on the beach, with the moon a few degrees above the peninsula, Hole in the Wall was clearly visible. The crashing of water surging through the narrow arch was loud, even though it was almost half a mile away. The reflection of the moon visible under its arch.

"It ain't gonna be easy," Rusty said, leading the way up a steep trail from the beach, as Pescador scrambled ahead of him. "Once we're on top, be real careful. The rocks along the trail are jagged."

It took fifteen minutes just to reach the top of the cliff, where Pescador waited. There was a narrow, rock strewn ribbon of a trail leading from there to the lighthouse and the keeper's quarters. The light loomed eighty feet above the surrounding land, its rotating beacon revolving once every minute. Rusty hadn't been exaggerating. There were a few scraggly bushes and patches of grass here and there, but it was mostly rock and looked very much like a different world in the moonlight.

As we approached the lighthouse itself, something got Pescador's attention off to the right side of the trail and he froze, staring that way. "That's far enough," I heard a voice call out, seeming to come from nowhere and everywhere at once.

"King Charles," Rusty called out. "Is that you?"

"Who is dat?" the voice responded.

"Rusty Thurman," he called back. "From Florida."

"How many are ye?"

"Dammit, Charles, I know you can see there's seven of us."

"Come on up di trail, Rusty," Charles finally called out. "Just you, by yaself."

Rusty left us standing there in the open and proceeded up the rocky trail to explain to his friend why he was here in the middle of the night. I'd seen movement about thirty feet to the right, where Pescador was looking, but saw nothing other than rocks and brush. Suddenly, someone stood up directly in front of Rusty, now twenty feet ahead of the captives. He was nowhere near where I thought I'd seen movement. Either King Charles wasn't alone, or he was able to move across these rocks without being seen, like some kind of apparition.

Both Rusty and I were still wearing earwigs. "Rusty," I whispered. "Charles isn't alone. Tango at your four o'clock."

"This isn't Charles," Rusty whispered back. "Fall back."

I sensed more than saw movement ahead and to the left of where Rusty stood, and I slowly reached behind my back and pulled out my Sig, holding it close to my leg. Deuce, who was directly ahead of me, behind the prisoners, had heard my whispered warning to Rusty and slowly drew his weapon also.

The man in front of Rusty moved suddenly, crouching and raising a rifle that had been concealed behind his leg. As Rusty dove to the left for the cover of a small

246

rock outcropping, Deuce stepped to the right, fired once around the captives, and then dove to the left.

As me and Pescador took cover behind a long-dead tree trunk also on the left side of the trail, I caught a glimpse of the man with the rifle as he suddenly jerked upright and fell backwards. Deuce had scored the first hit with a single shot.

Small-arms fire erupted from three locations. Knowing Deuce had heard me warn Rusty about the guy on the right, I searched out the muzzle flash on the left and opened fire. Deuce began laying down suppressing fire to the right as Rusty scrambled to get back to us.

The two women screamed and knelt down, getting as low as they could. I heard a sickening thud and Lopez moaned, then fell sideways, hitting his head on a jagged rock. Reynolds scrambled for what cover he could find, hampered somewhat by having his hands restrained behind his back.

"Rusty," I whispered loud enough for Deuce to hear. "Where's the fourth guy?"

"Top of the light," Rusty replied. "Not a rifle, though."

I fired four more shots where I thought the guy to the left was, then five quick rounds at the catwalk below the light at the top of the tower. Rusty was up and moving fast. He dove for cover next to Deuce and began firing at the man in the tower.

Engaging all three of the men left standing at once, we quickly worked our way back down the trail toward the cliff. Cut and bleeding from several places, I made it to the cliff first just as I heard the engines on the *Revenge* start up. A second later, Deuce and Rusty joined me.

"Let's get down this cliff quick!" Rusty said. "If they catch us going down, we're dead."

"You first!" I shouted as I scanned the trail behind us. "Go with Rusty," I shouted at Pescador. He and Rusty started down as Deuce and I laid down cover fire at anything that looked out of place, concentrating on the trail. My Sig locked to the rear and I quickly dropped the magazine out of it, inserted a fresh one, and began firing again.

"Go, Deuce!" I shouted.

I fired blindly, aiming to the left and right of the trail just a few degrees. When I was out of ammo again, I holstered the Sig and started down the steep path as quickly as possible. Rusty and Pescador were already on the sand, firing up at the top of the trail. Seconds later, Deuce joined him as bullets began to ping off the rocks around me.

Suddenly, I heard a familiar sound over the small-arms fire. A sound that can instill either terror or relief, depending on whether the guy making the sound is friend or foe. I immediately felt relieved, knowing that Tony and Bourke had mounted the .50 caliber machine gun and chambered a round. Ma Deuce began singing.

Either Tony or Bourke was opening up on the top of the cliff, chewing it up and sending rocks tumbling down the face. I scrambled down the rest of the trail under their covering fire and we all hit the water. The *Revenge* was slowly backing towards us, just thirty feet away, and for the moment there was no return fire from the cliff.

It only took a few seconds to reach the swim platform. Tony was at the fifty, firing three- and four-round bursts all along the top of the cliff near the path. Bourke was backing him up, making sure the belt feed from the ammo can didn't snag as it fed into the hungry machine gun. Doc and Julie were on the bridge, Doc at the helm, while Charity and Nikki crouched on the dive platform to help each of us up onto it. Staying low, we scrambled aboard, and Doc hit the throttles, bringing the *Revenge* quickly up on plane, powering away from the beach as Tony continued firing at the top of the cliff.

"Take out the Cigarette!" Deuce shouted.

Tony lowered the barrel and opened up on the boat resting on the beach. It only took him a couple seconds to move the rounds onto target. Suddenly the Cigarette erupted in a fireball that illuminated the cliff face as it rolled upwards in a billowing mushroom of orange and black above the spot where the expensive boat had once rested. Pieces of fiberglass floated back down to splash into the water all around the beach. We were well out of range of their small arms, but Tony fired another couple of quick bursts at the top of the cliff.

"What the hell just happened?" Bourke shouted.

"We were ambushed," Deuce replied. "Four people, not very well trained."

A moment later, we were all gathered on the bridge. I took the helm and jammed the throttles, turning the wheel toward the deep water I knew to be at the south end of the point. I rounded the promontory and turned north just a half mile off the coast. I stayed close to shore for a mile and then turned due east for five more minutes, putting us a good three miles offshore. I slowly brought the boat down to an idle and then shut the engines, drifting in the eerie silence.

"You're sure there's no other bugs anywhere on this boat?" I asked Bourke. "How'd you think to look for one in the first place?"

"He's paranoid like that," Charity said. "He occasionally sweeps for bugs, wherever he's at."

Bourke just shrugged. "Paranoia is an irrational fear that someone's out to get you. Doesn't mean there isn't sometimes."

"They knew we were coming. Make a lot of noise and sweep it again." Deuce said.

Bourke climbed down the ladder to the cockpit, loudly reciting King Henry's Saint Crispin's Day speech, assuming that any more might be the same voice-activated type. Tony pulled a small device from his cargo pocket and switched it on. Three green lights lit up on the front of it. He began sweeping it back and forth, starting at the windshield in front of the second chair. As he did, he carried on a loud argument with himself about the pros and cons of American-made cars over European. When he finished, he shook his head at Deuce and started down the ladder.

"Here's a thought," Nikki said. "What if the rental boat had one of those Lojack things?"

Pescador barked from down in the cockpit. Looking down, I saw him standing with his front paws on the gunwale, looking toward the lighthouse.

A flash of light from the coast, which was out of synch with the sweep of the lighthouse, caught my attention. "Damn! Just what we don't need."

Deuce looked toward the island. "A chopper?"

Sure enough, a corporate-type helicopter with a bright spotlight was flying out over the point. I reached for the ignition but Deuce stopped me.

"Wait," he said. "He's turning north along the coast."

"If he turns that light off he's sure to see our wake in all this phytoplankton," Tony said, as he climbed back up the ladder. "The boat's all clear, Deuce. There aren't any more bugs."

As we watched, the chopper moved out over the water about a half mile, sweeping the water with its spotlight.

"You might be right, Nikki," I said. "Renting out a high-dollar boat like that, I'm sure the owner has some way to track it."

"Okay," Deuce said, "someone bugged the *Revenge*. Maybe the Cigarette, too. Who? My gut tells me Lopez was telling the truth when he said he didn't know any-thing about a bug. I'd also bet either the guy who hired him also hired another contractor to do it, or the guy that bugged you is somehow associated with that guy. But how?"

"I check the bright work on the hatch just about every day I'm aboard," I said. "Even the most careful locksmith is going to leave scratches. Nobody picked the lock and besides, I check the alarm system's history at the same time and it's always set when I'm away. Nothing. It had to be someone that was invited aboard."

"And that someone has to be connected to the Maggio law firm in Miami," Julie said. "That chopper didn't come out here for the view. Not with guns."

"That pretty much rules out those Secret Service guys," Deuce said. "Nobody's been aboard since then?"

"Nobody that's not here right now," I replied. "Except my daughter."

"I think we can rule Kim out," Charity said. "We talked quite a bit those two nights we bunked together. All she wanted to know about was what kind of man her dad was. I told her what I could and I felt she was genuinely proud of you, Jesse."

"What about before the fishing trip?" Doc asked.

The chopper had disappeared into a cove three or four miles up the coast. I thought about Doc's question while I started the engines, turned east-northeast, and brought her up to cruising speed. I wanted to head even further out to sea before turning in to Elbow Cay. It would mean a later arrival but I didn't want to get there before sunrise now, anyway. I figured whoever it was in the chopper was poorly trained at best and thought like a landlubber. Using the light, they were target fixated and couldn't see outside of its cone, where we would have been visible by the light of the moon. Landlubbers only expect to see people, and therefore boats, near the coast and that was where they were concentrating their search.

Suddenly, it hit me. "The day we sold the Confederate gold!"

"Conner!" Deuce said, snapping his fingers. "He was the IRS guy. What was that other guy's name?"

"Bradbury!" I exclaimed. "With the Florida Historical Society."

"How are a tax guy and a history nerd connected to either an escort service or this Maggio guy?" Bourke asked in his deep baritone as he climbed up the ladder. Then to Deuce he said, "I even swept the foredeck, Boss. Nothing."

"Conner didn't strike me as the kind of guy who would utilize an escort service," Deuce said. "Not in his home-town, anyway. Did any part of that treasure discovery find its way into the courts?"

"No," Rusty said. "It was a straight-up cut. The state got its share and the income tax forms were all filed proper-ly along with the tax payments."

Noting our direction by a quick glance up at the stars, Deuce asked, "Are you going to run way outside and get to Elbow Cay in the morning?"

"Yeah," I replied. "We're not due until noon, anyway. We'll make the cut about zero seven hundred."

"I'll go below and shoot an email to Chyrel. Have her find out what she can about Conner and Bradbury. Any-one else you can think of?"

I thought back over the last few months since the wed-ding and before that. The influx of cash from the Confed-erate gold we sold the Historical Society meant I didn't have to take out any charters.

"The last time anyone else was aboard was a marlin charter four months ago."

Deuce looked at Bourke for an answer. "The battery in that device couldn't have lasted three months, Boss. Nev-er mind four months. Based on its power level, I'd say it was activated ten to twelve weeks ago."

"I'll go send the email," Deuce said.

# CHAPTER TWENTY-SIX

Nick Maggio hung up the phone, puzzled. "What happened?" his father asked him, noting his expression.

Nick looked up slowly. "Lopez and Serrano are dead."

"How?" Alfredo asked, sitting forward. "You just spoke to Serrano an hour ago when they got to the lighthouse and Lopez an hour before that, while McDermitt was undergoing customs inspection."

"When they arrived at the lighthouse," Nick said, still puzzled, "Reynolds and the others were McDermitt's captives. A gun battle erupted and one of McDermitt's people killed Serrano. Reynolds and the others were caught in the crossfire. Lopez was shot and the Cigarette destroyed."

"What?" Alfredo said, rising from his chair in his son's office and raising his voice once more. "They were only supposed to stop there to get guns and fuel. How did McDermitt know?"

Still puzzled by the strange turn of events, Nick looked up at his father on the other side of the desk. "Purely a coincidence. One of them knows the lighthouse keeper. McDermitt captured Reynolds and the others at sea and planned to drop them at the lighthouse for the keeper to guard, while they conduct the treasure search."

"The helicopter?" Alfredo asked.

"All six are onboard and it's in the air, searching along the coast for McDermitt's boat," Nick replied.

"The bodies?"

"Had to be left behind. The helicopter couldn't carry all eight. Reynolds had them moved inside along with the light keeper's."

Alfredo walked across his son's office to look out over the South Beach skyline. How it had changed since he arrived here as a young man, crowded with fifteen others in a small boat. He'd done well for himself in the thirty-six years since then. He'd worked hard when he arrived, scraping a living out of the cane fields west of the city. For three years, he'd cut cane and done any kind of job the overseer asked of him, and his reliability and hard work hadn't gone unnoticed. His employers soon recognized his ambition, his sense of honor, and his intelligence, taking him out of the fields and sending him to college. He represented the sugar company for ten years after he received his law degree and passed the bar. Even after the change in ownership that brought in some unsavory people. *When did I become a criminal?* Alfredo thought as he gazed out over the bright lights of South Beach.

Turning back to his son, he said, "Have Reynolds and the two women dropped off on Elbow Cay as planned.

Then have the helicopter go back and dispose of the bodies. Tell them to refuel first and go far out to sea. They don't have to locate McDermitt. We know where he's going. Tell Quintero to contact you when it's done. Round up four more people. Professionals. And get them over there."

# CHAPTER TWENTY-SEVEN

I sent everyone to get some rest and plotted a course on the GPS for Tilloo Cut, with a waypoint fifty miles east-northeast of our current location. At twenty knots, this route would get us to the cut at sunrise and we'd hopefully elude the chopper. We had to sleep on the boat anyway—might as well do it out on the blue, where we'd be just a speck.

We figured out sleeping arrangements to everyone's satisfaction and set up a bridge watch. Me and Bourke would take the first two hours, then Rusty and Tony would take over. Doc and Nikki would take the sunrise watch as we were nearing the coast again. After the adrenaline rush of the last several hours, everyone was tired.

"I'm still not convinced the bug and these people are connected," Bourke said after ten minutes of silently staring out at the stars. When I know someone's deep in thought, I try to let them work that thought out themselves.

"Why's that?" I asked.

"Think about it. After we made those four at Hurricane Hole, we sat right down there in the salon getting the information from Chyrel, with all nine of us talking and making suggestions."

"That bothered me, too," I said. "With four of them captive, why would they send only four more to try to free them, knowing how many we are?"

"Exactly," he replied. "Tactically, it's never a good move to attack an enemy that outnumbers you more than two to one. Waiting for more manpower would have been the better idea since they knew where we were ultimately going. That's why I don't think the ones on the island knew our strength, and therefore they weren't there to free the prisoners at all."

He looked out over the water to the east, thinking, and I let him come to his conclusion on his own. "They were cohorts, though. Before Tony opened up, I could see muzzle flashes from at least five guns on that cliff and y'all said there were four before Deuce dropped one. That means Reynolds and the others knew the guys in the chopper and took up arms with them. But, then again, they made quite a few tactical errors besides that."

"How certain are you about when the bug was activated?"

"Ninety-nine point nine percent. If we were at Homestead I could run a diagnostics check and see when it sent the first data burst, to get an exact date. But it was definitely eleven weeks ago, give or take a few days."

"That'd fit perfectly with when Conner and Bradbury were aboard," I said. "To what end, though? Neither of them struck me as a criminal."

"I don't know, man," Bourke sighed. "Maybe one or both of them just got bored with their humdrum life."

"Makes as much sense as anything else," I said. "Then, when they found out we had a lead on a treasure, maybe one or both of them hired people to try to take it from us? But at one point I know we talked in the salon about doing this through the proper channels. They'd have to know the treasure would be turned over to the Bahamian government the moment it's found."

"It's hard for law-abiding people like us to think like a criminal," Bourke finally said. "Chyrel will come up with something. That gal can run circles around the best computer analysts the Agency has."

We rode on in silence for a few minutes, and then Bourke asked me about my family and what it was like to reconnect after such a long absence.

"I never thought I'd see either of my daughters again," I said. "My ex took them when I deployed to Panama and divorced me when I was deployed again for Desert Shield. You have kids?"

"I did," he said. "I lost my wife and four-year-old son five years ago. I was on recruiting duty, Lower Manhattan. We had a little brownstone in Red Hook. Nice neighborhood, quiet. Know where that's at?"

"Brooklyn, right?"

"You know it, huh? Anyway, my wife took a job as a receptionist for a shipping firm in the North Tower of the World Trade Center. She was happy to have a job and they had a daycare just a floor below. We'd take the

Brooklyn Battery Tunnel to Manhattan every morning and I'd drop them off before going to the office. Then I'd pick them up when I left work. Now and then, we'd have lunch together."

"September eleventh?" I asked hesitantly.

"Yeah, we were running late that Tuesday morning and I dropped them off at the North Tower a few minutes after eight and then went on to work, just like any other day. I was just walking into the office when I heard the explosion. A few minutes later, the Chief I worked with turned on the radio and we heard the announcer say the North Tower was on fire."

I didn't know what to say. I thought I'd had it rough with my wife taking off with the girls. It explained a lot, though. Bourke was a career Coastie if ever there was one. Most men after twenty years with the Coast Guard would retire and take a part-time job or take up golf or something. Not take a job in a clandestine organization at the age of forty. "I'm really sorry, Anthony."

We rode on in silence, Bourke having given me more to think about. *Think like a criminal*, I thought. I'd always had the ability to get inside the head of the enemy. They were usually narrow-minded zealots of one kind or another, so that was pretty easy. I'm out of my element trying to figure out what your average, run-of-the-mill criminal would think or do. But what had happened back there made no sense whatsoever. The only conclusion I could come up with echoed what Bourke had been thinking. The four who ambushed us weren't there to ambush us and free Reynolds and his people.

At zero three hundred Rusty and Tony joined us on the bridge. Bourke gave Rusty his night vision goggles and climbed down the ladder to turn in. I quickly brought Rusty up to speed on our current location, heading, and distance to the waypoint. The radar was clear, nothing anywhere near us. Seas were flat calm and no chance of weather coming up. All they had to do was stay awake and not hit anything floating in the water.

"Doc and Nikki will spell you guys at zero five hundred," I said, handing Tony my goggles. "Tell Doc to wake me when we're five miles out, if I'm not already up."

"Will do," Rusty replied. "Go get some rest."

I climbed down the ladder and went into the cabin. With limited berths, we were forced to hot bunk on the pull-out sofa in the salon. Doc and Nikki had the forward stateroom, while Deuce, Julie, and Charity had the guest cabin with its fold-down Pullman-type bunk. Pescador was curled up under the settee, where nobody would step on him. Bourke was already snoring and I lay down, thinking. Soon, the gentle motion of the boat on the waves and the drone of the big diesel engines just below the deck lulled me to sleep.

It seemed like only a few minutes later when I woke up, but the light streaming in from the rear porthole told me otherwise. I rose and went forward to the galley. Someone had seen fit to set up the coffeemaker and I could see from the little tube it was still half full. I filled a mug and a thermos, then headed up to the bridge.

"Morning, Jesse," Doc and Nikki said at about the same time.

Checking the GPS and seeing we were about ten miles from the cut, I handed Nikki the thermos and sat down on the port bench.

"Any sign of the chopper?" I asked.

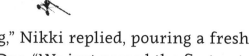
"No sign of anything," Nikki replied, pouring a fresh mug for both her and Doc. "We just passed the first outbound fishing boat a few minutes ago."

"This is your gig," I said. "We can cancel everything if you guys want to. After what happened last night, do you still want to continue?"

"We've been talking about it for the last two hours," Doc replied. "Whoever those people are, they surprised you guys up there on that cliff, but I'm betting they got the bigger surprise. I know that's not gonna happen again. If we do find this treasure, it means our kids and their kids will be set for life. It's a lot to give up, knowing what we know."

"Trouble is," I began, "they, whoever they are, also know what we know. At least a good bit, anyway. That many zeroes will make people do some really desperate things. It could get a lot more dangerous."

"Then give me a gun," Nikki said. "I'm a Marine, too."

I grinned and looked at Doc, who nodded. "Okay, when we go ashore everyone will be armed."

A moment later, Rusty climbed up to the bridge. "Somebody drained the coffeemaker," he growled, holding out an empty mug. "I put more on."

"Sorry," I said, handing him the thermos as I slid over on the bench for him.

"You want the helm, Jesse?" Doc asked.

"No, but let Rusty take the second seat, Nikki. He's been through this cut a few times."

One by one, the others came up to the bridge, making it standing room only once more as we approached the cut. Doc slowed to ten knots and looked north and south along the beaches we'd just flown over a couple of days ago. Both were deserted.

Gazing up the beach to the north, I had the strangest feeling. I'd heard people talk about déjà vu, but I'd never experienced it myself. Until now. Suddenly, I felt a rush of foreboding as I looked at the white sand beach stretching away to the north and felt certain I'd been here before, though I knew I hadn't.

Death had visited these shores, I remembered. Every person on this island had died. And it had happened not once, but twice. The Spaniards killed the original inhabitants by the hundreds. A few were taken captive, mostly women and children. After that tragedy, the wind blew through the trees and the blue-green water lapped at the white sand with nobody to hear it for a whole generation. Then the Spanish returned, this time wrecked somewhere up that very coast I was looking at. There, they died of either thirst or starvation. Otherwise, the coconut and the treasure would have been found. Death by either thirst or starvation is a horrible way to go. *Better a quick thrust with a Spanish sword*, I thought.

We idled slowly through the cut, Rusty pointing out the nearly invisible markers and guiding Doc to the south for about a hundred yards. "That's Tahiti Beach," Rusty said. "It turns into a sandbar with some shallow cuts, there where the water's shoaling. Swing tight around that marker at the end of the sandbar."

The channel turned one hundred eighty degrees to the north and we entered the Sea of Abaco, the shallow body of water between the many barrier islands and the mainland of Great Abaco.

The resort owner had given us GPS coordinates for the channel and we soon found it. Slowly idling through an opening in the sheltered reef into a small deep-water harbor with three docks, Doc pointed to a house on the bluff and said, "That big blue house on the hill is where we'll be staying and that's the resort's dock on the left."

"Turn her around here," I said. "It looks like we have the whole dock to ourselves. We'll tie up to the tee on the end."

A few minutes later the *Revenge* was tied off and we went down to the salon. All but Pescador, that is. He ran to the nearest tree as soon as we were close to the dock.

"Until we know the area better," I said, "let's stay together. If it's all right with you, Deuce, I'd feel better if everyone was armed. At least for a little while."

"Do you have enough aboard?" he asked.

I've always been kind of a gun nut and had a pretty large collection of sidearms and rifles, all stored away in waterproof boxes under the bunk in my stateroom. "Yeah, I have enough."

I went forward and retrieved two more Penn Senator reel boxes, each holding two Sigs and four magazines. I also grabbed a smaller reel case that held Pap's old Colt 1911 that I'd first learned to shoot with. I was issued a 1911 my first year in the Corps, but they soon replaced it with the Beretta 9mm.

I set the two larger boxes on the settee and those still unarmed passed around the magazines, clip-on holsters, and pistols. I gave Nikki the Sig I'd been carrying, along with its holster and extra magazine, then holstered the Colt and clipped it inside my shorts at the small of my back.

Doc had been on the phone with the resort owner to tell them we'd arrived early. When he ended the call, he said, "She's calling the caretaker and he'll be here in a few minutes with a golf cart for our stuff."

"Let's get going, then," I said. "I hear a shower calling my name."

When we had our gear unloaded, a golf cart appeared at the foot of the narrow pier, turned, and backed expertly down to where we waited by the boat.

"Welcome to Crystal Waters," the young man said as he got out of the cart. "You're early, but it doesn't matter. The house has been empty for two days and is all ready for you. Only one of the villas is occupied. Some other folks are due in today."

He said his name was Thom, "with an *h*." I introduced myself and the others, telling him we were from the Keys and were going to be doing some fishing and sight-seeing around the Abacos for a few days. The real reason we were there, we would keep secret as long as possible. Thom was in his late twenties maybe, with blond hair and a dark tan. He said he'd been working for the owners for just a year, but charter boats were fairly regular customers.

When we got to the top of the hill, I immediately noticed two things. First, it wasn't a resort as most resorts go. It was more like a private residence. Second, it was elevated. High. From the water I could tell it sat at least fifty feet above the docks. Maybe the highest part of the whole island. A huge two-story house, painted light blue and perched at the top of the hill. The steep climb up from the dock provided an excellent view even from the driveway. Standing there, I could see the bridge of the *Revenge* down below.

"Not to worry, Captain," Thom said, coming back out for two more bags. "You can see the whole dock clearly from any of the west-facing windows. We've never had a problem here."

"Thanks, Thom," I said. Looking east down the driveway and out over the five villas, I had a partial view of the Atlantic. *Yeah*, I thought, *clear some of these trees and this place would be a fortress.*

As Thom led us up the steps to the door, he said, "The master suite is the whole second floor. It has a king-sized bed and a private bath with a shower and bathtub, plus a pull-out sofa. The other three bedrooms are on the main floor, two with queen beds and one with double singles. There are a couple of pull-out beds in the living room, too. More than enough for all of you."

While Thom brought in the last bags from the cart, we went inside and looked around the house. It was really beautiful with lots of tongue and groove walls and ceilings. The kitchen and one of the bedrooms looked west toward the docks. Each had glass sliding doors opening onto a deck, with a pool and gazebo below.

After Thom left we gathered in the large dining room, which had a breakfast bar big enough to seat all of us. Deuce received a text message from Chyrel and pulled out his laptop. Once he'd connected to the satellite and the connection to Chyrel was made, her face appeared on the screen.

"It took a while," she said, "and I had to get Jim to help, but we finally found a connection that might interest you." Jim Franklin is a semiretired CIA surveillance expert. He created a device and a program that, when given a target phone number, can trace and extract other phone numbers called and even identify any active phone that is near the target phone on more than one occasion when a call is made or received.

"First off," Chyrel said, "I did like you asked, Jesse, and checked Conner's and Bradbury's phone records for calls to one another about the same day that Doc came out to the island with his coconut. You were right—Conner called Bradbury early the next morning. The call lasted less than two minutes and it was the first time either of them had called the other.

"Conner's dirty," Chyrel continued. "Though we didn't get any direct connections from Bradbury to anyone other than regular business and personal connections, he's dirty by association. Conner called a particular number three times in the last week that belongs to one Valentin Madic. The first call was just a few minutes after calling Bradbury." A surveillance photo appeared showing a man in his fifties, fit-looking and well dressed, with a pocked face. "Madic's Croatian. Arrived in the States about ten years ago and started building what is now a growing Eastern European mob presence in south Florida. The two goons you guys rousted at the bar work for him."

Pictures of the two men from the *Anchor* came on the screen. "This is Borislav Varga and Ivo Novosel, both former Croatian military. Varga was drummed out of their army when he was connected to a string of prostitute murders, apparently killing them during intercourse. Novosel was a pilot in their air force, similarly discharged for suspected serial rape against underage girls."

"That's a couple of sick pervs," Charity said. "That's all they got was a bad discharge?"

"Pretty much," Chyrel replied. "The Croatian Army looks the other way about certain things that might bring bad press and just gets rid of the offender."

"Aside from the phone call, how is Bradbury connected," I asked.

"Madic's been under surveillance by both Miami-Dade and FDLE for some time. He's slippery, though, and they haven't been able to get anything on him. I hacked their files and found surveillance photos of Madic and his two goons, along with an unidentified woman, entering Conner's office in Cutler Ridge the day after we were all on the island. Bradbury was at the meeting."

Four photos appeared on the screen. One was of the same pock-faced man with the two guys from the *Anchor* and a dark-haired woman. They were walking toward a door in a strip mall. Madic and his goons were looking around as though searching for trouble. The woman's back was to the photographer and all that could be seen for certain was that she had dark hair. In the second one, Madic was holding the door open for the woman while he and the two guys were again looking around the parking lot. The third photo showed Bradbury getting out of an older Buick sedan, carrying a briefcase and with his coat over his arm. The shadows suggested this picture was taken an hour or more after the first two. The fourth photo was of Conner, shaking hands with Madic just outside the door. The two big men were standing at the open doors of a black sedan, looking in opposite directions. The woman was getting in the backseat of the car, with one long, attractive leg sticking out.

"Apparently," Chyrel continued, "both Conner and Bradbury had a meeting with Madic."

"So how do the Maggio law firm and Consuelo Reynolds figure into this?" Deuce asked.

"And who's the babe?" Tony chimed in.

"There's nothing in either the Miami-Dade or Florida Department of Law Enforcement files on her, Tony. There's really not much of a connection, Deuce. The Maggio firm is highly respected in the Cuban community in Miami. They do represent some bad people, though. One of them is Madic and another is Madam Reynolds. There are calls made between Madic and Maggio going back a long time and Madic was surveilled a number of times entering Maggio's building, but none of those occasions really correspond with the times of the calls to Bradbury. As far as I can tell, Bradbury has never had any contact with the Maggio firm at all. FDLE has been trying to get a wiretap warrant for a while, but so far they haven't produced enough evidence for a Judge to grant one."

"Stay on it and tell Jim thanks," Deuce said and ended the connection.

Deuce looked at Doc, "Together or separate, we're looking at possibly eleven bad guys that we know of. Maybe more."

Doc gave it some thought, then said, "Maybe we should call the whole thing off. I don't want to endanger any of you guys."

Tony chuckled and said, "We're not the ones in danger, Doc."

"It's your call," Deuce said. "I think I can speak for everyone here when I say we've got your six. Speaking for myself, I don't like being followed and I really don't like being shot at. If it was up to me, I'd hunt them all down and make them rue the day they decided to do either."

"Let's stick with it, Bob," Nikki said.

Doc looked at his wife, then nodded. "Okay, let's do it."

Our first order of business was setting up sleeping arrangements, then a shower and some rest. Deciding to maintain the appearance of three couples, a Captain, and two crewmen, Bourke and I would stay aboard the *Revenge*. Doc and Nikki protested their room assignment, but since this whole idea was theirs, they finally relented and headed up to the master suite on the second floor. Deuce and Julie took the west-facing bedroom with the queen bed, while Charity took the other queen room that faced the Atlantic. Rusty, as the Captain, would also stay in the house and bunk with Tony in the middle of the three downstairs bedrooms with the two twin beds.

We agreed to rest up for a few hours and then have an early lunch before taking the boat to Hope Town Harbour to refuel and arrange to rent a few golf carts to get around on. Once back aboard the *Revenge*, I showered quickly, and after switching on both the generator and water maker, I crawled into bed for some much-needed rest.

# CHAPTER TWENTY-EIGHT

James had discreetly stopped at Ettaleigh's cottage at her beckoning twice during the day and both times she'd offered him her energy concoction after they'd had sex. When he left that afternoon, she'd made him promise to meet her at the post office dock precisely at seven that evening. She wanted to go to Bluff House on nearby Green Turtle Cay for dinner. While he'd agreed reluctantly, mumbling something about fishing, she knew from past experience that by the time he got off work, he'd be ready to mount anything that moved and was sure to be at the dock at the appointed time.

Her employer was due to arrive in the morning and this would be her last chance to have fun, possibly for quite some time. After tonight she'd have no further use for James and would be throwing herself back into her work.

She opened the bureau and took out a black leather briefcase and placed it on the table. She spun the little wheels to the correct numbers and opened the case. Removing three binders, a notepad, and a few unfiled work-related papers, she carefully pulled on the identification tag that seemed to be sewn into the bottom edge. The false bottom unsnapped and she lifted it out and set it aside.

The inside of the hidden compartment in the briefcase was only an inch thick and lined with red velvet. It contained twelve small bottles in recessed holders, along with an eye dropper, a syringe, a length of rubber tubing, and three very small measuring spoons of different sizes. She removed three of the small bottles and opened them. Retrieving her flask from her purse she filled it nearly full with bottled water and carefully measured in the precise number of drops from each of the three little bottles, then replaced the caps and put them back in the case. After putting the false bottom back in place, she replaced the business contents and locked the case, securing it back in the bureau.

Shaking the flask a few times, which now contained a more powerful dosage, she removed the top and took a small sip of the sweet liquid. *This should be perfect*, she thought.

Putting the flask in her purse, she showered and dressed for the evening. She decided on a black knee-length halter dress with a neckline that nearly reached her naval. It was slit up the right side all the way to her hip. Sitting on the edge of the bed, she put on her best black open-toe high heels. She had every intention of driving the poor boy out of his mind with lust. And then some.

Checking herself in the mirror quickly, she grabbed her purse and left the cottage. It was already seven o'clock, but she knew the young man would be waiting. She doubted he'd be waiting patiently, however.

A few minutes later, as she walked between the two rows of cars in the dock parking lot, she saw James half-way out on the dock. He was dressed in khaki shorts and a light blue button-down shirt, his blond hair ruffled by the light breeze.

Turning the corner and walking slowly down the dock toward him he heard the click of her heels and turned toward her. As she walked seductively toward him under the sparse dock lighting, he became obviously aroused, which excited her even more.

"I'm sorry I'm late, James," she said with a pout, biting on her lower lip.

"L-late?" James stammered, eyeing her hungrily.

"I'm famished, how about you?"

"Yeah," he replied, his eyes glued to her cleavage.

She leaned on him and started to remove her heels, then seeing three fishermen watching her, she pretended to stumble and fall into his arms. As he held her she could feel his excitement through the thin material of her dress.

"Oops, maybe I should sit down to take these off."

She sat on a bench and slowly undid the straps on her heels and removed them. Out of the corner of her eye she saw the three fishermen craning their necks for a look down her loose-fitting dress. She put her heels in her purse as she stood up and with a seductive smile asked, "Are we ready?"

"Very ready," he said hoarsely as he held her hand and helped her down into the little boat. He saw the fishermen and recognized them but was no longer concerned about it getting back to his boss. Right now, he had only one thing on his mind and it'd been that way most of the day.

Once he was seated beside her at the wheel and started the engine, she turned slightly so that her bare thigh was against his. The heat between them was almost unbearable. She knew they weren't going to arrive at the restaurant anytime soon.

A few minutes later, they were out of the harbor and skipping across the Sea of Abaco at nearly forty miles per hour, headed toward Green Turtle Cay thirty miles to the north.

"Do you think anyone will be at that little beach we visited?" she asked while holding her hair over her left shoulder with one hand and clutching the inside of his thigh with the other.

Without a word, James changed course a few degrees and pushed the throttle a little further. Fifteen minutes later, he slowed the boat as they approached the beach.

"It doesn't look like anyone's here," she said. "Can we go ashore? Do you have a blanket or a towel? The stars are beautiful way out here."

"You'll ruin your dress," he replied.

She moved her hand a little higher on his thigh. "I have no intention of wearing it."

He slowly approached the white sand beach and, seeing no sign of anyone around, he gently nudged the boat up onto the sand and shut off the engine. Silence immediately engulfed them, only the slight wash of their bow wave as it continued down the beach breaking it. Putting one bare foot over the side, he stood up in the knee-deep water.

"I have a blanket in the fish box," he said.

"It doesn't smell of fish, does it?"

"I just washed it. Give me just a second."

He walked forward and grabbed the gunwale, pulling the boat higher onto the beach. Opening the fish box he pulled out a large red beach blanket, walked up to a clear, flat spot, and spread it out on the sand.

When he turned back to the boat, Ettaleigh was standing on the casting deck, backlit by the rising moon. She slowly reached up and untied the top of the dress and let it fall slowly to the deck.

Thirty sweaty, passion-filled minutes later, the two lay next to one another, looking up at the stars that seemed to fill the sky from horizon to horizon. Though he was exhausted, James's obvious excitement hadn't dissipated in the least. *Time for round two*, Ettaleigh thought as she rolled over on top of the young man.

When they were underway again, Ettaleigh took a small drink from her flask and offered it to James. The immediate sensation caused by the concoction excited her senses. James took it from her hand and after a long drink, she had to take it back.

"Easy there, big boy," she said with a knowing smile. "You don't want to overload your heart."

When they finally arrived at Bluff House, they were both very hungry and ate ravenously, washing their lobster down with rum cocktails. They spent an hour on the dance floor, gyrating in wild abandon. Every man in the place watched them enviously as they ground against one another during a slow song.

When they finally left and were heading south in the Sea of Abaco, Ettaleigh said, "Slow down a little, I want to ride on the front." James did as she asked, bringing the little boat down to just a few miles per hour.

Ettaleigh took the flask from her purse and carefully made her way up to the casting deck, where she sat sideways, turning her body and facing forward. Looking back at James, she took a small sip from the flask and smiled seductively in the moonlight.

"Is there a way you can make the boat go straight, without you at the wheel?"

James needed no further prodding than the look she gave him when she drank from the flask once more. His heart began to pound in his chest as he pulled a bungee cord from under the helm and lashed the wheel in place. Standing up, he moved toward Ettaleigh as she rose to a kneeling position on the elevated deck with her back to him. He came up behind her, embracing her and cupping her breasts as she arched her back, pushing back against his groin.

Ettaleigh removed the cap from the flask and took another sip, instantly feeling the rush and tingling sensation it brought on. She turned her head and kissed James passionately as he ground himself against her. When their lips broke free, they were both panting like dogs. While pulling down the zipper of his shorts with one hand, she offered him the flask.

This time, she didn't stop him or even caution him. Instead, she tugged him free of his shorts, lifted her dress, and guided him, pushing back against his groin. He took her long black hair in one hand and, pulling her head back, began thrusting with wild abandon while he tilted his head to the stars and drank down every drop of the sweet nectar.

# CHAPTER TWENTY-NINE

Madic came into the cockpit as soon as the plane landed at the airport on the island of Great Abaco. Since he was the boss, Ivo chose not to remind him to stay seated until they stopped.

"There's been a change in plans," Madic said as Ivo turned onto the taxiway. "McDermitt's boat arrived on Elbow Cay early this morning. The three of us will take the ferry to Hope Town and check in at the lodge. The women will go straight from the airport to the villa just below where McDermitt is staying. We can't take the chance of them seeing the two of you."

"What about Miss Horvac?" Borislav asked. Secretly, he hoped she had returned to Florida. Upon meeting her, he sensed she was one to steer clear of. Cold and calculating in business dealings, she rarely spoke and seemed to take in everything around her, showing no outward appearance of emotion. When she did speak, she cut no corners and went straight to the point. Madic had full faith in her and had told everyone in the organization that dealing with her was the same as dealing with him. When Borislav learned more about her past, he avoided any contact with her as much as possible.

"You have her bag aboard?" Madic asked, and Borislav nodded. "Good, she arrived at the villa late last night and has been keeping watch."

"She's at the villa?" Ivo asked. "What if they see her?"

"McDermitt seeing her is part of my plan. It is the two of you that they know. They have not seen Tena before, or the two women," he said, nodding toward the back of the cabin. "Tena has one villa to herself and Sabina and Elana will be in another. The three of them will befriend these men in whatever way they must to get invited aboard their boat, where Tena will plant a tracking device. If possible they'll get the men to invite them to join in the search."

"How will we know when they find the treasure?" Ivo asked.

"Tena will inform us," Madic replied. "Once McDermitt finds what he is looking for, they'll leave soon after. I have two boats waiting on Chub Cay with the tracker's frequency. It will alert them in time to intercept McDermitt when he passes near there. When he gets out into the shallow water to the east, these men will destroy his boat with rocket-propelled grenades. Then all we have to do is send divers down to retrieve the treasure."

"Are the men on the boats divers?" Borislav asked.

"No, Elana and Sabina are. That's one of the many reasons they were hired," Madic said with a sadistic grin.

After clearing customs, they split up. The women took a cab to a nearby marina where Tena had arranged a boat rental for them. Madic and the three men took another cab to the ferry dock on the north side of the city. They had to wait ten minutes for the ferry to return to make the twenty-minute crossing to Elbow Cay.

When Elana Galic and Sabina Duric arrived at the marina, they presented their fake passports to the boat rental agent. They'd been transformed through the magic of technology into Melissa Johansen and Yvette Paulson, from Orlando.

"We have a boat reserved," Elana said.

The man looked at her passport and then at his rental reservations. He couldn't help notice they were both very attractive and neither wore a wedding ring. "Yes, Miss Johansen. I have a twenty-six-foot Dusky all ready for you. Will you need instructions?"

"No," Sabina replied with a smile, noting his name tag. "We're both avid boaters, Brighton. It's a Dusky inboard, correct?"

"Yes, ma'am, Miss Paulson," Brighton replied. "I just need one of you to sign the rental agreement and provide a credit card."

Elana produced a cloned credit card with the name Melissa Johansen imprinted on it and quickly scanned the rental agreement before signing it.

"You're all set," Brighton said with a smile. "It's full of gas and waiting at—"

Sabina interrupted him. "You mean diesel, right?"

"Oh, um, yes of course. It's fueled up and waiting at dock twelve. You have it for five days and the return time is four o'clock. Will you need bait, tackle, or anything else?"

"No, thanks," Elana said. "We're divers."

"Ah, of course," Brighton said as he handed over the key, which was attached to a little red float.

The two women went out to the dock and loaded their baggage and dive gear on board. Elana started the engine as Sabina cast off the lines, then stepped aboard. A moment later the two were skimming across the Sea of Abaco, following the course on the GPS toward the position the villa owner had given Tena.

Fifteen minutes later, they arrived at the dock and easily recognized the big boat that would be their target. It was the only boat tied up to the dock. Elana slowly idled past the big boat and chose a slip halfway down the dock, where she turned and expertly backed the boat into place. Sabina jumped to the dock and tied off the stern line to a cleat, fully aware that she was being watched from the bridge of the bigger boat.

Once they had the boat secure, the two women started moving their belongings onto the dock. "You see him watching?" Sabina whispered.

"Yes," Elana replied, lifting her dive gear bag onto the dock. "He's coming down now."

# CHAPTER THIRTY

I woke after about two hours and put on a clean pair of cargo shorts and a *Gaspar's Revenge Charter Service* tee shirt, then went up to the galley. Rusty brought five pounds of a new coffee he'd bought for the *Anchor* and I decided to give it a shot. He'd told me it was grown on a tiny farm in central Costa Rica called La Minita and said the farm managed the growth of the beans from seedling, to cultivation, to harvesting. *That's a lot of work to go to for a coffee bean*, I thought. I usually buy whatever the least expensive Colombian coffee is at the little grocery store on Big Pine. Rusty swore I'd like this better. But to me coffee is coffee.

While it was brewing, I went out to the cockpit with Pescador to call Kim. Pescador vaulted to the dock and headed straight to his new favorite tree, a large cluster of mangrove roots to the south of the small private beach.

Kim didn't answer, so I left a message saying we'd arrived at the resort safely and a little early. After I ended the call, I started back inside. As soon as I opened the hatch, I was struck by the coffee's aroma. *If it tastes half as good as it smells*, I thought, *I might just have a new favorite coffee.*

Pouring some into my favorite mug, I took a tentative sip. "Damn," I said out loud.

Filling a thermos with my new favorite coffee, I headed up to the bridge to get my bearings and study the local navigation chart I'd bought in Nassau. Electronics are a great aid, but I've learned to appreciate the old school ways more, like a compass, sextant, and paper charts.

Many years ago, while going through yet another land nav class in the field taught by a crusty old Master Sergeant by the name of Jake Steadman, a young Second Lieutenant pulled out a newly acquired GPS. It was the dawn of the digital age, but Steadman was old school and insisted on teaching map and compass to new Officers and Enlisted. I was taking the refresher class with a bunch of brand new butter bars and Privates. When Steadman saw the Lieutenant's GPS he strode up to him and asked what he was doing. The Lieutenant said something to the effect of it was almost the twenty-first century and the Corps needed to keep up with the times.

Steadman rolled out the Lieutenants map on the ground and placed a rock on one corner and the young Lieutenant's brand new GPS on the opposite corner. "What do you see, Lieutenant?" Steadman had asked.

"Modern technology on top of old school trash," the Lieutenant replied brashly.

Steadman unholstered his sidearm and put one round through the center of the GPS and the map under it. Handing the ruined device back to the Lieutenant, he said, "This is now a piece of shit, Eltee." Pointing to the map with a nine millimeter hole in it, he added, "That's still a map."

So I studied the many channels, reefs, and obstructions marked on the chart while I enjoyed the quiet peacefulness of the lagoon and the very good coffee.

Soon, the sound of a diesel-powered boat coming around the northern tip of Lubbers Quarters Cay got my attention. Lubbers Quarters is a small island just east of Tilloo Cut. Looking out over the spit of land behind the *Revenge*, I saw an open fisherman about twenty-five or twenty-six feet in length running about twenty-five knots. I sat back in my chair and could soon see that it had two women aboard, both dressed in bikini tops and cut-off jeans. The one at the helm was slightly taller than the other, with shoulder-length blond hair pulled back in a ponytail. The smaller woman had darker hair, cut short.

They slowed and then turned, idling into the lagoon right in front of the *Revenge*. When they reached the halfway point along the pier, the blonde spun the wheel right, reversed the engine, and spun the wheel back to the left, backing the boat expertly up to the dock before shutting off the engine.

I assumed they were the guests Thom had mentioned were arriving today. When I noticed they were unloading dive gear, I decided to be neighborly and help them up the hill with it. I climbed down from the bridge and with Pescador tagging along at my heel, I walked over.

"Hi," I said. "Name's Jesse. Is Thom, with an *h*, meeting you here?"

The dark-haired woman looked up and put a hand over her eyes to see better in the bright late-morning sun. "Oh, hi, there. I didn't see you. Who is this Thom with an *h*?"

"He's the caretaker of the villas and has a golf cart that goes up that hill much easier than carrying heavy dive gear on foot."

The blonde stepped up to the dock and extended her hand, which I took, noting she had a firm grip. "Hi, Jesse," she said, smiling. "I'm Melissa and this is my friend Yvette. How do we get this Thom with an *h* to come and help us?"

"His number should have been on the brochure they mailed you. Doesn't matter, I'd be glad to volunteer to be your slave."

Yvette stepped up to the dock and we shook hands. "Oh, we couldn't ask you to do that," she said, with a crooked smile and a wink. "At least not until we get you drunk."

I've had women come on to me a few times, but usually not so brazenly. "Be only too happy to do it sober," I replied, which brought a bit of a giggle from both of them.

I grabbed the two heavy dive bags and said, "Right this way, ladies."

Pescador led the way to the foot of the dock and started searching along the edge of the beach, where the lush foliage came right down to the sand.

"Is that your dog, Jesse?" one of the women asked as I started up the steep hill. Their voices were similar, so I couldn't tell which one it was

"He is, but he thinks it's the other way around," I replied over my shoulder. "His name's Pescador."

When we got to the top of the hill I stopped and set the bags down, thinking they had lagged behind me a little on the climb. I nearly got knocked over by my assumption—they were right on my heels.

"Thanks, Jesse," Melissa said. "We can handle it from here, I think."

"Be glad to carry these on down to your villa. I assume that's where you're staying?"

"Yes," Yvette said. "We're in the first one, just below here. Stop by for a beer later this evening."

The two women picked up the heavy dive bags, slung them easily on their shoulders, and started down the path to the villas. I stood watching, admiring their retreating forms until Yvette looked back over her shoulder and smiled.

*This could be an interesting few days*, I thought and then headed back down to the *Revenge*.

Rusty was just coming out of the hatch when I started up the ladder to the bridge. "You found my stash, huh?"

"Yeah," I replied. "Where you been hiding this nectar from the tropical mountain gods?"

He climbed up and joined me, pouring us both a fresh cup before sitting down on the port bench. "That the boat I heard pull in?" he asked, pointing with his mug.

"Yeah, two very attractive young women aboard. They're staying in one of the villas below us."

Rusty's eyebrows danced upward at the mention of the women. Looking up the path he said, "I see movement up on top of the hill." Following his gaze, I could see Doc and Deuce coming down the path.

When they got to the bottom, Deuce said, "Charity, Nikki, and Tony are going to walk up the road to a grocery store to get food for this evening. Did I hear you talking to someone a few minutes ago, Jesse?"

"He's puttin' the moves on a coupla young lady tourists that just arrived," Rusty said, answering for me.

Deuce gave me the eye. "There weren't any moves made," I said.

"Uh huh," Deuce replied. "How long's it been since Jackie last visited you?"

Jackie is a friend that saved my life last winter. She's a Navy Doctor and was the surgeon on call at the Navy hospital on Boca Chica when Deuce and I got shot up in Cuba. We got involved a little, but she was transferred to Bethesda over the summer.

"Jackie and I are just friends now," I said, wondering why I was being defensive.

"Yeah," Bourke said, coming out of the cabin. "Friends with benefits."

"It was over a month ago," Rusty said, answering Deuce's question.

"A month's a long time," Doc mused.

Changing the subject, I said, "Is Jules coming with us?"

"No," Deuce replied. "She's got a headache and is trying to get some rest."

Rusty looked up, concerned, but said nothing. "Don't worry," Deuce said to his father-in-law, "she just needs a little rest. We didn't get much coming back to the Keys and then all the adrenaline last night. She said she might go down and float in the pool for a while."

"Ya know," Rusty said, looking up at the big, blue house, "I ain't had a chance to swim in a pool for about twenty years. Maybe I'll hang out here, too. You know, just until you guys get back."

Deuce and I exchanged knowing glances. After all it had been just the two of them against the world for more than a quarter of a century.

"The water does look real enticing," Deuce said.

With that, Rusty climbed down the ladder and started up the dock. "Pescador," I shouted. "Go with Rusty."

Pescador leaped the gunwale and ran after Rusty, nuzzling his hand for an ear scratch before racing up the path ahead of him.

"Let's get underway," I said, starting the engines. "If we hurry, you can meet them at the store and haul the groceries back."

Bourke and Doc untied the lines while I plotted a course to Hope Town Harbour. Even running out around Parrot Cays, a small group of very tiny islands just west of the harbor, it was only five miles, but I don't take chances when running a big boat in unfamiliar waters. I double-checked the GPS against the chart and adjusted the waypoint to a spot just north of the northernmost of the little islands.

Just as I was pulling away from the dock, Bourke said, "Is that one of your new girlfriends, Jesse?"

I looked to the left and saw a woman walking out onto the small private beach, but she wasn't one of the two I'd met earlier. This woman had black hair to the middle of her back and was a few years older, maybe late thirties. She was dark-tanned, wearing a bright yellow one piece and one of those tropical-looking sarongs around her waist, which covered her legs completely. Although it was extremely unlikely, I felt like I'd seen her somewhere before.

"No," I replied. "The two women I met earlier looked a bit younger with shorter hair. That must be one of the other guests that Thom spoke about."

Turning east and leaving the lagoon, I took one last look back and she was shading her eyes, looking out over the water. Once we reached ten feet of water I pushed the throttles and brought the *Revenge* up on plane, turning due north. The feeling that I'd met the woman on the beach or seen her somewhere before kept nagging at the back of my mind.

"Once we have the golf carts at the house," Doc said, "a couple of us should go to the first property and talk to the owners, tell them what we're here for and why. Within hours, the news will probably be all over the island. Maybe we can search it this evening, before the whole island gets wind of a treasure hunt."

"That will be your and Nikki's job," I said. "She can be a lot more tactful than either me, Bourke, or Deuce."

"Hey," Bourke said, feigning insult. "I can be tactful."

I laughed and said, "Sorry, but telling someone to go to hell and making them feel happy to be on their way, just to be away from you, isn't tact."

"Jesse's right, Doc," Deuce said. "The three of us are probably a little too scary-looking to ask a homeowner if we can search their property with metal detectors."

We were approaching the southernmost island of the Parrot Cays. This one and the next one to the north are the only two that are inhabited. It was maybe three acres, not much larger than mine. The next one was about an acre and had only one house on the east side. As we approached the next island, a glint off of something reflective caught my eye just ahead and to the right.

Sitting ten feet above the water has its advantages. As we passed the northernmost island, I saw a boat beached on the far side of it. Lifting the binoculars I always keep close at hand, I trained them on the island. There was only one person in the boat, kneeling in the forward cockpit and leaning over the casting deck.

"What do you make of that?" I asked Deuce, handing him the binos. "Far side of that little island." Deuce stood and trained them on the island as I made a long, sweeping turn around it, heading toward the mouth of the harbor.

"A guy in an eighteen-foot flats skiff, beached. He's not moving and the outboard is down."

Anyone who operates a flats skiff knows to raise their engine before going into really shallow water. Easy way to shear a pin if you don't. Something didn't smell right. Literally. We exchanged quick, nervous glances and all four of us were suddenly very alert. We'd all smelled it before. Too many times.

I pulled back on the throttles and brought the *Revenge* down off of plane. Idling forward, I turned toward the skiff with the corpse on board while reaching forward and switching the sonar to forward scan.

Quickly, I pulled out the chart from the cabinet under the helm and unrolled it across the wheel. "Water's deepest on this side, but the three-foot line is still twenty feet from shore. The wind's out of the south, so I'll nudge the bottom, drop the anchor, and pull back ten or twenty feet. Doc, go unstrap the Zodiac. Bourke, the engine and gas tank are under the ladder down in the engine room. Deuce, grab a few earwigs from under the bunk."

By the time I'd dropped the anchor and pulled back, setting it in the shallows, Doc had the inflatable in the water and was walking it by the painter to the transom door.

While he and Bourke were mounting the engine, Deuce came out of the cabin and tossed one of the little communication devices up to me. I put it in my ear and turned it on. As the three men climbed into the Zodiac, I heard Deuce say over the earwig, "Com check."

The three of us answered back as Bourke started the little outboard and went racing off toward the island. A few seconds later, he shut off the outboard and raised it out of the water, coasting forward until the boat beached about ten feet from the skiff.

"Hey, mister," I heard Deuce shout. "Are you all right?" The man on the boat didn't move. Not that we expected him to. I was watching through the binoculars and could see that he was only wearing a pair of khaki shorts. A light blue shirt and some other black clothing, maybe a jacket, were laying on the casting deck.

Doc got to the man first, moving around to the upwind side. He checked his neck for a pulse, but even from here it was obvious the man was dead. He had long blond hair and his face was turned my way. His skin was pale and his empty eye sockets stared at everything and nothing at all.

"He's dead," Doc confirmed. "Skin's splotchy and blistered and it looks like a sea bird or three have been nibbling at him. They always go for the eyes first."

Bourke picked up his shirt and checked the pockets, then set it back down. Then he picked up what I'd thought to be a black jacket and held it up in the breeze. "Is that a woman's dress?" I asked.

Turning it inside out, he examined the label. "Yeah, an expensive one, too. Badgley Mischka, size two."

Deuce was checking out the boat aft and said, "Ignition's still on and the gas tank is bone dry. The prop's dug into the sand and nearly worn off. He beached at a good clip and left the motor running, engaged."

"Anything under him?" I asked.

Doc lifted the dead man by the hair until he was nearly upright, then both he and Bourke turned away, retching.

"His package is hanging out of his shorts and crabs have eaten half of it!" Bourke exclaimed between retches.

I grabbed the mic and turned the VHF radio to channel sixteen. "This is motor vessel *Gaspar's Revenge* calling the Royal Bahamas Police with an emergency."

A second later a voice came over the radio. "Royal Bahamas Police. What is the nature of your emergency?"

I told him where we were and that we'd found a dead body on a boat, beached on the northernmost island of Parrot Cays. He asked if I was sure he was dead, so I described how he looked.

"We have a police boat heading out of Marsh Harbour right now. They should be there in less than thirty minutes. Please remain at the scene, *Gaspar's Revenge*."

*Awesome reaction time*, I thought. "You guys see what you can and get back to the boat," I said. "Local LEOs are on the way, ETA twenty-five minutes."

They searched the body and found a few Bahamian dollars and coins, but no identification. Then they searched the whole boat, being careful not to touch any-thing, before moving back to the Zodiac. Bourke started it and they were back on board well before the cops got close enough to see us. I've had to deal with local cops enough to know that they really don't like anyone, espe-cially outsiders, even getting close to a crime scene.

"Only the dress," Bourke said. "No other sign that a woman was aboard. Maybe she fell overboard in just her underwear."

"Or maybe she wasn't wearing any," offered Doc. "The dress was a halter-type thing, so no bra."

The police boat came alongside and shut down their big outboard engines. The two officers on board grabbed our railing, the one that was riding passenger wearing the stripes of a Sergeant on his immaculate uniform. He first looked over at the body on the skiff, then looked up to where we all sat on the bridge and said, "Have you dis-turbed the body in any way?"

"No, Sergeant," I replied, climbing down from the bridge. "The guy on the radio said to stay put, so we just dropped anchor."

The boat's pilot, a black man in an equally sharp uni-form, tied a line from their boat to the port cleat and was talking in low tones on the radio, which was turned way down.

"Do you mind if I come aboard, Captain?" the Sergeant asked in the singsong accent of the islands.

Knowing that it really didn't matter if I minded or not, I nodded. "Sure thing, come aboard."

He stepped across the gunwale and I offered him my hand. He took it and said, "I'm Sergeant Cleary. What's your name, Captain?"

"Jesse McDermitt, out of Marathon, Florida."

"How long ago did you find di body?"

"We were just coming into the harbor for fuel," I replied. "It looked like the boat had run aground, so I stopped to help. When the guy didn't respond, I looked through the binoculars and could tell he was dead, so I called you guys. Couldn't have been more than a couple minutes before I called."

"And how long have you been in di islands?"

"Came through customs on Nassau yesterday evening," I replied, knowing that he'd probably already checked this before getting out here. "We refueled there and arrived on Elbow Cay early this morning. We're staying at Crystal Waters, just south of here."

"Why didn't you clear customs in Bimini, if you came from Florida?"

"There was a bit of a storm and they advised me that the approach was rough and I should continue to Nassau."

Another police boat was slowing as it approached and went straight to the skiff and the body. There were three black men aboard, two in police uniform and one older man wearing a plain white dress shirt and black tie. *Probably a Detective*, I thought.

"It's him," the other officer said to the Sergeant after hanging up the radio mic. "At least it's his skiff."

"You know the guy?" I asked the Sergeant.

"I know who owns the boat," he replied, looking back over his shoulder at the corpse on the skiff. "My kid brudda, James."

# CHAPTER THIRTY-ONE

The price has gone up," Jose Reynolds said into the phone. "And I'm taking full control of anyone you send over here. You guys don't know a whit about what's going on."

"I told you he was dangerous," Nick Maggio replied. "You chose to ignore my warning and got sloppy. I have four people on their way, professionals. I'm very sorry about Mister Lopez. I lost a man, also. The four men coming to meet you will be led by a man named Richard Michaels. If you and your people decide to stay on the job, there will be a bonus when this is over. As to who is in charge, you can take that up with Mister Michaels when he arrives."

"How much of a bonus?" Reynolds asked, the two women listening closely.

"Five percent, when the treasure is recovered and brought back here. Now, tell me. How did you end up in the same hotel as Madic and his two men?"

"They checked in a few minutes after we did," Reynolds replied. "They didn't see us, but we saw them. We're in adjacent second-story rooms, and we watched the older man and his two bodyguards go into one of the beach cottages. After a minute the two men came out. I closed the curtains so they couldn't see in. They walked right past our rooms and are in the two rooms next to ours. One of them is on the front patio, I assume watching over the older man's cottage."

"And Madic saw your faces at the restaurant," Nick said. "You'll have to get out of there somehow, find another place. When you do, I'll let Mister Michaels know where you are and you can bring him up to date. With McDermitt's people numbering twice what we originally figured on and being well armed, we've decided to take a different approach. Michaels is going to capture one of them and hold them until the others deliver the treasure."

"I'll call you back," Reynolds said and ended the call.

"You heard?" he asked the two women.

"I had my head turned," Faye Raminez said. "The other night in the restaurant? Madic and his two men never saw me and Gary."

"That's right," Bianca Garcia said. "Your backs were to him. He only saw me and Jose. What do you have in mind?"

A few minutes later, after Faye had changed and stuffed her clothes and running shoes into her bag, she was ready. Reynolds and Bianca went through the interior door to the adjacent room, further from the two bodyguards' rooms. Faye stood at the exterior door, looking through the little peephole. The large man was standing on the balcony, looking out toward the cottages. Even though he was wearing a sports coat, she could see the muscles flex as he moved. She could also see the slight bulge under his left arm where she was certain he carried a gun.

Faye stepped back from the door, put on a pair of oversized sunglasses, took a deep breath, and tossed her hair over her shoulders. She opened the door and stepped out, turning straight toward the bodyguard and nearly running into him as he straightened and turned toward her.

"Oh!" she exclaimed. "I'm sorry, I didn't know you were standing there." Then, smiling and lowering her sunglasses slowly to the tip of her nose so the man could see her dark, smoky eyes, she said. "You certainly are a big man."

Then she slowly walked past him, allowing a little more than the normal sway to her wide hips. She was wearing a blue bikini with a pair of very short cut-off jeans and three-inch heels. Ridiculous attire for going to the beach, but perfect for getting a man to take his eyes off of what he's supposed to be doing. After four steps she looked back at the man who was staring after her, unabashed lust written all over his face. She smiled as she slowly lowered her sunglasses again and saw Jose and Bianca leave the corner room and disappear around the corner. They planned to meet up later at Turtle Hill Villas, just a little way down the road. Jose and Bianca were taking the road and she was to make her way there on the beach.

Half an hour later, Reynolds and Bianca were in a three-bedroom villa. It was only a five-minute walk from the lodge they'd barely escaped. Fortunately, September is considered the slow season and there were rooms available just about everywhere through a quick Internet search.

"She should be here already," Reynolds said.

"Do you think those men caught her?" Bianca asked in her clipped Puerto Rican accent. "Maybe they did see her at the restaurant."

Reynolds checked his watch. Maggio's men were probably already on the ground and heading to the ferry on Great Abaco. He took out his phone and called Nick Maggio as Bianca disappeared into one of the bedrooms.

"We're at Turtle Hill Villas," he said into the phone when Nick answered, "just half a mile south of the docks. But we may be down to just two."

"What happened?"

"We assumed Faye hadn't been seen by them since her back was turned at the restaurant. She decoyed the bodyguard and allowed us to get out unseen."

"They caught her?"

"Maybe," Reynolds replied. "I don't know. How soon will your men get here?"

"They were just boarding the ferry before you called," Nick replied. "I'll let them know where you are. They should be there in thirty or forty minutes. How well do you know her?"

"Not well," Reynolds said, closing the door to the bedroom that Bianca had gone into. "No great loss. She came to work for my mother just two months ago."

# CHAPTER THIRTY-TWO

They held you guys all this time?" Julie asked once we'd returned and settled into the living room.

I was getting a bottle of water from the fridge and replied, "When the forensics team came out, they sent us into the harbor so we could get fuel but told us not to leave the dock area. They even had an officer posted there."

"The dead guy was the brother of the cop that came out to where we were," Doc said. "He identified the body by a dolphin tat on his back. When the word got out, a bunch of people started gathering at the docks. When they brought the body in an hour later, I overheard several fisherman say they saw the guy leaving last night with a dark-haired woman who's now presumed missing, a tourist that had been seen around Hope Town Harbour Lodge."

"You said her dress was found on the boat?" Nikki asked.

"And the dead guy was shirtless with his johnson hanging out," Bourke said. "Doesn't take a rocket scientist. The coroner thinks the kid had a heart attack and she fell overboard trying to get to the wheel, which was tied off."

"They were doing it on the front of the boat while the boat was moving?" Charity asked. "Pretty kinky."

"Pretty stupid, if you ask me," I said, shaking my head and taking a stool at the large breakfast bar. "The throttle on the boat was wide open."

"Anyway," Deuce said, "the coroner finally placed the time of death at around midnight. The Sergeant asked for a readout from the GPS on the *Revenge* and it showed our arrival here at dawn, so he cut us loose."

"Well, today's shot to hell," Rusty said. Turning to Doc he added, "There's still enough daylight for me, you and Nikki to get to that first homeowner and get permission."

"Good idea," I said. "You guys head out. Maybe we can catch a break and get started on the search in the morning. I'm going down to the boat to think."

"Think?" Deuce asked.

"Yeah, I think better on the bridge. Something's been nagging at me all day and I can't put my finger on it."

I left and started down the path with Pescador trotting ahead of me. When I got to the boat, I unlocked the hatch and turned off the alarm system. The generator was running quietly and the air conditioning was humming as it moved the cold air through the cabin. There was still a little coffee left and I poured myself a mug, setting the thermos aside while I set up the machine for another run. While waiting for it to brew, I powered up my laptop and connected to the boat's Wi-Fi.

My former first mate, Jimmy Saunders, is an electronics wizard who set up a satellite internet account for me and turned the whole boat into a hotspot. The Wi-Fi was also connected to the boat's security system, so I could check it when I wasn't aboard. I logged onto the security system and checked the alarm history. I could tell at a glance there hadn't been any unauthorized tampering today, since it'd only been armed and deactivated twice, once while we were sleeping and just now, when we went up to the house. Yesterday showed the same—no access other than myself.

I shut the laptop off, poured my thermos full of Rusty's new coffee, and headed up to the bridge. As I watched the sun sinking closer to Lubbers Quarters Cay, I sat back at the helm, swiveled it to face the port bench seat, and put my feet up.

This was such an idyllic setting. Beautiful tropical plants lining the shoreline, crystal clear water beneath the hull, and a soft tropical breeze blowing out of the south, gently rustling the coconut palms on the beach. *So why have I been experiencing such a strong sense of dread since we got here?* I wondered.

Suddenly it hit me, like a bowling ball right between the eyes. The woman I saw earlier on the beach. I'd been racking my brain trying to remember where in the Keys I might have seen her. It had to be there, I'd originally thought, because I'd never been to this island before.

Except when we flew over the other day.

The woman on the beach was the same woman that had waved at me and I'd waggled the wings in response. I was sure of it.

I slapped myself on the forehead, then put my coffee in the holder and nearly jumped off the bridge before running up the dock and hill to the house.

"Turn on the TV," I said. "Deuce, pull up the local news service on your laptop. While you're at it, pull up the pictures you took on the flyover."

"What's up?" Tony asked as he switched on the TV.

"See if there's a local news channel, Tony," I replied. "If there is, they'll be running the story of that kid's death all day."

Deuce found the story on the local paper's website just before Tony found the local news channel. The missing woman was identified as Ettaleigh Bonamy, but they didn't have a picture. The local news finished the weather forecast and went straight into the top news of the day, a young man who worked at Hope Town Harbour Lodge was dead and a guest of the lodge was missing and presumed dead. They didn't have a picture of the woman either.

"What am I looking for?" Deuce asked.

"The flyover of that rock out in the water," I replied. "You took pictures all the way back to the beach. Any shots of the beach itself? Hope Town Harbour Lodge is just south of there."

"Okay," he said, clicking through the images on the screen. "That still doesn't tell me anything."

"There!" I said. "Back up one and go to full screen."

The image I'd hoped for came up full screen as the others gathered around. "That middle structure of the three at the top of the frame—can you zoom in on it?"

With Deuce's super-high-resolution digital camera, you could almost count the grains of sand on the beach.

"Get as close up as you can on the woman standing on the deck."

Deuce dragged a box across the deck and hit enter and the woman came into fairly clear view. "That's the woman that was on the beach when we left," Bourke said. "She's even wearing the same outfit."

"Okay, Deuce," I said. "Let's get Chyrel on the horn and have her hack the Hope Town Harbour Lodge's registration."

A minute later, Chyrel's face appeared on the screen. "Hey, Boss. What's up?"

"Hi, Chyrel," Deuce said. "We need you to hack into a hotel registry here on Elbow Cay. It's called Hope Town Harbour Lodge."

"Okay, give me just a minute."

Deuce turned toward me and said, "What are you thinking?"

"I'm thinking when you're up to your ass in alligators, it's time to drain the swamp, or get the hell out."

"Okay," Chyrel said. "I'm in. What do you want to know?"

"They have three beachfront cabins, or cabanas," Deuce said.

"They call them cottages. Nice place."

"Okay, cottages. Since there's only three, I assume they're numbered one, two and three, or maybe A, B, and C."

"One, two, and three," Chyrel said.

"Who's in number two?"

"Unoccupied."

"Makes sense if the cops have it sealed off," Bourke said.

"Most recent guest?" Deuce asked.

"Ettaleigh Bonamy."

"Thanks, Chyrel," Deuce said, snapping his fingers. "Have a good night."

"Wait a second," Charity said. "Who's in the other cottages?"

"I thought you'd never ask," Chyrel said with a grin. "Number one is currently occupied by Valentin Madic."

"Let me guess," I said. "Number three is his two goons?"

"Nope," she replied. "A Mister and Missus, Franklin DeMetri, two retirees from the Windy City."

Chyrel was still grinning. "You should never play poker," I said. "Give it. What cottage, cabana, or hotel room are they in?"

"Rooms three and four in the hotel."

"I think it's time we paid those two a visit," Rusty snarled.

Chyrel was still grinning ear to ear. "What else you got, Chyrel?" I asked.

"Also in the hotel, in rooms one and two, are none other than Jose Reynolds, Bianca Garcia, and Faye Raminez."

Deuce grinned up at me. "Up to our asses in alligators, that's for sure."

"Thanks, Chyrel," I said.

Deuce stood and began pacing as he often does when he's working something out in his head. "We have Reynolds and the two call girls that were following us staying at the same hotel as Madic and his two hired muscle. Madic is staying right next door to a woman who was seen leaving the island last night with the dead guy and is presumed missing, yet turns up right here the next day. Something's missing."

"Pull up that surveillance photo of the meeting at Conner's office," Tony said.

Deuce sat down and clicked a few keys. The four surveillance photos came up and Tony said, "Isolate the one of the woman getting in the car and the full shot of her from behind."

After a few more keystrokes, two of the photos disappeared and the other two took up the whole screen. "It's the woman on the beach," Bourke and Tony said at once.

"How can you tell?" Charity asked. "You can't see her face in either picture."

Bourke looked at Charity over his reading glasses and said, "I know you'd like to believe none of us guys objectify women, but in all honesty we don't just look at a pretty face. When she was on the beach, one very fine-looking leg was visible under her sarong."

"That leg," Tony said, pointing at the photo of the woman getting in the car with her leg sticking out. "The hair's the same color and they're the same build, too."

"Too much coincidence not to be the same woman," Julie said. "She's supposed to be missing at sea and was staying in the cottage next to Madic. In actuality, she works for Madic, may somehow be responsible for the death of the island guy, and is now staying down in one of those villas?"

"What I don't get is how a twenty-something island guy dies of a heart attack," Nikki said. "Maybe she killed him for some reason."

"She could cause a heart attack," Tony said, grinning and pointing at the two pictures. "Heck of a way to go."

"I think we should just pack it in and get out of the swamp," Deuce said. "Too damned many alligators."

"No," Nikki demanded. "That clue has been in my family for generations, unsolved. We don't know exactly how much these other people know."

"And they don't know how much we know," I said with a crooked grin. "Right now there's at least nine of them, counting the three guys at Hole in the Wall, maybe more coming. We know where they are and who they are. If they're working together, and I don't believe they are, they know how many we are, but not very much more about us. If they're not working together, then only Maggio's crew knows our strength."

"What makes you think they're not working together?" Rusty asked. "I mean, they're staying in adjacent rooms."

"I don't know," I replied, getting up and looking out the kitchen window. "Just a hunch I have and can't put a finger on. The chance at instant riches brings them out like palmetto bugs when the lights go off."

As I looked down at the docks, I realized I'd been in such a hurry to get up here that I'd forgotten to lock up the boat. The reminder came in the form of the woman from the beach coming out of the cabin on my boat. "I know how we can find out, though. Rusty, Doc, and Tony, stay here—everyone else, go upstairs. Quick. Ettaleigh Bonamy is coming up the path."

The others hustled up the stairs as I grabbed four beers from the fridge and we went out on the deck. Hidden from her view by the overhanging trees, I quickly surveyed the deck. Picking a spot in the corner nearest the path, where it was obvious we couldn't see the boat, the four of us sat down.

"I'm telling you, Rusty," I said louder than necessary, "it was a marlin or a stingray, definitely a game fish. Not a shark."

Rusty picked up on my *Jaws* reference and immediately engaged Tony and Bourke in a heated debate about game fishing as the woman approached. I watched her out of the corner of my eye as she stopped and looked up, then looked back at the *Revenge*. From her vantage point, it was obvious we couldn't have seen her sneak onto my boat, so she continued walking up the path, secure in the knowledge that she hadn't been seen. She was wearing the same yellow one-piece bathing suit, but a solid blue sarong now. Up close she looked even more beautiful. Her jet-black hair fell to the middle of her back and a few strands blew across her face in the light breeze.

Pretending to see her for the first time, I stood up. "Hi, there," I said, smiling. "Great sunset, wasn't it?"

"Why, yes, it was," she replied with just a hint of an accent, pushing her hair back behind her right ear. "I was watching it from down on the beach. Is one of those boats yours?"

"The big one," I said. "I'm Jesse. Are you staying in one of the villas?"

"Yes," she replied. "For a few days."

The other three men had stood up as well. As she approached, I said, "These are my friends, Rusty, Doc, and Tony. Care for a beer?"

She hesitated for a moment then said, "Another time, maybe."

"Ah, come on, we're just four harmless fishermen," I said, studying her face now that she was only a few feet away. Her skin was dark. Not tanned, but sort of a dark olive. Her hair was fine and straight, but it was her eyes that drew me. They were a very dark brown, almost black, and deeper than any eyes I'd ever seen.

"Oh, it's not that," she said, her facial expression not reflecting any knowledge of anyone else being here. "I'm sure you are all nice gentlemen, but I have some business to take care of." Then she smiled brightly and said, "But perhaps you'd care to join me for a drink later, Jesse?"

"I'd love to. Where would you like to go?"

"Stop by villa three in an hour," she said. "We can figure that out then."

"I didn't get your name," I said as she turned and started down the path toward the villas.

"Constance," she replied, looking back over her shoulder. "Constance LeBeau."

"Jesse McDermitt," I replied. "At your service, Miss LeBeau."

She stopped and turned her head, tossing her long, jet-black hair over her shoulder. Smiling very seductively, she said, "We'll see." Then she continued down the path to the villas. The four of us picked up our beers and went inside.

A moment later, Deuce and the others came down the stairs as I pulled the curtains on the east side of the living room.

"You might be right," Deuce said. "By her response she thinks it's just the four of you. That, or she's a very good actress."

"The bitch was on my boat," I growled. "I forgot to lock up when I came up here."

"Tony," Deuce said. "Get down there and check it out. Covertly."

"Roger that," Tony said, grabbing his small bag sitting by the door.

"Are you going to meet her?" Charity asked.

"It'll look extremely suspicious if I don't," I replied. "I don't think this bunch wants anything more than the treasure. The other group might be pissed at us now that they seem to be a man short thanks to Deuce."

"Anthony, do we have any of those listening devices left?" Deuce asked.

"Four," Bourke replied. "The short-range, peel-and-stick units."

Bourke went over to the line of go bags by the door and brought his back. Opening it, he removed four small boxes. Inside each one was what looked like flattened-out used chewing gum. "These only have a range of one mile," Bourke explained. "They're activated when you remove the backing and will stick to just about anything, including cloth."

"Take a few of those with you when you go to meet her," Deuce said. "Two can play this game. All you have to do is peel the backing off and stick it under a table or something. When the backing comes off it activates the transmitter and will send a constant feed for six hours."

Tony came back in just then and said, "There're two. A constant transmit listening device under the helm and a combination tracker and listening device just above the frame of the hatch inside the hanging closet. Both are activated and both are very sophisticated long-range devices. Nothing like the one before. Want me to deactivate them?"

"No," I replied. "We don't want them to know we're onto them. But people better stop bugging my damn boat."

# CHAPTER THIRTY-THREE

Tena Horvac called Madic, who picked up on the first ring. "You have something to report?"

"Your divers have reported that they made initial contact earlier. The tracking device has been installed. A second listening device, also."

Madic thought for a moment, then said, "There's only the four of them, right?"

"It appears so," Tena replied.

"Our people on Chub Cay are ready," Madic said. "All we have to do is wait for them to find the treasure and leave. The tracker will alert the men on Chub Cay when they get within thirty miles. Still, it would be nice to have some advance notice, to give them a heads up. You said you've made contact with the two women divers?"

"Yes," Tena replied. "They are in the first villa directly below the house and are watching it. However, their view is not very good. Should I have them make further contact, also? To plant listening devices inside the house?"

"They're both very good at what they do," Madic responded.

"I thought you'd appreciate their abilities," Tena said into the phone, with an evil sparkle in her eyes.

"Yes, very much," Madic said, thinking back. "Have them move to get closer to at least one of them. Not McDermitt or the bar owner. One of the two younger men."

"I'll let them know right away. How are things there where you are?"

"Not good," Madic replied. "Police are everywhere. McDermitt was the one that found the body earlier today. Hopefully the police won't go to the villas to question them further."

"I'll relay that to the divers," Tena said and ended the call.

She immediately made another call. The voice on the other end was bubbly and cheerful, until Tena spoke. "Mister Madic says to proceed as planned. Try to get close to one of the two younger men. He also said to be alert—a body was found this morning and McDermitt is involved. The authorities may come to the villas to question him further."

"Consider it done," Elana Galic responded.

When Elana put down the phone, she sat down next to Sabina Duric on the sofa, tucking her feet up under her. All the lights were off and Sabina had her body twisted over the arm of the couch as she looked through a small telescope on the end table. It was trained up the hill at the big house, but only the top floor and the bedroom side of the first floor were visible. Occasionally, the wind would move some of the trees and she could catch a glimpse of the deck or the living room, but the curtains were drawn there.

"We are to get close to the two younger men," Elana said.

Sabina kept her eye to the telescope. "That's too bad. The tall one looked to be more fun. Isn't one of the younger ones married?"

"It won't matter," Elana replied. "He's miles from home. You know how American men are. Horvac also said to be careful. They found a body this morning and the authorities may come here to question them."

"There's someone coming down the path," Sabina said.

Elana picked up a pair of binoculars sitting on the table. Leaning lightly across Sabina's hip, she trained them out the window and up the path.

"It's the tall one, McDermitt," Elana said. "Is he coming here?"

"I did invite him for a beer."

They both watched as he passed the villa they were staying in, continuing down the hill. Moving from window to window, making sure to stay in the shadows, they followed his progress to the next villa, where he went up the steps and knocked on the door.

"For a minute, I thought we might have some fun with him anyway," Sabina said. "He seems to be more interested in the older woman staying alone."

"Go back to watching the house," Elana said. "I'll watch him."

Sabina went back across the room and took up her position on the sofa, watching the house for any more movement. A light went on upstairs and she saw the fat man pass in front of the window. A moment later, the light went off.

"I think the fat man just went to bed," Sabina said.

"The tall one has gone inside," Elana replied. "The woman looked like she was ready to go out for the evening. They must have a date."

"She's very beautiful," Sabina said. "He doesn't stand a chance." Elana came back across the room and sat next to Sabina once more.

"Now would be a good time to visit the two younger men," Elana whispered as she again leaned over the other woman's hip, looking up at the house, but without the binoculars.

Tracing small circles on Sabina's exposed thigh, the smaller woman sighed and said, "Perhaps in a little while."

# CHAPTER THIRTY-FOUR

I t was dark when I made my way down the path toward the villas. Passing the first one, I noticed that it was dark. The two women staying there must have decided to go into town. I reached the next two and went to the door of the only one that had lights on. I knocked and after just a moment the porch light came on. A few seconds later, the door opened.

Constance, or Ettaleigh, or whatever her name was stood in the open door, silhouetted by the living room lights behind her. She was wearing a loose-fitting top made of lightweight silk with narrow spaghetti straps. It did very little to block the light behind her, clearly showing the shape of her body beneath it. Below an exposed inch of her tan, flat belly, she wore a pair of tight-fitting black jeans. Standing in heels, she was only an inch or two below my six three. Her long black hair fell down in front of and behind her bare shoulders.

"Mister McDermitt," she said. "At my service?"

"Miss LeBeau," I said, bowing theatrically. "If you were serious about going out for that drink, I am."

She smiled and her dark eyes seemed to smolder. "I was trying to force myself to work," she said. "Which isn't easy here. Please, come in."

She led me into the living room, where a laptop sat open at a desk. On the screen were a number of pie charts and the desk was covered with what looked like business documents. *If she works for Madic, maybe she just handles his legitimate business matters,* I thought. *Yeah, and occasionally B and E of people's boats to bug them.* I couldn't help but wonder about the dead man, though. Could it be just as it appeared? An overly amorous coupling resulting in a heart attack? Did she panic about the thought of being involved with a much younger man and stage the disappearance?

She gathered up the assorted papers, arranging them into a neat stack and placed them next to the computer, not even attempting to hide any of it.

"My employer insists that I work through my vacation," she said, by way of an apology for the mess. "It's okay, though. Our business is nearly complete and I have several more days here. Would you care for a drink?"

"A beer if you have it," I replied.

"Have a seat," she said and seemed to glide across the room to the kitchen. "I'm afraid I didn't buy any beer when I went to the grocery. The bar is well stocked, though." She moved like a dancer, with very little wasted movement. She opened the refrigerator in the dimly lit kitchen. The light inside caught the profile of her body, showing every detail of her breasts as she bent to get a bottle of wine and set it on the counter.

"I prefer wine, usually. But you strike me as a rum man. They have seen fit to stock quite a few here."

I sat down in a rattan chair, with plush, tropical cushions, that faced both the kitchen and the exit door. "A dark rum, then," I said as I watched her pour a glass of wine.

Reaching up to the top cabinet for a tumbler, her shirt rode up, exposing quite a few more inches of dark, flat belly. *Focus, McDermitt*, I told myself.

She carried her wine glass and the tumbler to the bar. "Ice?" she asked.

"Just one," I replied and she used a pair of tongs and dropped a cube in the tumbler from an ice bucket.

"Let's see. There's a couple of dark rums here. Mount Gay or Pusser's?"

"Pusser's will be fine," I replied. She poured two fingers and brought the drinks into the living room, swirling the dark rum to chill it. Handing it to me, she sat on the adjacent sofa, crossing her legs, and took a tiny sip from her wine glass, running her tongue over her lips to gather any stray drops.

"So, I take it you're a professional fisherman?" she asked.

"Yeah, we're out here for the annual white marlin migration just off the coast," I lied, taking a long pull on the chilled rum. I looked around the room, trying to decide where to plant the first bug. "My clients are anxious to get out there tomorrow. What kind of business do you do?"

"Exporting," she replied. "I'm sort of a freelance go-between. The people I am currently contracted to, wish to expand their business here in the islands and I was sent to learn of the viability of their product here. Very boring, actually."

Taking another drink, I looked around the room. It was decorated similarly to the house we were in, but the tongue and groove walls and ceilings were a slightly darker shade. *Near the desk*, I thought.

"A very nice place to be forced to work in," I said.

"It does have its advantages at times," she said with a smile.

I drained my glass and set it on the table. Leaning back in the chair, I felt the rum starting to lighten my head. But the feeling wasn't exactly right. When Constance took another sip of her wine, her eyes seemed to glow with an inner hunger. I watched as her tongue once more licked the stray droplets from her lips, but the moment seemed to drag out very slowly.

She leaned forward to place her glass back on the table, revealing a good bit of cleavage. Her every move seemed to be catlike in nature. I found myself becoming mesmerized by her eyes, even more so by her other attributes. The excitement I felt just looking at her was almost overpowering.

We made small talk for thirty minutes or so , during which she made me a second drink and I sipped it more slowly. Mostly she talked, because I was having a hard time putting a cohesive sentence together. I was that distracted by her beauty. It seemed that no matter what she said or did, I found it enticing and as the minutes ticked by it seemed she was purposely trying to get me to notice her body. I'd never felt this kind of animal attraction to a woman. Every fiber of my being wanted to tear off her clothes, pick her up, and carry her into the bedroom.

Far in the distance, I heard the distinctive sound of a gun being fired. That immediately brought my mind back into focus. The single shot was quickly followed by another, then a moment later, two more in rapid succession. I could tell they were a different caliber—the first sounded like a small-caliber handgun, with the loud crack of a supersonic round. *Probably a .22 long rifle cartridge in a revolver*, my mind intuitively surmised. The subsequent shots were the deeper booms of larger-caliber handguns like we carried. *Maybe even a .40 or .45*, I thought.

"What was that?" Ettaleigh or Constance asked.

I shook my head to clear it and was instantly on my feet, crossing the room in quick strides to the open sliding door to the deck facing east. I stood beside it, listening for a moment, my hand instinctually going for Pap's big Colt tucked under my shirt.

"Gunfire," I replied. "In town."

# CHAPTER THIRTY-FIVE

Faye quickly made her way down to the beach. Pulling on a tee shirt and swapping her heels for running shoes, she looked both ways along the beach. Seeing no one, she ran out onto the sand. She ran daily on the hard-packed sand back home in Miami and knew exactly how long it should take her to reach Turtle Hill. She found a path that led to the road in front of the villas and hid in the bushes to wait for Jose and Bianca.

They came up the street a minute later and went into the office. Faye remained hidden in the bushes. A few minutes later, the two came out and Faye followed them at a distance, keeping to the shadows along the edge of the tropical jungle. They soon arrived at one of the larger villas on the bay and went inside. Faye found a spot among the foliage where she could see the house clearly and waited.

She didn't have to wait long. Fifteen minutes after Jose and Bianca went into the house, four men appeared from the main road, moving quietly toward the house. Faye could tell by the way they moved that they weren't there to party. They moved with precision, using hand signals. Faye ducked back deeper in the bushes as one of the men reached the door to the house and knocked before pulling a gun out of his pocket.

When Reynolds opened the door he must have seen the gun in the man's hand. Stumbling backwards he fired a quick shot at the man from his own gun. The shot hit the man in the shoulder and spun him around as he fired harmlessly into the door jamb.

Instantly, the other three men swarmed into the house, firing two more shots, which made Faye cringe. A moment later, the three gunmen came out and helped the first man to his feet, then moved toward where Faye was hiding in the bushes, stopping just a few feet away.

"Just a flesh wound, Colour Sergeant," the injured man said with a British accent. "Weren't there supposed to be three of them here?"

"Reynolds texted me just as we were approaching," another man said, also with a British accent, but with the timbre of authority in his voice. "Madic got the other slag. Break up and head for the next target."

"Right away, Colour Sergeant," the first man replied and they split up, all taking different routes away from the crime scene, but all heading north and not south, which was the way Faye was going to go.

When they were well gone, Faye made her way quickly past the villas and took a different path back to the beach. People were coming out of some of the rentals, so she walked casually. Once there, she could just make out someone moving north along the bottom of the dune, half a mile to the north. She waited until she was sure he was out of sight and started running south again. She wasn't exactly sure how far it was to where McDermitt was staying, but she had a fair idea. She also knew the main house and the cluster of villas below it should be visible from the road.

It took her fifteen minutes to cover nearly two miles of beach. Her normal morning runs were five miles on the hard-packed sand of south Florida. Two miles on this powdery sand left her short of breath when she started up the path from the beach to the main road. When she got to it, she knelt on the sand at the edge of the path to catch her breath and look around. There were very few cars on the island, but a lot of golf carts and bicycles. She waited, watching the villas and the big house above them. All of the villas were completely dark, as was the house. She checked her watch and saw that it was just after ten o'clock. *Someone should still be awake*, she thought.

Seeing and hearing nothing, she quickly darted across the road and into the shadows along the left side of the path going up the hill. Moving as quietly as possible, she made her way past the smaller villas and neared a large house on the left. The lights were on and would illuminate her if she continued.

Faye knelt in the darkness for a moment, the blood pounding in her ears. Finally, hearing nothing, she darted across the path and into the lush tropical foliage between the villas and the house. The grounds were well manicured and she moved from tree to tree, staying in the shadows as much as she could.

She stood next to a large coconut palm catching her breath and looked up at the darkened house. As she started to step away from the tree and proceed further, she felt cold steel pressed against the side of her head and warm breath on the side of her neck.

"Don't even think about moving," a rough voice whispered in her ear.

# CHAPTER THIRTY-SIX

When I looked back from the open doorway, Et-taleigh was reaching for her purse. I drew my Colt and leveled it at her, saying, "That's far enough, Miss Bonamy." She looked up, surprised. "Yes, we know who you are," I added. "Now step back away from that purse real slowly."

She took two steps back as I came back into the room. "How did you know?" she asked.

"Recognized you from the plane," I replied. "We also know you work for Madic."

This revelation really surprised her, as her mouth fell open and she began to stammer something. I picked up her purse and looked inside. It didn't surprise me when I found a Serbian-made Zastava .357 Magnum, just like the ankle gun I took off one of the bodyguards at the *Anchor*.

"Into the bedroom," I said as I motioned with the Colt. A gleam came to her eyes and I realized I'd had an erection for the last half hour. "Just to turn off the lights," I added.

Once she'd turned off the lights in the bedroom, I motioned her toward the front door, turning off lights behind us as I went. Once outside, I turned off the porch light and motioned her in the moonlight to go down the steps.

"Head up to the house," I said. "And be real quiet."

We walked quickly to the house. Tony was at the northwest corner of the house and saw us coming. "Welcome to the party, Ettaleigh," he said, startling her. Stepping partly out of the shadow, he grinned, his white teeth gleaming in his dark black face. Then he turned to me and said "The two women from the other villa are inside."

His last statement excited me and that in turn sickened me. *What the hell is wrong with me?* I wondered. Then it hit me. *The bitch drugged me.* I wasn't stumbling or slurring words. My mind was clear, but it seemed to be fixated on one thing. Sex.

"Who is on perimeter?" I asked, to get my mind off it.

"Me, Bourke, Rusty, and Deuce," Tony replied, handing me an earwig.

I put it in and, switching it on, I said, "Com check."

Everyone responded that they could hear me. "Are you all right?" Doc asked.

"She drugged me, Doc," I replied, pushing Ettaleigh up the steps. "Nothing debilitating, though."

Julie opened the door to let us in, wearing her Sig openly outside her pants with her shirt pulled up and tucked behind the holster. This, too, seemed to be both a turn-on and revolting at the same time.

Doc stepped into the dining room from the living room. "If it's not debilitating, how do you know you've been drugged?"

"Sit down over there," I said, shoving Ettaleigh onto the couch, where Charity held the other two women at gunpoint. Again, the urge to just jump into that pile of feminine flesh nearly overwhelmed my brain.

I turned to Doc and, pointing to my crotch, I said, "That's why."

Doc looked down and tried real hard to hold back a laugh. Finally he said, "What'd she give you? Viagra?"

"It ain't funny, Doc!" I walked over to where the three women sat on the couch. "What the hell did you give me?" I growled.

"Nothing," she said with a seductive smile and those smoldering black eyes. Looking into them, I had the urge to turn and shoot my friends so that I could be with her.

"Charity," I said, turning toward her and turning my gun around in my hand. "Take this. I'm not in full control."

Charity reached out slowly and took the gun from my hand. The touch of her fingers on mine was like electricity. I turned and went back through the dining room, motioning for Doc to follow.

Outside, in the soft breeze, with the moonlight shining down on us, I felt a little better. I reached up and switched off my earwig, motioning him to do the same. "Whatever she gave me, Doc, it's made me horny enough to hump a fence post. Charity's hand touching mine just now excited me like all hell and just looking into that woman's eyes made me think that shooting everyone so I could be alone with her wasn't such a crazy idea."

"You're kidding, right?"

"No, I'm not kidding, dammit. Even Julie's open carry holster turned me on. What the hell did she give me, Doc?"

He thought about it a moment and said, "There are any number of drugs on the market to boost a man's virility, but what you're describing goes way beyond any of that. Almost like ecstasy."

"Look," I said. "She works for Madic and they want to either beat us to the treasure or take it from us. Taking me hostage, or even killing me and saying I was their hostage, would make sense. So why would she give me some kind of drug that'd turn me into her own personal stallion?"

"That's it!" Doc said, snapping his finger. "I bet that's what caused that island guy to have a heart attack. Let me check your pulse." He put two fingers to my neck and after a few seconds, he said, "Your heart's racing. Come inside. I'm going to give you a sedative. Any exertion now could cause you to go into cardiac arrest. She did want to kill you, but in a really sick way."

We went inside and I sat down at the dining room table. A moment later, Doc handed me two pills. "Swallow these, then go in the bedroom and lay down. I'll be in there in a minute."

I washed them down with a bottle of water he handed me and did exactly as he told me to do, keeping my eyes off of Ettaleigh as I went through the hall to the middle bedroom and lay down.

The sedative he gave me was strong. Coupled with the rum and whatever drug she gave me, I was soon drifting off to sleep.

A moment later, I heard the door creak and Doc said, "You all right, Gunny?"

I mumbled something as I tried to open my eyes, but even I didn't understand what I said. Gradually, my eyes opened and I could see that it was light in the room. I lifted my left arm and strained to focus on my watch.

"You've been out for six hours," Doc said. "I checked your pulse every hour and even dead asleep, your heart was pounding like a racehorse. It finally came under control about an hour ago."

I groaned as I tried to sit up, but only fell back on the bed.

"But you still have a hard-on," he added with a chuckle.

"You looked?" I groaned. "Don't ask, don't tell, Squid."

"Didn't have to look," he added, still guffawing. "Looks like you're sleeping under a tent."

I saw movement behind Doc and Charity's face came into focus. "Oh my," she said, covering her mouth and turning away, giggling like a schoolgirl.

"Get the hell outta here," I snapped. "I gotta hit the head."

Doc closed the door, and only when I heard his footsteps retreating down the hall did I throw off the covers and get unsteadily to my feet. I went down the hall to the bathroom, where I relieved my straining bladder for a full minute. Soon, after splashing cold water on my face, everything was back to normal and my head was clearing.

All eyes were on me as I walked into the living room and made a beeline for the coffeepot. Just by the smell, I knew Rusty had retrieved his La Minita stash from the boat. I poured a cup and drank about half before I turned around. The three women were now tied up on the couch, the two younger women asleep.

I walked into the living room and held my hand out to Charity. "Give me my Colt."

She reached behind her, pulled my gun out and handed it to me, butt first. I removed the magazine and checked that it was still fully loaded, reinserted it, and racked a round into the chamber.

I turned and crossed the room in two strides to where Ettaleigh sat primly on the sofa, her hands bound behind her and her breasts poking at the fabric of her silk shirt. The view did nothing.

I gripped her throat with my left hand and brought the Colt up and put the barrel against her forehead and roared, "What's your real name and what did you give me?"

Pescador was immediately at my side, the hair on his back up and his lips pulled back in a vicious growl.

"Easy, Gunny," Doc said. "That sedative is still playing tricks with your brain."

"We'll get to what the hell you gave me in a minute, Doc," I snarled, pushing the woman back against the cushion of the couch with the barrel of the gun and pulling back the hammer. "Answer me now, or I swear I'll blow your head completely off." Ettaleigh's eyes no longer held anything remotely resembling a smolder. They were suddenly wide and filled with terror.

"There's no need, Captain," a strange voice said. I looked across the room and couldn't believe my eyes. It was one of the prostitutes we'd left at Hole in the Wall.

"Her real name is Tena Horvac," the call girl said. "She's been under surveillance by both Miami-Dade and FDLE for several months, along with Consuelo and Jose Reynolds, Gary Lopez, the Maggio firm, and Valentin Madic."

"And who the hell are you?" I asked.

"My real name is Linda Rosales. I'm a Special Agent with Florida Department of Law Enforcement, working undercover."

"It's true," Doc said. "Chyrel verified it last night while you were asleep."

I decocked the Colt, holstered it at the small of my back and said, "Why didn't you say something at Hole in the Wall?"

"I tried," she replied. "But you said to 'Shut up and wait here' when you carried me ashore. That was the only time I was alone with any of you and didn't want to blow my cover."

"I still want to know what the heck it was that she gave me," I said, pointing at Horvac.

"We only identified her last week," Rosales said. "The word on the street is that she's supposed to be some kind of sorceress—a Chovani, as they're called in Romania. Her people are the original Gypsies. She's from Croatia, though, and the drugs she gave you are probably a mixture of several that were hidden in a secret compartment of her briefcase." Rosales turned a briefcase around on the table, showing me its contents in a red-velvet-lined false bottom.

"Okay," I said, even more confused, "someone needs to bring me up to speed. There were gunshots in town last night. What happened?"

Just then Deuce walked in with the cop, Sergeant Cleary. "Four unknown gunmen shot the hell out of my town," Cleary said. "Their first target, the shots you heard, was supposed to be Agent Rosales here, along with her recently deceased companions, Jose Reynolds and Bianca Garcia. At least, that's who the room was reserved for half an hour before the shooting. Both Reynolds and Garcia were killed by a single gunshot wound to the head. In the case of Garcia, the back of the head, execution style. Reynolds got one of the gunmen, it looked like, but probably only wounded him. About half an hour later there was a running gunfight on the beach, where four men were killed. The news this morning said that three of the men were guests at Hope Town Harbour Lodge and the other one had just arrived on the island. The news didn't release their names, because we haven't given that information out yet."

Opening a notebook, he continued, "The three guests are Valentin Madic, Borislav Varga, and Ivo Novosel. All from Miami, according to their passports. Based on Agent Rosales's description of the four gunmen she witnessed kill Reynolds and Garcia, the fourth dead man on the beach was one of them. He was shot and killed by Royal Bahamas Police and had no identification on him. Agent Rosales said that two of them spoke with British accents and one was referred to as Colour Sergeant. Agent Livingston has identified all of you as working for the American Department of Homeland Security. Does Colour Sergeant mean anything to any of you?"

"British Royal Marines," I said, rubbing my forehead. "It's Colour with a u. A Colour Sergeant is the same rank I was in the Marine Corps, E-7."

"There are three of these men still running loose on the island," Cleary said. "But we'll catch them. It's a small island. Now, I must ask. Why didn't you identify yourselves as American Federal Agents when you found my brother's body?" Horvac looked at Cleary quickly, which drew his gaze to her.

"I apologize for that, Sergeant," Deuce said. "All this is somewhat our fault. We're not here in any official capacity, nor for the fishing and diving. Petty Officer Talbot's wife's family held a secret clue to a buried treasure and we traced it to a Spanish vessel that wrecked here on your island in 1566. We think we know where it is and went through the Bahamian government to get permission to look for it. These two factions somehow learned about it and were planning to take it before we had the chance to turn it over to the proper authorities."

Rusty stepped up and handed Cleary his American and newly acquired Bahamian salvor's licenses, along with the certificate to salvage on land.

Cleary examined the documents and said, "I'm satisfied with that. But you should have come to the Police and informed us. Now, what about these three women you're holding?"

"FDLE has reciprocity and extradition agreements with the Royal Bahamian Police," Rosales said. "Tena Horvac is in my custody and will be going back to Florida to stand trial. That is, unless she's arrested here first. Then we'll wait our turn."

"Arrested here for what?" Cleary asked.

"For starters, drugging me," I said.

"With the same drug she probably used on your brother," Doc added.

Cleary's head snapped around. "My brother?"

"Tena Horvac was registered at the Hope Town Harbour Lodge under the name of Ettaleigh Bonamy," Deuce said.

"From what Jesse described the drug doing to him, I feel pretty confident that you'll find one or more of these drugs in your brother's system," Doc said, pointing at the open briefcase.

Cleary looked at Horvac then at the case and finally at me. "What did these drugs do to you, exactly?"

Charity and Nikki both giggled as Rusty chuckled at my discomfort. "If I remember correctly," Doc said, "Jesse claimed it made him want to 'hump a fence post.' His words."

"It's some sort of aphrodisiac?" Cleary asked, annoyed.

"Far beyond that," Doc said, getting serious. "It apparently attacked Jesse's circulatory system, causing his heart to beat at double strength and double speed. It's also a mild hallucinogen, which caused him to see and feel everything as being suggestive and sexually exciting. Sort of like the drug ecstasy. Combined and given to a man in a large enough dosage, he'd want nothing more than to literally have sex until his heart exploded. And the drug could very well give a man that ability."

I could almost see the light go on inside Cleary's head. His head turned slowly back to Horvac and he said, "You screwed my brother to death?"

"Feel free to take this briefcase, Sergeant," Deuce said. "I'm sure your ME will be able to do a comparison and determine if that's what happened."

"What of these other two women?" Cleary said, never taking his eyes off of Horvac.

"We know nothing about them," Deuce said. "They are staying in one of the villas below here and when the shooting started, we thought it best to keep them here where they couldn't be hurt." Looking directly at Rosales, he added, "Since there seemed to be a lot of people running around who weren't who they said they were, we thought it best to restrain them."

"None of you know who these women are?" Cleary asked, looking around.

"We're just a couple of tourists here to do some diving," Yvette said.

"Yeah, you need to let us go, or we'll sue you for false arrest," added Melissa.

"No," Deuce replied. "We have no reason to believe they're anyone other than who they say they are."

"Release them," Cleary said.

Tony went behind the couch and used a pair of wire cutters to cut the zip ties that secured their wrists.

"No hard feelings, ladies," Tony said and the two women left in a huff.

"Tena Horvac," Cleary announced, "you are under arrest for suspicion in the murder of James Cleary."

He went on to read her pretty much the same rights she'd have had in America and then took her into custody. Before leaving he gave Deuce his card and said when we were ready to start our search, to let him know and he'd contact the homeowners and pave the way.

"Cleary's wrong," I said to Deuce after Cleary left with Horvac. "There's two groups of three running loose out there."

Turning to Rosales, I asked, "Why didn't you tell him about the other three men and what happened at Hole in the Wall?"

"They probably wouldn't find anything there," she replied. "I overheard Reynolds tell the pilot to return there, clean up, and dispose of the bodies."

"Bodies?" Rusty asked.

"Yes, bodies. One of their men was killed in the firefight, along with Gary Lopez, Reynolds's partner. The light keeper was killed before we even arrived. By now, their bodies have been dumped far out at sea."

"They killed King Charles?" Rusty asked, standing suddenly. "That old man wouldn't hurt nobody."

Deuce turned to Charity. "Sit down with Agent Rosales and do sketches of anyone she can identify." Then he asked Rosales, "I don't suppose you know what kind of chopper it was?"

"Yeah," she replied with a smile. "It's a Bell 407, white with a red stripe. It's owned by Maggio and the pilot's name is Quintero. Madic has a Bombardier Challenger at the Marsh Harbour airport, also."

# CHAPTER THIRTY-SEVEN

**W**hat should we do now?" Sabina asked when she and Elana got back inside their villa.

"Do?" Elana replied. "We get out of here. Now!" She started toward the bedroom to grab a few essentials.

"Wait, Elana," the dark-haired woman said. "There may be something else we can do."

"Are you out of your mind?" Elana exclaimed, spinning on her heel. "Our employer is dead, Sabina!" Pointing toward the house, she continued. "There are nine of them up there. All well-trained American agents. And they have the backing of the local *politia*. You heard what their leader said. Whoever killed Valentin numbers three and then there are three others somewhere. Someone is cleaning up the mess. In case you have not noticed, that makes fifteen of them against just the two of us."

"Yes," Sabina said with a smile. "But we know all nine of the ones here. That makes eleven against six."

Elana walked over to a chair and flopped down in it to think about what Sabina had just told her.

Sabina walked around her and sat down in the chair across from her, leaning forward with her elbows on her knees. She waited until Elana reached the same conclusion on her own, knowing she would.

Elana looked up at her companion and smiled. "We bide our time? Work our way into the Americans' trust?"

Sabina smiled and said, "They're sure to hide the treasure on that big boat of theirs. All we have to do is take over their boat somehow."

Elana looked across the room, through the open window and up at the big blue house. She slowly looked back at Sabina, smiling. "And kill them all. It might work. Here is what we should do." The two women leaned toward each other conspiratorially.

# CHAPTER THIRTY-EIGHT

Wearing a clean pair of khaki pants, docksiders, my one and only short-sleeved white dress shirt, and a pair of aviator shades I picked up at a gift shop, I strode into one of the fixed-base operators at Marsh Harbour airport. Both Madic's plane and Maggio's chopper were parked right in front of it.

"You need fuel, sir?" the young man behind the counter asked. He was wearing a white polo shirt, with *Cherokee Air Services* embroidered on the pocket. His name tag said his name was Clifford.

"Thanks, Clifford," I said, looking around and seeing that he was apparently working alone. "We got fuel when we arrived a few days ago." It was a busy airport and I knew from my own experience that to locals, most tourists' faces seem to blend together after a while.

"What can I do for you? Mister..."

"Madic," I replied. "I think my friend's cell service must not work out here." Jerking my thumb over my shoulder toward the white Bell chopper on the apron, I continued. "The Bell 407 out there? Mister Maggio's people? I can't find them anywhere and it's a small island."

"Four men and two very pretty women?" Clifford said with a grin. *Most tourists' faces blend together*, I thought, *but not all.*

Knowing that a pilot always leaves contact information with an FBO in case they need to move his plane, I grinned. "Yeah, that's them. They're supposed to stay at the same place we're staying, but they're not there. I figured I'd find Quintero either at the nearest bar, or right here. He's particular about Mister Maggio's chopper."

He glanced down at his ledger, flipped back a couple of pages, and ran his finger down the list of incoming flights, stopping twice. "Here it is, Mister Madic. Arrived the night before you. Mister Quintero said he would be staying at Abaco Inn, at White Sound."

"Abaco Inn?" I asked. "He told me they'd be at Hope Town Harbour Lodge."

"Is that where you're staying? What happened there?"

"From what I heard, some rival drug gangs," I replied. "Abaco Inn, huh?"

"Yes, sir. I can call the desk if you like."

Pulling my satellite phone out, I said, "So can I." I slipped a twenty across the counter and, after looking left and right, Clifford snagged it and stuck it in his pocket.

"Thanks, Clifford," I said as I turned and headed toward the door.

"Any time, Mister Madic," my new best friend replied.

Outside, I climbed into the waiting cab and was whisked back to the ferry dock. An hour later, I was back at the house. Deuce and Julie were there with Linda Rosales.

"They struck out at the first site," Deuce said. "At least the homeowner was willing to let them search the yard with the metal detectors."

"Where's Tony?" I asked. Tony had stayed behind to spear some fish in the lagoon for supper.

"Those two women staying in the villa stopped by," Julie said. "They asked if anyone knew anything about diesel engines, so he went down to the dock to see if he could help."

"They're still here? I figured they'd have cleared out pretty quick after last night."

"Me, too," Linda said. "The blonde said that they understood you were only trying to protect them." Just then Rusty came through the door, his bald head beaded with sweat.

He went straight for the fridge and drank down a bottle of water in one pull. "This treasure hunting is hard work," he said as the others came in.

"We did a preliminary check," Doc said, "with the metal detectors set for precious metals at max depth. All we found in a thirty-foot grid from where the treasure should have been was a few Bahamian coins."

"What'd you find out, Jesse?" Deuce asked.

"The chopper and Madic's plane are both still at the airport," I replied. "Quintero is staying at Abaco Inn, just a little north of here."

"Get a room number?" Bourke asked.

"No, but that shouldn't be hard," I said, smiling at Linda.

She looked up at me and asked, "Having a flashback from the drug Horvac gave you?"

I blushed slightly, remembering the previous night and this morning. "No! Sorry, I didn't mean anything like that."

"Just pulling your leg, Jesse," she said. "You want me to persuade the desk clerk at Abaco Inn to give me Quintero's room number, right?"

"And maybe get him to open the door," I said. "Without a gun in his hand."

"The way he kept ogling my legs on the flight up from Hole in the Wall, it shouldn't be any trouble. What's your plan?"

I looked over at Deuce, who said, "While you were gone, I called Sergeant Cleary and offered our assistance and told him we might have a lead on where his gunmen are staying. He said he'd come by here after he gets Horvac booked and in a holding cell."

"Kind of a reach, isn't it?" I asked, sitting on the stool next to him. Usually it's me making rash connections based on a hunch. "I mean, Maggio obviously sent those shooters to eliminate not only Madic and his people as rivals, but also the three that could connect him to anything. My guess would be he'd want to eliminate Quintero and the two men with him as well."

Deuce's laptop beeped and he opened it. A window opened saying that he had a video call from Chyrel. He clicked the connect icon and Chyrel's face came up on the screen.

"Hi, Deuce," Chyrel said. Then, in what I'm sure she considered a sultry voice, she said, "How's it hanging,

Jesse?" She quickly covered her mouth with her hand, laughing.

I glared at Deuce. "Is there anyone you guys didn't tell?"

"I'm pretty sure the First Lady doesn't know," Chyrel said, laughing even harder.

Getting control of herself, she said, "The information you asked for just came through, Deuce. I forwarded it to the Director and emailed it to you. Checking immediate family and known associates I found that Alfredo Maggio has a cousin in Kendall by the name of Rodrigo Quintero and another cousin in North Miami named Manuel Serrano."

"Everybody's got a cousin in Miami," I said, which caused Chyrel to start laughing again.

"I didn't know you were a parrot head, Jesse."

"A what head?"

"Never mind," Chyrel said and continued. "Rodrigo Quintero has a helicopter pilot's license and sometimes flies Maggio's Bell for him."

"Good work," Deuce said.

"Hey, when are you guys coming home? It's too quiet around here."

"With any luck, by the end of the week," Deuce replied. "Contact the Director and let him know what happened here last night and that, as shorthanded as the local LEOs are, I volunteered our services."

"Will do. Talk to you later." The screen went blank and Deuce closed the computer.

"Who is Manuel Serrano?" I asked. "And what's a parrot head?"

"Manuel Serrano is the other man that was killed at Hole in the Wall," Rosales replied.

"That's the hunch I had," Deuce said. "Maggio isn't going to kill his cousin. But he will send mercs to help his cousin, when someone kills a family member."

"So you think Quintero is hiding the Brits?"

"We're the only ones that know who Quintero and the other two from Hole in the Wall are. For that matter, we're the only ones that know they exist."

I thought about that for a minute. It would be best if we had the local Police support, to clear anyone else out of the hotel.

"Are you going to stay for supper?" Julie asked Linda. "We have plenty. That is, if you like fish."

"Hadn't really thought about it," she replied. "Nor where I'm going to stay."

"You'll stay here, of course," Charity said. "It'd be dangerous for you anywhere else. Tony can move into my room and you and I can bunk in his, where there's two beds."

I looked out the large glass sliding doors to the southwest. "It's almost sunset," I said. "I think I'm gonna go get a shower and give Kim a call, then have a beer and watch the sun go down."

"Keep your phone handy," Deuce said. "And see what's taking Tony so long."

I headed down the path with Pescador trotting ahead. When I got to the dock, I could hear Tony laughing and talking to the two women.

"Deuce was wondering if you'd been kidnapped," I said, approaching the women's boat. "What was the problem with the engine?"

"Believe it or not, as clear as the water is here, the intake strainer was fouled, causing the engine to overheat.

Guess they don't check them over all that well at the rental marina."

"I'm gonna hit the showers. Deuce was asking about you—I think they're about to start supper."

"Hope it's all right," Tony said. "I invited Melissa and Yvette to eat with us. Figured it was the least we could do, after last night."

I nodded at the two women, grinned, and said, "Hope this Squid didn't hurt you ladies."

They both looked puzzled for a moment, and then the blonde said, "Oh, no, we're both fine. We slept through most of it."

I continued up to the dock and stepped down into the cockpit of the *Revenge*. Pescador went over by the transom door and, after making a couple of turns, settled down for a nap. I unlocked the hatch, turned off the alarm, and went straight forward to my stateroom.

Ten minutes later, after a shower and fresh clothes, I was sitting on the bridge with a cold beer, thinking over everything that had happened in the last few days. Looking over the starboard bow at the sun slowly sinking toward the horizon, I took out my phone and called Kim.

She was excited to hear from me, explaining that she'd gone to the gun range early the day before, which was why she didn't get my call. I told her about some of the things going on here, leaving out the dangerous parts. She was excited about the treasure hunt and part of me wished she were here to share the experience. The irrational part. The rational side knew it was still far too dangerous. We talked for a few minutes more, when I heard footsteps coming down the dock.

Linda had changed clothes. Her feet were bare and she was wearing khaki cargo pants and a long-sleeved plaid shirt that I recognized as belonging to Julie. I told Kim I had to go and ended the call, with her saying, "I love you, Dad."

"Mind some company?" Linda asked when she got to the end of the dock.

"Come on up, Agent Rosales," I replied. "You'll need to ask the dog's permission first, though. He's picky about that, thinks it's his boat."

"May I come aboard?" she asked Pescador, as if talking to a dog was an everyday occurrence. He looked up and barked once.

"I take it that's dog talk for 'permission granted'?"

"Far as I know, yeah."

She dropped lightly down to the deck and climbed quickly up the ladder. She sat down on the end of the port bench and looked out over the water toward the setting sun.

"Care for a beer?" I asked, nudging the small cooler with my foot.

"Thanks," she said, opening it and taking a bottle. She twisted the top off and took a long, slow pull on the ice cold Kalik. "Since we're drinking buddies now, do you think you can drop the 'Agent' part? Just Linda will do fine."

"Okay, Linda," I replied. "Welcome aboard *Gaspar's Revenge*." I held my bottle out to her and she clinked the neck with her own bottle.

"Hard to believe any kind of violence could ever happen in such an idyllic place as this," she said, watching the sun sinking lower. "I don't think I've ever seen a more peaceful sight."

She was right; this was one of the most tranquil, beautiful places I'd ever been to. But even though it's very small, this island had seen its share of violence over the centuries. I kept dwelling on the Spanish sailors that met their end in a storm a couple of miles from here and the survivors finally dying of thirst, starvation, or injuries they'd sustained in the wreck. Maybe a combination of all three. I suddenly felt a chill and shuddered.

"Can I ask you something?" I asked.

She looked at me and smiled. "You're wondering how a forty-year-old woman could pull off getting assigned to go undercover as a call girl?"

"You're forty?" I asked. "I'd have guessed quite a bit younger. But that's not what I was wondering."

"What is it, then?"

"You have kids?"

I guess with all that had happened over the last couple of days, she was slightly taken aback by the personal question and it showed in her expression.

Understanding seemed to light her brown eyes and she said, "Your daughter, Kim? Sorry, when you said you were going to call her, the curiosity got the best of me and I asked Charity who she is. Are you rethinking your lifestyle choice now that your daughter is in your life again?"

"Something like that," I replied, watching the bottom of the sun meet the trees on Lubbers Quarters Cay and seem to set them ablaze while brushing the high, almost transparent clouds with a pastel pink-orange hue.

"I have a son," she said. "He goes to University of Florida, a sophomore."

"You find having a kid makes it harder to focus on the job?"

"He went to live with his father when he was fourteen," she replied, staring blankly at the horizon and taking another pull from the beer bottle. "That was when I applied to FDLE. I was with the Highway Patrol for ten years before that. This was my third undercover op, my first deep cover."

"My lifestyle isn't really a choice," I said, not comprehending why I wanted this perfect stranger to understand without knowing. "It just sort of happened. When I left the Corps six years ago, all I wanted to do was enjoy the down island life, do some diving, catch a few fish, and maybe bed down a pretty tourist woman every now and then."

She laughed heartily, with a sparkle to her dark eyes I hadn't noticed before. "What happened to change that?" she asked.

I took a long pull from my beer and watched the sun as it disappeared behind the island. In just a few weeks it would be a year since the only woman I'd ever really loved came back into my life, unannounced. She arrived about the same time as Hurricane Wilma. Things moved really fast over those few days and we decided to get married. She'd been murdered the night we were supposed to be honeymooning. There'd been a couple of other women in my life since then, but my mind was never in the right place for a relationship. Maybe it never would be.

"A lot of things," I lied.

In the dim light I could see in her eyes that she didn't quite believe me, her eyes seeming to say, *go on*. Just then, my phone chirped. A text message from Deuce: *Supper's on.*

"We better get up there if we're going to get anything to eat," I said. "Those Squids have huge appetites."

She laughed and said, "I once dated a Sailor for a while. I know just what you mean."

After supper, Sergeant Cleary arrived. We filled him in on the events that happened at Hole in the Wall, leaving out the part about the Browning machine gun. He was understandably upset that we hadn't told him earlier. Charity provided him with pretty good sketches of Quintero and the two men with him and Deuce provided him with the printout of the email Chyrel had sent, outlining the connection between the three men and the Maggio law firm. Cleary came to the same conclusion we had. The three remaining British mercs, and we were pretty sure that's what they were, would be holed up with Quintero and his men at Abaco Inn waiting for us to find the treasure, or the heat to blow off, before leaving the island.

"I have a dozen police officers arriving in the morning," Cleary said. "As you might expect, we're spread quite thin and I won't be able to move until morning."

"Can you empty the inn and surrounding buildings tonight, without tipping Quintero off?" I asked. "Then maybe turn your back for five minutes?"

"Your superiors have also offered assistance," he replied. "As much as I'd like to accept, it's just not possible. We'll arrest them in the morning."

After Cleary and the two women from the villa left, we assigned watch, having two people outside the house and one person on the bridge of the *Revenge* at all times, pulling three-hour watches. Linda volunteered to help out and Deuce gave her the last watch with Charity. Nikki protested not being included, but Deuce pointed out that we had an odd number of people and Rosales was a law enforcement officer.

"At least it'll only be for one night," I said. "With Maggio's people out of the way in the morning, we won't have to look over our shoulder while we're looking under rocks."

"Do you really think you'll find treasure?" Linda asked.

"We're pretty confident," Doc replied. "We have three other places that look good."

"We'd better all get some rest," Deuce said.

I headed down to the boat with Rusty and Bourke and took first watch, sitting on the bridge with a thermos of coffee and night vision goggles. Through our earwigs I could talk to Tony and Doc in low whispers, although I couldn't see either of them. They had the first watch up at the house and posted themselves at opposite corners, where they could see all four sides.

We kept all the lights off inside the house, especially the outside lights. It was highly doubtful that Quintero and the mercs would come here. They obviously wanted to wait until we found the treasure. Having the advantage of three sets of night vision goggles, the darkness was our friend.

We talked about the hunt for the treasure and who the mercs might be. Finally, Tony asked, "What do you make of Agent Rosales, Jesse?"

"Seems pretty competent," I replied.

"I don't think he meant her professional ability," Doc said.

"She's all right, I guess," I replied. "Seems nice enough."

"I overheard her asking Charity about you," Tony said. "When we were moving our gear from room to room."

I didn't say anything. True, she was a good-looking woman and technically I was single. Jackie's job in Washington pretty much nixed any chance of a relationship there. She couldn't pass up the opportunity and there was no way I was going to live in a city, especially not one that got snowed in several times a year.

"What about those two in the villa, Tony?" I asked, changing the subject. Sort of.

"Very nice," he replied. "Gonna be hard to choose. Maybe I'll just take 'em both."

"Yeah," Doc said. "In your dreams."

We lapsed into silence for a while and soon I felt someone moving around down below. Glancing at my watch, I was surprised at how fast the night had passed by. It was almost midnight.

A moment later, Rusty came up the ladder with my second thermos and said, "Go get some rest, bro." I handed him the goggles and said goodnight, then climbed down and went to the galley. He'd already set the timer on the coffeemaker for 0230, so I cleaned my thermos and left it for Bourke. I went down to my stateroom and, stripping down to my shorts, climbed into bed.

# CHAPTER THIRTY-NINE

Nick was in his office very early. Well before daylight, in fact. His wife was becoming suspicious about his late hours and early mornings. She didn't think he should be away from home so much with her being eight months pregnant. But until this situation was resolved, he needed to stay right on top of it. His father was depending on him.

The mercenary he'd hired two days ago had been instructed to check in at least every twenty-four hours and also as soon as the treasure was found and recovered. The previous morning, he'd called before six o'clock to say, in his words, that "all six targets had been neutralized."

Nick was still at home when the call came, so he decided it would be best if he were in the office the next day. He'd immediately gone to his computer and wired the second of the three payments they'd agreed on to the man's numbered account in the Caymans. Michaels called back just as quickly, accepting the second part of the job even though he had lost one man already.

"This part won't be dangerous," Nick had told him.

When McDermitt finds the treasure, Nick figured they'd leave the island almost immediately. He'd instructed Michaels to contact him again in twenty-four hours if McDermitt didn't find it before then. Nick had people in South Florida that could easily intercept the slow moving fishing boat, kill everyone aboard and take the treasure.

At five-thirty Nick's cell phone rang as he sat at his desk. He answered it immediately. "They didn't find anything yesterday," Michaels said, as soon as Nick answered the phone. "My man was close enough to hear that much last night. They'll be looking in a different place today."

"Stay on it," Nick said. "All we need to know is when they depart. I have people in place that will intercept them before they reach Florida."

"Roger that," Michaels said and ended the call. He was next up on the rotation and needed to get going. They were working in six-hour shifts, using the property next to the one the targets were staying in. The house was unoccupied, so they had no trouble breaking into the small boathouse on the property's dock after disabling the alarm system. From that vantage point, they had an unobstructed view of the other dock, the boat and much of the house.

"I'm going to relieve Fletcher," Michaels told Quintero, who was up and making coffee. "Make sure someone rousts Hailey by eleven."

"How long do we need to be cooped up here?" Quintero asked.

"As long as it takes, mate. Just make sure you don't order more bloody food than what three hungry men would normally eat for a meal. I imagine the proprietor would take a dim view of six of us staying here when there's only supposed to be three. Fletcher will bring back some extra supplies."

Twenty minutes later, he arrived by bicycle to the back of the boathouse. The path and the back side of the boathouse were completely hidden from both the blue house they were watching and the boat tied at the end of the dock. Having the rear windows open, Fletcher heard Michaels signal with a low whistle and opened the door for him.

"There's a few more of them than the four we were told about, Colour Sergeant," Fletcher said. "I counted the original four and two more. On top of that, the two birds from the villa seem to be getting on well with the black bloke."

"Eight?" Michaels asked. "Who are the two more?"

"Coupla ladies," Fletcher answered. "One seems to be with the big bloke with the short hair. The other one is a tall bird, with short fair hair."

"Just the four men and now they've picked up some lady friends? No problem, we're just here to watch and let the man know when they leave."

"Right, Colour Sergeant," Fletcher said. "I'd best be on my way. Everything all right at the inn?"

"That Quintero bloke is getting on my nerves," Michaels said. "Always going on about needing more food and wanting to go outside."

"Right," Fletcher responded. "I'll stop at the grocer and pick up a few things."

"Don't forget to drop that Cockney accent when ya do, mate."

Fletcher left him then, took the bike and headed to the small grocery store on the way to the inn. Michaels settled in and looked out the window. It was dark inside the boathouse and the windows were covered in a reflective screen to keep out the heat. *Still gets bloody hot in here,* he thought.

Looking over at the boat through a pair of binoculars, he could see the man sitting on the bridge in the dim, gray light of dawn. It was a man he hadn't seen before. He was about the same age as the tall man who owned the boat. His hair was darker, slightly graying at the temples, and he wore a bushy mustache. Though he appeared shorter, he was slightly broader in the chest and shoulders and about the same weight as the tall man. *So, there's five men,* Michaels thought.

A moment later, the tall man came out of the cabin and climbed up to the bridge and the two stood side by side in the dim early morning light. *What the hell,* Michaels thought. *For ten grand a day, we'll watch a whole bloody rugby team.*

# CHAPTER FORTY

I woke early. It was still dark inside my stateroom, but through the port hatch I could see it was just starting to get light outside. I pulled on a tee shirt, went to the galley, and filled a thermos before heading up to the bridge.

Bourke stood up as I climbed the ladder. "Don't look around, Jesse," he whispered, so low that I barely heard him. "We're being watched."

I stood next to him and took a sip of my coffee. "Where?"

He looked down into the cockpit and I followed his gaze, knowing that wherever the watcher was, we now had our backs to him. Bourke removed the night vision goggles and handed them to me. I made a great show of putting them on and looking up, down and all around the stern.

"One person in the boathouse at the boat's ten o'clock," Bourke whispered. "Left window."

I pretended to look all around, as if getting used to the night vision, as I slowly turned and my gaze drifted past

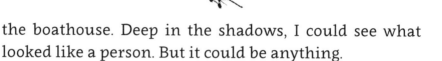

the boathouse. Deep in the shadows, I could see what looked like a person. But it could be anything.

Over the earwig, I heard Deuce say, "We have no visual here, Jesse."

Turning back aft, I whispered, "What time did Cleary say he was going to take those guys down?"

"He's moving against them in about ten minutes," Deuce replied. "I talked to him just a few minutes ago and told him about our boathouse guest. He suggests we do nothing until he can get here. He's going to call me back as soon as he takes the men at the inn into custody."

"I suggest we do nothing until he calls," I whispered. "And decide then. All six of them might be in there and none at the inn."

Turning to Bourke, I said loud enough to be heard over the water, "Go on up and get some breakfast, I'm just gonna sit here and enjoy my coffee for a while. Rusty's probably hungry, too."

Bourke nodded his understanding and went down to the deck and into the cabin. A moment later, I heard Rusty over the earwig. "You sure, Jesse?"

I swiveled the chair lazily and when my back was turned to the boathouse, I whispered, "Yes, go ashore."

A few seconds later, Rusty and Bourke headed up the dock, coffee mugs in hand. It was getting lighter and the goggles would be ineffective very soon. I slowly spun the chair back forward and slouched down in it, resting my chin on my chest.

Night vision goggles have a major flaw: tunnel vision. Your head has be pointed at what you're looking at and you have no peripheral vision at all. So it was impossible to turn my head slightly away from the boathouse and keep my eyes toward it. The next best thing was to slowly swivel the chair back and forth as if I were bored, so that my gaze fell across the boathouse and away from it.

I stopped the back and forth now and then to sip my coffee and look closer at the boathouse. The second time I did this was when I saw movement. As much as I wanted to hold my gaze on the window, I looked away.

Without moving my lips, I whispered, "Saw movement."

"They're real crafty," Bourke said. "I saw the first guy about zero five hundred and he rarely moved. Just before you came up, another person entered the boathouse and the first guy left."

"Watch schedule," I whispered, fully aware of how well sound travels over water.

"That's what we figure," Deuce said. "One guy on at a time."

As it grew lighter, the optics automatically reduced the amount of light and within minutes, nothing was visible through the boathouse window.

"Who's on watch at the northwest corner of the house?" I whispered, removing the night vision headset.

"I am," came Charity's voice over the earwig.

"Deuce, have someone take Charity's position above her on the deck and call out to me," I whispered. "Charity, move quietly down to the foot of the dock, but stay hidden."

"Roger that," she said.

A second later, Tony stepped out of the sliding glass door and moved over to the northwest corner of the deck and called out, "Hey Jesse!"

About the same time, Charity said, "In position."

I stood up on the bridge and leaned over the port rail and shouted, "Is breakfast ready?"

"Yeah, you coming up?" Tony shouted back.

"I thought we were going to wait for Cleary's call," Deuce said.

"We are," I whispered, as I climbed down the ladder. "I just wanted someone watching the boat and boathouse." Then shouting at Tony, "Be there in just a minute."

In the cockpit, I stepped inside and set the alarm, then locked the door. Turning back, I held up my hand at Pescador, staying him. "Stay here a minute, buddy. I'll bring you some bacon and eggs."

He looked up at me and whined. "Okay, I'll bring you fish, then." He barked once, his thick tail thumping the deck.

When I went into the house, Deuce was on the phone. "I understand," he said and ended the call. He turned toward me and said, "That was Cleary. There were only five of them at the inn. One's dead and two wounded. One of his cops took a round, but luckily it was in the vest and he'll be okay."

"That leaves one bad guy," I said. "And he's sitting right out there, watching my boat."

"Here's the bad news," Deuce said. "Cleary can't come for at least a couple of hours. He didn't actually have a dozen guys like he said he would. It was just him and four others. He says so long as the guy in the boathouse doesn't do anything, he'll come and check it out before noon."

"Noon?" I nearly shouted. "Hell, I can crawl right up next to this guy before noon and he'd never see me coming."

"This guy might," Deuce said. "Cleary listened to a conversation before busting in the door at the inn. The Colour Sergeant's name is Michaels, and he's the only one they didn't get."

"You think there's anyone else here more qualified to sneak across thirty feet of open, white sand beach and sea grass?"

Deuce knew my background very well. As a Scout/Sniper in the Corps, I'd taught cover and concealment to the best shooters the Corps had. Patience is the best quality of a good sniper; taking hours to move just a few feet is a hard task to learn.

Deuce looked at Tony. "No way," Tony said, holding up both hands. "A black man sneaking across white sand?"

"Hey, guys," Charity said over my earwig. "I might have a solution."

"Go ahead, Charity," Deuce said. "We're listening."

"There's a blind spot on this side of the dock and a lot of sea grass. A sea grass float could hide a snorkeler."

"Stand by," I said. "Let me look from the deck."

I walked out into the morning sunshine with a cup of coffee and moved across to the far side of the deck where the view of the dock was best. I leaned on the railing, pretending to look out over the Sea of Abaco. While my head was stationary, my eyes were measuring the distance from where I knew Charity was hunkered down over to the other dock.

Turning to go back inside, I whispered, "Great idea, Charity." Once back inside, I said to Deuce, "Looks to be about forty yards, with small clumps of sea grass most of the way. The only other approach is like I said, thirty feet of open beach. Too risky."

"What will you need?" Deuce asked.

"One ten-yard stretch is devoid of grass," I said. "I'll need a diversion to get past that. On that white sand, a pair of white trousers and white socks might help to conceal my legs."

I looked around at everyone at the table, all of them shaking their heads. "You mean nobody has a pair of white pants?"

"White shorts," Deuce said. "Your tan legs will stick out like a sore thumb, though."

"I might be able to help," Agent Rosales said over my earwig.

"Come on up," Deuce replied. "Tony, go relieve Charity and keep an eye on the boathouse. While you're down there, see what you can find for concealment."

A moment later, Rosales came up the side steps to the front door, the only part of the house hidden from view of the boathouse. She went straight to her and Charity's room, returning a minute later with a small bag. She set it on the counter and started rummaging through it, finally pulling out a pair of white stockings.

"Stockings?" I asked and everyone laughed.

"They are white," Rosales said. "And you wouldn't need socks."

"They'd fall off," I said. "Unless you have a garter belt in there that'll fit me," I added sarcastically.

"No, they won't," she said. "These are thigh highs. They have three rubber grooves around the top that stick to your skin."

"You gotta be kiddin'," I said, looking around at the others. "Nobody has a pair of white pants?"

"It's after Labor Day," Rusty said with a chuckle. "Nobody wears white after Labor Day. Well, except maybe them high-class call girls." Everyone got another good laugh at my expense as Rosales tossed them to me and they draped over my shoulder and head.

Thirty minutes later, wearing a white tee shirt and white shorts and feeling really creepy wearing women's stockings, I made my way around the far side of the house and down to where Tony had taken Charity's place. Being a SEAL sniper, he'd anticipated my needs and had already begun constructing the blind. We took a heavy life ring that he'd punched holes in with his pocketknife and festooned it with sea grass, sea grapes, and slime from under the dock, and soon had a pretty decent ghillie raft.

Donning my mask and snorkel, I went under the edge of the raft and lay prone in the shallow water. There was enough cover that I really didn't need the snorkel, but I used it anyway. If I needed to say something over the earwig, I only had to raise my head a few inches and drop the snorkel.

"Looks pretty good," Tony said. Then he chuckled and added, "But then, I've always been partial to white stockings."

"Just keep a close eye on the boathouse," I snarled.

"We're ready here, in case he sees you," Deuce said.

I shoved off, crawling slowly across the bottom with the benefit of a few pounds of lead weight I wore on a belt around my waist. Allowing my legs to just drag in the sand, I used my fingers for propulsion, moving a few inches and stopping for a minute or two. As a sniper, not being seen comes second to not being remembered. Even a trained mind won't register a clump of grass that's a few inches from where it was before. Given a long enough time frame, a properly concealed sniper can move across an entire field while a whole platoon watches from the edges and never be noticed. Forty yards doesn't seem like a very far distance, but at less than a foot per minute, it was going to take nearly two hours to get to the boathouse.

Forty-five minutes later, I was at the edge of the sea grass, the predetermined spot where Deuce would start the diversion.

"Okay, Rusty," I heard Deuce say over the earwig. "You guys are on."

Doc, Rusty, and Bourke began talking loudly as they walked out onto the deck, then down the path to the dock. When they reached the *Revenge*, I started moving again.

Although I couldn't hear them, I knew that the women were all heading out to the deck for a little sunbathing at the same time. With three men arguing loudly at the end of the dock and three women wearing next to nothing on the deck, Michaels was sure not to be paying attention to the water.

Rusty's argument started getting more and more heated. None of them were using earwigs, so it'd be impossible for me to hear Deuce or Tony if they needed to warn me. But I could still hear them with my ears just under the surface. Tony, who had a direct line of sight to the boathouse, said, "It's working. He's moved closer to the window and is looking back and forth from the deck to the boat."

I increased my speed and soon made it to the next clump of sea grass, where I froze in position for three full minutes. I was only thirty feet from the dock by the boathouse. There was a boat in the first slip, lifted up out of the water and with the sea grass at the water's edge angled toward it. I slowly followed the bed of sea grass.

Thirty minutes later, I was under the boathouse in five feet of water and ducked silently out from under the raft. I also reached down and shed the damned stockings, the rubber things snagging on about a million hairs as I pulled them off. *Me and my big mouth,* I thought.

Surfacing, I made an exaggerated *O* with my mouth and tapped twice on my forehead with my middle finger. The sound was lost to the lapping of the small waves on the pilings, but inside my skull it echoed, sending the prearranged signal through my earwig that I'd made it across.

"We have company," Deuce said over my earwig. "You're not going to believe who just rode up on a bicycle. It's Owen Bradbury."

I sat under the boathouse and listened to the one-sided conversation for ten minutes. Apparently, Bradbury had had second thoughts about being involved in murder, grand theft, and probably a dozen other crimes and had come to warn us.

The three men went back into the house and Deuce told Rusty to keep an eye on our new guest. I slowly crawled through the accumulated detritus you'd expect to find under a boathouse and made my way over to the far shore. Coming out of the water was going to be the hardest part. I was only feet away from the door and any water dripping off my body might alert him. I lifted my head slowly out of the water. Removing the mask and laying it aside, I plastered down my hair to get the water out.

Ten minutes later, I was standing up in knee-deep water, my Colt drawn and pointing at the door. Thankfully, it was a windowless door and the only window on this side was at the far corner. I slowly shuffled sideways toward shore and was soon standing at the corner of the boathouse with my back to the wall. By now, Rosales, Bourke, and Doc should be in place, hidden in the shadows at the edge of the foliage thirty feet away. Julie, Nikki, and Charity were still on the deck and would create a second diversion when Bourke said we were all in place. I glanced toward the bushes but couldn't see them. Which meant that Michaels couldn't see them either. I gave a thumbs up in the general direction I thought they'd be and waited.

"We're in place," I heard Bourke whisper over the earwig. I waited ten more seconds for the diversion to start. When I heard the women up on the deck begin screaming, laughing, and splashing water, I took the steps quietly up to the landing at the door. On the landing, a board creaked and I instantly took a lunging step forward, bringing my right foot up and planting it just above the doorknob.

The jamb splintered and the door gave, flinging in and banging against a chair. I followed it, my gun aimed straight ahead. He wasn't where I expected him to be, just an empty chair facing the window. I realized too late that he'd heard the creaking board and I started to turn to my left. Something came crashing down on my forearms and as my Colt fell from my grip, I realized it was a wooden barstool.

I followed the force of the blow and summersaulted forward into the room, coming up and turning, just as Michaels connected with a hard right to the side of my head. The room started spinning and lights flashed in front of my eyes. I'd been clocked a time or two, but this guy caught me in just the right place. I saw stars.

In an instant he was behind me, jumping up and snaking a forearm around my neck, forcing my head down into the crook of his elbow, while pushing me forward and down to my knees. I couldn't breathe and knew that if he held this hold for just a few more seconds, I'd never breathe again. I struggled against the hold, thrashing left and right, but he was very powerful.

I saw Rosales framed in the doorway and a shot rang out. Michaels's arm went limp and he fell back away from me as I fell forward in a heap, face down, struggling to get air into my lungs. Instantly, Doc was at my side, gently rolling me onto my back and placing two fingers against the side of my throat.

"He's got a pulse," I heard Doc say as he started to pull me up into a sitting position.

Then someone shouted, "Gun!" Doc moved instantly, rolling in front of me and forcing me down. I heard a sickening thud and Doc's dead weight fell on top of me as I was deafened by the sound of three more guns all going off at once.

# CHAPTER FORTY-ONE

Sabina bolted upright in the bed she now shared with Elana, who rolled onto her side. "That was a gunshot!" Sabina exclaimed.

Suddenly, three more shots rang out and both women instinctively rolled off the bed on opposite sides.

"It came from down by the water," Elana said. She got quickly to her feet and pulled on the tee shirt and shorts that lay in the chair by the bed.

"What time is it?" Sabina asked, also dressing quickly.

Elana picked up her watch from the night stand and replied, "It's after ten o'clock!"

"It was stupid of us to stay up so late," Sabina said as she hurried into the front room. Opening the door, she heard frantic shouts from down by the docks.

"I told you we should have left," Elana said as she joined Sabina at the door. "What's going on down there?"

"I don't know," Sabina replied. "The voices seem to be coming up the path now."

They listened for a moment and the shouting died down, as the people who were shouting got to the house on the hill and went inside. The silence was deafening.

They waited a full five minutes before deciding to head down the path to the road. "We can go to the ferry dock on foot," Sabina said. "It's only two miles."

They grabbed their backpacks, which held what they needed for a fast getaway, and left the villa. Once they reached the main road they turned north, walking at a quick pace, casting furtive glances over their shoulders.

"What do you think of that?" Elana asked, pointing to a tiny house on the left that was part of the Abaco Inn resort. The door of the house had yellow tape across it and the whole house was surrounded with more of the yellow tape.

Suddenly, a golf cart came careening around a curve thirty yards ahead and the two women quickly reversed direction. The golf cart was followed immediately by two more. As the first one approached, it came to a sudden stop.

"Aren't you the two girls staying at Crystal Villas?" the driver asked. Elana recognized him as the policeman that was at the house two nights earlier and ordered them released.

Knowing it was useless to lie, Elana smiled and said, "Yes, we are. Is something wrong?"

"Get on the back," he ordered. "There's been another shooting up there."

They started to protest and the policeman again ordered them to get on the back of the cart. They were barely seated when the driver took off.

Minutes later, they turned off the main road onto the path Sabina and Elana had just come down minutes earlier. Going past the villas and continuing up to the main house, the other two golf carts close behind, they came to a sudden stop at the steps to the house.

The policeman in charge got out and said to the driver and a second policeman, "Stay with these women." Then he went up the steps to the deck, followed by the other two men from the other golf carts.

# CHAPTER FORTY-TWO

Doc sat on a stool with his shirt ripped open while both Deuce and Tony worked on him. The bullet hit him high, just above the right shoulder blade, and exited just above his collarbone. Charity poured anticoagulant into both wounds as Deuce and Tony held him upright.

Doc winced in pain, gritting his teeth. "Hey," he grimaced. "Not so rough with the patient."

Julie ripped open two large gauze pads and, handing one to Charity, she slapped the other onto the exit wound.

"Good thing he didn't use hollow points," Deuce said. "That exit wound would've been a lot worse."

Nikki was watching as they worked on her husband. Finally, Doc lifted his head to her and gave her a small grin as Deuce wound sterile tape under both his arms and across his right shoulder. "Just a flesh wound, babe. Nothing to worry about."

Nikki instantly began crying and screaming at the same time. "Damn you, Bob! Why do you have to keep playing all this macho bullshit! I'm pregnant!"

Doc's mouth fell open. I looked at Nikki, standing there in a black bikini top, a towel around her narrow waist, with her feet firmly planted and her hands on her hips. Her face was full of concern, but her eyes flashed with fury.

"P-pregnant?" was all Doc could say.

Nikki stepped toward him, as Deuce finished wrapping sterile tape holding the two bandages in place. She took his face in both hands and stared into his eyes.

"Yes," she said gently. "You're going to be a father, Bob. Not a gun-wielding warrior father. Not a here today, gone tomorrow father. But a nine-to-five, home for dinner every night, push the stroller around the block kind of daddy."

Doc pushed himself up off the stool and put his hands on his wife's waist. "I'm gonna be a dad? For real?"

With tears running down her cheeks, she nodded and said, "Yeah, for real."

Ignoring the pain, the blood, and everyone in the room, Doc took his wife into his arms and held her close to his chest for a moment, then lifted her chin and kissed her passionately.

"I don't mean to break this up," Deuce said, "but the cops will be here any minute."

Doc suddenly realized he and Nikki weren't alone and looked around the room at all of us. Finally, his gaze stopped on me. Before my eyes, his whole demeanor changed. "I'm gonna be a dad," he said with a crooked grin. I knew then that we'd lost him.

"Yeah," I replied, grinning, "we heard. Congratulations, Bob."

He tried to raise his right hand to shake my hand but winced in pain, sitting back down on the stool.

I heard a commotion outside and went over to the open door. Cleary was headed up the steps with two of his men. All three men had their guns drawn.

I held up my hands and said, "Easy, Sergeant, it's all over. Follow me, I'll show you where the last of your gunmen is."

Leaving Deuce to clean things up in the house, I led the three cops down to the beach and over to the boathouse. They entered it tactically, guns drawn. When Cleary came back out to the landing, I explained what happened and how we tried to take the man peacefully.

"Who shot him?" Cleary demanded as Rosales came up the steps behind me.

"I did," she replied. "Four times."

Cleary looked down at the dead man. He had one dark stain on the top of his right shoulder, close to where Doc's exit wound had been. He also had a second, much larger stain on the left side of his chest where three holes were visible in his shirt. All of them could easily fit under a silver dollar.

"I had no choice," Rosales continued. "He had Jesse in a choke hold and was trying to kill him."

"He would have, too," I added. "If Agent Rosales hadn't stopped him."

Cleary looked inside at the dead man, past me at Rosales and finally looked up at me. "How much longer are you people going to be on my island?"

"Three more days," I replied. "Tops."

"I have half a mind to deport all of you today," he said. "But in the interest of continuing relations with both the American government and the state of Florida, I'll allow you to stay. For three days."

Half an hour later, having taken both my and Rosales's statements, Cleary left. Two of his men stayed behind at the boathouse until the coroner arrived.

"Thanks, Agent Rosales," I said as she and I walked back up the path to the house.

"Hey, I thought we were drinking buddies?" I stopped and turned toward her at the bottom of the steps.

"Thanks, Linda. I owe you."

"And I'll collect," she replied, with a smile. "One of these days." I watched after her as she went on up the steps to the house. At the top, she turned and smiled again.

"What are you going to do with me?" Bradbury asked Deuce as we came through the door.

"What we ought to do," I said, crossing the room toward him, "is feed your ass to the sharks."

"He did come to warn us," Julie said. "That took some guts."

The two women from the villa below the house were there, probably having heard the shots and all the commotion.

"A day late and a dollar short," I growled. "A lot of people are dead now because of your and Conner's greed."

"I am sorry about that," Bradbury said. "It's something I'll have to live with. But if Chase hadn't brought me in, they'd be just as dead. I'm here now and can tell you all you need to know."

Over the next hour, Bradbury explained how Conner had approached him about planting the bug after our first meeting on the boat. He said he never thought it would amount to anything but went along anyway. When they heard our conversation weeks later, Conner contacted Madic without Bradbury's knowledge to provide the funding and manpower. Madic in turn planted a bug in the bar at the *Anchor* and contacted Maggio to have him dig up more information about us. It turned out that Maggio's son had more connections to the crime world than Madic realized and took steps to beat Madic to the punch. As he was winding up his explanation of the snowball of events, Deuce's phone chirped.

"It's Cleary," he said, before answering it.

He listened for a moment then said, "Thanks for letting us know." After another moment, he said, "No, we're going to continue with our plans. If she's smart, she's long gone by now."

Deuce ended the call and turned to me. "Tena Horvac somehow coerced Cleary's one-man guard force into opening her cell. He's in the clinic, experiencing hallucinations and a very high pulse rate. Horvac and her little magic briefcase are gone and a Cigarette boat was stolen from a marina in Hope Town Harbour."

"Oh, great," Charity said. "That's all we need is a necrophiliac pharmacist on the loose."

The two women from the villa exchanged surprised glances and Bradbury's head drooped.

"What?" I asked him.

"I did some checking after meeting her," he said. "She was some kind of cult leader in her home country. Practiced witchcraft. Mostly harmless spells that were supposed to increase a farmer's crops or a fisherman's catch. But she was said to be a dark witch. Not that I believe in such nonsense, but when she was a young woman, she was gang raped by ten men. They were arrested and tried but never convicted. Over the next year, each one died of an apparent heart attack. Most of them naked in bed."

"Well, if she's smart," Deuce said to all of us, "she's long gone from here. We have work to do." Finally, he turned to Bradbury. "Mister Bradbury, we're going to hold you here until we figure out what to do with you. My guess is, you'll be turned over to the Police when we get back to Florida."

Rusty volunteered to stay and keep an eye on Doc and Bradbury while Deuce and three others headed to the second site, the house on the rock. Tony, Bourke, and I would get the boat ready if they struck out at the house. The third site was the offshore rock and we could work it well into the night if we had to.

Melissa, the blonde woman from the villa, asked Tony, "Do you think it would be possible to sort of tag along? We won't get in the way. Just watching a treasure hunt sounds like a lot of fun."

Tony looked over at Deuce. "Just stay out of the way," Deuce replied.

With Doc resting, Nikki taking care of him, and Rusty watching over Bradbury, we were down to seven people. Charity, Julie, and Rosales went with Deuce to the house on the rock, while Tony and Bourke helped me get the boat ready. The two women from the villa proved to be helpful also, as they were familiar with dive gear.

Within an hour, we had the mailboxes mounted above the swim platform on the *Revenge*. I'd had the pair made after using just a single one with great results on a Confederate shipwreck last summer. They were mounted on special swing arms that would drop them down over the platform to the twin propellers, redirecting the wash from the props straight down.

Before leaving for the third site, I went up to check on Doc, Pescador racing up the hill ahead of me. He was sleeping, having taken some pain pills and self-diagnosed himself as being fit enough, if he could just get a few hours of rest.

"You're going to make him quit the team, aren't you?" I asked Nikki as she walked to the door with me.

"I won't have to," she said. "He already told me that's what he wants to do. Carl still hasn't sold *Miss Charlie* and Bob thinks he can talk him into hanging onto it and letting him skipper it. It's not a nine-to-five job, but it's a lot less dangerous. I'm sorry, Jesse."

"Don't be," I replied. "He's got a family to think of now." My own thoughts turned to Kim. I was already rethinking my own involvement with the team. Colonel Stockwell was putting together another team to work out of Key Largo and had asked me to help him find the right boat, Captain, and location. Maybe I'd just have to find him two. I made Pescador stay with Rusty and walked back down to the *Revenge* to get underway.

It was thirteen hundred before we arrived at the rock a mile off the coast. The water on the lee side of it was fairly shallow, only ten to fifteen feet deep. We anchored about a hundred and twenty yards, or what we'd calculated would be the greatest distance that "eighty forceful advances" west of the rock would be. We put out two heavy Danforth anchors with plenty of rode astern and the main anchor nearly on the rock. The idea was to first blast sand from the bottom at the furthest place we thought the treasure might be. Then we could work our way closer to the rock by letting out ten or fifteen feet of rode to the stern anchors and taking up the slack with the windlass. Melissa and Yvette would be useful when we had to move, by letting out the stern lines.

Tony and I got our scuba gear ready, adding extra weight to our belts to help us hold our ground against the force of the churning water.

"What will you do if you find the treasure?" Yvette asked Tony.

He glanced at me and I nodded. "First, we have to call Cleary," he told her. "He'll in turn contact the Interior Minister, who will send out a survey team to lay out a grid and catalogue everything."

Melissa looked shocked. "You mean you won't be bringing anything up?"

"Maybe one or two things," I said. "Anything that might easily be overlooked or lost. If we find anything that we're sure wasn't on the ship's manifest, well, that's fair game. We'll have to wait for the survey team to finish the excavation, catalogue everything, and report it to both the Bahamian and Spanish governments."

"How many days will that take?" Yvette asked.

Tony and I both laughed as we rinsed our masks. "Days?" Tony said. "More likely months or years. Eventually we'll get credit for the find and probably ten percent of the total worth."

The two women exchanged nervous glances. "Years?" they asked as one.

"That might be a stretch," Bourke told the women. "Depends on how much is down there, if it's there at all. Getting governments involved will cause a lot of red tape, so maybe eighteen months at the outside."

Turning to me, Bourke said, "Just got off the horn with Deuce. They struck out at the second site. Not even a single Bahamian coin. Good luck."

I gave him a thumbs up and nodded at Tony. Wearing full face masks equipped with communications on the same frequency as Bourke's earwig, we rolled backwards off opposite gunwales and descended to the sandy bottom.

"They seemed real disappointed," I heard Tony say over the com.

"You take the north side, Tony," I said. "Get a good twenty feet away from the target area and make sure you keep that lanyard around your wrist."

"Roger that," Tony replied. We each had a small pick with a lanyard tied to it that we could jam in the sand to help hold us in place as Bourke engaged the engines and blew the sand away from the bottom.

When we were in position, I told Bourke to engage the engines and bring them up to about nine hundred rpm. The force was stronger than I'd counted on, as the twin props forced tons of water down at the bottom. It was all I could do to hang on. After thirty seconds I told Bourke to go to neutral.

There was a pretty good current flowing north and the sand was quickly swept away, exposing a ten-foot-deep crater about thirty feet across and twenty feet wide. Tony and I swam down into it and circled slowly, checking out the newly exposed rocky bottom.

"Nothing," I called up to Bourke. "That really blasted the bottom clean, though. Next time, just eight hundred rpm. Go ahead and move the boat twenty feet forward. This hole is huge."

Watching from below, we could see the two stern lines go slack and a few coils dropped into the water. Slowly, the boat inched forward using only the windlass until the stern lines pulled tight once more.

"We're in position," Bourke said.

"Same thing, Tony," I said. "Twenty feet away."

We got into position and I told Bourke to engage the engines again. Once more the force of the water gouged another hole in the sand, sending it mushrooming all around us.

"That's good," I called up to Bourke.

Tony and I waited a moment, while the sand was swept away in the current then descended into the hole.

"I got something here," Tony said. I looked over where he was fanning the bottom and swam over to him, not quite ready for what I saw.

"What is it?" Bourke asked over the com as a chill coursed through my veins.

I looked at Tony as he crossed himself reverently. "A grave," I replied. "Bones and a few metal pieces. Looks like four bodies were buried here. Nothing else. Move the boat fifteen more feet."

"How did anyone bury someone that deep?" Tony asked as Bourke and the two women went through the process of moving the boat again.

"Maybe they didn't," I replied. "Didn't Chyrel mention something about a lower sea level and that rock being the east end of a spit of land? This was all dry land then." I checked my console and added, "We're only ten feet deep here."

"Okay," Bourke said, "we're in position."

"We're ready here," I replied. "Blast away."

Once more, we were enveloped in swirling sand and suddenly something landed right in front of me.

"Shut it down!" Tony called and Bourke stopped the engines instantly.

Right in front of me was another skeleton, this one much shallower than the others. It had been in a sitting position and was knocked over nearly on top of me by the force of the water.

"It's another body," I said as Tony swam over to me. "Let's move it to where the others are."

We positioned ourselves side by side and as gently as we could, we moved what was left of the bones over to the previous hole, where the others now lay resting at the bottom of the partially filled grave.

"What do you want to bet this guy buried the others?" Tony asked while looking at me.

I stared at the empty sockets in the skull and was overcome with an emotion I'd never felt before. *This is how we will all end up one day*, I thought.

"You're probably right," I replied. "Let's put him with his crew." Somehow I knew this man was the leader of the others. Responsible for their fate and ultimately for their deaths.

I placed a three pound lead weight with a line attached to it next to the bodies and inflated a small balloon with air from my buoyancy compensator, allowing it to drift up to the surface. Somehow I felt the need to recognize this man and with Tony kneeling beside me, I saluted him. Out of the corner of my eye, I saw Tony do the same.

A moment later, we were back in position and I told Bourke to hit the blower again. We were quickly enveloped in the swirling sand, our visibility cut to nothing.

"That's enough," I called up to Bourke.

He stopped the engines and we waited for the current to carry the sand away. This time, we didn't have to swim around searching the inside of the crater. We both knew we'd found the spot as soon as we reached the edge of the crater.

Tony let out a whopping yell and started laughing so hard I thought he'd choke.

"What is it?" Bourke asked. "What's wrong?"

"We found it," I said. "The Captain was sitting right next to where he'd buried it."

Tony and I swam down to the bottom of the deep pit. There, sitting on the rocky bottom which hadn't seen the light of day for four hundred and forty years, were four large chests and five smaller ones. They were obviously very old, but well preserved. Each seemed to have been covered in pine tar, or something like it, and buried side by side.

I looked at Tony over the larger chests. "Want to take a peek?"

He nodded and I pulled out my dive knife, inserting it into the crack beneath the lid. It took some work; the pine tar seemed to have been poured over each chest after they were placed there.

Finally, the top cracked open a little, the hinges on the opposite side instantly crumbling, as I lifted the lid.

"Holy mother of God!" Tony exclaimed.

The chest was filled almost to the top with gold bars, each one gleaming like the day they were struck. There must have been hundreds of them. Excitedly, we worked on cracking open the other chests. After fifteen minutes we had them all open. Only the one held gold. The other three large chests were filled with silver pesos, some slightly encrusted. Thanks to the pine tar seal, not as much as I would have expected, though. The five smaller chests were filled with what appeared to be rough green stones of varying sizes, with flat areas all over them, mostly the size of marbles. *Emeralds,* I thought, *no doubt about it.*

I looked over at Tony once more. "Didn't Chyrel say there were three chests of emeralds?"

Tony looked up from the huge mound of wealth that lay before us, his eyes dancing behind his mask, knowing exactly what I was thinking.

"That's right," Bourke said. "The manifest said three small chests of uncut emeralds. Hang on, I got Chyrel's printout right here. Yeah, three chests, twenty libra each. She told me a libra was pretty close to a pound, so twenty pounds."

"Yep, and that's exactly how many we found," Tony said. "Three twenty-pound chests."

I nodded and gently picked up one of the small chests. Clutching it close, I slowly filled my BC. It inflated nearly to bursting before I began to rise from the bottom, Tony doing the same thing next to me.

"Meet us at the swim platform, Bourke," I said. "And bring two of my goody bags from the dive locker next to the engine room hatch."

At the surface, Bourke helped us get each chest into its own bag in case the ancient wood split open. A goody bag is a heavy canvas bag that divers use to hold their catch when spear fishing or lobstering. They can easily hold thirty pounds out of the water.

"Put these in the fish box for now," I said, pulling off my mask. "The manifest said three chests of emeralds and there's five. This is contraband treasure, never recorded on the manifest. We're going back down to look around for anything else, but it's all piled together and I don't think we'll find anymore. Call Deuce and let him know to get Cleary started on arranging things with the Interior Ministry."

I looked beyond Bourke at Melissa and Yvette, who were both smiling broadly. "Feels good to be a witness to history, huh? If you ladies promise to keep what's in these two bags under your hat, there might be a little something in it for you."

They glanced at each other, then turned to me and smiled again. "That won't be a problem," Melissa said.

I put my mask back on and Tony and I headed back down. I was pretty certain the chests in the hole would be all we'd find, but wanted to make sure.

When we reached the bottom, I heard Bourke yell, "What the hell!" His yell was quickly followed by a large splash. I looked up and saw Bourke struggling in the water. Thinking he'd fallen in, I started up toward him. Suddenly the engines on the *Revenge* started and all hell broke loose.

In seconds, I saw the lines to the stern anchors fall into the water, as if they'd been parted at the cleats. Those were soon followed by the main anchor line. Then, before I'd moved even a few feet toward Bourke, the engines raced and the force of the water surge pushed me down and tumbled me and Tony both away, along with a ton of sand and debris.

A moment later, I heard a shearing noise, then the unmistakable sound of my boat roaring away, as the two mailboxes fell away to the bottom. The force of the downdraft stopped and I quickly surfaced, only to see my boat rising up on plane and turning south. In minutes, it was almost out of sight. Tony surfaced twenty yards to the east and both he and Bourke were swimming toward me.

# CHAPTER FORTY-THREE

Are you sure you know what you're doing?" Sabina asked as Elana steered the big boat southward.

Surprised at how fast the boat could go, Elana pointed to the radar and GPS, showing their position in relation to the smaller barrier islands and the larger Great Abaco. "This boat has everything. All we have to do is go south to the tip of Great Abaco and then southwest to Chub Cay. After that, it's a straight shot to Florida. Do you know anyone in Florida that can fence forty pounds of emeralds?"

"Not in Florida," Sabina replied. "But I know just the person in New York. Head to the nearest port in Florida. I'll call him and have him fly down to meet us. How long do you think we have?"

Elana checked the GPS and started playing with its settings. A course was displayed that showed they had just over one hundred and forty miles until they reached international waters, west of Chub Cay. Checking the electronic display on the helm, she saw that they were traveling at almost forty knots.

"We'll be in international waters in three hours. Those three will be lucky to make the swim to shore in that time. We were over a mile out."

"What if the police send out a helicopter?" Sabina asked, worried.

"A helicopter? The *politia* drive around that island in golf carts and bicycles. There's only the one airport and I did not see any police helicopters there. Besides, there are many boats just like this all over these islands. They'll never find us." Smiling, she added, "I bet there's some champagne down in the cabin. Why don't you go see?"

Sabina climbed down the ladder and entered the cabin. She was amazed at how beautiful it was inside. It was a shame they'd have to abandon it in Miami. She didn't find any champagne, but there was a nice bottle of white wine. She took it and two wine glasses back up to the bridge. Sitting next to Elana she poured a glass and handed it to her before pouring one for herself.

"I had no idea this boat would be so fast," Elana said, pointing at the digital speedometer. "We're going over forty knots. That's seventy-five kilometers per hour."

"It doesn't seem so fast up here," Sabina said, stretching her legs out and placing them on the console while taking a sip of her wine. "How much do you think those emeralds are worth?"

"Probably more than a million American dollars. But a fence is only going to pay half of that, at best."

"Well," Sabina said with a wicked smile, "we won't have to split it with anyone and the two of us could retire in Mexico and live quite well with that much."

Gently placing her hand on Sabina's inner thigh, Elana smiled and said, "I do like the way you think, my love."

# CHAPTER FORTY-FOUR

By the time we made it to shore, a whole hour had passed. The current was pulling us north so hard that we had to swim at an angle or risk drifting out to sea, north of the island.

We finally found a house where someone was home and called Cleary. He agreed to send one of his men to pick us up and call Deuce to meet us in town.

"They have an hour-and-a-half head start," I said once we were all together in Cleary's office. "What do you mean you can't get a chopper in the air?"

"We don't have a helicopter here, Captain McDermitt, and we're already spread very thin, thanks to all the trouble you and your people have brought to my island. The nearest helicopter is in Nassau and I already checked. It's out on a hunt for a missing boat. It will be hours before it's available."

"What about Maggio's chopper over at the airport?" Deuce asked. "Have you confiscated it yet?"

"I've contacted the airport and instructed the people at *Cherokee Air* to make sure it stays there. But, as far as actually confiscating it, no. We really have no need."

"The people on that chopper fired on American government officials," Rosales said. "That's more than enough reason in Florida."

"This isn't Florida, Agent Rosales. Besides, we have nobody to fly it."

"I can fly it," I said. "I'm a pilot."

"Then feel free, Captain," Cleary shouted. "And when you run low on fuel, keep going all the way to Miami and never come back here again."

"Wait, Sergeant," Deuce said, in a calm voice. "Are you saying you'll release custody of Maggio's helicopter to the Florida Department of Law Enforcement?"

Picking up the phone on his desk, he said, "Yes, I'll call them now, if it will get you people out of here. While the Bahamian government appreciates you finding that treasure and turning it over, you and your people have caused more than enough trouble here."

In minutes, the deed was done and we left his office, heading straight to the ferry dock. Deuce was on the phone with Rusty as we got there and the ferry was just boarding.

"The four of you stay put," he told Rusty. "The chopper can only carry six passengers. We'll let you know if we find them."

I got a sudden idea and stopped dead in my tracks. "What's wrong?" Deuce asked.

"Tony, please tell me you remember the frequency of that tracking device Horvac put on my boat."

Tony smiled and we ran the last few steps to the ferry, climbing aboard just as they cast off.

Half an hour later, we arrived at *Cherokee Air Services* and I walked in with Rosales as the others waited outside.

"Mister Madic," Clifford said. Then, smiling at a confused Rosales, he added, "I see you found your friends."

"Hi, Clifford. Did you get a call from Sergeant Cleary?"

"Yes," he replied, looking confused himself. "He said to fuel up your friend's Bell and that an Agent Rosales was going to be taking it."

Rosales produced her identification and badge and showed it to the stunned man. "I'm Agent Rosales. Mister Madic is going to take me and my friends up."

As I did a quick preflight, Deuce asked, "Are you sure you know how to fly this thing? It's not a Huey."

When I was in the Corps, I got about eighty hours of seat time in a UH-1 helicopter. Not really as part of any training, like the air crew—just some overly friendly chopper jocks I was able to con into letting me fly. Also not enough to get a civilian pilot's license, either, but enough that I was comfortable at the stick.

"A chopper's a chopper," I said. "This one's just got a few more bells and whistles."

Tony knelt between the front seats, dialing in the frequency of the tracking device on the chopper's secondary VHF receiver. "The antenna's on the tail. When we're pointed directly at the boat is when the signal will be weakest, because of the interference from the airframe. But it can't tell us which way to go."

"I know which way they went," I said. "South."

"That tracker only has a thirty-mile range and they have almost a two-hour head start."

"I know, I know," I mumbled as I started the turbine.

"That means they're nearly ninety miles away," Deuce said, strapping in. "At this thing's top speed, it'll take close to an hour to catch them."

"That's if we follow the same course they took," I said, increasing the throttle and pulling up on the collective a little too much, causing the bird to jump into the air and wobble. Getting control, I said, "We're headed straight for the Northwest Channel. They'll have to go almost due south to Hole in the Wall before turning west."

"You're assuming they'll head for Florida?"

"They can't stay here," I replied as we gained altitude and I pointed the nose of the chopper to the southwest.

Deuce's phone chirped and after checking to see who it was, he answered it. He listened for a few minutes and said, "Okay, Chyrel. I'll tell him." Deuce ended the call and looked over at me.

"Tell who what?" I asked, glancing at him and seeing the distress in his eyes.

"That was Chyrel," he began. "She kept digging into the connections of both Madic and the Maggio law firm."

"Kind of a waste of time with Madic," I said, grinning.

"Jesse, Alfredo Maggio's son's name is Nicholas Maggio, married, with a child due in one month."

"So? I don't give a shit if he has ten kids and an orphanage he supports. His ass is going to prison."

Deuce didn't say anything for a moment. When I glanced over at him, he was still staring at me.

"Give it," I said. "What else?"

"Nick Maggio's wife is Eve Marie McDermitt Maggio."

"What?" I yelled.

"Your daughter, Eve, is married to Alfredo Maggio's son," Deuce said.

We flew on while I considered this. I remembered Kim telling me that Eve's husband's name was Nick and he was a lawyer. I remembered thinking at the time that it was a good thing she'd married a successful young man. And now that successful young man was responsible for the deaths of a lot of people. Almost forty minutes later, a faint ping started coming from my headset, pulling me out of my thoughts.

"That's it!" Tony said, kneeling and adjusting the radio. "Yaw left, then right."

I pushed on the left pedal, causing the helicopter to crab a little sideways and slow down. The sound of the pinging became fainter.

"They're at about eleven o'clock from our course," Tony said. "You timed it perfect! We'll catch them just as they pass Chub Cay and enter Bahama Banks."

"There's Chub Cay five miles dead ahead," Deuce said. "Looks like a couple of fun-seekers heading out." Sure enough, I could just make out two go-fast boats coming out of the marina on the west side of the island.

"There!" I shouted. "There's those two bitches with my boat!"

"Okay, what do we do now?" Deuce asked.

Pushing forward on the stick, I dropped the nose, sending the chopper into a dive. "We can't shoot them," I said. "Might hit a fuel tank. We still have plenty of fuel, so we'll get low and slow and follow them in. If they see us on radar, they'll think we're just another boat."

I leveled off just thirty feet from the wave tops and dropped the airspeed to forty knots. My boat was just threading the needle in the underwater canyon and heading onto the Bahama Banks a few miles ahead. Deuce watched through a pair of binoculars. I saw the two Cigarette center consoles that we'd seen leaving the marina on Chub Cay turn, following the wake of my boat a mile ahead of us. It looked like each boat had only two people aboard, all four of them looking forward. They both increased speed and began to veer away from one another, accelerating to overtake the boat thieves.

"Oh my God," Deuce mumbled.

"What?" I asked.

"The guys in those two Cigarettes have RPGs!"

I watched in horror as the two boats quickly overtook my boat and trails of white smoke emanated from the bow of each one. The rockets streaked toward my boat, both of them reaching it about the same time. The explosion was horrific, as a giant fireball erupted and rolled up toward the sky. The *Revenge* was lifted from the water and thrown over on her side, breaking into thousands of pieces, as the orange and black cloud spat what was left of it out the side.

I instinctively pulled back on the cyclic and raised the collective, slowing and gaining altitude as the main part of the fire quickly burned itself out. What was left of *Gaspar's Revenge* quickly sank below the surface.

# CHAPTER FORTY-FIVE

Amazingly, the two goody bags were thrown clear of the wreck. Art Newman, another of Deuce's team members and previously part of his SEAL team, found one and Julie found the other one.

It'd been two days since the sinking of my boat. We'd called Cleary and given him the GPS coordinates of the wreck and a description of the two Cigarettes, which had immediately turned and headed west as we hovered over what was left of my boat.

Cleary said he'd advise the Coast Guard since it was outside his jurisdiction. Since we were low on fuel, we flew directly to Homestead, where Deuce's team was headquartered, arriving there ninety minutes later. By then, the Coast Guard had arrived on scene and reported there was little left of the bodies of the two boat thieves.

Chyrel had contacted Colonel Stockwell and he'd pulled some strings and arranged for us to salvage the *Revenge*, explaining to the Coast Guard that it was a DHS vessel and contained sensitive documents. The Coasties remained on station to keep anyone from diving on the boat until we got there.

Art was visiting the island when Deuce called Chyrel. He quickly provisioned *El Cazador* and headed to Miami, arriving there late that night.

The following morning, we loaded up dive gear and equipment and six of us headed to the scene of the wreck, arriving before noon. Besides me and Deuce, we had Art, Tony, and Julie with us, being the best divers on the team. Bourke piloted the boat and acted as liaison to the Coasties. They agreed to pull off a mile away and stay on station as we worked through the day. By nightfall, we hadn't recovered very much and put into Chub Cay for the night.

We were back on station early the next morning and resumed diving to recover what we could. Art and Julie were working the perimeter when they found the two goody bags. Miraculously, although the chests were destroyed by the blast, the bags held and the gemstones were still inside.

Tony and I were working the bow section, trying to get to the bunk in the forward stateroom. After two dives in the very shallow water, we finally were able to get inside. The bunk itself was ripped from its mounts and laid on the port bulkhead. One by one, we removed the dozens of fly rod cases and reel cases, passing them to Bourke on *El Cazador*.

Deuce was working solo on what was left of the cockpit. The boat was basically broken in two pieces just forward of the engine room. The bow section lay on its port side and the stern lay upright on the sandy bottom just a few feet away.

By noon, we'd recovered everything from under the forward bunk and although the mount for the machine gun was twisted by the force of the blast, the M-2 machine gun itself was completely intact, although one of the barrels was obviously bent.

Sitting on the gunwale of *El Cazador* dripping wet, Bourke looked over at me. "Doc just called," he said. "They arrived at Marathon Airport an hour ago."

"How's he feeling?" Deuce asked.

"Said he'd seen better days but was going to be fine," he replied, glancing at Deuce. Then to me he said, "Doc said to tell you Pescador didn't much like riding in cargo, but he's okay. Outside playing with the Trents' kids."

"Is there anything else you think we should try to salvage?" Deuce asked me.

I looked up from where I was sitting. "Electronics are all toast. Engines, too."

"I got a couple of things," Tony said, pulling a bag over to where he sat. "They're wet, but I think you can dry them out and they'll be okay." He opened the bag at his feet and I looked inside.

I'm not much of a sentimentalist and didn't have many things I really cherished. But in his bag were several framed pictures of me with different people, the President among them. Also, my collection of challenge coins and a few other mementos that once decorated the bulkhead of my stateroom. I picked up the newest one, a picture of Kim and me taken just last week. It seemed like a lifetime ago.

"Let's shove off," I said. "There's nothing left down there that's worth anything."

"Doc said to tell you one more thing, after I'd told him what we'd recovered," Bourke said.

"What's that?"

"He said he was advancing you one chest full of emeralds to replace your boat." We all began laughing. It seemed to be the first time in a long time.

Bourke started the engine and as he turned east, brought the big boat with its wide Carolina bow flares up onto plane. He picked up the mic and told the Coasties that recovery was complete.

Four hours later, we tied up at the slip Deuce had arranged at the marina on Rickenbacker Causeway. There was a government van there to pick us up and we loaded the equipment and what we'd salvaged into it and went directly to Deuce's headquarters. We parked in a secure garage and left everything in the van for the trip down to Marathon tomorrow.

I showered and put on fresh clothes, using an empty dorm room. It was still early, not even supper time. When I got to the van, Deuce was there waiting.

"Where do you think you're going?" he asked.

"I have to go see a lawyer," I replied. I opened the back door of the van, removed one of the waterproof Penn Senator reel cases, and opened it.

As I reached inside and removed one of my Sigs, Deuce said, "Not alone, you're not." He reached into the case and removed the other one.

"This doesn't involve you," I said.

Racking the slide a couple of times to check the action, he inserted a fresh magazine and turned to me.

"Jesse, I've known you almost my whole life. As a kid, I thought you were bigger than life. I knew Eve and Kim when they were little, too. I also know what you're going to do."

"You do, huh?"

"Yeah, you're going to make your son-in-law wet his pants," he said with a grin. "Then you're going to point out how you'll be watching his every move for the rest of his life and how he should stop taking on cases involving low-life scum."

Inserting a magazine into my own Sig, I holstered it and leaned on the bumper of the van and looked up at him. He was right and we both knew it.

Ten minutes later, we were in a black Ford Crown Vic, headed to South Beach. We found the building where Maggio's law firm was located and took the elevator up to the top floor.

Stepping out of the elevator, a pretty receptionist looked up from her desk. I looked left and right and saw that there was one closed office door across from a glassed-in meeting room down each corridor.

"May I help you, gentlemen?" the receptionist asked.

Deuce pulled out his wallet and flashed his badge and identification. Glancing down at the nameplate on her desk he said, "Take a coffee break, Gina. A long one. Downstairs. In fact, why don't you just call it a day?"

She started to reach for the phone and I put my hand on top of hers. "You might also look into finding another job, Gina," I growled. "The guys you work for are dirty." She looked at me, then got up from her desk and quickly stepped into the elevator.

"You take the left and I'll take the right?" Deuce asked.

"If you find Junior, bring him to Daddy's office. I'll do the same."

I headed down the corridor on the left and stopped in front of the office door. Looking down the hall, I saw Deuce was at the other door. I opened it and stepped inside.

The man at the desk was surprised. He looked up and said, "What's the meaning of this?" Then he called over my shoulder, "Gina! Get in here."

"Your receptionist took a coffee break, son," I said as I walked over to Nick's desk. "Get on your feet."

"Who the hell do you think you are, mister?"

I slowly reached behind me and drew the Sig Sauer from the holster at my back. "My name is Jesse McDermitt. Now get on your feet, dammit!"

He stammered for a moment, trying to say something as the realization dawned on him. He started to reach for a desk drawer, but I moved quickly around the desk and put the barrel of the Sig against his temple.

Reaching past him, I opened the drawer and took out a Smith and Wesson .38. "A little advice from a professional? Mount a holster under your desk." I grabbed him by the collar of his expensive coat and yanked him to his feet. "There's a meeting in Daddy's office. I don't think we should keep them waiting."

When we walked into Alfredo Maggio's office, I couldn't help but be awed by the view outside the window. Deuce was sitting in Maggio's chair behind the desk, his Sig laying on the desk right in front of him, and the older man was seated in front of it. I shoved Nick down into the other chair as Deuce got up. I walked behind the desk and sat down.

Looking from one man to the other, I snarled, "Your greed has caused the death of nearly ten people. All but one were just as dirty and greedy as you two."

Nick started to say something, but Alfredo cut him off. "Shut up, Nick."

"Now that's smart," I said. "Probably the only smart thing either of you has done in a week."

Looking at the older man, I said, "Do you know who we are?"

"Agent Livingston has identified himself," Alfredo replied.

"I'm Eve's dad," I said, letting it hang there for a minute.

Finally, I said, "I can't help but wonder. What would you have done to us, if your plan had worked?"

Both men stared at me. "Never mind," I said. "Fifty million bucks will make a man do just about anything. You see, the problem we had was that we couldn't think like you. A friend pointed that out to me a couple of days ago. You're criminals and my mind doesn't work the same way yours does."

Again, Nick began to speak. I leveled his own gun on him and cocked it. "If you say one damned thing, I'm liable to start, though."

He changed his mind about whatever he was going to say and I continued, "You two made some pretty stupid mistakes. Not the least of which was not knowing the type of people you were trying to steal from. My friend here works for the federal government. I work for him, along with about thirty others."

I opened the cylinder on Nick's .38 and dumped the cartridges in my hand, transferring them to my pocket.

I tossed Nick the gun and said, "Our job is to protect the American public from scum like you. You see my predicament, don't you?"

I looked to the elder Maggio. "Your son is married to my daughter, who will soon give birth to our grandchild."

Maggio looked down at his lap and I continued, "We did a complete background check on you, your son, and this firm. We had analysts scouring every document that's ever been produced in this office and every case either of you have handled, individually and collectively. We know when you became criminals and it wasn't that long ago, was it?"

"No," Alfredo said. "It wasn't."

"Here's the deal," Deuce said. "Against my better judgment and in deference to Jesse's relationship, you two get a second chance. Each of you now have a ten-million-dollar life insurance policy, naming Eve McDermitt Maggio as the sole beneficiary. Compliments of the man in front of you. If you take this deal, you'll both live to be old men. If you don't, or if you stray just a little bit off the straight and narrow, there won't be any arrests made. No lawyers. No Miranda rights. No trial. You won't see us coming. And you won't live to be old men."

"From now on," I said, "you won't be representing degenerate scum like Madic. The only cases you'll take will be for the betterment of the community. You'll take pro bono cases whenever someone needs help. You'll become fine, upstanding citizens even if you never get rich. If you don't, we'll know. You're not to speak a word of this to anyone."

"How do we know you can do all these things?" Alfredo asked.

Deuce reached over and turned the phone to Alfredo. "Dial information and ask to be connected to the Department of Homeland Security in Washington." I looked up at Deuce and he winked. Maggio reached for the phone and dialed. "When you're connected, ask for Associate Director Stockwell's office and put it on speaker."

Once he asked for Stockwell, he punched a button and put the phone back in the cradle.

"Travis Stockwell," a familiar voice said over the speaker.

"Hi, Colonel," I said.

"Jesse! How are things in the Keys? President Bush asked me when you were going to take him fishing again."

"Anytime the President wishes, sir."

"I assume Deuce is there with you?"

"Yes, sir," I replied.

"Am I also to assume that your son-in-law and his father are seated there, as well?"

"Yes, sir," Deuce replied.

"Good evening, Misters Maggio," Stockwell said. "My name is Colonel Travis Stockwell, US Army, retired. Deuce and Jesse are part of a very elite anti-terrorist group that I'm in charge of. Deuce asked me to take this call and against my better judgment, well, here we are. The two men in front of you are two of the most dangerous men employed by our government. I bet you didn't know that, did you?"

"No, sir," Alfredo said. "We did not."

"Either or both of these men can end someone's life very quickly, or in some very slow and unpleasant ways. And I can have the whole matter completely swept under the rug. Permanently. I hope I make myself clear. Do I?"

"Yes, sir," Alfredo said, again speaking for both of them.

"Good," Stockwell said. "Deuce, Jesse, I'll see you two tomorrow."

"Have a good evening, sir," Deuce said and reached over to end the call.

"We're going to leave you two to talk about your future," Deuce said and headed toward the door.

I got up and followed after him. Waiting for the elevator, I turned to Deuce and said, "How'd you arrange that?"

He just shrugged and said, "He likes you."

"And what was that crap about seeing him tomorrow?"

"Call Kim," he said. "Tell her to meet us at zero eight hundred where *El Cazador* is docked. And tell her to pack a bag."

# EPILOGUE

Stockwell met us the next morning at the dock. Kim arrived just minutes after we did and Stockwell gave me the keys to a loaner I could use until I was able to find a replacement for the *Revenge*. It was a forty-six-foot Viking convertible, only a year old. Though not as fast as the *Revenge*, it was very well laid out and handled great.

I contacted the guy that Deuce's dad and I had gone through many years ago to unload some silver bars we'd found, and arranged to sell the emeralds. After a lot of back and forth, he agreed to pay a nice cool million dollars for them. We knew they were worth at least half again as much, but we also knew we wouldn't be able to get that in a fast turnaround.

The recovery of the treasure on Elbow Cay would continue for weeks. The people running the operation found more treasure scattered a little further offshore and north of where the main cache was located. Apparently, the survivors were unable to recover all of it after they wrecked and what we'd found was only what they were able to recover. In all, the research team found more than a million pesos, twenty-two hundred pounds of gold, and of course the three twenty-pound chests of emeralds, which were on the manifest. The gold and silver was quite a bit more than was reported and they attributed it to being contraband. In all, our ten percent was going to be somewhere in the neighborhood of six million dollars. But we'd have to wait quite a while to get any of it. Well, except for the cool million we got for the contraband emeralds.

Kim and I spent the following few days boat shopping online. I finally found a 2004 forty-five-foot Rampage convertible, almost like the *Revenge*. It was in Galveston, so we flew over to take a look at it. It had the same monster eighteen-liter Cat engines my old boat had, but the owner had modified them with twin turbo chargers, so they produced nearly twelve hundred horsepower each. On a run out of Galveston Bay, the GPS recorded a top speed of an even fifty knots and the owner said with the twin turbos, forty knots was a good economical speed. The interior and bridge layout are the same, with a few upgrades, and the hull is a deep, midnight blue. It still needs a few more upgrades and those will come later. After a little haggling, we agreed on a price of four hundred thousand dollars and I bought it on the spot.

The stolen Cigarette from Hope Town Harbour was recovered in Fort Lauderdale, adrift in the Intracoastal Waterway. Tena Horvac and her briefcase had disappeared, without a trace.

Bradbury and Conner were both turned over to FDLE, arraigned, and released on their own recognizance. Conner immediately disappeared into thin air.

Linda Rosales was promoted and transferred to a desk job in Miami. She came down to Marathon the weekend Kim and I returned from Galveston and we took her out fishing. Kim was fast becoming a very good First Mate and we started taking out charters again aboard *Gaspar's Revenge II*. As it turned out, Rosales was a pretty good angler in her own right, loved to swim and ran five miles a day on the beaches of Miami. On her weekends off, she came down and stayed with us on the island, bunking with Chyrel.

Chyrel became a one hundred percent island girl, moving out of her apartment in Homestead and into the little bunkhouse on a permanent basis. Between her and the Trents, they enlarged the aquaculture garden and produced more food than we could eat.

Doc was feeling better and better by the day. After putting together a crew, he and Nikki took to the sea. Carl made him Captain and her the First Mate of the *Miss Charlie*. At least that way, he was sure to be a "home every night" kind of dad, even though home was sometimes out on the Gulf. Everyone agreed that due to the loss of the *Revenge*, the replacement cost should come off the top, so I was off the hook for the half a million he'd fronted me. The other half million from the emeralds was split equally between everyone, including Rosales. She protested, but Nikki insisted. Once the insurance pays up, I'll split that with everyone as well.

A week after we got back, Deuce was promoted to Commander. There was no official ceremony, since on the books he was no longer in the Navy. Along with his promotion, he was put in charge of both the team that operated from my island and the team that was going through training at Homestead and would operate out of Key Largo.

Me? I'm just enjoying the time I have with Kim, teaching her about the sea, fishing, and scuba diving. She's taking flying lessons and I'm still looking for a King Air. Maggio's Bell was never returned. It's now officially a Department of Homeland Security aircraft. Eve still thinks I'm a knuckle-dragging Neanderthal, but Kim is slowly convincing her I have other redeeming qualities. Although she doesn't understand her husband's new stance on what cases he and his father are now taking and not taking, she's happy that they are helping others who need it. She's due any day now.

I spoke to Stockwell and told him that moving forward, I was going to be more concerned with the welfare of my immediate family and there might be times I'd just tell him a flat no. He didn't like it, but he went along. We found another boat and Captain in Key Largo, a recently retired, salty, old Navy Master Chief who operates a struggling charter fishing business in Lower Key Largo.

# THE END

If you enjoyed reading this and would like to receive my newsletter for specials and updates on upcoming books, please sign up at my website:

## www.waynestinnett.com

### Jesse McDermitt Series
*Fallen Out*
*Fallen Palm*
*Fallen Hunter*
*Fallen Pride*
*Fallen Mangrove*
*Fallen King*
*Fallen Honor*
*Fallen Tide (November, 2015)*

### Charity Styles Series
*Merciless Charity*
*Ruthless Charity (Winter, 2016)*
*Heartless Charity (Fall, 2016)*

The Gaspar's Revenge Ship's Store is now open. There you can purchase all kinds of swag related to my books.
WWW.GASPARS-REVENGE.COM

Made in the USA
Middletown, DE
05 August 2021